WHAT HER SICILIAN HUSBAND DESIRES

CAITLIN CREWS

SECRETLY PREGNANT BY THE TYCOON

BELLA MASON

MILLS & BOON

First published in Great Britain 2023
by Mills & Boon, an imprint of HarperCollins*Publishers* Ltd,
1 London Bridge Street, London, SE1 9GF

www.harpercollins.co.uk

HarperCollins*Publishers*, Macken House, 39/40 Mayor Street Upper, Dublin 1, D01 C9W8, Ireland

What Her Sicilian Husband Desires © 2023 Caitlin Crews

Secretly Pregnant by the Tycoon © 2023 Bella Mason

ISBN: 978-0-263-30678-1

05/23

This book is produced from independently certified FSC™ paper to ensure responsible forest management.
For more information visit: www.harpercollins.co.uk/green.

Printed and Bound in the UK using 100% Renewable Electricity at CPI Group (UK) Ltd, Croydon, CR0 4YY

WHAT HER SICILIAN HUSBAND DESIRES

CAITLIN CREWS

MILLS & BOON

CHAPTER ONE

IT WAS A beautiful day for a divorce.

Chloe Stapleton smiled to herself as the private jet winged its way down over the mountains of Sicily that rose up from the gleaming Mediterranean Sea, jutting proudly high and covered in sprawling vineyards and crumbling old temples to honor gods long lost.

That felt appropriate too.

She kept her gaze trained out through the window as the plane came in for a brisk landing on a remote hilltop strip, carved into the mountains with a certain brutal efficiency that reminded her of the owner of not only the plane, but the landing strip too. And the whole bloody mountain, the better part of Sicily, not to mention an ever-widening swath of the whole wide world beyond.

For there was no part of the planet, however isolated and far away, that the might and power of the Monteleone family did not reach.

Chloe was already feeling a bit nostalgic that she was very shortly going to be asked to resign from her place as one of them.

Or rather, one of them in name only, she amended.

She had been to this estate only once before. Five years ago, when she hadn't known what to do, so she'd reached out to the darkly powerful man who had once been her stepbrother to beg him for help.

He had been her only hope—and Lao Monteleone had not hesitated. She always thought of him as a smooth coil of a man, forever holding himself back from the unwary—which only made his ruthless ferocity all the more apparent. When she knew, as did the world, that he did exactly what suited him when and how he liked.

But he had always been kind to her, if distant.

She had come all the way here five years ago, banking on that kindness, and Lao had not let her down.

As she stepped out of the plane and allowed his always excruciatingly well-trained staff to usher her into the waiting car, she could admit that Lao's kindness—and the protection he had offered her immediately—had made her feel safe when she hadn't believed she would ever feel such a thing again. She would never forget that.

In the darkest hour of her grief, when she had lost her father and with him, the one person who had always loved her and championed her in all things, Lao had stepped in. He had taken care of everything, allowing Chloe to take care of herself.

It was truly bittersweet to return here today, knowing full well that this must be the end of that safety. That she would need to find a way to be her own safe space from here on out.

Surely this is simply called learning to be an adult, Chloe told herself stoutly. *Get a hold of yourself, girl.*

She tried to brush the strange melancholy away as the car took her down from the landing strip on narrow track roads that wound around the exuberantly wild mountains, giving her sweeping views of the ancient Sicilian cities down near the water and the many historic villages tucked into the hills. Back home in London, the weather was predictably vile, making the sunshine appear even more bountiful here. It seemed like a blessing, pouring down through the trees and making the leaves gleam brightly as she drove through.

Even five years ago, when she had still felt so inside out in the face of her father's loss, it had been impossible not to notice the beauty of this untamed island. While she had spent many holidays in the more refined parts of Italy before then—the hills of Tuscany, the canals of Venice, the beaches of the Amalfi Coast—she had never come to Sicily before or since. And it made that nostalgia within her seem to ache all on its own to find it just as she remembered it. A wild tangle, not quite civilized, and in no way as manicured as the Italy thought she knew.

But then, the same could be said for Lao himself.

He had married her here five years ago, quickly and without ceremony. It had been more like a business meeting than a wedding, she thought, though at the time it had pleased her, for it was a demonstration of his kindness. They'd stood together in Lao's office, here on this mysterious island in the ancient castle he had renovated and made the base of his operations.

The castle, he had informed her offhandedly five years ago, that had been in the Monteleone family for some untold number of centuries. That had made their marriage seem even more like a safe haven, she'd thought then. As if all of those centuries, steeped in Monteleone might and power and influence, would cocoon her, too.

She supposed it had.

When Chloe thought back to that day, it was all tearstained and blurry. She had the impression of Lao's steel gray eyes and his powerful form, so much broader and taller than she was. As if he intended to block out the sky if that was what she wished. And the way he held her pale hands in his, belting out the appropriate words.

"A marriage such as this, naturally, will be in name only," he had told her in that powerfully grim way of his.

"Naturally," she had murmured in reply.

And it was between her and the dreams she'd never shared with another living soul that she might have found that *just* the slightest bit insulting. That there had been a part of her, even then, even so lost in the terrible clenching fist of that grief had not left her for another year or so, that had been…not exactly *insulted* that Lao had not even bothered to seal their marriage with a kiss. That he had glared at the priest as if even requesting such a thing was an affront.

She hadn't been *insulted*, of course she hadn't in the face of his going so far above and beyond any possible duty he might have felt, but she had felt ever so slightly *indignant* all the same.

But that was pure silliness and well did she know it.

What mattered, as she intended to make certain she told Lao when she saw him, was that it was a gift. All of it, when he'd owed her nothing. When he could so easily have refused to even see her that day. He had given her the gift of his protection, and her silly, foolish little fantasies were a secret she would take with her to her grave.

The car turned in through an imposing gate, flanked by ancient bits of marble, though the gate itself was decidedly modern and clearly high-tech. Once through that gate, the dirt track became smoother, so there was less jolting and jumping, and she no longer needed to grip the handle in the back seat so tightly.

Chloe settled in as the car headed up the drive toward the man—the *husband*, mad word though it was to describe either Lao or his relationship to her—waiting for her. Cypress trees marched in dutiful columns on either side of the lane, olive trees were set into neat lines down the flank of a rolling hill, and she could catch glimpses of the cultivated Monteleone land in all directions. But it was the old castle that made her hold her breath when she caught sight of it, rising in its ancient, imposing way there at the top of Lao's own, private mountain.

The place where he had taken the sobbing mess she'd been, married her, then set her free to do as she liked.

"As your father would have wished," he had told her, almost formerly, in the brief moments they'd stood together after the quick ceremony.

And so Chloe had spent these years that Lao had gifted her doing her best to find her own place in the world because that, she knew, was what her father would have wanted for her if it had been up to him. If he'd been here to listen to her stories and laugh away her hurts until they felt minor.

But the truth was that she'd always been a bit too dreamy. Maybe a better word was *sheltered*, but either way, she'd drifted from one job to another, forever trying to find her *passion*. She'd done a bit of literary PR, because it had sounded so grand to swan about London, talking of books to whoever would listen. But the job hadn't worked out that way. It was much less about talking, very little about loving books at all, and a whole lot more about tracking campaigns across the internet and avoiding angry emails from authors. She'd dipped in and out the charities and nonprofits that a great many of her school friends were involved in. But they all seemed to be more about being photographed at parties than actually doing any good in the world. None of her friends had understood when she tried to tell them how she felt.

"It does good in the world," her best friend Mirabelle had argued with a roll of her lacquered eyes. "People like to look at pretty things, Chloe. Why not be one of them?"

Chloe had eventually ended up working in an art

gallery, which she found fun. Because the gallery was filled mostly by the sorts of people who enjoyed making the most spectacular mountains out of any given molehill.

"That's how you convince a rich man with no taste to buy a splatter of paint on a crap canvas to bung up on the guest room wall," her jaded boss, the sleek and slinky Moriah, had told her.

Maybe, Chloe had started to think, she was onto something with the art world. Because, at the very least, she wasn't as bored as she'd been in publicity. Surely that was worth *something*. Maybe it wasn't *her passion*, but then, maybe it was deeply unsophisticated to spend so much time worrying about finding something no one else seemed to care about or value at all.

Maybe she needed to worry more about upping her sophistication game, she'd been thinking in the days before she'd received Lao's summons.

Strange, then, that the only thing she could seem to think about as the car wound ever closer to Castello Monteleone was passion, after a fashion. She was already working on her arguments. The same way she did every time she received a summons from Lao in whatever city they both happened to be in, because he always knew where she was. Once, memorably, she'd met up with him on a beach in Brazil. He usually took her for a meal, quizzed her on her life and plans as if he was taking over the role of her father and guardian despite being her legal husband, and then left her reeling in the wake of all of that rampant virility, and seething, incalculable power.

She always had the dreams after those dinners.

But this was the first summons she'd received to the castle in all this time. Chloe had known the minute she'd received it that it could only mean one thing.

The one thing she'd known would come, sooner or later.

Lao had given her the gift of these five years, held securely there between his might and influence.

It was high time she stood on her own two feet, however unsophisticated. She knew that.

But knowing it didn't make those feet seem any more steady or sophisticated when the car pulled up to the castle's grand entrance, and his staff swung the door open to wave her out.

She was dearly tempted to crumple into a swoon like one of her favorite heroines from a book, but she didn't.

Because that would be taking advantage. And would cheapen, somehow, the care Lao had taken of the truly beset girl who had shown up here in pieces the last time, uninvited and wholly uncertain if she'd make it through the week.

She made herself smile at the poker-faced servant who held the car door for her, and again at the extensively trained butler who bowed her into the castle's great hall before personally leading her deep within.

Chloe wasn't much for architecture, and she hadn't paid much attention to her surroundings five years ago, but she could see now that this place was a true wonder. No doubt it helped to have all the money in the world, but she thought that Lao must have a particularly keen eye for detail as well. Because he had taken this ancient castle and made it a showpiece of timeless style and incomparable grace. There were stone walls all around, complete with ancient hung tapestries and priceless art in museum-quality frames. At the same time, there were also boldly modern steel girders and the feeling of brightness, airiness, and more windows than there could possibly have been originally. She had read once, after visiting this place the first time, that he had essentially taken a ruin that had stood on the property for generations—instead of the family villa that was stationed somewhere else on the land—and transformed it into his own personal palace.

A feat of architectural time travel, the article writer had gushed. *A heady, dizzying example of taste and vision, refinement taken to perfection.*

Yet when she thought of those words, she pictured Lao himself, not the castle that loomed all around her now.

The butler led her over the glassed-in bridge that spanned a deep crevice winnowed into the side of the mountain, allowing her to gaze down for what seemed like miles. She felt a shiver start deep within her, winding around and around with every step until it took her over. She could feel the goose bumps all over her skin. And when they reached the other side and found themselves in another hall, she could *see* the way her skin bristled as they walked along what seemed like an entire wall of antique mirrors. Chloe took the opportunity to smooth down her hair and straighten the clothes she'd worn on the flight down from London this morning.

She'd dressed for her imposing husband, despite the fact that he was soon to be her ex.

Because no matter what he was to her, he had always rendered her a bit breathless. Whether he was wearing a dark bespoke suit in the grim rain of a London summer or lounging beachside in Brazil with an indolence she hadn't been able to look at directly.

Or maybe it was less the indolence that had been so blinding and more the acres upon acres of lean, golden muscles that had been on display, with the dusting of dark black hair, and that entrancing V etched into his lower abdomen that led the eye directly to one of those astonishingly small bathing costumes stretched to capacity over his—

But thinking of that meeting in Brazil made her cheeks burn. She couldn't recall a single word he'd said. It was possible she hadn't spoken at all, but had merely been sat there in a tumultuous daze.

Thinking only of the color blue.

The color of that bathing costume.

It haunted her still.

And again, Chloe found herself smiling at her own silliness as the butler murmured something she didn't quite catch, then beckoned for her to precede him into the room she remembered so well.

She had been married here, on this edge-of-the-cliff office that could only be called such a thing because there was a desk on one end, surrounded by crisp white bookshelves, all of them filled—but not bursting. Every item on every shelf was precisely placed *just so*. But then, everything in this part of the castle was new, from the poured concrete floor tossed here and there with rich, deeply hued artisanal rugs, and the grand wall of windows that aped the castle next door, but were all in glass.

It was there, standing before that glass that she knew gave way to the cliff side itself, that she saw him.

Right there where she had married him five years ago.

Lao Monteleone himself, standing with his back to her.

Chloe wondered if it was possible to be jet-lagged when she had only flown a few hours down to Sicily from England. Because she couldn't think of any other reason why she suddenly felt so weak.

He turned, then, and the sunlight poured in from above, illuminating the harsh planes of his stern face. And then she found she wasn't simply weak. She wasn't even breathless, as usual. She was holding her breath. Completely.

Because it was always like this, and yet always seemed new. Lao was a hard, shocking blow to her solar plexus every time she saw him. As if she'd fallen down and had the breath knocked straight out of her.

He was widely called handsome, though he wasn't. He was too imposing. Too forbidding. Taken apart, his features were too strong for the kind of male beauty that most admired and therefore graced magazine covers and the like. Those high cheekbones, that ruthless blade of a nose. Starkly sensual lips that were forever pressed in a faintly disapproving line, as now.

He was imposing, though she knew by now that was as much the power that emanated from him as his actual skeletal structure. He was at least six feet and muscled, everywhere, like so many of the statues in the halls of this castle. But his shoulders were wider than anything carved in the Renaissance or since.

Today, he was not dressed in his usual bespoke suit or, mercifully, a thong bathing costume in cobalt blue, though Chloe would not describe him as *casual*, either. Even lounging mostly naked, gleaming in the Brazilian sun, he had exuded all the might and formality that he always did.

At least today there was no need to swallow her tongue.

Even if she could see a hint of his sun-gold skin at the top of that crisp white button-down shirt he wore.

She had no idea why merely *looking* at him should make a raw swath of a nearly unbearable ache widen within her.

Only that she was certain he could see it. Just as she was sure that he could see the bright spots of heat still on her cheeks.

"Hello, Lao," she said, and felt the absurd urge she

always did, to break out into giggles like a schoolgirl. She felt that fluttery thing inside her take over, filling up that aching part until it was hard to tell where one bit began and the other ended.

Looking at him felt the same as peering down into the jagged Sicilian canyons that could easily eat her whole.

"Chloe." Her name on his lips was the same dark poetry it always was, inflected with the magic of his accent, like so much spice. It was a chore not to lick her lips. "I trust your flight was pleasant?"

"Yes, thank you. Very pleasant indeed."

"I have ordered you some tea," he said, and she did not miss the emphasis on that last word.

Lao was entirely Italian. He did not understand the English obsession with tea, much less diluted with milk. But was providing it anyway, because that was what he did, she knew. He took care of things, always. It made a different sort of shiver work its way through her that she, alone in all the world, should know this man for the protector he truly was. Not the dark mage of the business world that so many feared, the inscrutable billionaire who had been, at times, the most hated man in Europe. She alone knew better.

His gray eyes flared with a touch of silver heat. "I know how you English rely upon your tea."

"That sounds lovely." Chloe would have said it was lovely even if it wasn't, but the truth was, she could do with a bracing brew to get her head on straight. She needed to stop shivering and aching and start remembering that this trip was supposed to be about gratitude. About thanks and divorce. Not cobalt-blue bathing costumes or that chiseled face of his.

Lao nodded to someone behind her, so she turned her head to see the same butler directing another diffident staff member to set up a full tea service on a polished wood table that looked as if it had been hand carved. Perhaps from the trees on this very mountain.

The silence in the room seemed to grow, then deepen, after his staff retreated yet again.

"You're very kind," Chloe said, because she'd promised herself she wouldn't let this get away from her. That she wouldn't let her overwhelming foolishness where this man was concerned leave her tongue tied the way it often did. "I want you to know that I appreciate it more than I could possibly express. These past five years have been a wonderful gift. I don't know what would have become of me without you. It's thanks to you that I feel ready and capable to carry on now. On my own. But I'll always remember this, Lao. It was a truly wonderful thing for you to do for me, when technically, you weren't even my stepbrother anymore."

He didn't move, so Chloe wasn't certain why it was that he seemed to *expand* then, taking over the whole world. Certainly this room, though the arched glass ceiling that must have been three stories high at least.

His gaze was a thundercloud. "Why do you think I've called you here today, Chloe?"

"Oh." She laughed nervously, though she wasn't

sure why she was laughing at all, or even why she felt so nervous in the first place. This was *Lao*. Sure, he was big and imposing and overwhelming, but he had never been anything but perfectly kind to her. Sweet, even. Her reaction was the *height* of exactly the kind of foolishness that had led to Mirabelle calling her a *right dozy cow* more than once. Mostly affectionately.

"Well. I assume that you're ready to go on with the rest of your life. And that an inconvenient marriage to the daughter of a man I don't recall you liked all that much anyway might get in the way of that."

But he only gazed at her, in that same stormy fashion and she found herself too hot, again.

"I'm perfectly happy for you to divorce me, Lao," she said hurriedly. "Really. You don't have to worry about me at all."

"I do not worry about you, because I know you are taken care of," he told her, in a low, stern tone that did nothing at all to take away that shivering inside her. "But things must change, Chloe. Because I think it is high time. Past time, even."

"Past time," she agreed, and once again, lectured herself not to feel that unreasonable sense of disappointment. "I agree."

"I need an heir," he told her, and she had the strangest sense that he was being gentle, though there was nothing about his demeanor that would suggest he was capable of it. "And as I already have a wife, I see no reason why she can't provide me with one."

"An heir?" Chloe was having trouble keeping up.

She swallowed, though her throat didn't seem to work and her body seemed to have taken itself off for some kind of riot. "Do you...do you mean with me?"

He looked as if he'd made from thunder and too much rain, as wild and untamed as the Sicilian mountain they stood upon. He looked *at her* as if she was a very small, glass thing he held in the palm of his hand.

She felt as if she was.

"I mean you, Chloe," Lao said, like he was rendering judgment. Though she was glass straight through and could only seem to concentrate on that brooding heat of his from across the room. "It is time you became my wife in full."

CHAPTER TWO

LAO MONTELEONE HAD waited what seemed like an unbearable lifetime or three for this moment.

Now it was upon him, it did not disappoint.

He had wanted Chloe Stapleton for a long, long while.

And Lao did not have much experience with *wanting*. What he wanted, he got, and long before he had spent so much as an instant in the *wanting* of it. He had chosen to view his obsession with Chloe Stapleton, perhaps the only thing he could remember waiting for in his entire life, as a lesson. One he had been pleased to learn.

Because it reminded him that he was something more than the current master of the vast Monteleone enterprise. The lord of all he surveyed, etcetera.

It reminded him that he was, beneath all of that, mere flesh and blood and mortal.

A man like any other where it counted most.

Not that he required these reminders today. Because Chloe stood before him the way she always did, with those dreamy, impractical dark chocolate eyes and soft lips that seemed forever on the verge of an exclamation. He knew that she usually dressed far more casually, just as he knew that she like to make an effort when she saw him. He approved, because it meant that she wore a dress like today's that highlighted the delicacy of her clavicle, the soft, elegant sweep of her neck.

All of that was as expected, and he enjoyed it.

But he enjoyed even more the way she looked at him now, a new gleaming thing in her gaze.

Did she even know she wanted him or would he need to teach her that, too?

Lao was more than ready to find out.

"I don't understand," she said, when he rather thought she did.

He crossed the room, not quite brushing past her to take a seat near the tea service that his staff had laid out. He was too Italian to fully understand the lure of endless cups of a milky liquid that was not coffee, and moreover, not confined to breakfast. But that did not prevent him from pouring out the tea, then taking his own cup—mercifully black—and watching as she drifted over to the chair opposite him, as if pulled by some kind of invisible thread.

The way she always did. He approved of that, too.

"I've always expected you to divorce me," she said as she sat, frowning at her teacup. She added the expected milk, then three sugars, and did not seem to note the arch of his brow as she took a big sip. "I assumed that was the plan. We both know that you only married me as a favor. No one on earth would expect you to continue doing me that favor for life."

"I do not wish to divorce you."

"Oh, but you have to." She looked up then, her gaze solemn. And direct, which always came as such a surprise when she wafted about otherwise. "If you want an heir, Lao. It's the only thing that makes sense."

"Not the only thing."

Her lips parted, and she blinked, confusion all over her pretty face. "I'm really not following you. All you have to do is announce that you're looking for a woman to have your baby, and the parade will form within the hour. A parade that could go on for days and days, across several continents."

"I have no need of parades. I am already married. And as I require that my heir be legitimate, this seems an easy solution, do you not think?"

"You're not making sense."

She frowned at him, the first hint he'd seen in some time that there was more to her than the hapless, lost girl she'd become after weathering a year of deaths. First his mother, the complicated and resplendent Portia, who he knew Chloe had adored. As had everyone who had encountered her. Six months later, her father, the brash, self-made Charlie Stapleton—who had lured Portia away from her Monteleone widowhood—followed, leaving Chloe devastated.

Lao had been something less than pleased at his mother's second marriage, a mere eighteen months after his own father's death. That his parents had never been happy together was neither here nor there, to his way of thinking. What did happiness have to do with the Monteleones?

"There is more to life than the Monteleones, Lao," Portia had said on the night she'd confessed to him that she was remarrying. There had been a great wisdom in her gaze, but he had not wished to see it. "Even for you."

He had not allowed her to see anything but the faint pulse of the muscle in his jaw.

"I have seen no evidence to suggest anything of the sort," he had replied.

And he had been surprised—not to mention outraged—that his mother had gone ahead and married Charlie Stapleton anyway. He and the man he had never referred to as his stepfather had never been close. They had suffered through the odd family event, but with precious little grace on both sides.

What Lao remembered most about his mother's wedding was Charlie Stapleton's little girl. She had been cross. And about as interested in their parents' marriage as he had been.

"I expect you are looking forward to having a new mother," he had said to the glowering seven-year-old who had, for reasons unclear to him, been left alone in his presence. He couldn't remember why. Was it the actual wedding, or some attempt at a family meeting before that? He couldn't pull those details into place, but he remembered Chloe. Her arms crossed, her mouth turned down, her hair in dark plaits.

"I already have a mother," the little girl had replied tartly. "She's disappointing. Why would I want another?"

Lao had laughed despite himself, when he'd been so certain that he would never so much as crack a smile while participating in such a farce. He would support his mother, as ever, but he'd had no intention of warming in the slightest to Charlie Stapleton, his new money, or the child he'd had from his scandalous tabloid marriage to an "actress" whose beauty far outstripped her talent.

But he had liked Chloe, was the thing. Despite himself, he'd always liked her. And he'd come to have a grudging respect for Charlie, too, because whatever his many sins, he had loved Lao's mother. In a way his own father not only hadn't, but—Lao was all too aware—had never wanted or attempted.

Monteleones were not emotional. So his father had always taught him. Emotions were for smaller men, who had less consequence and more time to indulge such foolishness. Monteleones had empires upon empires to keep running so smoothly that they were nearly invisible, unless someone knew precisely where to look.

"Real power is never showy," his father had always told him. "That is a performance. Real power does not require a stage."

But Chloe was not a Monteleone. Not back then.

And he had found he liked the funny little girl who was always rattling around the great mansions they found themselves in, her eyes full of dreams and her arms usually piled high with books. She had always amused him, when Lao was not easily amused.

He had not seen her in some while when, not long after her eighteenth birthday, her father had died and she had come all the way to Sicily to seek his aid.

Lao would have given it to her without question, in honor of that funny kid he remembered. The only child he ever had any interaction with. And because it would have pleased his mother to imagine he might do something, not because of what he might gain from it or how it might enhance his standing or portfolio, but simply because it was the right thing to do.

Portia had been married to Lao's father, a sheer icicle of a man, for years. Yet had still maintained her warmth. She had been a marvel of a woman indeed.

He would have helped Chloe no matter what.

But she'd been standing right here in this room. She had been waiting for him. And she had turned to look at him when he came in.

That was all. Even now, he couldn't have said what it was that had changed everything for him. It had been raining outside, so there had been no convenient shaft of light to illuminate her features. He thought— and he had gone over it so many times in his head by now, again and again and again—that perhaps it was her grief, carving the woman she was becoming indelibly across the features he had only ever seen as that of a girl.

One way or another, a bolt of sheer lust had struck him, so hard he was still shocked it hadn't taken him to the ground. It was as if he had never laid eyes on a woman before, and he had not known whether to be shocked that he was capable of feeling something so intensely—or shocked far more that she had caused it. *Chloe Stapleton*, of all the women alive.

He had assumed he was ill.

Even so, he had handled everything, from summoning a priest to "donating" the appropriate funds to hasten along what was normally a more drawn-out wedding process, here in Italy. Then he married her, sent her on her way, sent a security detail to England to keep eyes on her—on the off chance anyone discovered she was the wife of *the* Lao Monteleone and imagined they could get to him through her—and got back to work.

He had been certain that the strange longing he had felt for Chloe would pass like any other virus, but it did not.

Every now and again, he had met up with his putative wife to see how she was faring, and that bizarre reaction to her had only gotten worse each time. Until he had been forced to face it head-on—after seeing her in a filmy sort of beach cover-up in Brazil that had only drawn attention to what she wore beneath it. And worse, that body of hers that had haunted him ever since.

Golden curves held tight in a blazing red bikini.

Everything since then had been a waiting game, bringing them here. To this moment. To this day, at last.

The day he had finally had enough.

If he must be plagued with this *longing*, he had decided, he might as well use it for a purpose.

Chloe was frowning thoughtfully. She took another sip of her tea. "I didn't think about the fact that, of course, people can make all the babies they like in a doctor's office these days."

Lao could have a disabused her of whatever notion she was having, but he did not. He found himself too intrigued by her, given that he had no idea where she was going when she spoke. Notably unlike everyone else in his orbit. His many underlings did not dare enter his presence unless they were fully vetted and his phalanx of assistants had ascertained exactly how they planned to waste his time.

If any one of them had ever surprised him, Lao could not recall it.

But Chloe was nothing like the people who worked for him, obsequious and sharp at once. He watched instead as some other thought occurred to her. He could see it break across her face, like a tide.

She leaned forward and set her tea down on the table between them, with a decisive sound that was unlike her. "I would love to have a baby for you, Lao. It's a bit extreme, I suppose, but I can't express how much your protection has meant to me all these years. Really, I'd be happy to be a surrogate for you."

"You will not be my surrogate." She frowned at him then, but he remained where he was, sitting untroubled in his chair. "I told you, Chloe. I want a wife. By which I mean, in every way."

That sat there between them, as much a presence as the tea things. The wall of windows. The whole of Sicily just there, outside.

Chloe seemed to freeze solid, and Lao use the opportunity to flip back through all the security reports on her that he had committed to memory, these last five years. He had expected that she would carry on as most eighteen-year-olds in her position—rich and pretty—would have. And it wasn't as if she'd locked herself away in a tower. Quite the opposite. She had attended all the same parties her friends had, but when they'd hopped into taxis with inappropriate men, Chloe had gone home.

He had begun to suspect—then begun to hope—that she was as innocent as she seemed.

It wasn't a requirement. But it was fast becoming an obsession.

Lao told himself it was the novelty, that was all, for a man whose lovers had always been women of great experience and even greater enthusiasm for the things he—and his vast wealth—could do for them.

But this was Chloe. His wife.

"Not every way," she argued.

He only waited.

Because she might be dreamy, and her father might have been so doting that he'd allowed her to grow up in a cruel world this naive, but Lao was neither of those things. His father had raised him the same way that he had been raised in his time. As harshly as possible, to prepare Lao for the enormous task before him. The Monteleone fortune was an entity so broad and so vast it was as if it lived and breathed on its own. It was nearly sentient, this many centuries along. One did not manage it so much as tame it, throughout the course of a lifetime that must necessarily be dedicated entirely to that taming.

Lao had always taken his role seriously. He had not, like so many of the heirs he knew to this kingdom or that fortune, wasted away his youth in the pursuit of foolish things. He had never been tabloid fodder. He was not given to flashiness of any variety. He made certain he did not frequent the kinds of places paparazzi might linger and he avoided the sort of people who trailed cameras and commentary in their wakes.

The Monteleone family had always preferred their power to rest behind thrones rather than upon them, because that way it could not matter if the regime changed, the way regimes always did with tedious regularity.

The Monteleones remained.

Yet that wasn't to say that Lao had not satisfied each and every one of his appetites in a way that he saw fit. He had, and did. It was only that he preferred that the things he got up to remained his own business and no one else's.

And he was certainly capable of recognizing a deep, hungry feminine interest when he saw it.

He'd been seeing it in Chloe Stapleton for quite some time.

He had not been certain it was real—until Brazil. And he certainly saw it now.

Lucky for her, he was finally ready to do something about it.

Her mouth worked a time or two, though no sound came forth. Her throat moved, and Lao saw goose bumps march up and down her bare arms.

"I think," she said slowly—very slowly, with a look in her dark eyes he could not call the least bit dreamy, "that I need you to tell me exactly what you mean by that."

"I think you know."

She studied him as if the glass walls had shattered and a dragon or two had flown in. As if he *was* a dragon himself. He did not find the idea the least bit outrageous. And he could admit that he did not mind the hint of awe in her dark gaze.

"You can't possibly mean you want *me* to be the sort of wife you want in *every* way," she said at last, her voice more thready than usual.

"I am unaware that I am married to anybody else," he said. He held the delicate teacup in his hand, and kept his voice bland. Though he knew the way he looked at her was nothing of the sort.

She flushed, as if he had his hands on her. "Lao. You can't mean that. You don't. I don't understand what you're going on about, because it can't be…"

But she trailed off, her lips parting as if she could taste the tension in the room, then. At last.

He sipped at his tea, hardly tasting the bitter brew

of water over leaves the English liked so well. When all he could see was the way she swayed, slightly, as if whatever images she had in her head were making her shiver where she sat.

It made him conjure up his own.

"What that means, Chloe, is that I want you in my bed," he told her in a low voice, watching with a hard sort of pleasure as her skin pinkened with every word. "Every night. And if it takes some time, all the better. I do not wish to rest the whole of the Monteleone legacy on one head as my parents did. I am thinking four, at the least."

"Children?" she asked, faintly. "You want *four* children?"

"I do," he assured her. And then made certain she understood him fully. "With you, Chloe. I want to have four children with you, the old-fashioned way. Not in a doctor's office. In a bed. Against the wall. Anywhere and everywhere. Is that exact enough for you?"

Lao watched her take that in.

He found himself braced, as if she might take flight. And he did not know that he wished to acknowledge the part of him that wanted her to do exactly that, so that he might have the pleasure of chasing her.

Like the kind of barbarian he had always known he truly was, deep inside.

He watched her chest rise and fall, and her pulse beat in her neck. He saw emotions he could not name chase across her face. He was a man who waited for nothing and no one, save this woman…

And so he told himself he could wait a little longer now. Just a little longer.

"I... I don't understand," she said again, but her voice was little more than a whisper and there was that wild pulse in her neck, telling him the truth.

"I think you do understand," he said quietly. "I think you understand me entirely."

Though for the first time in his adult life, Lao Monteleone found himself wondering if a woman actually wanted him.

A notion so astounding, so impossible to conceive of, that if he hadn't been standing here—feeling an odd sensation that it took him long moments to recognize as a touch of *uncertainty*, another first—he would have laughed at the very idea.

As he watched, Chloe moistened her soft lips. She blinked, again and again, as if that might give her clarity.

"You have never given me any indication that you harbor these feelings," she said, with the tone and expression of someone wandering through a meadow who had only just realized she was weaving her way through land mines.

He could not say that he cared for it. More, it was not the reaction he had expected.

"I do not *harbor feelings*, Chloe," he said abruptly, as if he really was some kind of land mine and she had activated him with her misstepping. "Do not confuse this for mawkish poetry. You are already my wife. I am already your husband. This relationship has been in name only for far too long. All I am proposing is that we shift it."

"Shift it," she repeated, but when she blinked again, her gaze seemed to narrow.

"I am a remarkably busy man, as you know," he told her, not liking the way she was looking at him. "Why should I go through the trouble of divorcing you only to turn around and marry all over again to create legitimate heir. It's a waste of time and effort, surely, when you are here, have nothing better to do, and bonus—are already married. To me."

"Heaven forfend your time and effort be wasted," she murmured, her dark eyes narrowed further.

"There is no reason not to approach this efficiently," Lao told her as if he had never been more at his ease. "Efficiency and circumspection, that's all I ask."

"Efficiency." Her voice was changing, going up an octave with each syllable, and there was an unfamiliar gleam in her dark gaze. He had not seen it in a long while, but he suspected it was…temper? "Circum-spection. And, of course, sex against walls, but let's gloss over that part."

That was the part he least wished to gloss over, but then, he had not anticipated that she would respond like this. He'd rather thought she would weep with gratitude the way she had when he'd married her five years ago and taken charge of all the details her father had left for her to handle. House, funds, bills, staff.

He could not see why this was hitting her so differ-ently. Or why she'd imagined he would call her all the way to Sicily to divorce her when he could have her served with papers anywhere she happened to be—

Though he thought better of saying so.

"You already enjoy the benefits of my protection," he pointed out, quite reasonably, since it was true. "The only change for you will be the physical aspects of the relationship." He very nearly let himself smile, then. "But I flatter myself that you will not find what I require of you too onerous."

Chloe held his gaze for a long moment, and there was something almost electric about it. It seared into him, making him tense. Making him think it was wiser to set the absurdly delicate teacup aside. But then she wrenched her eyes from his and looked down into her lap. He followed her gaze and saw how she gripped her hands before her. Twisting her fingers together, as if agitated.

Lao could not conceive of a single reason why she should feel even the slightest hint of agitation.

Not when he—*he*, Lao Monteleone himself—was standing before her, offering her something most women would kill to experience. It was not vanity that made him think so, he knew. It was a simple fact.

Perhaps she was overwhelmed, he reasoned. Perhaps it had never occurred to her that he might make such a generous offer. She likely had to pull herself together, for she was no longer eighteen and might imagine it was childish to weep the way she had, throwing herself into his arms and sobbing until she'd soaked the front of his shirt.

He waited, certain that in a moment she would look up again, wreathed in soft and yielding smiles, and accept what could only be seen as a remarkably generous offer on his part.

Again.

Because as irritating as he might have found it to think that she had expected him to divorce her today, he could concede that it would have been a reasonable expectation in a situation such as theirs.

This, however, was a gift.

Chloe looked up then, but there was no smile. No hint of moisture in her gaze. It was as if she had turned into a stranger before his very eyes. It was almost as if he didn't recognize her, so dark was her gaze, so oddly set was her jaw.

"No," she said.

Too distinctly for his taste. Too definitively.

That word seemed to squat there between them, as if she'd tossed it into the middle of the room tied to a rock.

Lao realized he could not recall the last time someone had said no to him, either.

She was a revelation. Not one he entirely enjoyed. "I beg your pardon?"

"No," she said again, and then blew out a breath as if she was trying to control her reaction. Or steady herself. "I will have to refuse."

Lao waited, but she did not elaborate. Instead, she looked at him for moment, then rose, looking as if she meant to march straight back out of the room. And possibly the house.

He was beginning to tire of all this novelty.

"You do not intend to tell me why you have chosen to refuse me?" he asked, sounding almost lazy. Which she could not possibly know was Lao at his most dangerous.

Chloe stopped walking toward the door, but she did not turn back around to face him.

"If you would like a woman to have sex with you at your convenience," she said in a low voice that he hardly recognized, so different was it from how she normally spoke to him—all stammers and blushes, "I'm sure that you can find any number of them. But none of them will be me."

As if he had asked her to be his whore. He, who had done nothing but protect her for years. Even going so far as to offer her the great honor of becoming the mother of the next generation of Monteleones. Lao could not account for what he was hearing.

Though he realized he had, indeed, heard her speak in a tone like this before. When she had been a cross little girl.

He didn't care for the memory.

Just as he didn't care for the way she stood there before him, her spine straight and her shoulders set in an indignant line.

He did not like it. He would not tolerate it.

"I think you have misunderstood me, Chloe," he said with a soft menace he did not attempt to hide. "It was not a request."

CHAPTER THREE

CHLOE COULD BARELY BREATHE. Her lungs seem to be working overtime, but she couldn't manage to get in a full breath. Every single nerve within her was alight, making her shake, deep down, in places she couldn't name.

Because for a moment…just for a moment…she had thought Lao had meant something completely different.

Something that had made everything inside her blaze hot and wild, like a comet leaving trails across the night sky—

But she should have known better.

A man like Lao did not have feelings, and certainly not for her. He had minions. And all he was proposing today was that she become one of them.

And then, while she was at it, produce no less than four children—the old-fashioned way—to follow his orders right along with her.

Later, perhaps, she would think about what she'd imagined he was saying today, and let the full force of the emotions she felt come out. Or let herself name them. But not here, where he could see her. She hoped she would never have so little pride.

If that was all she was left with today, it would be enough. Chloe told herself it would have to be enough.

She had been *so close*. So close to that fluttery, shivery dream inside of her that she'd pretended not to have for more years than she could name. So close that for a moment, she had seen the unvarnished truth of who she was. Who she had always been, perhaps.

Worse still, the truth of what she felt about Lao. What, deep down, she thought she might always have wanted from him—even back before she had the vocabulary to express it.

Or the ability to look at any of these things directly.

Things she would have said she didn't even know how to express *now*, and for a moment, she hadn't needed to worry about what she could or couldn't manage to say because it seemed as if he was saying it all for her. As if he was taking care of that for her, too. The way he taken care everything else. For all these years.

She should have known better.

Truly, Chloe thought, she really should have *known*, and that she hadn't expected this at all was galling.

More than galling, if she was honest with herself about him, for once. It hurt.

It *hurt* that he wanted nothing more from her than for her to act as his convenient broodmare.

It was not a request, he'd just said, and that hurt too.

All of this hurt a whole lot more than she'd thought

it would. Even when she'd thought he was divorcing her. At least a divorce made sense. This was…too close and too far away from too many things she should have known better than to entertain. Especially here.

No matter what he'd said to her.

"I want you in my bed every night," he had said.

And she'd thought… God, what she'd thought and what she'd *felt*.

In a bed. Against the wall. Anywhere and everywhere.

Like all her dreams were coming true—but she should have known better. She should have remembered that she wasn't the girl whose dreams came true. She was the girl who had a mother who wanted nothing to do with her and had lost everyone on this planet she'd ever loved.

Save one, but he was…

Well, he was impossible, and she knew that. She had always known it. As a child she'd thought of Lao as an *immensity*, not a man, as huge and overshadowing as a mountain.

Now she knew that the truth was far more complicated. He was all the things she'd imagined he was back then. But he was *also* a man, and that made everything…delicate.

Inside you, maybe, a tart voice inside piped up. *He seems anything but.*

Chloe turned, then.

And the expression on Lao's face made everything inside her go still. Then begin to…hum.

As if she was a tiny little creature, nothing more than prey, and he had her in his sights.

What she couldn't understand was the part of her that wanted nothing more than to be what he chased. And better yet, caught.

That seemed to land in her too hard, because Chloe felt something like winded.

"You don't control me, Lao," she said, and hated that her voice was far softer than it should have been. She made herself stand taller, as if a straight back would take the place of the spine she should have grown years ago.

She told herself there was no time like the present.

Lao only gazed at her, his hard face a study in arrogance. "Do I not?"

Chloe couldn't get her head around what was happening. How different this was from what she imagined. What she'd expected today.

The Lao who stood, slowly, before her was familiar in a thousand ways, and yet a stranger all the same. She should have been appalled. Offended, even. But she felt nothing so simple.

The way he looked at her was pitiless. She found that everything inside of her seemed to pull tight and then hold. Making it almost impossible to breathe.

Or do much of anything else, for that matter, like give voice to some of the things swirling around and around inside her and seeming to settle there, low in her belly.

"You can defy me if you wish," he said. In a tone

she might have been tempted to believe was offhand if she hadn't been looking at him. If she hadn't been too able to see the intensity in his gaze.

"Thank you for your permission," she said, and felt fleetingly proud of how close to scathing she sounded.

"But what will become of you, Chloe?" he asked in that same low, deceptively casual manner at total odds with that glimmering steel gaze. "I think you'll find it a Pyrrhic victory at best. I control your funds. Here, on the grounds of this estate, I control your body. You cannot leave without my permission. Even if I did allow you to go, I could cut you off immediately and you would not have the necessary monies to make it to the sea. What then?"

"Are you really suggesting what I think you're suggesting?" She shook her head, but it didn't clear. Not even the slightest bit. "I feel as if I've stepped into an alternate universe."

"It is more that you have finally woken up, *dusci mia*." He had never called her that before. It made the concrete beneath her feet seem to buckle and she didn't even know what it meant. "You have finally opened your eyes and seen what has been in front of you all this time."

She felt something move inside of her, blooming outward like some kind of internal tsunami. Fury, perhaps, though she wasn't sure that she'd ever experienced a fury like this, a burning, melting heat that coursed through her and seemed to glow, deep in her core. She was terribly afraid there was something more to it. Something more like grief.

"I thought you were my friend," she said quietly, though it was a fight to sound so calm. So…unbothered by what was happening here.

Because it was true that she had often imagined he might be her friend. That being his friend was the most she'd hoped for, even if there was that glowing thing inside her every time she thought of him. It was also true that *friendship* was not all she had imagined when it came to him, and that the idea of making their marriage real in a physical sense when it could not be real in all the other ways she craved him…*hurt*.

And she had the sneaking suspicion he knew it.

That he knew every thought she'd ever had about him. Every dream. Every stray notion.

She told herself what she felt then was horror, but it was much too hot for that to be true.

"Some would say I am the best friend you've ever had." He did not move closer to her, and yet she felt as if he had closed the distance between them and encircled her neck with one broad, hard hand. She felt that breathless. And as if he knew that, too, Lao thrust his hands in his pockets. It should have made him look more casual. It did not. "Have I not been at your beck and call these last five years? Have I not done everything you've asked of me? Can you think of a better friend to you than I?"

"How depressing it is to realize that even the great Lao Monteleone is only nice to a woman when he has an ulterior motive." She blinked away that great wave inside her, because it didn't matter what it was. Grief. Fury. That glowing thing she didn't want to look at directly. A kind of shame that she had let herself believe anything he said in the first place. That she had delivered herself directly into his hands.

That she had hoped, however briefly, that he might have been sharing something of himself with her when he'd said he wanted her to be his wife in full. That it might have meant something.

"I cannot make sense of this reaction, when it is clear that there has always been an attraction here," he said, though he did not sound the least bit insulted. But Chloe could not find that a good thing, because it meant only that he was a stranger to her here. The one she read about in the papers. The formidable opponent, on the few occasions he actually allowed others to note what he was doing, out there in power circles so lofty most didn't know they existed. More often, he was talked about as he might be some kind of ghost, forever moving in and out of the shadowy doors of power.

She had never recognized the Lao she knew in the accounts she'd read of him.

But she saw him now. As he spoke of *attraction* as if she was being childish for pretending otherwise. Or for wishing there was something less clinical in the way he said it. "Then we are both of us surprised. Because I cannot recognize my stepbrother in a man who would threaten me the way you have today."

For a moment he considered her, and she thought that just possibly, she might have gotten through to him—but then he laughed.

She would not describe it as mirthful.

"You must breathe rarefied air indeed if you find the notion of becoming my wife in full a *threat*, Chloe." That steel gray gleam became a part of the humming inside her, making it almost impossible to stand still. "I would be tempted to find this insulting, but the trouble is, I don't believe you."

"You don't…" She shook her head, ordering the clamor inside her to die down, though it only seemed to get louder. So she had to talk a little more fiercely "It's not a matter of *belief.* It's true you've controlled many things about my life for these past years, but it's *my* life. I thought you were helping me, not…collecting evidence to use against me like this!"

To her surprise, she found that he looked almost… proud. "And here I was beginning to think your personality died with your father, Chloe."

She felt as if he'd slapped her. Or perhaps she would've preferred it if he had. "Are you truly trying to use my father's death against me?"

It seemed as if he moved closer, or perhaps it was simply that he took over the whole room by just…existing. Especially when he shrugged, so languidly, as if none of this affected him at all.

Why that should bother her almost more than the rest was a question she did not intend to answer.

"I remember you as a child," he said, though he was

not looking at her like she was a child. At all. "You said what you felt with little consideration for anyone around you or any false notions of courtesy. That is not a complaint. It was refreshing. But when you came here five years ago, it was as if you were lost at sea. And as far as I can tell, you have been lost ever since." She opened her mouth to defend herself, but there was something about the way his dark eyes gleamed that kept her from it. "You have no purpose, Chloe. You waft about aimlessly, from one pointless enterprise to the next. What is it now? You adorn some SoHo art gallery?"

"I'm an assistant, not an adornment."

"And how, precisely, do you assist? What do you know about art?"

"I know I like art, which is more than I can say for you."

"I cannot tell if you mean you do not think I like art myself, or if it is me you do not like," Lao said with ferocious unconcern. "But either way, it will not last. Whatever this enthusiasm is, it will end and you will wander into something else equally meaningless. What future do you see for yourself? Where do you think you will be in ten years?"

Chloe had no idea why she was shaking. She only knew that she was no longer containing that shaking inside of her, and that was a shame. Because he could no doubt see the way she trembled, and would likely attribute it to the wrong cause.

Or the right one, came that unflinching voice within her.

But no. She was certain it was fury. A deep, bracing, shivery and melting *fury*.

"It doesn't matter where I am in ten years," she told him, and she might have been trembling like a cursed fawn, but she couldn't remember the last time she'd been so *aware* of…well, everything. The way he looked at her, and the heat in it. The competing waves of emotion that buffeted her. That blaze inside her, bright and impossible to ignore. As if it had been waiting a long while to shine. "Because I came here for divorce. I thank you for looking out for me these past five years, even if it turns out you weren't doing any such thing. But I'm perfectly capable of handling my own affairs from here on out."

She thought that hit all the right notes, but Lao seemed unimpressed. He did not move, only considered her. "Are you? I don't think you have the slightest idea what your affairs entail. Do you have the slightest idea what it is I do for you?"

"I can figure it out."

"Because you are under the impression that you—lacking any kind of education and having spent these last years pretending to work at public relations or swanning about an art gallery because they find you pretty—are prepared to take the reins of a multinational corporation, with all its implications and financial considerations. To say nothing of your own personal fortune, about which you have never inquired, not even once, in the whole of the past five years I have managed it and grown it. Tell me, Chloe, do you even know what you're worth?"

She flushed then and knew it to be a corrosive kind of shame, the sort that might take her down to her knees if she let it. So she did the only thing she could. She opened her mouth and came out with a number she'd read in a gossipy magazine a year or so before.

And did not feel any better when Lao only shook his head as if he was disappointed in her, which was almost as bad as the rush of shame that she'd let this get so out of control. "You don't even know enough to know that I enjoy feeding numbers like that to amuse myself. I like to see what happens when I let go of certain balloons and let them rise. I like to see what goes where."

He let out a sound that was not quite a sigh, but it made her wish she could sink through the concrete floor and topple straight down into the wild heart of one of the canyons below them.

And he wasn't done. "Yet you stand here in my house and parrot my own fake numbers back to me. In the same breath as you try to tell me you're prepared to handle all that I have done for you yourself. I could let you do it, of course. I'm almost tempted to, because I know what you are perhaps too stubborn to see today." Again, that deep, bone-rattling gleam in his gaze that made everything feel precarious, even her own skin. "The only thing you will accomplish is wasting your own time, and then, later, mine. When you come crawling back to beg for my help once more."

"That, Lao, will never occur."

"Indeed, it will not." His voice was so dark, then. His gaze was so hard. "Because I have no intention of allowing any of that to happen."

"You're not thinking straight."

"Am I not?"

"No." Though Chloe knew she wasn't, either. Maybe there was no straight thinking to be had. Maybe she just hadn't noticed, too busy trying not to swallow her own tongue at the sight of him in that bathing costume. Or the memory. She found her hands outstretched, palms up, imploring him, and wanted to hate herself for begging—but couldn't quite get there. Not under these impossible conditions. "You don't really want this. I know you don't."

"What interests me far more is why you think that you don't want it," he said. One of his dark brows rose, and there was the faintest hint of a curve in one corner of his mouth. "Do I disgust you?"

He did not look as if he was overly worried about how she might respond to that, so she knew she should tell him that he did. That she was *disgusted* with him. That the very notion of being *a true wife* to him revolted her, that she had never thought of him as anything but a kind of distant brother figure. She knew, instinctually, that if she said any of that, he would divorce her within the hour and she would never see him again.

Not ever.

All she needed to do was *say* it, and yet she couldn't.

She couldn't bring herself to open her mouth and lie to him.

Especially not about that.

Not when the many ways she'd lied to herself over the years seemed so obvious to her now and more, throbbed insistently between her legs.

He only watched her, much too closely, while the space between them seemed to join in the throbbing she could feel all over her. It felt like a kind of madness.

There was something electric in the space between them. There was something almost terrifying.

"Because," Lao continued quietly, as if she'd answered him. As if she'd dared. "I would give you the same advice I gave you when you wanted to begin drinking spirits."

Chloe remembered that far too well. She had always liked when Lao gave her the full force of his brooding attention. She had been perhaps fourteen. The friend from boarding school she'd had with her that Christmas had gotten very drunk and silly, and Lao had taken it upon himself to make certain that she did not intend to behave in the same manner.

"Men get drunk all the time," Chloe had said crossly, because she had always been so *cross* then. And never afraid to show it. "Why is it the end of the world if a girl does too?"

"Because the world is unfair," Lao had replied with his typical bluntness. "Drunk boys tend to be loutish. Drunk girls, by contrast, easily turn into victims. One way to avoid this is to never drink beyond elegance, Chloe. And never seek oblivion."

She hadn't wanted to tell him that she was always the one who was careful in her group of friends. The one who never allowed herself to get as foolish as the rest. She'd thought it would make her seem unsophisticated, and she had dearly wanted him to find her anything at all but that.

"If in doubt," Lao had told her quietly over the sounds of the grand party in the distance and her friend moaning on the bathroom floor in the next room, "I would advise you to sample whatever it is everyone else is drinking, but sparingly. How can you know if you like it otherwise?"

"How does anyone know if they like anything?" she had demanded, but she had been breathless by then. That was what he did to her, and much too easily. Even back then.

He had not smiled. He did not smile, not Lao, but she had felt as if he had. And in any case, he had reached over and tapped the very tip of her nose.

"Mind you, never drink anything you don't see opened and poured with your own eyes, please."

Yet what she remembered was not the advice, but that tap. And how she had felt burned alive by a casual touch that he could just as easily have used on a pet cat.

But he didn't, she remembered telling herself, lying awake much later while her friend snored. *He touched me instead.*

Like it meant something.

"I can see you remember as well as I do," he said now, and his words seemed engraved into her bones. As he wasn't speaking to her, but from within her. Once again, he didn't smile. Once again, there was only that faint suggestion of a curve in the corner of his sensually stern lips. "I'm not going to club you over the head, Chloe. Or drag you off to my cave like a Neanderthal. But I would invite you to sample what I am offering before you dismiss it out of hand. Is that so terrible? Do you think that deserves the level of drama we have seen here today?"

She could tell that he was being deliberately condescending. That he wanted to provoke her, and he was succeeding. What she didn't understand was why she didn't simply turn around again and march off. She could put it to the test, couldn't she? She could see if it was true that she couldn't escape his estate without his permission.

But she didn't move.

"I think of you as a brother," she lied, when she never had. Not really. He had always been more to her. Always. "Nothing more."

"I don't think that you do."

He did move closer then.

And Chloe felt her pulse take over the whole of her body. As if it changed her where she stood, making her the pulse itself. Part of that gleaming way he gazed at her.

Proving what a liar she'd turned out to be, that easily.

"I don't think you know me better than I do," she threw at him, maybe a little too fiercely. "I don't even know why you would think that you could. You hardly know me as it is."

"Chloe, you are my wife." Lao's voice was too intense. It moved within her like a kind of smoke. It wound around and around inside her, making it impossible to think of anything else. As if it filled her up. As if it had already changed her on some fundamental level it made her shiver to consider. "You might have spent these last years lost, but I have not. I have always known exactly where you are. And exactly who you are."

Her mouth worked. She swallowed, hard. "You followed me?"

"I have protected you in every possible way I could," he shot back at her, his voice rough. "Just as I promised you that I would."

He came even closer and then he reached out.

At last, something in her whispered.

Then he made it worse—or better—and smoothed a hand over the fall of her hair.

And there was something about the way he did that. So softly, when everything he'd said so far was hard. Demanding.

So softly that she found herself trembling all over again.

"Lao," she whispered. "I…"

"Dusci mia," he murmured, that big hand of his warm against the side of her face. Like sunshine in his palm. "Kiss me."

CHAPTER FOUR

CHLOE WANTED TO RUN.

But not away from Lao. *Into him*, if such a thing was possible.

His hand was so warm, the look in his eyes so commanding, she almost thought it was. That he would make it so.

Everything inside of her felt stretched out between those two extremes—his hand and his gaze—as if they were extremes in the first place instead of simply Lao Monteleone in all his considerable glory.

She wanted so badly to fight this. To fight *herself*.

Not because she didn't want him. But because she did. Oh, how she did.

And this, she understood, was not likely to be a tap on the nose, like she was nothing more than a house pet.

She would never know how it was that she had stood here all this time, pretending that what upset her was the notion of making their relationship real. When the truth was, what bothered her more was that she might lose herself in all these feelings she had so deliberately kept at bay all these years. Feelings she had resolutely refused to name.

What if she lost herself, getting entirely swept away, while he was unaffected?

The very notion was unbearable—

But Lao's hand was on her cheek. His eyes were so stern, so compelling.

And Chloe, for once, did not feel the slightest bit lost.

On the contrary. She had never felt more *found* than she did right now.

It was as if she had never had any other choice but this.

She eased herself forward, her heart drumming so hard in her chest that it actually *hurt*. Then she reached out a hand so she could balance it—gingerly—on the sheer rock wall of his astonishing chest.

For a moment, Chloe could only stand there, amazed at her own temerity. Or maybe what truly amazed her was the way so simple and light a touch seemed to re-bound back into her. Lighting her up.

Making her glow from within.

Some part of her—maybe all of her—expected him to take control. Maybe she wanted him to. Bend his head, sweep her into his arms, carry her off…

Maybe she assumed that he would do exactly that.

But for all his talk of keeping her here, and all his threats—implied and direct—Lao did nothing.

He merely waited.

And, second by second, that made everything more intense. More electric.

It seemed to take Chloe an age or three to lift her gaze from where it rested, there on the hand that nestled between the planes of his hard pectoral muscles. She could feel the heat of his skin. His *body*.

And something about the simple wonder of that, of him, was so erotic it made her feel near enough to giddy.

She could have stood there, just like that, forever.

But Lao had told her to kiss him. And she knew that it was unlikely she would make it through another day if she did not obey him.

Because deep down, there was the truth that somehow Lao had known all along.

It was that Chloe had wanted to kiss this man—and do a good deal more than merely *kiss* him—forever.

Even when he had been her lofty stepbrother, always clearly in a state of deep disapproval over his mother's choice to remarry.

And even if, left her own devices, she would never have admitted such a thing. That didn't make it untrue. It didn't change the inexorable pull she felt now, so close to him at last. *Touching him*, after all these years. It was so overwhelming she wanted to simply… close her eyes and disappear into him.

Instead, she lifted her head and let his magnetism guide her. Pull her.

Take her over.

So that it seemed only natural to bring her head up, then go up on her toes so she could angle herself against him. Into him.

Then, and only then, could she strain up that last little bit to press her mouth to his.

And for a stretch of time that could have been a second or an eternity, that was all there was.

The press of her lips to his. The scent of him, spice and sunshine. The way her own heart was a jarring force in her chest, a deep thunder she could feel washing through her, over her, and making a ruckus in the strangest places. Spiraling around and around and shooting out a kind of spun gold into all the recesses of her body only to settle with great heat between her legs.

Making all the rest of her seem to glow.

Chloe surged against him, desperate and seeking and *wanting* things she didn't even know how to name. *More*, whispered something inside of her. She just wanted *more*, whatever that was. Whatever it looked like, felt like—as long as it was Lao.

And when his hands shifted at last, guiding her mouth where he wanted it to and allowing him to change the angle and the slick slide of their lips against one another, it was as if something in her began to sing.

She couldn't forget, not even for a moment, that this was Lao.

This was Lao. Her Lao.

This was *Lao*, and he was *licking* his way along the seam of her lips, then dipping inside. She was stroking her tongue against his, following his lead. And she couldn't tell what was more intoxicating—his taste that flooded her mouth and her senses, or the sensation itself, or the fact that this was happening at all.

His other arm came around her back and held her there as he leaned in, so she was no longer on her tiptoes but bent back into his hold.

And he kissed her, again and again, and she kissed him back.

And it was Lao, and this was *them*, and too many things made sense to her now, colliding inside her with every new slide of his tongue.

The dreams she'd had for years. How she'd gone out of her way to contrive to be near him, no matter how flimsy the excuse.

Even here, five years ago, she had come running as if he was the only man on earth. The only *person*.

As if Lao alone could help her.

He kissed her and he kissed her. And it was fire and it was light. It was golden and it was heat.

It was far, far better than all the things she'd pretended she hadn't been imagining since she was much younger than she was now.

Chloe wanted to dance in the flame of this forever. She wanted to crawl along the length of him, to swing herself into his arms, to strip them both of all the clothes they wore so she could get her skin all over his.

And then see what happened.

When he set her away from him, there was still that hard gleam in his gaze. There was also the hint of a deep triumph over his face, but she didn't mind that as perhaps she should.

Because she was feeling triumphant herself.

Because for a moment—just the faintest moment

before his typical harshness took hold—the great Lao Monteleone looked just as shaken as she felt.

In the next instant it was gone, but Chloe decided she would hold on to it anyway. She would hoard the memory of that scant little breath of time, because even if she'd only imagined it, well. It still felt like everything.

It still felt like the kind of treasure she'd long since stopped believing she might ever find.

He smoothed his hand over her hair once more. Though this time, when he finished, he brought his fingers down the side of her face. And his thumb diverted from the line of her jaw to trace her lower lip.

"I think we will do nicely," he said in a low voice.

He did not sound as if that was up for debate.

And Chloe meant to argue. She did. If only because he shouldn't make such assumptions… But somehow, she couldn't get that message from her brain to her mouth, and that triumphant look on his face only intensified.

Another bolt of heat seemed to simmer there between them, but Chloe stepped away. She had to *make* herself step away from all that brooding heat and steel gray intensity.

And she really didn't know if she wanted to start spinning herself around in circles, like a little girl gone giddy, or if really, she wanted nothing more than to curl up in a ball and sob out all these messy feelings churning inside her.

But either way, didn't matter. Because clearly, Lao saw what happened between them as capitulation on her part. He moved past her, stepping out into the hall and summoning his staff, issuing instructions in rapid Italian. Only then did he look at her once more.

"You will need to settle in," he told her, and she noted that he did not ask her if she'd *like* to settle in. He was telling her to go and do it while he did whatever it was he did here—like run the world from his mountaintop, presumably. And again, she wanted to argue, but her mouth no longer felt like hers. She could taste him on her tongue. She could *taste him* and all she could do was stare back at him, wondering why no one had ever told her that kissing a man like Lao could make her whole, entire body feel like someone else's. Like his. "My staff will see to any needs you might have, Chloe, and we will meet again this evening."

He did not wait for her to comment on that. Much less mount any sort of argument. He turned and started back across the great expanse of the room toward his desk while Chloe was politely swept off by a waiting phalanx of his servants.

She wasn't sure she really came back to herself until they were walking down a corridor she'd never been in before, all modern lines and expansive white space to show off the edgy modern art that somehow worked in this ancient setting. Before she could comment on the juxtaposition of old and new, they were beckoning her into a grand suite of rooms that she knew at once belonged to Lao.

It all belonged to him, obviously. But this was where he *lived*.

The last time she had stayed here, it had been in the lovely, cheerful guest apartments, all bright yellows and blues and polished antiques.

This was something else again. The art gallery feel of the hall gave way to a great deal of old stone and dark wood that somehow contrasted beautifully with so many sweeping windows and French doors that opened out over the island, letting in the sky and the mountains and, far off in the distance, the sea.

Chloe assumed they would drop her here and then, no doubt, lock her away until Lao was ready for her. Instead, she found herself surrounded by a set of female attendants, who very happily took it upon themselves to buff and shine every part of her.

They removed the varnish from her toes and fingers, and then reapplied it in a gleaming red. She was led into a room with a massage table, where aestheticians worked over her. First a bit of waxing, then a facial, then a massage to soothe it all away.

Chloe had always liked a spa. She and her friends had been to some lovely ones. But she couldn't recall ever having had a private spa arranged all around her before. It would have been overwhelming, she reckoned, if she wasn't so boneless.

Hours passed before it occurred to her to realize that this wasn't a gift that Lao was giving *her*.

He was preparing his own gift.

He was preparing her for later.

That made her so weak, everywhere, that she was happy she was already lying down.

Eventually, they led her into her bedroom at last. She expected to find Lao there, but it was empty. And more than that, she could tell with a glance that it wasn't his.

She didn't know how she knew that, but she was certain all the same. It was a pretty enough room, with a canopied bed, an antique chaise, and a selection of priceless furniture kept in pristine condition. One door led to a large, sprawling bathroom suite with a great big copper tub in a glass alcove. Another led to a dressing room that looked like a high-end Marylebone boutique, but it was through a different door entirely that she found what she was looking for.

Another bedroom, next to hers. Separated by not only that dressing room for her, but one on his side as well, filled with beautiful clothes that smelled of his sunshine and spices.

Chloe understood at once that Lao had placed her in the bedchamber adjoining his, the way men of his station like to do with their wives. "Only peasants share their grubby little queen beds," one of her friends had said once—the sort of joke that wasn't a joke at all.

And Lao was no peasant.

She knew she'd found his actual bedroom immediately. It was more masculine, for a start, than her canopied bed and floral accents. But more than that, there was some faint hint of that same scent that told her it was his. Some little hint that made every part of her seem to shiver.

Especially when she looked at that big, wide bed that commanded most of the space against one wall.

It took her a long while to get her breath back to normal.

She went back into the room that had been allocated for her on polished feet that felt unsteady beneath her. Once there, she made her way to the grand windows so she could stand there and gaze out at the rolling hills of the Monteleone estate, spread out there for her.

Her breath was closer to normal, but it took longer still to make all that giddiness and sensation subside. She would nearly get there and then she would think, *I am his gift* and it would start all over again.

But eventually she managed to tamp it all down just enough she could think straight. Or try.

She hadn't expected this. She'd come down this weekend because he'd asked, and she'd been sure she knew exactly what she was walking into. She'd expected divorce papers and perhaps a polite dinner. She'd intended to express her gratitude and be back in London by noon the following day.

There was no way she could have expected his proposal that they make this marriage *real*.

Much less that kiss.

God. That kiss.

But she couldn't lose herself in that wave of sensation again. Not yet.

Chloe tried to think critically, never her strong point. And certainly not when in Lao's direct orbit.

But surely there was no real reason that she couldn't

make this marriage work. For her as well as for him. Lao wasn't the only one who could expect to get what he liked out of this. *Four* children, for God's sake.

She had always intended to have children, the way everyone seemed to *intend* to have them—in a very distant way, set off sometime in the future. Not *now*. But she didn't have to worry about that no matter what Lao had planned, because every three months, without fail, she went and got a shot of birth control in her hip. Not because she'd ever put it to the test, but because she'd always thought that at any moment she might decide it was time to begin a wild and crazy sort of life.

Chloe had been waiting to make that particular decision for a long while. Because it turned out that Lao was the only man she'd ever met who could call up this kind of response in her. She couldn't deny that it was thrilling. It was every silly fantasy she'd ever had, finally coming true in the form of that kiss—and whatever came next.

She felt that heat in her again, winding tight and yet managing to reach every part of her at once so she couldn't think of anything to do but lay her forehead against the cool glass. And think about the fact that while she fully intended to surrender to whatever this marriage, in name only until today, brought her, she also knew she could do it fully only because she didn't need to worry about the very consequences Lao claimed to want.

He might think he knew her every move, but she

had to think that wasn't entirely true. Because she'd seen her doctor for her three-month shot only last week, which meant that she had three months to explore whatever happened here without having to worry about getting pregnant. Three months to see how she felt about this man who only wanted heirs when she wanted…so much more. But she couldn't help thinking that if Lao knew that she couldn't get pregnant right away, he wouldn't have started this. If he really did know everything about her, why would he have begun this now?

What that meant to Chloe was that she could… throw herself into this. She could chase down every last one of these daydreams she'd hardly ever admitted she had. She could finally see what all the great fuss was about, and then, if she didn't like any part of this, she could leave.

Because she could lull him into a false sense of security. She had no doubt of that. He was so sure of himself. Better yet, he was so sure of *her*. He would expect her to fall in line because she always did, and because that was what everyone did in his presence.

So there was no reason at all she couldn't let him think that.

For as long as it was convenient.

Then do exactly as she pleased. But this time, without wondering what it was she was missing.

Later, the staff descended upon her again and bore her off with great flourish to the dressing room where they made as if to start outfitting her for the evening.

"These aren't my clothes," Chloe said, stopping short in the doorway.

"Mr. Monteleone wanted to make sure you have as many options as possible," one of the women said. She smiled knowingly. "He is so generous."

Her fingers found their way to her own lips, then. Teasing out the leftover sensation of Lao's kiss that only seemed to get deeper as the hours passed. She would have expected the opposite—but it was as if the kiss had spent the day settling deep into her flesh, becoming part of her.

Doing what Lao did so well and changing her from the inside out.

She reminded herself that she was reclaiming the situation.

"He is very generous," she had to agree, and she even smiled. "But I can trust myself tonight."

As lines in the sand went, it seemed silly. Pointless, even. But she'd drawn it and she would stand by it, Chloe thought. She needed to remember that it had started off like this. That his kiss had sent her spinning, perhaps, but she was still *herself.*

She didn't know what she expected after her announcement. The team of women who gazed back at her to fight her on this, perhaps? Instead, they all smiled and nodded as if they'd expected this all along.

"As you wish, Madam," the same woman said. "We will simply enhance your natural beauty, shall we?"

What that meant, Chloe discovered, was that when she pulled out the simple, workhorse of a black dress she wore to everything—because it could be crumpled up into a ball and tossed into the bowels of any given suitcase, but still look chic and unmarred with a single shake—the women gathered around her transformed what she thought of as a certain quiet pulled together-ness into elegance. They did something understated yet complicated with her hair, twisting the dark mass of it back and fastening it to the nape of her neck, so that it looked deceptively simple and breathtakingly sophisticated. They smudged shadow on her eyelids and dusted something like gold over her cheekbones until she looked as if she was lit up from within.

They capped it off with a hint of diamonds at her ears, her neck, and one wrist. And would not hear of it when she protested. They even switched out her shoes for something a bit flashier, and then shooed her from the bedchamber with a whole lot of Italian and laughter, making it clear that they would not let her back inside.

So there was nothing for it but to head downstairs to dinner.

Where Lao would be waiting for her.

Everything seemed to spin around and around in-side of her then, building up that heat that had stayed at a constant simmer throughout the day.

She felt nervous, she realized as she walked down the long hallway again and found her way to a stair that led her down to the castle's main level. Where, she knew, there were any number of little salons and dining halls as befit the grand place this must have been in the past and was again now.

But all she could think about was Lao.

Once again, she got glimpses of herself in the mirror as she passed. She could see the flush of excitement on her cheeks and the indisputable artistry that the women had practiced on the rest of her, making her shimmer as she moved.

She couldn't tell if she felt like an elegant bride, or a sacrifice.

Why not both? a voice inside her asked.

And she laughed a bit at that, only to swallow it down hurriedly when she turned the corner to go down the last flight of the grand stair, because Lao was there at the foot—his steel gray gaze slamming into her so hard she had to stop and regain her balance.

But it didn't occur to her to stay there where she stopped. She started moving again as soon as she was steady, as if she was helpless to do anything but go to him.

Not helpless, she lectured herself. *Curious.*

And it was as if she was gliding, caught up in that dark heat he aimed her way, all the way down to the bottom step.

Where he took her hand at last.

And for what seemed like forever, simply held it.

"Truly," he said, in that low voice of his that wound around and around inside her, "you are a thing of beauty, Chloe."

She had never before felt beautiful. Not like this.

Not when all she could see was that frank male appraisal, and feel all of that dark, stirring heat inside her.

She had never before *believed* that she was beautiful, but she believed him. She believed he thought so. She could feel the truth of it.

Lao was wearing one of those dark suits that was hand-tailored to the exact width of his shoulders, the precise leanness of his hips.

"So are you, Lao," she said softly, then found herself smiling when he looked surprised that she should compliment him in return.

It made her wonder if he was so overwhelming, so wildly intense, and so astronomically remote in every way that mattered, that no one bothered to offer him compliments. But any such thoughts splintered, because he carried her hand to his lips and pressed a courtly sort of kiss to her knuckles.

It should have made her laugh. It should have felt silly and old-fashioned, but it didn't. Not in an ancient castle, perched here above an island so steeped in history.

And not when the faint brush of his lips across the back of her hand made everything inside her seemed to curl up tight, then begin to boil.

"Welcome, little one," he murmured, the heat in his gaze making everything inside her take notice, especially the tender flesh between her legs. And that heart of hers that would not stop its wild thundering. "To our wedding night. At last."

CHAPTER FIVE

LAO HAD SPENT the whole of the day distracted, which was unacceptable on every level. The point of having a wife, as his father had always told him, was so that a man could focus *more*, not less.

"Too many men's lives are wasted in the pursuit of women," the old man had told his son when Lao was barely thirteen. "And who can begrudge a man a judicious sowing of oats, wild or otherwise? But a wise man settles on a wife early so he can turn his attention to things that matter."

Meaning, things other than Lao's mother. But for all that Lao knew that his father had been the sort of old-school figure who would have done well in a previous century or two—and who hadn't been kind to the wife he'd settled on—he also knew that a man in his position needed to pay attention to his work. A little eccentricity was permitted, even encouraged.

But the moment he lost focus was the moment the Monteleone reputation could suffer a critical hit. Once that happened, the work of centuries of his ancestors could be gone. Just like that.

Power was perception before it was anything else. His father had taught him that, too.

Lao had finally concluded—halfway through a phone call he had hardly heard a word of and could not have recalled if his life depended on it—that it was part and parcel of this waiting that he had been doing for far too long now.

But the waiting was at an end.

And he intended to enjoy tonight in every possible way.

It helped the Chloe looked like a dream come true. And that, better still, she looked at him as if she felt the same. He led her through the castle's great halls, but did not take her to the grand dining room, because tonight he was after something far more intimate. Something memorable and even a bit magical, come to that. He walked her outside and then down a well-lit path that followed what remained of the castle's old walls, hugging the side of the cliff.

"This used to be a stop along the soldiers watch each night," he told her as he led her around to the remains of a medieval tower, the one that sat on the furthest edge of the cliff that stretched out over the slope of the mountainside. "They could see any enemies coming from far off."

"And then fight them?" Chloe asked.

Lao slanted to look down at her. "One of the great boons of Castello Monteleone is that its position is such that a great many fights could be avoided before they occurred. Some generations of my forebears simply barricaded themselves here and kept the mountain roads impassable, so that any enemies who might have wished to confront them died out before they did."

That was not the strictest interpretation of his family's history, but it was true enough.

And Chloe smiled. "Here I thought that Sicily was stitched together entirely of blood feuds."

"Vendettas are as life, *ovviamente*. No Sicilian would ever tell you otherwise. But those stitches fall apart if none of the offending blood remains. My family has always preferred the longer view."

He took the last turn in the path and was perhaps more pleased that he should have been when he heard her indrawn breath beside him. And when he turned, he saw the look of pleasure that washed over her face.

And liked it a bit more than he should if his only goal was *focus*—but he shoved that unhelpful notion aside.

Because the tower he had brought Chloe to was a ruin, but it had been transformed according to his specifications. His staff had strung up too many lanterns to count from what was left of the roof, taking advantage of the temperate evening to create a dinner for two, here not quite beneath the stars on this warm night.

Lao was not a romantic. There had never been a call for such sentimentality, not in the whole of his life.

But it did not take much to understand that Chloe, dreamy and lost Chloe, was nothing but.

He led her to the table and took his time settling

her into the seat that waited there. He sat opposite her, across the cozy table he had requested.

"This is magical," she said in a hushed sort of voice, looking around. There were candles on every possible surface, flickering in the night breeze. Tapestries hung over the holes in what once had been walls on three sides of the remains of the tower, leaving the fourth wall open. Letting in the sweet Sicilian air, the sparkling night sky, and the sea far off in the distance.

The little sigh Chloe let out sounded like music.

"Molto bene," Lao murmured, and then inclined his head toward the shadows where his staff waited, so that the meal would begin in earnest.

And then he set about an enterprise that was entirely new to him. Seduction.

As they ate the pine delicacies his staff had prepared, he played with her hand. He leaned closer. He listened intently to every word she said, asking her question after question. He made her laugh. He made her consider her replies. By the time their big plates were served, she looked more caught up in him than any meal.

What he had not considered was the possibility that he, too, might feel as caught up in her.

"You must feel out of step with the world up here," she said at one point, her gaze out toward the stars. When she turned back to him, she seemed to have them in her eyes. "Or maybe that's what you like about it?"

"I do not worry much about keeping time with the world." But he softened his tone. "It is not arrogance to suggest that the world keeps time with me, whether they know it or not."

Chloe laughed. "No, not arrogance. Not from you, Lao. Perish the thought."

And he had never wooed a woman in his life. Normally all he needed to do was glance at a woman and she would follow him about until he was no longer interested.

But for this one, he would make an exception to all his usual rules.

He felt it was the least he could do on this, their wedding night. To this woman who was already his wife.

So he did not comment on the fact that she dared *tease* him. *Him*. Instead, he asked her question about her art gallery. Not about what, exactly, she thought she was doing there. That could wait. But rather what drew her to an art gallery in the first place.

Chloe sat back in her chair and smiled as if she was truly happy. Not that Lao had much of a reference point. Happiness was the province of lesser men, or so his father had always told him.

"This is the most excited I can remember seeing you in some time," he told her after she'd gone on for some time about the *feelings* art kicked up in her. When all he could really focus on was the sensation that surged in him whenever she leaned closer to make a point. "It seems you really do like art, after all."

"You have quite a bit of art," she said, one hand playing with the stem of her wine glass. Her hair had begun to come out of its twists, so that tempting tendrils fell about her face, begging for his fingers. So he reached over to twist one tendril around and around his finger. To watch the way her eyes lit up as he did, then went unfocused.

"The place is stuffed full of art," he agreed, though he was surprised he could track the conversation. "It's hard to keep track of it all."

That, too, was not exactly true. His father had felt strongly that Lao needed to know every single piece of what was his, or how else could he protect it? His education had required a great many tours through the family collections, even back when this castle was little more than a moldering old ruin on the edge of the property.

"But do you *enjoy* the art you have stuffed into every nook and cranny?" Chloe asked with the sort of intensity he found made him think of what she would be like in bed. This fierce, he hoped. This laser-focused on her need. And his. "When you pass one of the Great Masters that simply hangs about, mostly unseen, one of your walls, do you pause? Are you swept up in the glory of it? Or do you take more pride simply in the owning of it?"

He studied her, letting go of that tendril of her hair and watching as it felt against her cheek. He could not have said what that faint sense of something like unease that crawled through him, then. "I appreciate all the things I collect. Or I would not trouble myself to collect them."

And he could see that look in her dark eyes. He

could read the question there as surely as if she'd asked it, though she hadn't. Perhaps it was the magic of this night. Perhaps she simply did not dare.

"Appreciation is not the same thing," Chloe told him with more of a serious tone than he would have thought a discussion of his art collection required. She even frowned at him. "Art is supposed to sweep you away, or what's the point of it? If it's nothing but a balance sheet, why bother with it at all?"

"We are speaking of *art*, yes? I wish to be certain."

The wind had made her bold, he could see. And there was a part of him that wanted to tap that down at once, because he knew where that led, that sort of irrepressible spirit. He had watched his mother try to bloom in the same circumstances, and fail.

But there was another part of him that liked it.

Even the way she waved a hand, dismissively, as if she expected him to argue with her. Or maybe wanted him to. What was curious was that he did. "Yes, whatever art is to you. Blah-blah-blah investments, I imagine. But, Lao." She leaned forward again, that intense expression on her face once more. "What *stirs your soul*? What makes you feel *alive*?"

And she had never sounded so naive to him. So filled with that fervor and certainty that he should have laughed. He should have told her that reality had nothing to do with souls and he should know, as he spent most of his days shaping it.

Yet he found, to his surprise, that his sex was deeply interested in all this talk of passion.

"Perhaps you can teach me," he said instead.

Her dark eyes searched his, as if looking for trick. Then a smile moved over her mouth, reminding him of her taste. And reigniting the bright flame of his hunger. "Perhaps I can."

"Do I disappoint you, little one?" Lao asked softly. "Did you imagine we could light our own sparks here, speaking of oils and canvas?"

Her breath seemed to take her a moment. "You asked me why I liked working in the art gallery. I'm telling you, Lao. That's all."

Then he watched her close up before him, like some kind of spring flower deprived of sunshine. Like he'd hurt her feelings. But *feelings* should have had nothing to do with this. This was about sex and the heirs he required.

And, too, this was about wanting her, when he had never wanted anything.

When he had never been given the experience of *having* to want.

But the part of him that was only and ever the man who wanted his hands on her perfect body, and his sex so deep inside her that he was tempted to forget his own august name, was perfectly happy to show her passion, too.

Better passion than feelings, he thought then.

He pushed back in his seat, enjoying the way her eyes widened as he rose. "I prefer a far different canvas, Chloe."

He did not wait for her to comment on that. He could

not *wait* a moment more. Instead, Lao reached over, lifted her from her seat, and drew her over his lap.

And he didn't wait for her to settle against him, he simply claimed her mouth with his.

This time, he asserted himself.

This time, he feasted on her, the way he had watched her feast on the art from his kitchens tonight. And she tasted heady indeed, wine and rich foods, and beneath it all, that taste that had driven him mad all day. That taste that was uniquely her.

That taste, something in him whispered, *that you will never escape, as long as you might live.*

But that was foolishness and Lao was no fool. Not even for this woman who made him want things for the first time.

Tonight, he intended to have them all.

He kissed her and he kissed her, angling his jaw to take more as he reached up and thrust his hand deep into the heavy, silken mass of her hair. He tugged until it all came free, falling down around them to cocoon them both in more scent, more heat.

Lao kept kissing her until he could feel her wriggling helplessly in his lap, telling him without words that she wanted him as much as he wanted her. He broke free of her mouth then, following the line of her neck.

He tasted his way across her delicate clavicle, then leaned back to he could slide his palms over the full curves of her breasts.

And gave himself over to the glory of this moment.

The glory of Chloe with her head thrown back, her eyes closed, as the candlelight danced over her face.

The sheer, sweet perfection of Chloe arching her back so that he could take more of her breasts in his hands—pressing herself into him with an intoxicating abandon that swept over him and through him like the strong spirits he rarely allowed himself.

And if she'd been any other woman, he would have cut to the chase, pulling her across his lap to straddle him so he could work his way between her thighs, then sink himself home.

But she was not any woman. She was his wife.

And more, Lao was quite certain that if Chloe had any experience at all, it was scant indeed.

When she whispered his name, he stood them both up, though it made him ache. Still, he put her on her feet and brushed her hair back from her face, and found it harder than it should have been not to get lost in her dark gaze. The heat there. The need all over her face that matched the same need in him.

"Come," he murmured, extending his hand.

Then waited for the heat and fire in her gaze to clear, just enough, so that when she laced her fingers with his, they both knew she meant it.

For a moment, there in the candlelight, there was only the sound of her breath, the steady beat of his heart, and the simmering heat where their hands were clasped together.

For a moment, and perhaps another, Lao simply let the heat between them swell.

But when he couldn't take any more of it he pulled her close, swung her up into his arms, and then strode with her to the spiral stair in the back of the tower that wound down to the room that waited for them.

"The magic goes on and on," Chloe whispered as he carried her into the small tower room that was done up with simple lushness. A fire in the grate to ward off the cold mountain air. A bed of iron, there against one stone wall. Piled high with soft linens and over-stuffed mattresses for their ease and soft rugs on the floor to soothe away the chill of the stone.

"You have no idea," Lao told her, laying her out gently on the bed and following her down into the mattresses' soft embrace. "This is only the beginning."

And then he showed her what he meant.

He luxuriated in the fact that he could spread out with her at last, stretching along the length of her body so he could explore her in full.

All of her. Finally.

Lao shrugged his way out of his clothes as they got in his way and the barrier of linen and cloth became too much. And he stripped Chloe, too, with far more care.

Until she lay before him in nothing but a scant bit of lace between her thighs.

"You have not done this before," he said as he crawled over her, having finally dispensed with his clothing entirely. Her chest was moving, her breath coming in hard pants, and her eyes were big.

But she was flushed.

Everywhere.

She opened her mouth as if to speak, but no words came out. Instead, she pressed her lips together, then shook her head. Side to side, as if in distress.

"I'm sorry," she whispered.

Lao settled in beside her, returning his attention to her perfect breasts. To the proud nipples that stood high, begging for his mouth.

He obliged. One, then the other.

"Why would you apologize?" he murmured against her flesh.

She was arching up against him, pressing her nipple into his mouth, letting out a kind of sigh he thought might play like a symphony in his head forever.

"Everyone knows you must have had a million lovers," she managed to say, though her voice was broken now. "There's no possible way I can live up to any of them."

"The only thing you need to concern yourself with is this," he told her. He waited until she looked at him, her eyes so dark they seemed nearly black. And wildly glossy. "With me. Whatever happens here, between us. There is nothing else, *dusci mia.*"

"But—"

"I will need you to say it, Chloe."

Though he didn't think she would, for a breath. Then one more.

Then, "You," she said softly. "Me. And nothing else, Lao."

He made a low sound of approval, then withdrew from her breasts so he could make his way down the length of her body.

And he remembered that beach in Brazil too well, so he glutted himself on the indentation of her waist, the rounded jut of her hips. He lost himself in circles around her navel, making her moan and shift against him.

Then, at last, he made his way down to that scrap of lace she wore. And while she bucked her hips against him, he wrapped his hands around her, holding her where he wanted her as he played. He used his mouth to taste her, finding his way to the softest part of her and sucking her in, fabric and all.

She made a broken sound and strained against him. And the sounds she made seemed to break something in him, too.

Lao helped himself to the glory she offered him, quickly stripping the lace off of her hips, down her legs, then tossing it aside. Then, finally, he settled himself between her legs, lifting her bottom into his hands so he could lick his way into her softness.

And then, once again, he feasted on the banquet of her.

He brought her to the edge, let her dance there, then pulled back.

It was not until her hands were sunk deep in his hair and she was sobbing out his name so that it echoed off the wall and came back at them. It was not until her heels drummed against his back that he threw her over, letting her buck and writhe beneath his mouth.

Then he only started all over again.

And Lao had waited for this moment. He had wanted her for far too long, so now that he had her, he took his time.

And when she had shattered again and again, and was making soft little noises in the back of her throat, he crawled up the length of her body once more. He gathered her beneath him, gritting his teeth at how easily she came to him. How she wrapped her arms around his neck and gazed up at him. Maybe even *into* him.

Only then did he notch himself between her thighs, ease himself into her softness, and then—without waiting any longer or giving her a chance to tense— thrust deep.

Chloe sucked in a ragged breath, the eyes she'd let fall shut flying open.

And Lao held himself still, watching in a kind of wonder as she let out a long, slow breath that he could feel ripple all through her body.

Which meant all through his, too.

She began to experiment on her own, moving her hips against his. As if testing his length, his depth.

And he let her, doing nothing at all except holding himself there above her. She grew bolder. She began to lift her hips to take as much of him as possible, then dragged herself back, slowly.

On and on she went, concentrating on what she did with a ferocity and focus that made Lao's mouth water. So he let her do as she liked. He let her play with this, with him, finding what she needed, and working her way toward that bliss.

Her intensity made him feel something like humbled.

But she couldn't quite get there, and he waited, the muscles in his arms beginning to shake—and not from the exertion—as he let her figure that out on her own.

"Please," she whispered, and it was the prettiest sound he'd ever heard. "Please, Lao."

So he took pity on her, at last.

And then he took control.

He took her wrists in one hand, hauling them up and over her head so her back arched once more and her breasts danced as he thrust into her.

Lao went deep. And hard enough to make her moan as he took her past where she'd reached on her own and straight on into the sweet heat only he could make for her.

For them.

He set a demanding pace and felt an enormous wildfire lick its way all over his body when she met it. Exulted in it.

Cried out his name like it was a song.

And this time, when she shattered, he lost himself right along with her, secure in the knowledge that he had gotten exactly what he wanted.

That he had broken the spell she had over him.

At last.

CHAPTER SIX

THEIR WEDDING NIGHT might have been five years late, but for Chloe, it was worth the wait.

More than worth it.

Because finally—*finally*—she'd gotten everything she'd ever dreamed of, and more, from her remote, forbidding former stepbrother. Everything she had pretended she didn't want in the light of day. Everything she'd pretended she didn't crave, when deep down, she'd always known better.

He taught her things she hadn't even known were possible.

She had never considered herself *truly* married these last five years. But she also knew she was, in fact, married. And maybe that was why she hadn't been in any great rush to experiment with the boundaries of their in-name-only arrangement.

Then again, maybe the mantle of his protection had been the perfect excuse to keep herself from succumbing to the urge to do something about her innocence with any of the uninspiring boys who were always hanging around her group of friends.

Lao was no boy. He was *man*, and she had learned

that with every touch, every scrape of tongue and hint of teeth. She had understood the entire purpose of her body at last, when he'd showed her what they could do with it. What they could feel, together.

She would have said that she preferred all the bare-chested, hairless men she'd seen so many pictures of over the years, but it was only when she was tangled up in Lao, her face buried in the places where his dusting of dark hair made everything *so much better*, that she got it.

That she more than got it. Some part of her wished she could live forever on that dancing edge of the world, lost in sensation and hurtling toward the next bright implosion, as close to Lao as it was possible to get—

She wished she could go back in time and have her wedding night five years ago, so they could have spent this time perfecting this new-to-her art at which Lao, clearly, was a maestro. She wished she could go even further back and assure the younger teenager with the unwieldly crush on her worldly, faintly disapproving stepbrother that it would all work out.

In the most glorious possible way.

Chloe hadn't held on to her virginity because it had mattered to her in any way. She hadn't consciously been waiting for Lao, for this. She hadn't let herself imagine anything like this could ever happen. But it was immediately apparent to her that she would have regretted wasting her time on some lesser man.

He took her again that night and he was there when

she woke up the next morning, lying beside her with a gleaming approval in his dark gaze that quickly washed away any impulse she might have had to feel ashamed about the previous night's wild abandon.

Instead, she felt a little bit like the goddesses that had once roamed these Italian shores.

She imagined he might take her all over again. She longed for him to do exactly that, amazed anew that she could feel her body's demands so acutely—and that he clearly knew, without her needing to tell him.

She could see it in the way he didn't quite smile.

Instead, he set about putting her clothes back on her body rather than removing them. Dressing her like she was his very own creation. Even helping her into one shoe, then the next, in a manner that left her feeling shivery. And flushed from within.

Then he threw on his own clothes and did not seem to notice or care that, for once, he looked very nearly...rumpled. Not his normal immaculate self, the very definition of male sophistication.

It felt like intimacy.

Especially when Lao led her out of that tower and back up the path they had come down the night before. As if they were walking, together, into this new day. This new version of *them*.

Chloe was absurdly grateful for the hand he held, leading her along the path. Because she felt so changed. So altered from the woman who had boarded that plane outside of London only the day before.

And she couldn't tell if the fact she felt remade was

what made the world sparkle as it did. Or if it was simply the beauty of the Sicilian morning, the ancient perfection of the Monteleone estate, rolling out before her as the man she hadn't dared dream about directly led her inside.

He took her back into the castle, but did not lead her to her own bedchamber. He led her instead into the bathroom suite that sprawled between her chamber and his. There, without a word spoken between them since she'd woken up to find him gazing at her, he set about stripping her of her clothes and his all over again.

When he was finished he lifted her into his arms, taking her to the great copper tub that stood watch over the fields far below. She thought to whisper something to him, some acknowledgment of what had passed between them—but didn't dare.

The expression on his face was too intense, his focus too fierce, as he set about washing her. Everywhere.

And when he had smoothed warm water and a soap that smelled of tangerine and woodsmoke all over her, even between her legs, he rinsed her with the handheld sprayer. Then he lifted her again and carried her, wet and slippery, to the distinctly modern shower stall that stood nearby.

He finally took her again there, his mouth against the nape of her neck, her hands braced against the tiled wall, her head tipped back to let her cries pour out.

Sometime later that morning, she'd woken in his

bed to find him dressed to his usual standard of bespoke perfection and heading toward the door.

"Where are you going?" Chloe asked in a voice gone rough from all the crying and moaning she'd been doing. Even hearing it made her skin warm all over again.

"The commitments I have wait for no man, be he a Monteleone or not," Lao had replied. He had sounded the way he always did, darkly untroubled by the concerns of anything around him.

Chloe pushed herself up on one elbow, shoving the heavy weight of her hair out of her way. She had not meant to be particularly provocative, but she watched as his gaze fell to where her breast peeked over the covers she had pulled over her sometime earlier.

His steel-gray eyes gleamed a fine, bright silver, but he did not come to her.

"I am sure you can find something or other to amuse yourself here, Chloe," he said in that cool way of his. "Though I can't promise anything as rewarding as the odd press junket or art show."

It was only later, after she'd napped again—and deeper—that she realized there was an insult wrapped up in that.

But she was entirely too sated, her body as brand-new to her as if it was her very first day on the planet, to care.

Later that afternoon, her attendants found her again. She was lying near one of the inlaid pools that dotted the terraced garden levels along one sloping side of the mountain, meaning at any moment to crack open the book she'd brought with her. Something brightly covered and fun-looking that she certainly hadn't found in his musty old library of tomes. She'd brought it with her from her last trip to a Waterstones to see what her former colleagues were publishing and promoting these days.

But the memories of last night were too delicious, too stirring, *too much*.

"Come," the attendants urged her as they stood above her, beaming with that same good cheer. "The master wants an early meal this evening."

Chloe understood that meant that the preparation for the master's early dinner needed to get underway as soon as possible. And she found she rather liked the idea that she could let them turn her into a party favor.

Up in her bedchamber, it seemed like great fun to let them go through the wardrobe that had been assembled for her. They settled on a confection of a dress that floated all about her and made her feel like a princess. They even fastened a sort of tiara in her hair that made her sparkle with every step.

She had to remind herself, as she moved through the castle a little too eagerly later, that she was the one who had decided to throw herself into this. Meaning she could remove herself, too.

You're not being swept away, she told herself as she walked. *You are simply enjoying a swim.*

But then Lao took one look at her, ordered his staff

out of the small salon where he had been waiting for her, and had her right there on the table.

As if she was a dessert he could not wait to sample.

And sweeter by far than the *sfincia* they had much later, curled up together in one of the chairs near the fireplace in Lao's rooms.

Another day passed in the same dreamy manner, sex and sun and Chloe's delight in both her own body and his, but then it was Monday.

She woke up early. So early that Lao, who never seemed to rest, was still asleep in the bed beside her. He was golden and bold against the pale linens, his eyelashes much longer than they seemed when she could see all that steel and thunder in his gaze.

There was no reason that should tug at her heart, Chloe told herself sternly.

No reason whatsoever.

She slid out of the bed, then padded over to the great glass doors that opened up to one of the many balconies in this castle that brought the island inside. The sky above, the sea below, as if they were all part of each other. As if they were all the same thing.

And then she stood there, looking out, feeling a kind of aching deep inside her that already felt like loss.

"What troubles you, Chloe?" came Lao's voice from the bed behind her, though it was gravelly just then, as if he was deliberately aiming straight between her legs.

She smiled as she turned to face him. Lao did not

pull his curtains closed, so the dawning light was already making its way into the room to find him on the bed, all that golden skin dusted with dark black hair like a dream come true against the sheets. Her dream. Her truth.

Chloe didn't understand how it was she'd spent days now, memorizing every inch of him, and still her mouth watered for more.

Still she felt as if she could never, ever get enough.

"I'm sorry this has to end," she said softly.

And meant it far more than she intended to share with him. Because she might have been a bit *dozy*, sure, but she hoped she wasn't that much of a fool. She hoped she wasn't silly enough to pour out her heart to a man she'd spent the weekend with, even if it was Lao.

Especially because it was Lao.

It wasn't playing games. It was because intimacy and pleasure were a tangle inside her and yet the dark steel of his gaze was the same.

There was a thread of feminine wisdom deep within her that made it clear that some things were better kept to herself.

His dark brow rose in that way of his. It was a quiet display of arrogance so intense it should have been preposterous. But this was Lao. It was simply who he was.

"End?" he asked, as if she'd lapsed into some kind of gibberish. "Why on earth would anything end? I thought I was clear. I have no intention of divorcing you."

Chloe blinked. "But it's Monday." When he only gazed back at her without comprehension, she found herself almost sputtering. "I… I do have to go to work, Lao."

Another man might have thrown back his head and laughed. That wasn't Lao. But still, she could see by the way he shifted in the bed that she amused him. Deeply.

"You do not have to work." He shook his head as if the very notion baffled him. "You are a Monteleone, in both name and fact now. You are my wife. The only work I require from you will take place here. In this bed."

Something about that seemed jagged within her, like broken glass. Chloe wanted to argue, but he was crooking his finger at her.

And it was as good as throwing a rope around her and tugging her across the vast expanse of the room toward him. She moved without meaning to, making her way to the side of the bed where he hooked his arm around her and tumbled her down with him.

The he rolled her over and lit them both up all over again.

Much later that morning, she texted the gallery to let them know that she was taking a bit of a leave of absence, and couldn't really have said why it was that their dismissive reply—No problems, love. Drop in when you can—left her feeling…almost listless.

As if there was a truth here she didn't want to see.

"You matter," her father had told her once, in a voice as close to stern as Charlie Stapleton ever got. She had been a young girl then, trying to process the fact that her mother had traded her role as a parent for a small fortune and a house to go with it in a distant country. "The world is a better place with you in it, my girl. That's true no matter what your mother chooses to do. No matter what anyone tells you or wants you to believe. You matter, Chloe."

She had held on to that as a child, the way some children held on to a much-loved blanket. Later, when she had been a newly minted teenager, her stepmother had found her stomping around the garden on a cold December morning and had slipped into place beside her.

"A bit of a moody morning," Portia had said. "Just right for brooding about in the cold, I'd say."

Chloe hadn't had much use for her mother and hadn't heard from her in ages. But still, she'd thought that maybe she'd better put on a good show and resist her father's marriage to Portia, because that seemed the sort of thing a decent daughter would do.

That had lasted all of four seconds. Portia had been a force of nature in the best possible way, sweeping up everyone she encountered in her irrepressible good cheer.

"Everyone I know has a plan," Chloe had burst out. "Everyone I know at school is either planning a brilliant university career, already has a gap year lined up, or has plotted out their whole life. Where they want to move. What they want to do. Who they want to be. When all I can manage is being thirteen."

"All you need to be is Chloe," Portia had said in that matter-of-fact way she had, as if she expected the planets would align themselves behind her at her say so.

By then, Chloe had believed they would too.

"But I don't have any idea who that is!" Chloe had cried.

Next to her, Portia hadn't rushed to offer a solution. She had considered Chloe's outburst thoughtfully, as if it mattered to her as deeply as her own issues must, and that was one of the reasons why Chloe had loved her so much. She had always, always listened.

Losing that had been like losing a limb.

"I don't know why you think you should know," Portia had replied eventually, the cold December air making both of their faces pink.

It had made Chloe imagine they were the same. Or could be.

"It seems to me that a life is the process of finding that out. Just because everyone else appears to be on a schedule, with everything sorted, that doesn't mean you need to do the same. All you need to do—all you ever need to do—is what works for you."

And now, here on the same land in Sicily where Portia had once lived, Chloe wondered if she'd been waiting her whole life for this without even knowing it. Because she hadn't been particularly good at any of the things she'd tried, no matter how much she might like talking about art. But what became clear to her, and quickly, was that she was excellent at being this new, full version of Lao's wife.

Like I was born for it, she thought a bit smugly as one week rolled into the next, so that a month swept by and into the next before she noticed.

Because he could hardly keep his hands off her. She wasn't sure he tried. Her days were spent recovering and her nights were filled with Lao. With learning all the different ways that they could make each other come apart.

Nothing was forbidden. Nothing was sacred.

They explored each other, chasing that explosiveness, that drugging release, that endless well of passion.

"I suppose this counts as the honeymoon," she said one evening, when they had both showed tremendous restraint and had made it all the way through dinner without tearing each other's clothes off. Now they sat in Lao's favorite salon in the main part of the castle, sipping at espresso to balance out the wine and the sweets while the stars outside gleamed down over the tangled slope of the mountainside. "Although perhaps not for you. Since you do insist on working all the time."

"Empires do not run themselves, *dusci mia*."

And for fun, Chloe liked to catalog all the ways that Lao was different now. Now that their relationship had changed so much. Now that he was sharing his life with her. He was still Lao, of course. He was still *stern*, but she had a much different context for that now.

Because *stern* now made her shiver, then melt. And perhaps because of that, he seemed less stern to her outside of bed, even unbending enough to lounge there across from her as he was now. As if he knew how to relax.

"What exactly is your empire?" she asked idly, when really, she was congratulating herself on not launching herself at him the way she wanted to. "I read a whole article about the Monteleone family a few years ago. If anything, it managed to make you and your history seem that much more mysterious."

"There's a lesson there, I should think. You'd be much better off not believing what you read."

"I was surprised there was any article at all, if I'm honest. I thought you were opposed to publicity in all its forms. As ancient Monteleone family policy."

"I am." He took a sip, then held the espresso cup in his palm in a manner that sent that same delirious heat dancing all through her body. And when he looked up, there was a considering sort of expression on his face, though he was aiming it out the window and further down the mountainside. "I was taught when I was very young to abhor the kind of flashiness and attention-seeking that so many aspire to these days. Yet at the same time, if we never allow anyone near us at all, we risk creating a sense of mystery that some find irresistible. This has played out in a thousand regrettable ways over the years."

She wanted to ask him how, but didn't. Because she had a sense he not only wouldn't answer, but might even have forgotten he was telling her these things. And Chloe did not want him to stop.

"It has always been my goal to make those who wish to solve the mystery, such as it is, of the Monteleone family feel as if they've already solved it. Hence, articles that pretend to expose me and my history, but these are never truly exposing. In the kind of circles that I run, less is always more and vulnerabilities are only ever seen as weapons to be used against whoever is so unwary as to show their bellies."

She found herself frowning at her own espresso, wondering if it was the rich brew that made her heart beat so fast. "You make it sound like some kind of game, to hide in plain sight."

"It is easy enough." He lifted his shoulder. "For one thing, I do not attend the sort of social events that end up in the papers in the first place. We live in an age where people believe existence only occurs if it is recorded and then disseminated. It is not so much that I try to be invisible but that I simply don't take part in the endless internet celebrity hustle. Monteleones existed long before there was any such thing and they will endure long after, too. If I have an empire, that is what it is. The knowledge of time, how it passes, and what is required of me to make sure my family continues on."

Chloe had no idea why that seemed to poke at her. As if he was insulting her, when he wasn't. "The internet is the new town square. It's how people communicate, like it or not."

"But we are not now seated in a town square, are we? We are at the top of a mountain, in a very old castle, overlooking an even more ancient island. My ancestors retreated from town squares generations ago. I don't participate in the kind of communication most people do. I allow people to find me or I don't."

His arrogance really should have knocked her out of her chair. She thought she really ought to despair of herself for finding it, instead, attractive. Her body was already clamoring for him—and the more arrogant he was, the more she seemed to want him.

Maybe she was broken.

Though...she didn't *feel* broken. She felt hungry.

"You can be looked up on the internet the same as anyone else, Lao," she said, frowning at him as if that might make all that hunger go away when, by now, she knew better. There was only one fix, and it was glorious, but it only made her hungrier. "You're not a ghost, no matter how you might wish you were."

"I control it," he said in that voice of quiet thunder that she felt as much as she heard. "That would not be possible to do if I allowed myself to become tabloid fodder. I control when I am mentioned, and by whom. And in so doing, not only control *how* I am discussed, but who takes part in the discussion." He regarded her then, a faintly curious look on his face. "Why does this subject interest you?"

And she wanted to tell him something lofty and analytical, something that would make her seem more on his level than some dreamy child bride he'd had to rescue more than once already. It astonished her, how deeply she wanted that.

"Because I don't want to be a ghost," she heard herself say instead, without realizing those words were on her tongue. But she'd said them, hadn't she? And now they hung in the air and couldn't be taken back, no matter how high his brow arched. "And I…don't want to have children who disappear in plain sight."

She hadn't told him about her birth control situation. He hadn't asked. There was something in that, too, that she supposed she ought to look at. That he had simply made pronouncements, then taken her to his bed, and clearly had every intention of fulfilling his own wishes as he saw fit.

Whether she had explicitly agreed or not.

Then again, she knew without having to ask that he would not take it well that she'd chosen not to share the fact she'd had that shot. And that in not telling him, she was deceiving him—especially when she mentioned children. Chloe liked to tell herself that was the reason why she didn't pursue these little threads of concern and disquiet that cropped up inside her, now and again.

But she didn't take this opportunity to correct the situation.

Lao was setting aside his espresso and rising to his feet. Once he did, he reached for her, pulling her to him and then hauling her up into his arms.

"The ghost life has much to recommend it," he told her, and she wanted to think that he was joking. But the truth was, she couldn't tell. There was too much behind those eyes of his, but he never shared it. "Let me show you."

And he did. This time he backed her up against the nearest ancient wall, without any kind of finesse. It was hard, deep, and wildly intense.

It was magic.

Because she was always ready for him, now. Because she wanted him more by the second. It only took him tossing her skirts up, holding her as he worked his zipper, then slamming himself home.

It was that easy. It was that *perfect*.

She had taken to biting down on his neck she rode out her pleasure, as if there was something in the quick violence of it that made her shake apart even more.

Or as if, something in her whispered as she panted in the aftermath, *you want to carry his taste on your tongue—the more intense, the better.*

Another night, weeks later, they walked outside after their evening meal. They took in the warm air and the lingering light, as summer waxed on all around them.

"I think of your mother here," she said, looking toward the riotous expanse of rose bushes that reminded her of the flowers Portia had tended so lovingly on her father's estate in England. "She must have loved how the gardens grow in this climate."

But Lao did not respond. His jaw seemed to harden as he looked off, down the mountainside the way he did too often.

"Your mother was no ghost," Chloe pointed out, because those jagged things inside her never went anywhere. They only waited for her to get fed up with the poking. "Of all the things someone might say to describe Portia, the word *ghost* would never come up."

Lao turned that dark look on her, and her breath caught, for there was something forbidding there. Something she would heed, if she were wise. "Still holding on to that conversation, are you? When I thought I taught you there are a thousand glorious ways to haunt this place, at the least."

Apparently Chloe was not wise, for she pushed on. "You said that was my role. And she was the only other Monteleone wife I ever knew." She let out a laugh, thinking of her stepmother and her many projects, from her roses to her stepdaughter to her numerous charities. "I doubt very much that she sat about all day, without any kind of purpose, waiting for your father's notice."

Lao stopped walking. "You did not know my mother as a Monteleone wife, Chloe. You knew her only as a Monteleone widow. They are not the same." And before Chloe could respond to that, much less the darkness in his voice and all over his face, as if he wanted to drown out the early stars and what remained of the summer light, he went on. "And you are mistaken. My father had extremely old-fashioned ideas about her role here. She was to oversee the various tutors he selected for the education he expected me to have here, before I went off to boarding school. She managed the house and the staff, but always according to his demands. She was otherwise expected to be available to him, silent unless spoken to, and charming to any guests." Something ugly seemed to pulse there, deep in the thunder she could see in his gaze, but he only pressed his lips together until it passed. "You, Chloe, already possess a greater degree of freedom than my mother ever did"

"That sounds hideous." Chloe's voice was low, but that didn't hide the hurt in it. Though whether she hurt for Portia or herself, she was ashamed to discover she couldn't say. "I can't imagine your mother locked away like that." She swallowed, hard, but Lao only gazed down at her in that affronted manner of his that made everything inside her...shudder. "She was so...vibrant. Alive. Why would anyone want to lock her up?"

"For precisely those reasons. Because Monteleones do not call attention to themselves." Lao looked back at the castle. "This was only a ruin, then. We lived down at the manor house on a lower part of the mountain."

"I've never seen it."

But she knew. She knew that this was what his eyes searched for in the dark, down that slope, again and again. She knew this was a huge part of the secrets he kept locked away inside of him. She *knew*.

"That is because I had it torn down," Lao told her, confirming what she knew already. And there was something in his voice, then. It made a prickling thing wind its way down the length of Chloe's spine. "This castle was where my mother liked to come when she wished to be alone. And be herself. Once my father died, I decided that I might as well reclaim its place as the family seat."

She felt the strangest rush of emotion tear through her, then. It was how stiffly he stood there before her. It was how little he said, and yet how much there was stuffed in all around the careful words, telling her far more. It was the way he frowned out across the darkness, always in the same direction.

"Lao," she whispered. "What exactly did your father do to your mother?"

It seemed to take him much too long to look back at her. And when he did, there was no hint of that frown. That darkness.

She could see nothing on his face but that same desire that marked them both.

"Lao—" she tried again.

"Enough talking," he growled, and then jerked her into his arms.

And she knew that there was something here. That she should fight. That she should protest, at the very least.

But his kiss was too marvelous. He knew her body too well. She was on fire within seconds, and then entirely wanton in his arms, right there in the dirt where the roses grew.

And it was not until a few days later, after she'd tried repeatedly to return to the topic of his torn-down manor house and his parents' relationship, that she realized there was a pattern here.

Lao didn't want to talk to her about anything of substance. He always changed the subject, and always in the same way. Very much as if what he wanted from her was the same thing his own father had wanted from a wife. Hadn't he told her so, more or less, already?

Sexual availability and obedience. And instead of one child, who could likely be managed easily enough and then sent off to school, Lao wanted four. She doubted that was an accident.

She doubted any of this was an accident. And he hadn't said that having so many children would give her something to do, but once she got that thought in her head she couldn't seem to get rid of it.

Good job you're on the shot, she congratulated herself heartily. *And that you kept that to yourself all this time.*

It was already August when he flew off for meeting somewhere else, leaving her for the first time since she'd come here at the end of May. She thought if she was someone else, she could put the time she was alone here to good use. She would…investigate him, somehow. Round up the staff, ask them questions, and take over the whole place. But she didn't.

Because they had all made it clear in a thousand small ways that they were entirely loyal to Lao. She took long walks around the property instead, heading out farther than the gardens. With him gone she had no one to answer to, so she wasted little time in finding an overgrown but clear path down the side of the mountain, heading straight toward that place where Lao's eyes were always drawn.

The path ended in a field, but she saw it from the path down and knew it for what it was—an overgrown footprint of the house that had once stood here.

It was a warm day, but she shivered. The house had been set on a flat expanse on the slope, the mountain and the castle up above with the better part of Sicily far below.

She stood there in the forgotten rooms, where grass now grew and vines tangled this way and that, trying to imagine what it must have been like to grow up here. Suspended between the sky and the sea and a mother and father who could be called, at best, harsh.

Chloe spent an afternoon there, as if the way the breeze whipped at her was some kind of evidence. As if the way the sun beat down with the birds singing could unlock the secrets of Lao Monteleone.

As if the way her heart ached for him could save them both from these ghosts she was beginning to believe were monsters.

The next day, when he returned, she told herself she would wait to be summoned. But she couldn't hold to it. She heard the car pull up out front and couldn't keep herself from racing down the stairs to meet him.

"I like this eagerness," he told her in that dark way of his, pulling her up against him, giving her a hard kiss.

Then he was tugging her along with him, back up the stairs and into his bedroom. He tossed her down on the bed, making up for those days they'd spent apart.

Making sure she hadn't forgotten him. Or this.

He didn't tell her where he'd been. He didn't tell her what sort of meetings he had to take. She didn't ask.

And it was hard to tell if she was playing along, or if she didn't quite dare.

Later, Lao had food brought to the room. They sat together, wrapped up in the softest robes, out on that balcony as the day's heat rose around them until the breeze rushed in to wash it away.

"I found your old house," she said, and watched him as she said it.

Because maybe she did dare, after all.

He didn't move. He didn't even look at her, and yet she could feel the chill, the dark, the hint of far-off thunder.

Then Lao turned to her—but there was nothing on his face. No frown. No disapproval. Just that hot, gleaming steel.

"That must have been a pretty spot to live in," she said, and she knew she was pushing him, she *wanted* to push him, and maybe she *needed* it—

Chloe caught her breath as he reached for her, but it was only to lift her from her seat and pull her over his lap.

Then his mouth was on hers, hot and demanding. His hands moved between them, arranging her body so she could straddle him and he could surge deep inside of her with one sure stroke.

And she didn't forget as he slammed his way in. She didn't forget as he lit them both on fire, letting that particular storm of theirs in again. And again.

She didn't forget as he took her tight nipples in his mouth, ratcheting up that sensation to near unbearable heights.

She didn't forget as he reached between them, finding the proud center of her need, and pinching it until she sobbed out her pleasure.

Not when she shattered that first time, or a time or two again for good measure.

Not even when he carried her inside and sank into that tub with her, holding her before him with her back to his front and kissing away the words any time she tried to speak.

She didn't forget, but to be certain, Chloe tried again and again over the next week or so. Until there was no denying that it was true.

Her husband wanted very specific things from her. Her body yes. Again and again and again. But when it came to conversation, he wanted it light, on the surface, and easy. Or he was happy enough with silence.

This man who had been the defining force in her

life for as long as she could remember, so long that the fact she was in love with him had been as unworthy of direct mention as the existence of the sky above, didn't love her back. His kindness had, perhaps, not been quite so kind after all.

Because all he wanted from her was sex. Perhaps an heir—or four.

But what he didn't want was Chloe. Not the reality of Chloe, the whole person who existed outside their bed and the white-hot fire of what they did to each other when they were naked.

And she wasn't sure that she could bear it. Not if he didn't see *her* when she looked at him. Not if the only man she'd ever loved, the man she'd dreamed about almost the whole of her life, didn't think she mattered beyond the children he wanted her to give him or the life he wanted her to live, entirely on his terms.

Not if the only way she could have him was to make herself another one of his ghosts.

CHAPTER SEVEN

"I'VE BEEN RESEARCHING the roses," Chloe announced at dinner one night.

"Have you?"

Lao considered her over his glass of wine. She sat, flushed and pretty, in the chair opposite him. The prettiness was a genetic gift, he knew, but he'd had a hand in that flush. He had decided that he fancied an *aperitivo* this evening and had found his way into her dressing room earlier, scattering her attendants with a tilt of his head. Chloe had been dressed in nothing but a strapless bra and matching bit of lace panties, a confection in human form.

She had made him feel drunk when he did not allow himself drunkenness.

He had knelt down before her, drawn one silky smooth leg over his shoulder, and drank his fill.

And then, to prove to himself that he was under no kind of spell, he had not taken his own pleasure in her.

Because he could wait, he had assured himself. He *kept* assuring himself. This was not about need. This was about the future he intended make happen with this woman. Not just any woman—his wife.

And that did not require his own release.

The results of his handiwork were before him now. All that glossy need in her gaze. All that heat in her cheeks that he knew reached every last part of her lush little body.

He had checked.

"I looked online, of course, but in your library too," she said. After clearing her throat and squirming in her seat. She looked edible—though he could see she meant to sound serious. "I can't find the specific variety of rose that grows here anywhere."

Lao did not precisely sigh. He sat back in his seat and considered her. "What I can't help but notice is that you seem determined to find a mystery here, no matter where it is you look. I am tempted to find this insulting. Perhaps you may have heard it said that a rose is…just a rose, Chloe. Sometimes they grow wild and mean nothing at all."

Her eyes flashed a bit at that but she didn't comment directly. She never did. He had never told her that she must keep any hint of her temper to herself, the way he could distinctly recall his own father lecturing Portia back in the day.

"Your silence must be gracious, woman," his father had thundered. "You must reflect the Monteleone legacy with every glance, every word, every expression on your face. What you think, what you feel—these things matter not at all."

Lao had never said such things to his wife.

Still, though he knew that he'd seen that flash in

her gaze, she spoke instead of the damned roses. "I hunted down your gardener. He does not have any English so I had one of the women who help with my dressing translate for me. But he agreed. It's a different sort of rose, Lao."

And a man who was not under this woman's spell might have laughed at that, because it was so obvious where she was heading. But Lao had never been much given to laughter, so he only sighed. "Stop dancing around whatever it is you wish to say to me, please. Simply say it, Chloe, so that we might eat our meal in peace."

There was no disguising the temper in her gaze, then. She looked nothing short of mutinous, and he told himself it was the reaction of a child—but try as he might, he could not truly think of her as a child. Oh, he would like to. It would suit him only too well to dismiss her as immature in every way.

But there was no doubt whatsoever that he had a woman in his bed, not a girl.

Lao could not quite bring himself to lie about that. Not even in the privacy of his own head.

Chloe did not glare at him. Not quite. "Your gardener and I agreed that these roses must have been cultivated. I think your mother made her own variety here."

And then she looked at him as if there were some significance in that. Some lesson that he should take to heart.

What a pity he did not have one.

"My mother was an avid gardener," he said off-handedly. Agreeably enough. "If I recall correctly, she maintained that a house was no home without roses set to bloom and planted them accordingly wherever she happened to find herself."

There was something about the way Chloe studied him, then. As if she was far shrewder than he liked to give her credit for and could see much more than he thought. A notion he did not choose to entertain. "But she did not live in the castle. You said she lived in the manor house, didn't you? That you all did, until your father died."

"My mother did her duty." Lao was uncomfortably aware that his voice was bordering on...tense. "She lived in the manor house until my father's death. Then she moved into one of the guest cottages. It made the decision to renovate the castle easy."

"What about the decision to raze the manor house?" Chloe asked.

Perhaps a touch too sweetly, as he considered it.

And as it happened, he found himself craving dessert. He reached across the table and took the wineglass she held from her hand. Then he pulled her up and into his arms, drinking in the little sighing sound she made, the little hitch in the back of her throat. The noises he found himself thinking about far too often when his attention should have been focused on more important things. The noises he was beginning to think might haunt him for the rest of his life.

"I thought we were speaking of roses," he said, his

mouth against her neck, letting his teeth graze the tender flesh he found there until she shuddered and broke out in goose bumps. The way he knew she would.

He chased her words and her mysteries and her canny questions away with the heat of his mouth, hauling her up against him, his hands already busy. He reached beneath her skirts, happy that she rarely bothered with panties any longer, and certainly wasn't wearing any tonight.

Lao had removed them himself upstairs.

Maybe he had known that he would need her in a fury, like this, angling her back onto the table and pounding into her, his thrusts so deep and so true that she was not the only one who shuddered.

She was not the only one who seemed ravaged by this unbearable heat between them.

But the only thing Lao cared about any longer was when she shattered in his arms, his name on her lips.

Like every night, he set her to rights when their breathing slowed again. He tucked himself away. Then he carried her upstairs to the bedchamber he had never intended to share with anyone and started it all over again, from scratch.

In the mornings, he rose as if he had not been up all night, desperate for her in the dark. He readied himself for work and put in his usual long hours of endless calls and meetings, tending to the only garden he had been taught to care about.

This ever-growing, ever-shifting Monteleone legacy, with its tendrils like vines, reaching this way and that. In his mind's eye it seemed to him that the influence of his name alone wrapped up the whole globe and held it tight.

Just as the legacy itself held him in the same way.

He sat in the office he'd built himself so he could always look not only at the sweep of Sicily and the world beyond, but the remains of the manor house below him. Every day, with only a steep cliff and too much history before him, he could comfort himself with the knowledge that this was only temporary.

Only and ever temporary, this summer. It would be fall before he knew it.

It always was.

This madness, this sensual hurricane, had already gone on longer than any of the affairs he'd ever participated in his adult life. His lovers had always been sophisticated women in possession of their own fortunes, with appropriately excellent pedigrees, so that, should news of their union get out somehow, it would raise no eyebrows. They had been universally overawed by him. Lao had chosen them carefully and pursued them quietly, and because of that, had always wondered why it was impossible to maintain any level of heat or interest much past the first month.

He could admit that it had been something of a relief to take those vows five years ago, and then demand of his own body that he ignore its own demands, his own needs, because above all else he was a man who did not break the promises he made.

And that was the explanation for his reaction to

Chloe. He had spent time telling himself this. Because it had been years. He had been pent-up in a manner that he never had been before. It was no wonder that he had confused that for some particular, unique spell that Chloe had cast on him.

It was no wonder that those first two months had been a pageant of blistering need and that undying desire for her.

He told himself that, now, what animated him was this driving need to see her pregnant. To get the issue of his heir sorted, so he could step back. So he could put this steamy summer behind him.

"You must take care with women," his father had barked at him. The old man had already been in the first flush of his illness, though no one would know it for years yet.

"I always take care, Father," Lao had replied, trying not to show that he was offended. Because he had been just out of university and the last thing he could imagine wanting was the trouble of a child.

Unless it was a woman who might make demands on him outside his bed.

"I'm not speaking of sex," his father had bitten out at him in his usual cold manner. "I should hope you are not so cringingly stupid as to foist one of your bastards on the world. Because I promise you, Stanislao, should that happen, I will cut the both of you off and sire a new heir by morning."

Lao did not doubt that at all. Not for one moment.

As far as he had ever been able to tell, his father was motivated by three things only.

Spite and money.

And, of course, the power that followed from each.

"I am very careful," he had replied. Stiffly.

His father had sat there in that oppressive study in the manor house, his heavy brows clapped together as he regarded his son. "What I am speaking of is the woman you will marry. And do not act as if you are unaware that you must marry to maintain the line."

That, too, was a deliberate slap. "I am aware of my duties."

His father had made a low noise, as if he had some doubts on that score. "I will tell you now, it will be a difficult choice. There are certain expectations of a Monteleone wife. She must be without peer. Her beauty must be a fact, not a debate. She must exude an old-world elegance without tipping too far over into that inbreeding that makes for horse faces and weak chins. Find a decently bred woman who other men might covet, but only if they possess enough sophistication to recognize her for the jewel she is."

Lao had nodded dutifully, while hoping he was not about to be sent off on a hunt for said jewel. "I had no idea that you held my mother in such high regard."

"Your mother is a cautionary tale," his father had barked, and had gone a bit red in the face as he'd leaned forward, jabbing one of the cigars he loved to smoke in Lao's direction. "She commands far too much attention. She has a magnetism that has always offended me and should offend you, too, my boy. Because it is never a single personality that should claim the spotlight, but the Monteleone name."

Always the name. Always the family legacy.

As if he could hear his son's less-than-honorable thoughts, his father had growled and continued, "It is always the name, Lao. Never the man. And certainly never that man's wife. If you do not choose wisely, you will live out your days in turmoil. And I do not mean the wild sort of passion young men might find intriguing." His gaze had been cold. Bracing. "I mean war."

War, Lao had thought then—and thought now, too—was not the least bit appealing.

He found himself standing at those grand windows in his office on another summer morning, awash in another sensual hangover. He scowled out down the mountainside, past the field where the manor house had once stood. The only thing that remained in that field, off to one side and down the cliff some distance, was his father's grave. Lao liked to stand here, high above it, and remind himself that whatever else he might gain in this life, he too was destined for a lonely grave on a mountainside where only the family name mattered.

Before Chloe had come back, he had found that notion a comfort.

It had been much easier when he'd thought he knew exactly how things would go with the girl he'd married.

What he hadn't been prepared for on any level was

that that lost, dreamy creature was entirely different when she was infused with the kind of confidence that came with regular, and regularly excellent, sex. Or a passion that he could not pretend, in the midst of it or outside of it, did not wreck him as it wrecked her.

He supposed that would give anyone an elevated sense of themselves.

It wasn't that he wished to crush it. He didn't.

But he could not encourage it, either.

Because his father had been difficult in a great many ways, but when it came to the care and protection of the Monteleone name, he had been right. Like it or not, he had always been right.

Lao knew that he could not afford to let his marriage take precedence over the Monteleone legacy. Especially when he had yet to make any inroads into the continuation of that legacy into the next generation.

But until he secured the line, he also could not dismiss his wife.

That the latter happened to align with his actual, personal desires only made him more suspicious of himself.

"It can't have been easy to grow up here, all alone," Chloe said another evening when they were walking outside in the garden. The scent of summer flowers perfumed the night air, the castle gleamed like a beacon up the hill from them, and Lao could pretend that he was civilized. Simply because he had not yet knocked her to the dirt and found his way between her thighs.

He told himself there were more and more of these moments, where he reacquainted himself with his self-control. And that they meant her hold on him was diminishing.

"I don't know what you mean," he managed to say with some semblance of good grace. "It is, as you can see very well, a true paradise. I had no complaints."

"You must have been very lonely."

"A Monteleone is never lonely," Lao replied mildly enough, intoning the words he had heard his father say a thousand times. "For he is forever surrounded by the deeds of his ancestors."

And he did not understand it when she laughed, then sobered quickly in response to whatever look he wore on his face.

"You're supposed to play as a child," she argued softly. "Not parrot back strange quotations about family lines. It sounds a bit creepy, don't you think?"

He stared down at her. "No, Chloe. I do not think."

"I told you." And there was a different sort of tension in her voice then. "I don't want to raise my children with ghosts. And I certainly don't want them to *become* ghosts."

That had struck Lao like a blow. "I am no ghost, if that is what you mean."

"If you say so" was her unsatisfactory reply.

And she was the one who lurched forward then, pressing her lips to his. Igniting that wildfire that always raged between them.

Lao responded the way he always did, though he

knew she had done it to forestall whatever he'd been about to say.

It did not sit easy in him, that she should use his own best weapons against him. But he did not push her away, either.

Much later that night—after they had ravaged each other in the bed he did not even pretend they did not share, though they both knew that, supposedly, she had her own—he lay awake. He stared up at what remained of the ancient ceiling, reinforced with the steel girders that helped him remember that he must be the future no matter how steeped he was in the past.

That he had a duty to perform. That he knew all the appropriate steps to take, laid out carefully by all his ancestors.

What he could not do was allow the cancer of emotion to destroy him. Because he already knew where that went.

They had buried his father with very little pomp or circumstance, as befitted a man who had always preferred the shadows to the light. His mother had walked away first and Lao had let her go, thinking that she needed some time to herself, perhaps some space for what he assumed must be an even more complicated grief than the one he had been experiencing.

He did not know how long he stood there. But he remembered the very instant he'd smelled smoke.

The rest of it was a blur. The smoke, the flames. That he had fought to get the fire out, working with members of his staff as if they had all transformed themselves into firemen overnight. And when they'd finally got the fire out, and had lost relatively little in the process—only, he could not help but note, the master bedroom and the wing in which it had stood— he had found his mother wrapped in a blanket, staring sightlessly off toward the sea.

"Did you love him so much then?" Lao had asked her, not sure what that terrible weight was inside him, but assuming it must be more of that same unknowable grief. "That you can think of nothing but following him into the afterlife?"

This despite the war he had always known his parents waged between themselves. The war he had witnessed long before his father had called it such.

"Oh," Portia had said, sounding nothing like her vibrant self, "I loved him once. He knew that, and he used it against me in every possible way. Just as he used my love for you against me. Just as he used anything and everything I loved against me, so he could be sure that the only thing I could ever depend upon was him, for good or ill."

"Mother…" he had tried to say.

But she had looked at him with a kind of fractured, hard-earned wisdom in her gaze that he did not like to think about, even now.

"I walked into that house a silly-headed bride who hoped against hope that I would have a happy life, and your father disabused me of that foolish notion as quickly as possible. And then he made me live in it for near on twenty-five years. And I find that I would rather sleep beneath the rosebushes, thorns and all, up at the castle than spend one more night in this accursed house that was never, ever a home."

Lao thought of that, and it kept him awake.

In the morning, he meant to take himself off to work as usual, but Chloe was stirring. She smiled at him, her eyes sleepy and her body so warm, and then she sang in the shower.

And he was only a man.

He was only a man, and perhaps not much of one, because he followed her into all that steam and heat and made them both groan their way into the morning, not once, but twice.

When they'd finished, boneless and clinging to each other as the water poured down, he wrapped her up so carefully, squeezing out the water from her hair and binding it up the towel. Then he caught himself looking at her as if she was something far more than merely a puzzle he needed to crack.

And she smiled as if she couldn't help it.

"You look as if you've gone a little silly there, *dusci mia*," he said, though he knew he shouldn't. Because he knew better.

He knew better, and especially when her smile only widened.

"The silliest," she agreed, and then she sighed, a big sound that seemed to well up from the deepest part of her. "Lao. I don't know how to say this…"

"Then do not feel you must," he replied sternly, because surely he had some premonition.

But she moved toward him, slid her arms around him, and smiled up at him as if he had placed the stars in their firmament.

And he was only a man, despite his father's best attempts to beat that out of him, and so he basked in it. He couldn't help himself.

He hated that he couldn't bear to step away...but he didn't.

"I love you," she whispered. "I don't know if that's allowed, but I do. I... I think maybe I always have?"

And he could not allow that.

He could not allow *love*.

No matter how his pulse became a drum, how he felt a terrible weight again that he thought he recognized, a vicious grief—

But he had always known his duty. Always.

So he looked down at her as if he pitied her. He told himself he did, and so he tapped her on the nose as he remembered doing, once long ago.

To remind them both of who they were.

"I need heirs, Chloe," Lao said coldly. "Not love poems. Let's remember who we are."

CHAPTER EIGHT

KNOWING SHE NEEDED to leave Lao was one thing.

Doing it was another.

Especially because, her broken heart notwithstanding, Chloe kept thinking that if she just tried a little bit harder, he would change his mind.

If she just kept at it, he would love her.

It was not lost on her that this was a very similar line of thought to the one she'd been swamped in years ago, when she was a little girl trying to make sense of her mother's defection. Somehow Chloe had come to the conclusion that Bianca Stapleton, always the center of her very own spotlight, was driven away by the child she'd always ignored.

That was the reason her father had given her that little talk about *mattering*.

"The truth is, my darling," he had told Chloe when she was older, "Bianca never loved a thing on this earth but herself and I doubt she ever will."

It was Portia who had loved Chloe, as if Chloe was hers. It was Portia who had raised her in the years they'd had together. It was Portia who had loved Chloe's father, too—just as it was Portia who had always rolled her eyes with her usual wisdom and good humor when Lao was around.

"My son was raised to take himself very, very seriously," she'd always said. "And heaven forfend those of us around him don't follow suit—the very fabric of the universe might be torn asunder."

Back then, it had not occurred to Chloe that it was *possible* to tease a man like Lao.

What she had understood, even as a small girl, was that it certainly wasn't *advisable*. And that the sort of teasing a man like Lao might accept from the woman who had given birth to him was likely not something that he would tolerate from anyone else.

But she tried that, too.

"You really must *try* to take yourself less seriously," she ventured one night. She even did her best impression of his mother. "Or you might actually turn into one of your bronzed statues, and then what will the grand Monteleone legacy do?"

As they had been walking along the castle's gallery, festooned with statuary in all directions, it had seemed like a reasonable thing to say. A bit funny, even. Especially as Lao was clearly in in a particularly glowering sort of mood and could do with some cheering up.

But she really wished she'd thought better of it when he looked at her in frozen amazement.

"I beg your pardon?" he asked, his voice soft in that way that meant he was on the verge of going fully incandescent.

And, because Chloe was at heart a coward when it came to this man, she cleared her throat. She felt herself wilt inside, and likely matched it outside, too.

"What I meant to say," she managed, "is that I'm not sure I fully understand your point? If you could repeat it?"

"I said what I always say." His dark gaze had been too brooding, too gray. "That when we began the real part of our marriage, I assumed that things would progress quickly."

"Bodies do as they like, regardless of our assumptions," she replied breezily.

"That is all well and good, but it is come September and you are not pregnant. Are you?"

"I am not," she agreed, when what she thought was *September*.

How had she missed the fact that she'd passed her three-month cutoff?

"We will fly to London in two days," he informed her coolly. "There is a doctor I wish you to see."

And that was it, then.

Chloe had to stop pretending.

He didn't love her, and there was no quiet way off this mountain—even if she'd wanted to go. There was no nipping out for a paper and failing to return. She didn't feel trapped, because how could she feel trapped when the man she loved was here?

But a trip to London meant her time was up. She already knew what his doctor would tell him, patient privacy be damned.

She'd had her experiment. She'd experienced more than she could possibly have imagined, going in. Surely she would find a way to be happy about that.

And in the meantime, it was time to leave him.

While she could still make herself go.

And before he learned what secret she had been keeping from him.

Chloe supposed that she'd known that the summer was ending, like it or not. There had been so many hints that she'd ignored. The breeze was no longer quite so soft. Some of the nights were downright chilly.

"London," she said faintly, focusing too intently on some or other bronze. "How lovely."

And she spent the time she had left saying her goodbyes.

To this marvel of the castle, stone and steel. To the tangled mystery of Sicily, these slopes and fields, groves and vineyards. The golden sunrises, like candy floss stretched across the horizon.

And in every spare moment, she said goodbye to Lao as well.

In the bed they had shared these last months. Sunk deep in that copper tub with its view of eternity. In the night, out near Portia's roses. She even took him by the hand and led him down that path he'd showed her on her first night here, down to that half-ruined watchtower, so she could show him all the things she had learned.

All the ways she had finally become his.

She didn't get much sleep, but that was a good thing. It allowed her to tell herself all manner of stories about why she was feeling so fragile when they finally boarded his plane. Or why, looking down at the castle and the whole of the island of Sicily from the air, she felt as if she was being torn in two.

You need a nap, she told herself, over and over again. *That's all.*

"You seem unusually subdued," Lao said as they soared high above the sparkling Mediterranean and headed north.

"I was thinking of the flight down months ago," she said, which was not a lie. She forced a smile, which was. "And how everything turned out so differently than I expected."

When he didn't respond, she glanced over at him, to see him studying her far too intently from across the table where they had taken their seats.

"Do you have a complaint that you would like to register?" he asked, his voice that mixture of mild disapproval and cool affront that made her sit up straighter even as it made the center of her need for him throb.

But today, maybe because she knew this was the end, it occurred to her that this was how this man who was raised to view feelings as a betrayal expressed his.

That felt like a revelation. She was almost tempted—

But no. He didn't love her. That was the beginning and the end of it.

"How could I have a complaint?" she asked lightly. "I am a Monteleone wife. Surely hordes fight daily for the honor. I am merely readying myself to defend my title on the streets of London."

Those steel gray eyes searched her face. And she felt as if he'd reached over and scooped out the contents of her chest, leaving her empty.

But no, said a voice inside her that sounded a little too much like Portia's. *He has no need to do that. You are doing it for the both of you.*

"Very droll," Lao murmured in reply. "But it is no joke, Chloe. My only task in this life is to support my family's legacy, not diminish it."

"I know," she said, the words coming out on a rush of breath. And this time, the way she curved her lips was no lie. "I think you're lucky, really, to have been born with a purpose. Some of us wander about our whole lives and never find any. You had yours handed to you at birth. I understand that comes with its own set of challenges. But still, I think you really are lucky in the end."

"My father would be offended at such a notion," Lao said quietly, but there was something about the way he said it. Some kind of new, dangerous heat that lurked there, just beneath the surface. "He would say there is no such thing as luck. There is only strategy, power, and good breeding."

"He sounds like a fascinating man." Chloe waved a hand when Lao frowned at her. "What? I've always been fascinated by him. After all, he was the other ghost who hung over my childhood. And he was the one who mattered. I'm not sure my mother really counts, because, as far as I'm aware, she is still quite alive."

"Your mother lives on a lavish Bel-Air estate in Los Angeles," Lao told her matter-of-factly. "These days she prefers a party circuit of well-placed lovers, who shower her with gifts because they think the settlement that pays her bills means she has some kind of power. All in all, I think she's quite as happy as she can be."

Chloe blinked. She let out a laugh, though it was involuntary. "That's…more information than I've had about Bianca in years."

"I started keeping track of her when my mother started dating your father. It seemed prudent, given her love of scenes and spectacles. And I continue to track her because she is, after all, the only living relative of my wife."

Lao raised a shoulder then lowered it as if in total unconcern, then returned his attention to his tablet and the work that waited for him at all times.

But Chloe…didn't quite believe he was as unconcerned as he pretended.

The trouble was, she knew him. She had known him for a long time. And the cold man who wished to compartmentalize everything and lock her away, his own Monteleone wife locked up in a tower awaiting his pleasure, was not the same man who had been surprisingly kind to a motherless girl.

She knew his mother. She had listened with avid attention over the years as Portia had told this or that anecdote about the boy Lao had been and the man he had become.

She knew the not quite stepbrother who had stepped in to take care of her when she'd been so lost in her own grief that she still didn't know what might have become of her otherwise or where she would be now.

And even now, with all his cool demands and orders, she still knew him. Looking back, she did not think she could possibly have surrendered to him so totally if she hadn't understood, down deep into her bones, that for all his thundering and all that steel, this man could never hurt her.

Hadn't she experienced that firsthand that night in the tower? When he had relieved her of her innocence and introduced her to a new version of herself she never would have found otherwise?

She was so different now, on this side of the most remarkable summer she'd ever had.

Chloe thought about her funny, brash, remarkable father and how open he'd been about his own mistakes. He had never savaged Bianca, but he'd made it quite clear that in his first marriage, he had allowed himself to be swayed by external factors. A mistake he had not made twice.

She thought about Portia, who had clearly suffered in her role as Monteleone wife and had made it clear, every single day she was with Chloe's father, that she had never been so happy before.

She thought of Lao himself, the way she always did. The way she'd been thinking of Lao since she was a kid. And maybe she was the one at fault here, looking for signs of love from him that he could not give. Not because he didn't feel things, but because he didn't know how to show them.

Then again, she told herself sternly, *maybe he just doesn't love you.*

She felt that churn about inside her, making her feel sick to her stomach. Because the truth was, she didn't want that to be true. She didn't *want* to leave him.

All she needed was the tiniest little sign and she would stay forever, living off the crumbs of Lao's affections, such as they were. It was clear to her now that he had intended she do exactly that from the start. He had sex with her to keep her quiet, to keep her content.

And the passion between them was real, she had no doubt on that score. It was overwhelming and it was glorious and she did not think that she would ever quite recover—

But that didn't make it love.

Lao had told her enough about his childhood for her to know that none of his reasons for the things he said he wanted were good ones.

He wanted an heir because his family legacy required an heir, not because he had looked at Chloe one day and wondered what it would be like if the two of them created another little being made of bits and pieces of the both of them.

The only thing he cared about was his legacy.

He had told her so himself, hadn't he? A thousand times.

She could sit here and argue herself into thinking that he said such things—even thought such things—because he didn't know any better. Naturally, she was tempted to believe that all he really needed was someone to love him.

And she could already feel herself wilting inside.

After all, it had only been a short summer. It would take years to love a man like him enough to wash away his past. Was she running away too soon? He would be upset about the birth control shot, sure, but he would get over that. She was sure he would.

But she couldn't quite convince herself.

And she might have been the dozy cow Mirabelle liked to call her, but she knew one thing beyond a shadow of a doubt. Chloe still might not know what she wanted to do with her life. She might have meant it when she told him that he was lucky that he had a purpose.

Chloe might not know a whole lot of things, but she knew that she mattered. And more, that she was supposed to matter to the people in her life.

She would love Lao forever, if he would let her, and she didn't even require that he do it the way she might.

What she did need was to know that he could love her. That he *wanted* to love her. She did need that little bit of encouragement.

She also knew that Lao was not going to give it to her.

And so, in the end, it was easier than it should have been, because he expected her to remain docile. *Dozy.* She had given him no indication she would ever be anything but.

He took a call in one of his gleaming, luxurious limousines as they pulled up outside the doctor's office. He waved her inside,

Chloe marched into the lobby and was halfway to the appropriate lift before it occurred to her that this was the chance she had been waiting for. And even then, she hesitated. She looked back outside, toward the car...

But another thing her father had told her, especially after Portia died, was that life was for living, like it or not. And no one ever claimed that living was fair.

So instead of going up the lift to meet a doctor who was sure to tell her husband exactly why she wasn't pregnant, she walked through the lobby until she found a different door. Then she slipped out onto a different street and walked away.

She chucked her mobile, then presented herself at the nearest bank, where she withdrew a significant amount of money in hundred-pound notes. She bunged it all in a bag from the boutique next door, then bought herself a ticket on the first train heading north.

Mirabelle or one of her other friends would have been only too happy to let Chloe stay with her, but Lao was sure to look at her friends. And if she was honest, she didn't want to explain her summer to them. She didn't even know how she would begin.

Funny story, I've actually been married for five years? Yes, you know him. I mean, you know of *him...*

She didn't want to reduce what had happened between her and Lao to a silly story she could tell over drinks. The very idea made her feel a bit sick.

Within an hour, she was chugging out of King's Cross, with the ticket that would get her all the way to Aberdeen.

Eventually.

It was raining, and that felt right, so she sat by the window and stared out at the row houses she passed in London neighborhoods she'd never visited. Then, as the train sped north, she saw whole towns and small cities filled with *lives*. Filled with people with purpose, and people without any, all of them hunkered down and *living* in the same cold rain.

She told herself it was a comfort.

She was almost convinced it really was.

Chloe got off the train in the first place that she looked at and thought, *I wonder what it's like to live here* instead of *who can possibly live like that*. It seemed like the right distinction to make. It was already dark, and the September night was much wetter and colder in Scotland than it had been Sicily. But she found her way to a hotel and stayed there that first night, where she curled herself up in the narrow bed and sobbed herself to sleep.

It took her very little time to find a little bedsit in

the city center—as it was amazing what cash in hand could do—and then she found a job waiting tables in a café, because it was that or spend her days becoming one of those ghosts she'd made it clear she wanted nothing to do with.

Every hour without Lao, she could feel herself becoming more and more see-through, as if she was disappearing by the day.

Yet the more she did a thankless job she didn't really fancy, the more she daydreamed about what she might prefer instead. Maybe infinite choice was a recipe for disaster. Maybe she would have been better off if her father had been strict with her. If he'd laid down the law about all the things she had to do and achieved to please him.

Maybe she could have had something to rebel against. Maybe that would have changed things.

But her father had loved her to distraction and had denied her nothing, and she knew that now the same as she'd known it then. With that same certainty and love. Just as she knew that if he hadn't, she would never have managed to do the necessary thing and walk away from a man who she might tell herself loved her madly—but he didn't want to.

And he would never say so anyway.

Chloe had to think that the bare minimum requirement she should accept from a man she was married to—especially one she had such intense chemistry with, which was really just a shortcut—was that he make her feel that kind of love. Not a father's love, but that kind of expensive, fundamental love, or what else was there to build life on?

Every day at the café, where she was in no way a great waitress, she gave herself rousing, private speeches about what she would and would not accept. She believed every word.

Still, she wavered.

The nights were the hardest. And she found that she'd become a bit of a night owl, because she did just about anything she could to stay awake. It was that or fall asleep and lose herself in those dreams. Dream after dream of the things she and Lao had gotten up to together. The taste of him in her mouth when she woke. The ache in her body because she wanted him so badly.

Sometimes she woke with tears pouring down her cheeks, sobbing, on fire, and so lonely she thought it might break her in half.

She *wavered*, and she was half ghost already, and it would be so easy to ring Lao the way she'd rung him a hundred times before. All she'd need to do was whisper his name and he would come to her.

He would save her from having to live with the choices she'd made. He would take her over and she would let him and she could convince herself all over again that he really was her purpose—

When he didn't want to love her, he just wanted babies. And obedience.

Chloe would never know what she might have done if she hadn't started feeling ill.

At first she just felt heavy. Then she began to feel

nauseated at the strangest times. The smell of the food in the café where she worked could suddenly set her off. A meal she been living on—beans on toast, say— suddenly tasted revolting in her mouth. And maybe she knew what that might mean. Maybe she didn't want to know.

Maybe she was her own wishy-washy self to the bitter end.

But when she found herself waking up in the mornings and having to race to the toilet to heave up her empty stomach, she knew.

She didn't need confirmation. She rinsed her mouth, then walked the two steps out into the middle of her little bedsit, her head spinning.

Yet even as it spun, her hands crept over her belly, and she felt herself…exhale.

A sense of calm seemed to envelop her where she stood, in a little city in Scotland, a stranger to everyone she encountered.

And she didn't feel the slightest bit of *wavering* at all.

She was going to have a baby. And she was Chloe Stapleton, Charlie Stapleton's much loved only child. Even if Lao could claim half of the fortune she'd had him manage, the other half was hers. And it was more than enough.

She thought about Bianca and whatever high life her mother thought she was living. She thought about Portia, who had walked through a fire and then had lived out the rest of her days in joy.

All this time, she hadn't understood. She hadn't *known*.

But now she did.

She was going to be a mother. And she knew that some women, having left their husbands and taken themselves off into strange and unlikely circumstances, would be scared. She would have been scared six months ago.

Yet today she was anything but.

Chloe had never felt a greater sense of purpose in her life.

This baby deserved all the things that Chloe had always wanted, and had only partly gotten. This baby deserved the world.

And Chloe intended to give it to her or him.

Whether Lao loved her or not.

CHAPTER NINE

LAO WOULD HAVE SAID, with the greatest confidence, that Chloe could not possibly evade him for a day. Much less an entire month.

And certainly not two.

Then again, he would also have said, with the same amount of confidence, that she would not *wish* to do anything of the kind.

Yet it was November when he finally got the call that he had been waiting for.

She had been sighted at last. After pulling off her exit from his life with an ease that made him wonder if he'd ever known her at all, she had reappeared in the same manner, as if in a puff of smoke. He waited, certain she would contact him the way she always had—

But she did not.

Moreover, she did not come back to Sicily, alive with apologies and explanations. She did not make any attempt to contact him at all. If he had not set his men in all the places he could think she might show, he might never have known, as he did not spend a great deal of time roaming about the neighborhood of that grand old estate outside of Winchester where Chloe had grown up.

Lao was tempted to conclude that his people were incorrect and it was not Chloe at all—but they were certain. And they had proof. Photographic evidence of a woman who was very clearly his missing wife, out for a walk in a misty British morning.

As if she had not abandoned him on a London street without so much as a backward glance. He knew. He had seen the CCTV footage.

And so Lao flew north from Sicily, consumed with that same rage they had eaten him alive since he had walked into that doctor's office and discovered that she had run off.

That rage that had been hot and bright and all-encompassing at first, but now it was…colder.

And it grew more frigid with every kilometer, he rather thought, as he sat in the back of the car that carried him through the frozen countryside of this bitter island she called home. This island she unaccountably preferred to his.

He could admit, if only in the privacy of his own head, that he had not spent these months without her gracefully.

Lao had spent three months with her, trying his best to keep her at a distance despite the demands of his own hunger. Then the next three without her, as much distance as it was possible to have, and he… had hated it.

The castle he had fashioned so that he might never

live in misery, the way so many generations of his family had done in the manor house, had betrayed him. He found himself listening for her light, quick steps in the halls. He woke, certain he heard her laughter, only to find himself alone. His body had become conditioned to her touch, and he was appalled to discover that he missed it almost more than he could bear.

That he missed *her*.

Her absence was more of a distraction than her presence had ever been, and Lao, who had dedicated his life to being precisely the same man every Monteleone heir had always and ever been, was terribly afraid that he was forever altered.

At first, after ascertaining that she had not been abducted, he had not looked for her.

He had been certain that whatever might have spurred her to run from him, she would call him within the week, filled with shame and almost too flustered to talk. He imagined all the ways he would accept her back, how magnanimous he would be, and exactly what recompense he would demand from her sweet body.

But she did not call.

At the end of September, he'd sent his men off to find her, certain he would discover that she was languishing in some friend's villa somewhere warm and undemanding. Or, if not, perhaps haunting an art museum or gallery somewhere, talking of perspective and chiaroscuro with great passion to the unwary.

But she was in none of the places he thought she might be.

She was nowhere at all, though his men tracked her to a northbound train headed out of London. Eventually, they found that she'd exited that train in Scotland. Lao had spent the better part of October fielding reports from his men as they traced her through the Scottish hinterland, never finding her—but finding where she'd been. She had stayed the night in a questionable hotel. She had rented a sad bedsit above a chip shop. She had become a waitress in what the British called a kind of café, though it bore no resemblance to any kind of café Lao might frequent in Italy.

If he ever frequented cafés, that was.

Every day, Lao was forced to face the unpalatable fact that he clearly did not know Chloe at all. Because the Chloe he did know would never have managed to conceal herself. She would not have thought to use only cash, so as not to be easily traced. She would certainly never have lowered herself to bedsits and cafés that served only weak coffee and fried food.

She would not have known that she could bank on no one recognizing her, because no one had been looking for Chloe Stapleton, late of the society pages, in a grubby little town of stone and rain so far from any part of her actual life.

It was impossible not to take it as an insult.

That she should go from Castello Monteleone to living a life a bare shred above the poverty level—willingly and deliberately—was an affront. Though

Lao could not pretend that he did not know that what outraged him the most was that he hadn't found her while she'd done these things.

Or that she was clearly no longer bothering to hide, which was the only reason he'd found her now.

He gritted his teeth and reminded himself that his temper had cooled. That it needed to stay cool.

But that was difficult to manage as he started to recognize the landmarks outside his windows.

Lao couldn't say he was pleased with this unwanted trip down memory lane he was forced to take as his driver navigated the increasingly familiar route to the old stately home where his mother had gone to live—with unseemly haste, in his opinion—after Portia and Charlie had gotten together.

This despite Lao's misgivings.

"You hardly know this man," Lao had argued when she had found him on the grounds of the castle, talking plans with his architect. She had chosen her moment deliberately, he knew. Because as little predisposed as Lao ever was to making a scene, his appetite for such things when there were witnesses was zero. "If you must date, Mother, surely you can do so without setting up domestic arrangements at the drop of a hat."

"Lao," Portia had replied, smiling in that way she had had…as if she was made up of too many secrets he could never possibly know. "I was not asking for your permission or even your blessing, though I would like it if you care to offer it. I was telling you what is happening, blessing or not."

She would not hear any arguments. There had been nothing for it. His mother had been remarried again before that year was out instead of living out her days as his *nonna* had done, wearing black only and asserting her will by whatever means she could. That was all unfortunate enough.

Worse, Lao had found he had no option but to come to this house in the British countryside far more than he liked.

Because his mother had refused to return to Sicily. Ever.

And he could admit that he had blamed Charlie Stapleton for that. Though now, as his car turned in the long drive that led up to the great old house, he wasn't sure why. It wasn't as if he didn't have a good idea why his mother had left Sicily. Why she had been unhappy as a Monteleone wife.

Or why she had tried to burn the manor house down.

And as the car drew up before the house, he found himself thinking that he could see his way toward a spot of pyromania all too easily.

The last time he'd seen this old heap, it had been in pictures sent by his staff after they'd closed it up five years ago. Chloe had been down in London, flitting about from one flat share to another with interchangeably pointless school friends of hers. There had been no need to keep the house open, so he hadn't.

It was instantly clear to him from the lights cutting through the November gloom alone that the house had been reopened without his permission or knowledge. For at least as long as it took to get a house this size up and running. There was smoke curling from the chimney. He could even see through the windows, meaning the shutters had been opened wide and inside, the furniture had been uncovered.

It looked a lot like Chloe—*his wife*—had moved back in.

When Lao knew this to be impossible, for *he* most certainly did not intend to live in England in this lifetime or the next.

He didn't wait for his man to open the door. He was out, sucking in deep breaths of the frigid November air as he stalked up to the front door and tried to open it.

Unlike his castle, which was of course protected by gates much lower on the mountain, the door to the old house was locked.

And so it was that he, Lao Monteleone, was forced to stand about in the cold, ringing the bell as if he was no better than a traveling salesman. Hawking his wares from house to house and hoping not to be run off by dogs.

He expected Chloe to open the door.

Or to shout at him through it while refusing to open it, more like, as that seemed to be the incomprehensible path this was taking.

But instead, the same ancient butler Lao recalled from his many visits here over the years opened the door and managed to look at him with a particular

English hauteur that made it perfectly clear that the butler, at least, did not approve of him.

The insult was so great that it was obviously intentional, and Lao took a moment to cast about for the correct thing to say. Something that did not involve the cold fury he could feel charging through his veins—

But the butler stepped back. Wisely.

"Mr. Monteleone," he said, by way of a frosty greeting. "Miss Chloe has been expecting you."

Lao then prowled through the old house in the butler's wake, not sure how he was meant to handle this increasingly bizarre situation. It had been a long while since he'd found himself outmaneuvered, if ever. And if he'd had to guess who it might be who would manage to leave him feeling as if he didn't know what was going on, he would not have chosen Chloe.

Not his lost Chloe, who had only ever seemed to find herself with him.

Perhaps, came his mother's serene voice inside him, *you are not quite as lofty as you like to think you are, my son.*

He chose to shove that aside.

Lao had spent entirely too much time in this house, close and crowded as it was—like all houses of its ilk. He would even say that all the time he'd spent here had helped him as he was designing the *castello*, because he had wanted the opposite of this particularly British experience with its small rooms and closed doors.

The butler seemed to slow down on purpose with every step, and Lao refused to give the man the satisfaction of indicating his own impatience. So he slowed too, though the last thing he needed was quite so close a tour of a place he had never cared for overmuch.

And he thought his jaw might shatter from the effort of clenching it as hard as he was by the time he was finally waved into a room he recognized only too well.

It was the atrium that his mother had made into a greenhouse here, so she might keep a garden all year long. And Lao had grieved the loss of Portia in too many ways to count. He might not have agreed with his mother's every choice, though he had understood them, on some level. Because for a long while, they had been the only allies each of them had. They had not needed to discuss in any detail what they'd lived through, because they had survived it together—if in different ways.

And when he had not been pondering what it meant for his family's legacy—which had then been his responsibility—that his mother had gone off and remarried in such haste, he had been able to admit that he'd enjoyed seeing her happy.

Maybe some part of him had even thought that if she could be happy, maybe there was hope for him, too.

Though Lao had long since dismissed that sort of thought as weak and unworthy of him. Men in his position did not concern themselves with *happiness*. There were far too many other important things to do.

Still, it felt like stepping into a little too much old

grief tonight. Because all of his mother's plants were gone. Of course they were. But he had found her here a thousand times, flitting from worktable to window box, deadheading flowers, cutting back this growth or that, and sinking her hands into the rich earth in her collection of pots.

It took him a moment to realize that she and her plants were not here. That the figure standing at the windows, her back to him, was not Portia. Those were memories.

This room, empty and cold, was real.

"It feels wrong that there are no plants here, doesn't it?" Chloe asked, without turning to face him, and that only made it colder. "If I thought I could grow my own roses here in her honor, I would."

Lao took in the sight of his wife…hungrily. He took in every detail. Her dark hair tumbled down her back in wild abandon instead of the more structured styles she'd worn in Sicily. He hated that he…didn't hate it. And though it was not warm, her feet were bare. And she otherwise wore a body skimming dress that made him entirely too aware the curve of her bottom.

Remaining where he was, and standing still, began to feel like something of a heroic act when all he wanted was to get his hands on her.

"What is this?" He kept his voice low in the hope that might keep the driving pulse of his temper at bay.

It was unsuccessful.

"Symmetry," Chloe said quietly, still looking out into the afternoon mist. "Does this not feel familiar to you, Lao? Only this time, I am the one standing in a window and you are the one in the doorway with no idea what's happening. It isn't pleasant, is it?"

And for the first time in as long as he could remember, Lao laughed.

Then had the distinct pleasure of watching his wife's spine straighten, as if the sound was an assault.

An assault with goose bumps, he could see. Which meant she was not as coldly set against him as she wanted him to believe.

"You are my wife, Chloe," he reminded her, and there was no concealing his temper any longer. He was not sure he'd tried. "I will tell you exactly what is going to happen. You will return to Sicily. You will resume your place at my side. And if you are very lucky, I might allow you to leave my mountain in another fifty years or so."

She turned around then, and he was struck at once by the way her dark eyes blazed. By that strange new expression she wore on her face. He hardly recognized it. Or her.

And he didn't like how that made his chest go tight.

"No," she said.

Very distinctly.

And for a moment, that was the only thing that he could focus on. That single syllable that hung there between them as if it alone might bloom here, in this greenhouse where so many other flowers had flowered before.

"I beg your pardon?" He spoke through his teeth.

"No," she said again, sounding even more defiant than before. Her chin rose. "And even though that is a complete sentence, Lao, I'll explain it to you. If you want me to come back to you, then you must say so. I will not be responding to orders or commands. If you have something you want from me, you can ask for it. You might or might not get it. But I can tell you right now that you absolutely will not get anything from me by acting as if you're my boss instead of my husband."

"I fail to see the difference."

Even as he spoke, his gaze was moving over her with that same consuming need, that same hunger—made worse by these months without her. He was drinking her in, making sure that she was precisely as he'd last seen her. That she was still his, whether she knew it or not.

But she was wearing that tight, stretchy dress.

And she was not the same.

That pulse inside him grew louder. It became a kind of drum.

Lao was crossing the room, bearing down on her before he knew he meant to move, and he could not imagine what look he must have had on his face. But he did not mind it when her eyes went wide.

"I hope you don't think you can intimidate me," she began, in a higher-pitched voice that suggested he could.

And there was a part of him that did not want to intimidate her at all—but that was lost in the wild drumming that had taken him over.

"I would suggest that you choose silence," he managed to say, his voice barely more than a whisper as he reached her.

He was not looking at her face. He was looking at her breasts, heavier now and rounded. He was letting his gaze skim down the rest of that body he knew better than his own, immediately noting the slight protrusion of her belly. The thickening of her hips.

Lao kept going, backing her up until she was pressed against the glass. Even then he didn't stop. He kept on until he could plant one hand beside her head and then he leaned closer, testing the evidence that his eyes had given him with his hands.

He took one breast in his palm, and ignored the startled noise she made as he weighed it against his memory and found it heavier. Then he smoothed his way down the length of her torso until he could find the new little belly she was sporting.

He kept his hand there as he felt her breath pick up. As he felt the heat of her bloom.

As he raked his gaze back up to stare her full in the face.

"Tell me I am mistaken," he growled out at her, not sounding at all like himself.

And, for once, not caring.

"I don't know what you are, Lao. I never have. What I do know is that you should not go around manhandling people—"

"You are pregnant," he bit out as if he could not believe the syllables that were coming out of his own mouth, because he could not. Because the betrayal was so deep, the cut of it so intense, that he was surprised he could still stand. "You are *pregnant*, Chloe. You ran from me. You hid from me. What game can you possibly think you are playing?"

He assumed she would crumple at that. That she would tremble.

But to his surprise, she straightened from the glass behind her, and pushed his hand away. He thought she might try to run again, but instead she stood tall, tilted her chin back, and held his gaze.

Without, it seemed, a single shred of fear.

When he rather thought she should have been significantly more worried than she appeared.

"I am pregnant, yes," she agreed, sounding significantly—and offensively—more calm than he had. "And do you know what that means?"

"What it means," he growled at her, his body alight with her betrayal as if she'd struck him with lightning, "is that you have made a terrible mistake indeed."

He saw the first hints of uncertainty then, a flash of it in her dark eyes, but it was gone in an instant. And her chin rose higher.

"I'm going to be a mother," she told him, in that careful, distinct way he discovered he disliked intensely. "And I don't care about your family legacy, Lao. I care about this child and the kind of life it will have. I'm not going to be like my mother. I'm not going to abandon this baby when things get difficult, or boring, or whatever her complaints were.

That will never happen. And I'm also not going to turn this child into the kind of robot that your father made you. I'm not going to do it and I'm not going to let you do it, either."

"Robot? You think I'm a *robot*?" He laughed again, a little more wildly this time. "You can say this despite all the many ways I have showed you that I am made entirely of flesh and blood?"

He could remember them all. Every touch.

He could see that she did, too.

But she said, "I've had a lot of time to think," instead of acknowledging what was between them.

And he had seen many versions of Chloe over the years. That cross little girl. That grief-stricken teenager. That sweet wife he'd had for so short a time, filled with wonder and need.

It settled in him like some kind of reproach that this was the first time he'd looked at her and seen the grown woman she had somehow become without him realizing it. No longer simply pretty, but objectively beautiful—with strength in her gaze and conviction in the set of her shoulders.

He felt it inside him like some kind of shudder.

Chloe was studying him with a kind of wisdom that Lao did not like at all.

"You don't want to know, do you?" she asked softly.

"Clearly," he belted out, "you have had entirely too much time to think. I cannot recommend it."

And he was not thinking at all when he reached

out, his hand around the back of her neck, jerked her close, and then slammed his mouth to hers.

Lao was not thinking. He was *feeling*—and he knew better than that.

But this was Chloe.

This was Chloe, and so the kiss was not simply a kiss.

It was an explosion.

This was Chloe, *his Chloe*, and so the instant, impossible conflagration swept them both away. Their mouths clashed, tangled. Her hands were beneath his shirt, her fingers grazing his chest, her fingernails leaving little pinpricks of pain that only made it better.

This was Chloe, and her body had changed, so he had to learn her all over again. He bent to put his mouth to these new breasts of hers, full and ripe. He kissed his way down to her slightly rounded belly, so he might worship her.

And this was Chloe, so she fought him—but not to get away.

To get closer. Her hands fumbled with his belt. Her breath was coming fast and loud. And she sank down before him on the hard floor, pulled length of him from his trousers, and then took him deep into her mouth.

The way he had taught her.

It had been too long. It was too good. His hips moved of his own accord, the pleasure so intense, so hot and wet and *good*—

But Lao wanted more. He wanted everything.

He pulled her off of him and then up to her feet, but that wasn't enough. So he lifted her up right there, in the center of this atrium that had once been alive with green things and blossoms. He yanked up that dress of hers up to pool around her waist, pulled her legs wide around his waist, and then impaled her where they stood.

Her body made the shape of a bow. Her head fell back.

And Lao felt the fist of her sex piston around him.

Then she came apart.

Again and again.

She came and she came, and only when she was soft and writhing did he begin to move her, up and then down again, and she kept coming. And with every stroke, the fire roared through her and through him, burning them both alive.

At last.

But it still it wasn't enough.

It still wasn't everything.

Even when she locked her ankles around his back, grinned down at him, and whispered, "Catch up."

Not even when he did, with a roar.

And then moved back toward the windows so he could brace himself there. Then set her on her feet.

He was still bracing himself as she caught her breath beside him, her whole body shaking.

But her gaze was sad when she looked at him.

"Does that not convince you?" he managed to say.

Something in him stuttered, then stopped, when

she reached over and smoothed one hand over his jaw. With that same heaviness in her dark gaze.

"We've always been good at that, haven't we?" she asked softly. "But look around, Lao. This atrium used to be filled with joy and love and light. Your mother spent hours in here, encouraging all of her plants to grow. To bloom. She would cut flowers and arrange them all over the house. There was no part of her life that didn't share in this happiness."

"Chloe."

He said her name in desperation, as if it was torn from the very heart of him—as if he had such a thing after all—but she didn't stop.

"Now it is empty. It is an old glass room that feels drafty. The floors are cold and hard. And nothing grows here any longer."

"Because the house was closed up." He didn't recognize that dark urgency in his own voice. Or the feeling in his chest, as if his ribs were against him. "If you wish there to be a garden here, I could easily see to it that there is always—"

"If I wanted a garden made out of money, I could buy one myself."

And it would have been one thing if she sounded angry. Or even bitter, but she didn't. Once again, she sounded nothing but sad.

For you, a voice inside him whispered.

"Tell me what you want," he urged her, his voice a growl. "Name it, and I will give it to you. I will get you ever flower in Europe."

"It's not the flowers that matter. It's how they were grown." She waited, as if she needed him to say something to that, but all he could do was stare back at her, his heart a mad riot within him. "Love. They were grown with *love*, Lao. So will this child be grown inside me."

"I don't understand." The words tasted like ash in his mouth, but he pushed on. "Did I not take care of you, for years? Was I not there for you when you had no one else? Is this how I am repaid?"

"I love you," she told him, the way she had once before.

And this time, she looked him full in the face. She didn't blink.

Lao did not know how he was meant to handle this. This...*outrage*. He kept telling himself it was nothing more than that.

And she wasn't done. "I think I have always loved you. I expect I always will. All I ask is that you care a little bit less about your legacy and a little bit more about the possibility that you might just love me back. Whether you know it or not."

He stared back at her, his chest heaving as if he suddenly found himself running a marathon. "And if I cannot?"

Though the words hurt.

She smiled again, though there was nothing but that same sadness in it. A sadness he could feel inside him, winding its way through him like too much smoke.

When he thought he'd extinguished that kind of fire a long time ago, and for good.

Her smile only grew sadder, as if she knew.

"Then I am afraid that you will have to go," she said, with a deep certainty that was almost more of an earthquake within him. Because he had never heard Chloe—his Chloe—speak like this before. With such offhanded authority. She hugged her own belly, where their child grew even now. And she meant every word she aimed at him, with devastating precision. He could tell. "Because I will not raise this child—our child—without *at least* as much love and joy, hope and delight, that your mother gave her plants. I won't even try."

CHAPTER TEN

THIS WAS THE hardest thing that Chloe had ever done. With every breath, she wanted to snatch her words back. She wanted to tell Lao that she didn't mean them. That however he might take her, however he might treat her, it was good enough.

Because it was better than not being with him at all.

And she might have done exactly that, before. She'd been wavering. She'd been weak, and she knew that.

If he had shown up at that little bedsit of hers in Scotland, who knows what might have happened? Well. She did know. He would have had her back in Sicily so fast her head would have spun. He would never have let her off that mountain again. She would have become yet another Monteleone ghost.

But instead, she'd found herself pregnant, and that had changed everything.

It had changed *her*.

"You talk freely of love for someone who, in the next breath, threatens to leave me, with my child, if I do not dance to your tune," Lao thundered at her. "What kind of love do you call this, exactly?"

"What does it matter?" She didn't know how she

was keeping her voice so calm, when everything inside of her shook so hard. "Whether it's a good love or bad love, you don't want any part of it. So no need to concern yourself with it either way, I would think."

Her body was still reacting to what had happened between them here, and that didn't help. She was melting, still, and she could feel that same mad passion ramping up inside her all over again, the way it always did when she was near him.

But the one slip was all she would allow herself.

Because they were other things to think about now.

She brushed past him, and marched toward the door, feeling slightly ashamed that it was wide open. Any of the staff could have seen them in here—and given that they'd all helped raise her, the very idea made her face flame.

But she didn't let that stop her. She made her way to the warmer parts of the house, that she could keep at any temperature she liked, now, and she didn't know if that made her want to laugh or cry. Her father had always complained about how warm the place was, at least until Portia had become ill, when he'd stopped complaining about anything.

She reminded herself that today, here and now, the baby she carried was the only thing that mattered.

Not who she missed. Not what the people who worked here could have seen. Not Lao, not her. Just the baby who she intended to make sure lived the happy life she and Lao had only ever had pieces of.

If that.

She went into the room that Portia had claimed as her retreat in this house, aware that Lao was following her, his frustration plain in every step.

It was a cold, dark, November afternoon day outside and the fire was crackling merrily in the grate, making the spines of all the pretty books on the shelves lining the walls seem brighter. The old butler who had served her father so well had taken charge the moment Chloe had tracked him down, opening up the house, bringing back the rest of the old staff, and doing the place up as Chloe had always liked it best.

Meaning that a lovely cream tea was already waiting for her here, in the very room Portia had taught her to love them as a child.

But Chloe didn't go and sit on the happy little couch, she went to the bookshelves instead, running her fingers over the much-loved volumes that Portia had always stacked haphazardly on the shelves, claiming that a neat bookshelf was a sign of a disordered soul.

"You know this was your mother's favorite room, don't you?" she asked Lao softly.

"I have been in this room many times, Chloe. As you are well aware. And I do not see what my mother's preferences have to do with this."

Chloe turned, her lips curving into something that wasn't quite a smile. "Do you not? Really?"

She had never seen Lao quite like this. His eyes were a wild quicksilver and for the first time in as long as she'd known him, he seemed to…*simmer*. As far from that cold, stern, and forbidding presence as it was possible to get without outright exploding.

And the way he looked at her made her think that all that thunder that was normally in his gaze was in her now. Sunk deep into her bones.

She was not sure she would ever get it out again. Or even if she wanted to.

Chloe kept her hand pressed against her belly, as if that could soothe the child inside. *We will be all right*, she promised the baby silently. *You and I will make it work, whether we are made of thunder or not.*

"Tell me what I have done to you, please," Lao grated out at her. "You disappear on the way to a doctor's appointment. You hide yourself in Scotland under an assumed name. You conceal the heir you know I have wanted for some time from me. Is this how you repay my kindness to you? A kindness you were once so grateful for that you offered to carry my child when there was no physical relationship between us?"

Chloe pressed her fingers into her belly a bit more firmly. "I will always be grateful for your kindness to me, Lao. This has nothing to do with that."

"This has everything to do with it." He had been standing in the door, but he came in further now, and in one step seemed to take it over. The little room, peaceful and happy as it has always been, seemed to disappear into him. As if he was a black hole that dragged everything it encountered deep inside of him.

She felt that same irresistible pull herself.

"I had no intention of getting pregnant," she told

him, and maybe her voice was a little less calm, now. In the face of that intoxicating pull. And Lao getting that much closer, making it hard to concentrate. She cleared her throat and reminded herself that this wasn't about her. "I know that was your goal, but it was never mine."

"What, pray, did you think would happen?" Lao shook his head, his eyes glittering. "I shudder to think what will become of you, Chloe. So lost, even now. And so unable to understand the very basics of human anatomy."

He might as well have slapped her. She felt as hot and furious, as wounded.

"I was on birth control, Lao," she snapped back at him. When she saw him take that in, his head jerking back as if she was the one who had landed a blow, she felt something in her light up. Like that was some kind of triumph. "Do you really think I'm that stupid?" But she let out a small laugh. "Don't answer that. I can see that you do. You truly believe that I'm such a fool that I would imagine I could have that much sex with you—with anyone—while taking absolutely no precautions, and imagine nothing would come of it?"

She expected him to fire back, and wasn't sure what to do when he only sighed, muttering something in Italian beneath his breath. "I do not think you are stupid. I assumed you wanted the same things that I did."

"You know that I didn't," she replied, her voice fierce. Because whatever that little pop of triumph was, it quickly turned into this. This bright fire inside her. "You knew all along how much I loved you, and what a dream come true it was to me that I could have you in that way. It never crossed your mind that you shouldn't use your power and your influence to get exactly what you wanted, and you know what the funniest part of this is, Lao? I don't mind that. Some part of me *likes* it. Because I know exactly who you are. I love you exactly as you are."

"Even as we stand here, discussing your lies," he said in that quietly furious voice of his that should not have affected her as much as it did. "You can understand, can you not, how pale the words sound in these circumstances?"

"I love you," she said again, and she didn't care if he could hear the fire in her. The fire she wanted very much to be temper, not need. "I love you, Lao, but not enough to set aside every weapon at my disposal. Not enough to give myself over to you like some virgin sacrifice and help you burn me to a crisp in some ritual fire."

"Monteleones have not required ritual sacrifices in some centuries, Chloe."

"But the result is the same," she threw at him. "Is that really what you want? Because sometimes, there's something else inside you, Lao. I've seen it." Or she liked to think she had. "Something more than the Monteleone legacy. There's more to you than that. I know there is."

His jaw worked. His eyes blazed.

When he spoke again, his tone was frozen solid. "You are mistaken."

"I'm sorry to hear that," she shot right back at him. "Because I will not allow you to flatten this child the way you were flattened."

More of that silver fire, aimed directly at her. "I would not call it *flattening*. I was raised very differently than you, Chloe. I was given responsibilities at a very young age and asked to live up to them. I was not coddled. No one cooed over me or applauded when I ran about, doing as I liked."

"Your mother did all of those things," she replied softly. "All your life. It's just that she was overruled."

It was like a new storm broke then, washing over Lao and making him...a whole electrical event. He scorched the sky, the room, *her*.

Chloe's pulse was skyrocketing through her veins.

His voice was so quiet it hurt. "You have no idea how I was raised."

"I do." She indicated the room around them. "Your mother used to tell me all about it, right here. Usually after you visited and she felt she had to make excuses for..." She waved her hand at him. "The way you are."

"The way I am?" He said the words in his typical affronted astonishment, but today it was worse. Today it burned. "By this you mean... What, dare I ask?"

"Shuttered," she shot back at him immediately. "Locked up inside yourself. Grim and forbidding and off-putting, as if, when you were still a young man, you had already made yourself over into some hermit on a mountaintop—counting your piles of money while the world turned on without you." She let out a small laugh at the expression on his face. "Those aren't my words, Lao. They were Portia's."

He moved closer then, so close that his scent seemed to wrap itself around her, teasing her. Tempting her.

It would be so easy to simply melt against him. To wrap herself in his arms and forget what she was trying to do here. What she knew she *needed* to do. Because she was standing here in Portia's favorite retreat, the one her stepmother had made after leaving Sicily and the Monteleone legacy behind. So Chloe already knew how this would end, didn't she?

She couldn't pretend she didn't, no matter how much she longed for Lao even now.

"I think you're relying too heavily on the words of a woman who wanted, very desperately, to create a tidy narrative of her own past." Lao did not exactly spit those words out, but they were like bullets, one after the next, slamming into her as he towered above her. "I am not certain my mother was the woman you wish she was, Chloe. Then again, I'm not sure anyone could be."

"Are you really going to try to convince me that your mother was…" She shook her head, feeling as if the room was suddenly spinning a little too fast all around her. "I don't even want to know what sort of twisted attempt this is to—"

"Do you know why I tore down the manor house?" There was something different in him, she could see it. He seemed to blaze at her, then. A lightning strike that just kept coming. "Because she did not merely burn down the wing she shared with my father. She went on a rampage, ransacking the place, and it was easier to take it all down then to repair it. Does that strike you as the actions of a well-adjusted woman?"

"Maybe she was a desperate one," Chloe whispered.

"My father was already dead." He bent toward her, his face as cold as his eyes were hot. "I assumed my mother was having a breakdown, so when she left the island—claiming she was going abroad for some rest and recuperation—I supported it. Instead, she announced she was marrying your father. And quickly."

"Yes," Chloe said, though it took everything she had to keep standing there, defying him, when it would be so much easier to simply... Melt the way everything in her wanted to do. "Because whatever else you might think about my father, or whatever you thought of him then, what's undeniable is that he made Portia feel safe. For the first time in her life, I think. That means something."

The strangest expression moved over his face then. Lao stepped away from her, which should have pleased her. It didn't.

Then, in one of the few hints she'd seen outside the bedroom that he was, indeed, a mortal man, he rubbed his hands over his face as if this conversation was finally getting to him.

Chloe couldn't decide if she was pleased about that or not.

"Do you really believe…" Lao shook his head, then wheeled around to scowl into the fireplace, though she doubted he was seeing the flames before him. "My mother was raised on a silver platter, wrapped in cotton wool, not too far from where we stand right now. She came from a very long line of proper English heiresses, all of them trotted out to marry this or that lord on command. Or, if he is of high enough status, not necessarily marry him at all. One of her direct ancestors was a particular favorite of one of your King Georges, or so her family like to claim." He turned back then, and she would have called the look in his eyes a kind of anguish, except he seemed so icily furious. "My point to you is that my mother was not some…random commoner who was swept up into a world she could not understand. She was bred for the role she took. From the time she was born, she and her sisters were raised to marry a very specific sort of man and become a very specific sort of wife. There was no expectation of a happy love match, an egalitarian relationship, God forbid, or anything other than maintaining the family profile and giving herself over to her husband's demands."

Chloe felt as if she was shaking apart from the inside out. "How unfortunate that instead of being an automaton, she was Portia."

"You are speaking of who she became," he told her in that same stormy way. "I'm speaking of who she was. Whether she liked her duty or did not, the vows she took meant she continued to do it. I'm not going to stand before you and pretend that my father was a kind, softhearted man. I do not believe that he ever pretended otherwise. It was my mother who changed. She could not accept that he would not change with her."

"Yet somehow, you're telling me this story to blame her, not him."

"Because she is the one who did not live up to her commitments," Lao threw at her. "She is the one who was forever bleeding her emotions everywhere, making nothing but a mess. And to what end? Nothing changed. Certainly not my father, who died as he lived, stern and uncompromising to the very end. And even then, my mother let her emotions lead her into appalling displays. Involving fire and wanton destruction. If she were anyone else but *my mother*, she would have been thrown in prison for arson. Rightly."

"Lao," Chloe managed to say, though she felt as if she was rattling apart. As if some sort of earthquake had started, right here in Winchester, and soon enough the fault would swallow her whole and leave nothing behind but rubble. Still, she tried to focus on the only thing that mattered here. "Lao, I think—"

"All she had to do was her duty," Lao thundered. "That's it. That's all that was ever asked of her, and it was too much. She had everything her heart could possibly desire. Money. Power. Influence. So many things that when she burned down half of them she still had more than plenty. I will never understand what made her think that she could change a thing.

Or why she'd want to." She ran her hand over his face again. "What could she possibly have thought she could gain from going head-to-head with my father?"

"You," Chloe said, with a deep certainty she could not possibly have explained. It had something to do with the baby inside her. With the new, proud jut of her own belly that made everything…clear. Maybe too clear. "She was hoping to gain *you*, Lao. She was losing her son, day after day, as you became more and more like him. Because you have, haven't you?"

She could see the way his chest moved as he stood there. She could see how wild and silver his gaze was.

"Portia was hoping to give you a choice," Chloe said, because she knew. She just knew. "To be like her or to be like him. And look what you've chosen. Look who you've become."

She had never seen Lao look so undone as he did then. So unlike himself.

And she wasn't sure she had ever loved him more—

But because of that, because of the baby she carried and had to protect above all things—even if that meant from him—she stayed where she was.

And no matter that it felt like she was hurting herself…

"Chloe…" he managed to say.

"Is fire what it takes?" she asked him then. "Is that what gets your attention."

"Chloe," he said again, with more force this time.

But she refused to listen. She stood with her back straight and her gaze steady. "Tell me, Lao, what do

I have to burn down to prove to you that I love you? Though I think we both know that's not the real question."

She thought he might argue further, but all he did was gaze back at her, as if she was haunting him.

Right here, in this happy room, in the middle of the afternoon.

"The real question," she made herself say, though it tore up her throat and seared her tongue, so desperately did she want to keep these words to herself, "is why you believe you can't love me back without the whole of Castello Monteleone falling straight off the mountain and into the sea?"

CHAPTER ELEVEN

IT WAS TOO MUCH.

There was a certain anguished *kindness* in Chloe's gaze—too close to pity, by his reckoning—and he couldn't take it. He couldn't allow it.

Instead, Lao found himself shouldering his way out of the room, then staggering through the cramped old house until he found himself outside in the cold.

He gulped in the damp air, as if that might save him.

As if that might make sense of these things raging inside him.

He thought of his father, never *quite* cruel, because true cruelty required a deeper level of attention than his father had ever given to anything that was not a part and parcel of the Monteleone estate.

His father, always talking of duty. Always making it clear that while Portia fell far short, it was still possible for Lao to prove himself.

If he worked hard. If he never strayed from the path laid out before him by his betters. If he got his unruly reactions to things he didn't like under control.

Lao had done all of those things and more, though he'd failed more than he'd succeeded, at first.

He'd gotten better at it after he'd been sent off to boarding school, where he'd received a crash course in locking up any stray emotions he might have attempted to have, lest they make him a target.

In time, he had forgotten he'd ever had any.

Just as he'd forgotten all the things his mother had told him that did not fit with his father's version of events.

"Why can't you stop?" he had asked her one night before his father had passed. After another dinner had gone south, in a hurry, because Portia had refused to sit there in the obedient silence his father required. "You know he won't divorce you. What is the purpose of defying him?"

"I do not have to stay here," his mother had replied. "This is not the only Monteleone property, as I think you know. I could live quite happily elsewhere."

"Then you should," he had returned, with all the arrogance of the younger man he'd been then, who had taken such pride in his inability to feel things the way Portia did.

He had told himself that the brightness he'd seen in his mother's gaze that night was her shame, not his.

And he remembered his father's deathbed, too. How his mother had tended to a man she could not possibly have esteemed in any way by that point. Without question, without a word.

A parody of the perfect wife she had never been, Lao had thought then.

Yet in the end, his father had laughed. His gaze had

been something like feverish then, his body already so changed that though he had not yet died, he already looked far too much like a cadaver.

"The Monteleone legacy always wins," he had cackled. "Always."

Then he had closed his eyes, taken one, last rattling breath, and died.

And all this time, Lao had believed his father had been speaking to him. That he had been passing on one last piece of advice, one last directive.

It had never occurred to him that his father had been doing no such thing. He'd been taunting Portia.

This seemed so clear to him now. The old man had been drawing his last breath, he'd known it, and he'd used it to announce to his wife that he had made their son into the image of him.

More importantly, that there was nothing she could do about it.

And suddenly, that his mother had chosen to set fire to the part of that legacy she must have hated the most did not seem in the least bit surprising. Nor in any way the kind of breakdown he'd been so sure she was having.

How had it taken him all this time to understand that?

But he knew. It was Chloe.

He had spent so much time and effort convincing her that she needed him, when all along, it seemed it had been the other way around.

Lao had been paying no attention to where he was

going, and it took him long moments to recognize that he was in the garden, hunkered down against the cold, though it was now, in late fall. The again, perhaps he'd meant to come here, he thought as he recognized his mother's rosebushes, cut back for winter.

To the untutored eye, they might even look dead.

But he knew better.

Because now, in a great rush of painful understanding, he knew why Portia had spent her days up in the castle ruins, tending to plants that died each winter and rose again each spring.

She had been fighting for him all along. She had been tending to him as best she could. Not, perhaps, doing her duty as a Monteleone.

But always—*always*—doing her duty as a mother.

Doing it so well that Lao had not even noticed what she did.

He reached down, brushing his hand over one of the withered-looking stalks—only to pull it back when his finger stung.

Somehow, it was as if the thorn that pierced his skin punched straight through him.

Lao saw a single red droplet of his own blood, there in the November gloom, and it was as if he was made new.

As if all the things that had seemed so out of control even an hour ago came suddenly back into focus.

Snapping off the bit of stem, he turned to make his way back up to this house that he had always told himself was too uncomfortable. Too English. He had always kept his visits short, to guard against too much of Charlie Stapleton rubbing off on him.

That was what he'd always thought. That was what he would have said—and probably had said—to his own mother.

Now he understood why she had always smiled so serenely, yet never engaged with him in the argument he'd clearly wanted.

Because she knew.

What he couldn't tolerate was love.

The love between Charlie and Portia. The love between Charlie and Chloe. The love his own mother lavished on the girl herself.

The love the Stapleton clan felt for their staff, who returned it in kind—and if he'd doubted that, it was proved well enough by the fact they had all come out of retirement to help Chloe now.

It wasn't that he couldn't tolerate all that love, he thought now. He hadn't even been capable of recognizing it for what it was.

No wonder Chloe had been so lost without it.

He found himself charging through the house once more, barely noticing the rooms that still looked sleepy from being closed up all these years. Barely noticing the canny-eyed old butler who nodded at him, or anything at all but the light that led him back the way he'd come.

The light that led him to Chloe.

She was where he'd left her in his mother's favorite room. While he'd been out facing reality in a stripped-down rosebush, she had taken herself over to the fire. She stood there, her arms wrapped around her middle, as if she was afraid that if she let go she might fly apart.

Or perhaps as if he had already broken her beyond repair.

She turned when he came in, and Lao had some sense of how it must seem to her that he should come charging back like this, the cold and the wet clinging to him as if he brought the coming night with him wherever he went.

He thought maybe he did. That he had done, and for years.

But this was Chloe, so what she did was take a look at him—a long, hard look, so that he expected her to order him away.

Instead she simply…opened up her arms, offering him nothing but that invitation and the sheen of a deeper longing in her gaze.

Because she knew exactly what love was.

And it was as if everything within him shattered to dust, that simply.

He came toward her, still gripping that strand of thorns in one fist. She made a soft noise when she saw it, and then her hands were on his. She was peeling open his palm, shaking her head as she peered down. "Lao. You're bleeding."

"But I can feel it," he said gruffly. "That must mean something."

She looked up, eyes wide and much too bright. As

he watched, she pulled the thorns from his hand and tossed them into the fire.

"You and I can agree that we should burn the things that hurt us," she told him softly. Solemnly. "But not the rest."

A single tear trailed down one cheek, and she leaned down to press her lips into the palm of his hand.

As if her kiss alone could soothe the cuts he'd made with the might of his own grip.

And the metaphor wasn't lost on him. The harder he held on to those thorns, the deeper they had pierced his flesh.

All it took was opening up his hand—and the one thing he didn't think he could survive losing was still right here, her lips against his palm, tears for him in her soft gaze.

"Chloe," he told her, though the words caught in his throat. "I think that you are the only thing I've ever loved."

"Not the only thing," she corrected him, with a smile that no longer seemed tinged with sadness. "Just the most simple thing."

He reached over with his unabused hand and smoothed it over her cheek, her hair. "There's nothing simple about you. And I love every part of you. Whether you are lost or found, as long as you are mine."

"Lao." She shook her head, and his stomach fell— until he saw the way her lips curved. "I always have been. Since I was all of seven, and you came to me, right here in this house, and made everything better."

"I doubt that. That is not the Monteleone way."

"But it's our way," she whispered, fiercely. "It has always been *our* way, if we let it."

And there, standing before the fire where the last of his mother's roses burned, yet would still bloom again come spring, Lao let go.

He opened himself up, and *let go*.

Lao let go of that wall he had been trying to build between himself and this woman…forever. He let go of the legacy his father had cared about above all else.

He let go of all the things that no longer seemed at all important and concentrated on this.

The woman who looked up at him with love and trust in her gaze, though he knew full well he had done nothing at all to deserve them.

The woman who carried his child in her body, and who had been prepared to fight even him to keep that child safe.

And he understood that this moment would be the one his whole life hinged upon. Everything that had come before, and everything that would come after— all of it depended on this.

On what he did now.

He could do his duty to a dead man who loved only his legacy, or he could do his duty to the child he already wanted to love with all his heart.

This was what his mother had known all along. He could not do both. No man could.

Not if he wanted to give his child the love that child deserved.

The love he knew Chloe had gotten from her father.

And of the two of them, it seemed obvious to him that she had come out better adjusted, with no Monteleone legacy like a noose around her neck.

So he gathered his beautiful wife in his arms. He held her there, before the fire.

"Chloe," he murmured. *"Dusci mia, sei tutto per me.* You are everything to me. I want you to marry me."

"I already have," she whispered.

"This time I want a spectacle," he declared, and this time when he felt his heart like a drum inside his chest, he called it joy. Hope. "I want to pry open my family's secrets and wash us all clean of the secrets and the lies. So that the only thing remaining is this. Us."

She looped her arms around his neck and tilted her head back while she looked at him, tears streaming down her cheeks.

But he knew that she was showing him love, complex and sweet, layered with too many feelings to count, right there before him.

He knew it was love. He could feel that, a brighter and better sting than any thorn could ever be.

"I promise you," she whispered. "I will be the best Monteleone wife there ever was."

"Mi amore," he replied, as he smoothed his hands over her belly, then raised them again to take her face in his. "Do you not see? You already are."

CHAPTER TWELVE

LAO WAS ABSOLUTELY true to his word.

He was a Monteleone, after all. But these days, he chose the legacies he wished to uphold.

He opened the whole of his mountain to the world. He tore down the ancient gates and invited them all in, with cameras aplenty, to witness his wedding to Chloe.

Because the only thing more powerful than the mystery of the age-old Monteleone legacy was love, and he intended to prove it.

The way Chloe proved to him, every day, that he was not the man he'd always thought he was.

She taught him how to laugh. She taught him how to *play*. She taught him that there was nothing to fear in the emotions he had tried to hold off his whole life—not while they were together.

Together they planted his mother's roses on his father's grave, then left them to do as they liked. They planted trees in the ruins of the manor house.

"So that one day, another Monteleone will stand right here," Chloe said as they held each other in his office one day. "And see only the island and the sea."

"No ghosts," Lao agreed, like it was a vow.

Their son was born six months later, and once again, the whole world shifted. Once again, Lao found he had to reassess not only who he was, but how he had ever considered having an heir nothing more than a cold-blooded duty to check off his list.

"I cannot understand it," he told Chloe, mere days after the heir he had always wanted had been born into his hands. But he was no *heir*.

He was called Gaetano. He was a miracle.

Lao held his son against his chest, skin to skin, and was in love. He didn't care that this was his supposed successor. He didn't care that this was what his own father would have wanted.

The woman he loved more than he had ever loved anything or anyone on this earth had fought and struggled and brought forth their child into this world, and now, together, they had no job at all but to love him. To care for him.

To do their best to nurture him, for all his days.

To take part in this journey that would, God willing take little Gaetano with his chubby hands and sweet red face, from the bundle of heat and wailing he was today to the man he would become.

Lao intended to enjoy every moment.

"What can't you understand?" Chloe asked softly, curled up next to him on the soft couch. She had never looked more beautiful, still round from her pregnancy, her breasts big with milk. "How it's possible to love anything as much?"

They had made the room next to theirs, supposedly her bedroom, the nursery. Because there was no point pretending that they would ever sleep in separate beds. They sat there now, close together basking in this small, perfect life they had made between them.

"That, yes," Lao said quietly, playing with Gaetano's tiny fists. "But then to act as my father did."

Chloe traced a gentle circle on the tender, soft spot on the baby's head. "For all we know, he was gentle and loving compared to his own father."

"I promise you, Chloe," Lao grated out, because now he was a man made entirely of emotion. He was not afraid to let it grip him, hard. He was not afraid of what love wrought in him. Not as long as they went through these storms together. "I will never let that happen to us. Or to our son."

"I know you won't," she said, her lips on his.

But as much as he loved her belief in him, Lao made sure to work on it.

He worried less about power and influence. He created his own legacy, by beginning to give away the money that his ancestors had spent so long amassing to those who needed it.

And there were so many who needed it.

Not to mention, it turned out that Chloe had a particular talent for giving his money away. And, like him, wanted that to be the secret of the Monteleone family.

The only secret worth keeping.

And as the years passed, they spent their time together dispensing joy where they could, and spending as much time as possible together—and with the children they made.

The four he had rashly demanded, and two more, for fun.

"It is incredibly unfashionable to have so many children," he told Chloe when their sixth was a toddler, incredibly full of herself and entirely feral. Sebastiana was a terror in every respect—but that only made them love her more. "We are no doubt the laughing-stock of Europe."

"Good," Chloe said. She covered her mouth to hide her laughter as red-cheeked, overly serious Sebastiana spun too fast and toppled straight over on the grassy stretch of hill before the castle. Then howled with rage before picking herself up to do it again. When Chloe dropped her hand, her gaze was soft, but serious. "I don't want any of them to ever think they're alone in this world, Lao. Not like us."

Never like them.

That was the mantra that Lao lived by. That was the promise he made himself, day in and day out.

His children would not be alone. His children would have the both of them. His children would never question whether or not they were loved.

Chloe taught him that every day. Just as his own mother had tried, over and over again.

And every year, one slipping by after the next more quickly than seemed possible, Lao watched his mother's roses wilt in fall and then bloom again in spring.

Each year, brighter than the year before. Each year more beautiful and more fragrant.

And thorns were inevitable, but none too sharp or too painful—provided he knew the trick of letting go.

Of choosing love instead.

Over and over again, the way Chloe had taught him. The way he wanted to love his children, so well that they would never know another way.

So that the legacy that he and Chloe left, in the end, was a love so right, so good, it lasted as long as the roses bloomed on Castello Monteleone and their descendants were there to tend them.

Which was another way of saying forever.

* * * * *

SECRETLY PREGNANT BY THE TYCOON

BELLA MASON

MILLS & BOON

For everyone who's ever had to hide a piece of themselves, and for Megan for helping me find Matt and Hannah's story.

CHAPTER ONE

CHROME AND GLASS surrounded Hannah Murphy. If it hadn't been for the obscenely expensive plush chair, she would have sworn she was sitting in just another high rise. Maybe even the one she herself worked at. But one glance out of the wall of windows and there was no pretending that she was any- where except London. Melbourne, her home, was thousands of miles away. Everyone she knew was probably asleep. Well, almost everyone.

With her foot bouncing at a rapid rate, her heart wanting to beat out of her chest, Hannah looked down at the phone clutched in her hand, Emma's message appearing under the last one she had sent.

You're doing the right thing. He deserves to know.

Hannah understood that. She also understood why she trem- bled at the mere thought of seeing Matt Taylor again—the man she had met seven months ago when he'd visited Melbourne. The man who had turned her world upside down in so many ways. Who had showed her pleasure she'd never dreamed pos- sible. Who'd made her feel like the most beautiful woman in the world.

Hannah brought her fingers to her lips, the force of their first kiss and the sad resignation of their last imprinted on the soft flesh for ever. Standing in the airport, it was as if he'd tried to brand the memory of himself into her. At that he'd been more than successful. She'd spent weeks after that lying awake in the flat she shared with Emma, thinking about him. Craving his touch while she touched herself, replaying their moment over in her head. It was a cheap facsimile of what she wanted, but it had to be enough, because they couldn't be together. Their lives were light years apart. That was why she had only contacted him once since he had left.

That was until everything had changed.

Hannah looked down at her rounded belly, her hand coming to rest on the very pronounced bump. The baby moved at her touch, making a soft smile creep onto her face.

Oh yes, Matt Taylor had definitely turned her world upside down and now she was about to do the same to his. Hannah had no idea how he would react to the news. She didn't dare hope for excitement—this would be a shock. At least *she* had had the last trimester to come to terms with it.

A trimester.

Just three months.

The world was unfair. There were women out there who could count on their cycle like clockwork. Hannah knew several such women and envied them all, never having been that fortunate. That was why she had thought nothing of missing three periods. Of course, she should have taken notice sooner of the extreme fatigue she'd been feeling…

Everyone always commented on her boundless energy. Whether at work or play, she was up for anything…until she wasn't. So, she had seen a doctor, who had uttered three little words that she was sure had stopped her heart.

'You are pregnant.'

Hannah had sat in the doctor's chair listening to everything she'd said but none of it had sunk in. Shock was all she felt in that moment. How was this possible? Motherhood was a dream she had long given up on, knowing it could never happen for her.

The doctor had handed her pamphlets and written out a prescription, while saying words that had not registered. There had to be a mistake. She couldn't be pregnant.

But she was. It had taken a while for her to come to terms with it. Only after her first scan a week later had the idea finally solidified. She really was going to be a mother.

She hadn't said a thing to anyone in that week. She couldn't. What if it really was just a mistake? She would have worried everyone for no reason.

And it wasn't as if anyone had really noticed a change in her body. Hannah wasn't slim and tall like her best friend. She was soft. She had curves that she loved.

Once she'd got that printout of the scan, everything had changed.

Emma was typing again.

At least you made an appointment so you two will have some time to talk.

Guilt curdled in her belly. She hadn't made an appointment. She'd meant to but she just hadn't been able to bring herself to make the call. What would she say? Especially when she had held onto the news for three months. When she'd sworn Emma and Alex to secrecy. Keeping Hannah's secret from his friend had not been easy on Alex, she knew that. After all, they considered each other brothers—another thing to stab at her conscience.

Those three months had been hell. Every single day she would torment herself about calling Matt, telling him, but what would she say to a man she had only known for a week? A man who had only come to Melbourne for a holiday? A man who was still pretty much a stranger. A man who'd said he didn't want to be a father.

Somehow, she'd managed to convince herself that pitching up unannounced would be far easier for everyone involved and, if Matt's highly efficient, slightly terrifying PA sent her away, at least she could say she tried.

Hannah stared down at her phone, trying to remember all that Emma and Alex had said. Trying to believe those words over the fear about what awaited her in that office…

Hannah had been curled up on the large, tan leather couch. A blanket on her lap kept the Melbourne chill at bay. A fluffy black cat had lain on her lap, purring contentedly against her belly. A steaming cup of hot chocolate was in her hands.

Emma had sat beside her, sipping at her own cup. 'He misses you,' she'd said, looking at her cat, which only had eyes for Hannah.

'I miss him too.' Hannah had scratched Lucky between the ears, making him purr even louder. 'It's weird how quiet the apartment gets.'

'It won't be for long.' Emma had smiled.

'I know.'

Hannah was nearing the end of her second trimester. She'd been equal parts scared and excited for the birth of her baby. It amazed her how much one night could change your life.

Just then, Alex walked into the lounge. Hannah watched him take a seat opposite them and smile at her friend in a way that made her indescribably happy for Emma and the love she'd found. It also made her heart break to know she could never find anything like it. The closest she'd come was the reason she was scared now. An unparalleled attraction to a man who neither wanted to be a father nor could be in any kind of relationship with her.

'You really do need to tell him, Han,' Emma said gently, picking up the conversation from where it had fallen before. 'Even if you think he'll reject you. You need to try.'

Emma didn't understand. Matt was gone. He didn't want any part of this pregnancy. 'He said he didn't want children, Em.'

'He still needs to know. What did he say exactly?' Alex was regarding her with an intense gaze that made her look away.

'He said that he didn't want to be a father. That he wasn't

cut out for it.' Hannah vividly remembered that walk on the beach when they'd spotted a young family playing with a beach ball that had landed at their feet. 'You didn't see his face. He was adamant. How can I force this on him?'

'Hannah.' Alex called her attention with his deep voice. 'I know Matt better than anyone. He would want to know. You wouldn't be forcing anything on him. He always steps up to his responsibilities. He won't leave you alone in this.'

Hannah looked down into her mug, suddenly losing her appetite for the rich drink.

'Let me ask you this,' Alex pressed on. 'What are you going to do when you see him again with a child that looks like both of you in your arms?'

Hannah opened her mouth but no sound came out.

'Do you want to avoid him for the rest of your life? Days that you want to spend with Emma given up because of this?'

No, Hannah could never sacrifice any part of her friendship with Emma. They were there for each other through everything.

'And what about when your child asks after him? What will you say then? Give him a chance, Hannah. You're not the only one who hurt after he left.'

Alex had made several great points. Hannah was logical enough to see that, but how would she tell Matt that he would be a father when she'd assured him that they were safe? And did he really miss her as she missed him?

'I want to, it's just that…'

Emma reached over, squeezing her hand. 'Han, Matt isn't Travis. He's a good guy.'

'I know no man better,' Alex added.

Her baby moved again. He seemed as restless as she was. God, she was tired!

With her back aching, Hannah adjusted herself in the chair. What she wouldn't give to have a lumbar roll right now!

Hannah prayed her friends were right. Straightening her dress with as much grace as she could muster, Hannah took a deep breath then typed out her response to her best friend.

I didn't make an appointment, but I am at his office waiting for him.

She could almost see her friend shaking her head. It was just that Matt was the ultimate bachelor. Theirs had been a holiday romance that had burned brightly but had had an expiration date. Hannah was already so stressed with the idea of being a single mother—going through the birth alone, having to give up work while on maternity leave, preparing her home for a new-born—that she couldn't deal with the possibility that Matt would reject her baby. That he would be furious. She just couldn't trust that he would be there for her. This situation was her own to figure out.

But now she had officially run out of time. Matt had to know about the pregnancy and this wasn't the type of news to spring on him in a call. Especially after she'd waited so long to tell him. No, this was face-to-face news. All she wanted was to tell him that he would be a father soon and that she wasn't coming after him for anything other than what he wanted to give. That she'd be perfectly fine raising this baby on her own—no pressure. She had a great job as a software developer at a respectable tech company, and a great flat in the city that was mostly hers now, with Emma having moved out. There wasn't anything she needed from Matt. How could she count on someone she barely knew, anyway?

She would tell him, get her answer and be on the earliest flight back to Melbourne. But, as she sat in that office, she realised that she had backed herself into a corner. What if he wasn't ready to wave her off with his baby in her belly shortly after she'd arrived with earth-shattering news? What had seemed like a good idea at the time now seemed like a serious lapse in judgement.

As if her body knew exactly where Matt was in the building, Hannah turned to face a corridor of glass-walled offices. She didn't see his. What she did see was the disapproving glare from his PA. She knew the prim woman in her black skirt-suit was judging her six ways to Sunday, but she couldn't bring herself to care. She was nervous enough without having to worry about strangers she might never see again.

Hannah looked at the smart watch on her wrist. She had been waiting almost an hour. Part of her wondered if the PA had even mentioned her name. Then a small, dark part of her wondered how many times Matt's PA had had to deal with women making some sort of claim on him. He obviously got around; his playboy reputation wasn't exaggerated.

He was rich, handsome and constantly in the public eye. How many women had he seen since he'd left Melbourne? Had he spared a thought for her? Had their fling meant something to him? Had it kept *him* up at night as it had her? Probably not. Despite what Alex said, men didn't value relationships the same way. That was a hard lesson she'd learned a long time ago.

Hannah tried to push away the thoughts. She and Matt had said goodbye. The memory of him leaving still wrenched her gut and stole her air but they owed each other nothing. What he did wasn't any of her business.

Except soon they would be linked for ever by the little life she carried. *If* he wanted to know his child. Taking a deep breath, Hannah tried to leash her out-of-control thoughts. It was only because she was forced to sit out here that they ran riot. She had nothing to do but wait and stare out the window. The view of London was magnificent, but even this city couldn't distract her from the enormity of what she was about to do.

When she was just about ready to burst, to grab her bag and

flee the building, cursing herself for coming here at all, the PA, whom she was quickly coming to dislike, approached her chair.

'Mr Taylor will see you now,' she said calmly as if Hannah wasn't in the middle of a crisis.

'Thank you.' Hannah pushed to her feet as elegantly as she could manage and straightened her red shirt-dress. She slung the strap of her handbag over her shoulder and slipped her phone into it before following the woman down the long corridor.

Hannah's heart was racing and it grew more frantic with every step they took towards Matt. She could no longer tell if it was because she would see him again or because she bore life-changing news.

She still tried to tell herself that logically he couldn't be too shocked. This pregnancy was the result of a goodbye neither of them had wanted to say. That last night would be etched in her memory for ever. And, even though she wasn't supposed to have been able to fall pregnant, she had.

Hannah couldn't remember a whole lot from that first doctor's appointment, but she did remember her saying that, while it was rare for an infertile woman such as herself to fall pregnant, it was known to happen.

Her baby had defied the odds to be here. He deserved the best life she could give him. Just as the thought settled in her mind, the baby kicked the hardest he'd ever done as if to prove a point. The gasp left her lips before she could stop it.

The PA halted mid-step, casting an eye over her shoulder. 'Are you okay? Do you require assistance?' she asked, in a patronising tone that irritated Hannah more than it should have.

'No, I'm perfectly fine.' She smiled sweetly. And she was. Hannah hadn't needed anyone when she'd come over to London. She had refused Emma's offer to travel with her. She had even refused Alex's apartment. She was doing this by herself—Matt, the pregnancy, everything.

They stopped at a large corner office. The glass walls were

opaque but despite that she could make out that the room was bathed in the gold glow of the afternoon sun. It was finally upon her. This was what she had to do for her baby.

Hannah watched the PA rap her knuckles on the door then open it and step aside.

And there he was.

With his shirt sleeves rolled up and black wire-frame glasses perched on his patrician nose, he took her breath away. But it was those green eyes that had her feet carrying her towards him when they landed on her. She didn't even notice the PA close the door, leaving them with complete privacy.

'Hannah?' A frown marred his forehead as he stood. He was tall and broad-shouldered, a physique from his rugby playing days that he'd never lost. His jaw was strong and smooth. She remembered kissing it and the smile it had brought to his face.

'Hi, Matt.' She smiled. Looking at him was like looking at sunshine, golden hair radiating a warmth she had forgotten.

CHAPTER TWO

IF MATT WAS SUNSHINE, Hannah was flame. Vibrant red tresses fell about her shoulders. The red shirt-dress she wore was vivid against her skin. Brown eyes that had ensnared him months before held so much apprehension, he ached to pull her to him. She was even more beautiful than he remembered. And, oh, he remembered!

His gaze raked over her, then he noticed what had changed about her and a stone dropped into the pit of his stomach. But he couldn't stay away from her. Not after all these months.

He went to her, watching as she craned her neck to look up at him, and for a moment all he wanted to do was kiss her. Make sure she was really in his office. Replace the memory of their last kiss with a new a one.

That memory had haunted him. The cold emptiness that had settled within him when his lips left hers. She was the best distraction he had ever had on holiday. So good, in fact, she'd continued to distract him months later. He knew, if he put his lips on hers now, he would devour her.

Seeing her now, it felt as if no time had passed at all, but her body showed the proof of it. And it was her fuller breasts and the rounded belly that threw him a lifeline of control.

'You never called,' he said, taking her hand. 'But it seems like we have a lot to discuss.'

He watched her swallow hard. Her mouth opened and closed but no words came out. Finally, she dropped her head and sighed. Clearly this wouldn't be easy for her. He pulled out the chair in front of his desk and helped her into the seat before leaning against the front of his highly polished table. Their knees were just inches apart.

'Thank you,' she rasped. Her husky voice fell on him like silk. When Matt had met Hannah seven months ago, she'd been full of life—confident and vivacious. The moment he had laid his eyes on her, he had been unable to see anyone else. That was who she was to him. a light so bright she'd rendered everyone else colourless.

But now he didn't see that confidence. It was that little fact that kept him from demanding answers immediately, but he needed them. Whatever happened now, she needed to say the words. A small part of him was hoping those words would be that she just needed the help of a friend and nothing more. After all, Hannah had an active social life. There was no reason to think that what was going on here had anything to do with him.

'I want to ask how you are, Hannah, but I think you need to tell me what's going on.'

Matt's deep voice was barely breaking through the pounding in her ears. She needed to take a breath and calm down. Reminding herself stress wasn't good for her or the baby, Hannah closed her eyes and did just that, and when she looked up at Matt again she saw nothing but him waiting patiently. His fingers were wrapped around the edge of the desk, his head cocked to one side. Why did those glasses make him look so damn sexy?

She cleared her throat to get the words out as quickly as possible. 'I think it's pretty obvious I'm pregnant...' She swallowed and rushed out the rest. 'And the baby is yours.'

His jaw twitched, the only indication he'd heard her say anything at all, but his gaze burned into her. Silent seconds stretched on for minutes or hours—Hannah wasn't sure. Eventually Matt reached over his desk and pressed a button.

'Yes, Matt?' His PA's voice crackled through.

'Hold my calls.'

'You have a meeting in fifteen.'

'Push it back an hour.'

'Yes, sir.'

Was that it? Was that all the reaction she would get out of him? Hannah didn't know if this was better or worse than she had expected. She had expected at least a little shock, maybe even some anger—a sensible reaction. But this calm was unnerving. Did it mean he didn't care at all? Had she wasted her time coming all this way?

The thoughts were starting to swirl.

'How did this happen?' he asked in that still-calm voice which was starting to grind at her nerves.

'Well, you see, when a man and a wom—' she began snarkily.

'Hannah.' It was a growl. 'You know what I'm asking. I thought this wasn't possible.'

'I thought so too. I've gone most of my life knowing I would never be a mother so I thought we were fine. And that night...' She trailed off, not wanting to relive a moment which still had the power to bring tears to her eyes.

Their last night in Melbourne was something Hannah would never, could never, forget. She had never felt a connection like that, not to a soul, not even to the man she thought she would marry. The man who had so irreparably scarred her heart. For just a moment, Matt had made her believe she could experience something deeper again but when the sun had risen and they'd had to leave for the airport she'd known she was just kidding herself. They'd barely known each other. Wasn't his reaction now proof of that?

Matt had just been told he was going to be a father but it was as if she just dropped off a file on his desk. Something he needed the facts about and nothing more. And it tore at a piece of her. She realised now that she wanted him to think she was special in some little way and not a summer tryst to forget. She'd been stupid to come. She should have sent him a message months ago and left it at that.

'Yes, that night when you told me this wasn't possible. And I bought it, didn't I?' There was a coldness in his eyes now she didn't recognise. 'The question is: what do we do about it?'

It? The baby who grew inside her, who she already loved more than she could bear, was an 'it' to him.

'*We* don't have to do anything,' Hannah spat. 'You needed to know. I came here to tell you and I've done that. *You* need to decide what *you* want to do because I'm perfectly happy raising him on my own.'

Beneath the calm exterior, Matt's head felt as if it was going to explode. He couldn't be a father! He had no road map for this. No example of how to be a good one. He closed his eyes. He needed a moment, but his mind kept flashing the word 'pregnant' in neon lights.

How could he have let this happen? He was always so careful. But he knew. On their last night he hadn't been careful. He'd just been desperate. Desperate to have Hannah. To carve out a memory so ingrained in him that even on his death bed it would be the one thing he would remember.

And now he was facing the consequences of losing control. His heart was galloping. He was furious at himself for allowing Hannah to play him like this, like the others who'd tried. He was disappointed because he'd thought she was different. And so, so frustrated because even now his body responded to her.

Matt knew he had to marshal some sort of control over what he was feeling. There was no way he could show any weakness, which was exactly what this fear was. It was a vulnerability. Something in no way acceptable to him. Calm control was the only way to find a solution. That was how he had lived his whole life—whenever he was presented with a problem, a bit of calm was exactly what he used to solve it. What his father had trained him to do. So have a moment of calm was what he did.

He pulled off his glasses and placed them on the table, pinching the bridge of his nose. 'That came out wrong, Hannah. I apologise. But you're sorely mistaken if you think you can come in here and attempt to trap me with this scheme.'

'Scheme?'

'What else would you call telling me you can't have children and sitting here, clearly pregnant?' He fought to keep his voice even. He wouldn't give anyone the satisfaction of knowing they'd got under his skin. Not even Hannah.

'Screw you, Matt!' she snapped.

He admired the fire still burning brightly within her, hiding under the exhaustion he could clearly see on her face, and in the way she held her body.

He didn't know why he should care, but he pushed to his feet and walked across the office, where he opened a cabinet filled with drinks. Fetching a bottle of water, he screwed off the lid and handed it to her. She reluctantly accepted it and he watched as she drank steadily, assuming she must have really needed it if she would accept his help despite her anger towards him.

She had no right to be angry. Not when she had so clearly lied.

'Then how would you explain it?' he demanded.

'I never lied to you, Matt. It wasn't meant to happen. This baby is a miracle,' she said, her tone harsh. 'Now, he can be my baby, or he can be ours. That's up to you.'

'You expect me to just take your word for it?' Obviously she was still lying. And what a gifted liar she was. Which made him wonder what else she was capable of lying about. 'Not likely. I want a paternity test.'

'What? The baby is yours! You are the only person I have

ever been with without protection and I haven't been with anyone else at all for some time!'

If he'd thought she was angry before, it was nothing to her fury now. She was incandescent in her rage.

It didn't faze him.

'Words, Hannah. It's all just words.' He leaned against his desk once more, crossing his arms over his broad chest. 'I will arrange the paternity test—and I'm warning you now, you won't like it if you've lied to me again.'

'I haven't lied to you at all,' she said, looking into his eyes defiantly.

'That's yet to be seen.' He couldn't allow himself to trust her. He'd done that once already. Now he wondered how far the betrayal went. 'Who's come to London with you?' Perhaps Emma; maybe Alex was here too. His friend, closer than a brother, who might have known about this and not told him. Might have hidden it from him just like Hannah had done, as if he had no right to know about what was potentially his child.

Oh, he would be calling his friend. He'd never felt anger like this before—not towards Alex, at least. After everything they'd been through, he would have thought his 'mate' would care enough about him to tell him the truth.

Matt watched Hannah's brows pull together as she answered. 'No one.'

'Where are you staying?'

Hannah told him the name of the hotel and he ran his fingers through his tousled blond hair, heaving a sigh.

'We have a lot to talk about. This isn't the place. I'll come by the hotel tonight.'

He was dismissing her. Hannah couldn't blame him. She'd dropped a bomb in his lap without even a 'how do you do?', but his reaction made her blood boil. It made her question the connection she'd felt to him seven months ago and wonder if that warm man was just a fiction.

Him wanting a paternity test made sense but, right now, she didn't want to be understanding. All she felt was anger towards this person she really didn't know.

She was scared. She still didn't know where he stood and she felt exposed, like a raw nerve.

'Fine.'

She placed her hands on the arm rest, ready to push herself to standing, but a strong arm wrapped under her shoulders and helped her to her feet.

Thank you was on the tip of her tongue, but she swallowed it back, holding on to her ire. She turned to face him and her heart skipped a beat as he grazed her cheek with the back of his fingers.

She saw his jaw twitch as he watched his fingers, as if he was annoyed at the touch.

'Goodbye, Matt.'

CHAPTER THREE

HANNAH FELT OFF-BALANCE leaving Matt's office. She stepped out into the afternoon sunlight, trembling with pent-up rage. Talking to Matt hadn't helped at all. The biggest problem was that he'd had almost no reaction. Well, until he'd accused her of lying, of planning this pregnancy to extort him.

How dared he?

Her eyes suddenly burned but she refused to allow a single tear to escape.

There was no way she would be a crazy, crying, pregnant lady on a street in London.

Hannah tossed her red hair back and hailed a black cab. It stopped right in front of her. She told the driver where to take her and settled back in the seat, still trying to make sense of all Matt said.

He had clearly seen she was pregnant the moment she'd walked in. Her pulse had quickened when she'd seen his eyes rove over her body. It was the same way he had looked at her seven months ago. Just that alone had made heat pool in her belly, a reaction that irritated her.

They were done. They had said goodbye. She hadn't needed Matt Taylor to wreak havoc on her system because she hadn't needed a man in her life. She'd had that once and never again. No, all she'd wanted was a temporary romance—a night, a week, an ephemeral affair. But now she was attached to Matt.

Or was she? He hadn't said he wanted to be in the baby's

life, had he? He hadn't really said anything. Maybe her baby would be just like her—not good enough. The thought had fire coursing through her. Her baby was worth the world.

This felt so much worse than not telling Matt at all.

She closed her eyes, thinking back to that fateful day when she'd first met him. She'd had no idea that she would end up here, in a London cab, more confused and angry than she had ever been.

Seven months ago

Hannah walked beside her friend as they cut through the crowd of gyrating bodies moving to the pulsing rhythm in Zephyr, the most exclusive VIP club in Melbourne.

The space was glossy. Almost every surface was black or gold. Even the wavy lights above their heads that meandered through the entire club cast a golden glow, oozing glamour and opulence afforded to the very fortunate. Tonight, thanks to Emma's new boyfriend and his friend—neither of whom Hannah had met—that included them.

The two friends pushed their way over to the private booths. The shiny floor turned into a plush carpet and in this area there was no mass of bodies. Cosy tables and chairs were dotted here and there. A bar tender entertained a group with his flairing skills at the backlit bar. Ahead of them every booth was fully occupied.

Except one. The only one surrounded by a gold curtain.

Emma said something but Hannah didn't know what. In fact, the whole world had gone silent. A golden and glorious man sat in the booth. He was tall and broad in a dark suit with no tie, and it was as if the very air bowed to him.

Something about him called out to Hannah. Maybe she called to him too, because he turned to look at her and the force of his light-green eyes left her breathless. Then his lips curved up and his smile was devastating.

This man was Adonis.

They arrived at the table and he stood, towering over her.

That smile fixed in place. Emma was about to make the introductions but he beat her to it.

'Matt Taylor.' His voice was deep and rich his English accent so very sexy. Hannah was suddenly overcome with thoughts of rich caramel.

'Hannah Murphy,' she replied, very nearly breathless.

He took her hand, bringing her fingers to his lips. Her skin sparked at the touch. 'It's very nice to meet you, Hannah Murphy.'

She wanted to hear him say her name again.

Hannah watched him walk around her and pull out her chair. Muttering her thanks, she took her seat and watched him sit down once more. Emma sat beside her but Hannah couldn't feel her friend's presence at all. It was as if a vacuum had swallowed Matt and her and they were all there was in this space.

'I'm glad you could join us,' Matt said.

Hannah blinked, forcing herself to behave as she normally did. She had never been so taken with a man. Yes, she had been attracted to men, and had had her fair share of dalliances, but none of them had ever rendered her speechless.

'I could never pass up a chance to come to Zephyr.' She smiled. Watching his eyes dip to her mouth made her shiver. She wanted to kiss him. She had said only a handful of words to the man and she wanted his lips on hers. Something in his darkening gaze said he felt the same.

'How are you enjoying Melbourne so far?' she asked.

His eyes snapped to hers, as if he'd been pulled away from the most engrossing puzzle, and when they landed the look in them speared her, pooling liquid heat in her belly. 'It's a great city. Lots to do and see but, I have to say, I like the view tonight a lot better.'

Hannah laughed. 'Oh, you're very smooth, aren't you, Matt Taylor?'

'I like to think so.'

At that very moment her phone pinged to life. Normally

the sound of her message tone made her smile, but this time it made a blush creep up her neck. She quickly placed it on silent and hazarded a glance at Matt, who was grinning.

'Sonic rings?' He was on the verge of laughing. Heavens, this man! He was dangerous to her self-control.

'One can never over-appreciate the nostalgia factor of a good game, Matt.'

'Oh, I don't dispute that. I just didn't expect this ravishing woman in front of me to pull out a Sonic the Hedgehog reference.'

'A lady has layers, you know,' she teased, feeling giddy that her inner nerd was appreciated.

He placed his elbows on the table, leaning forward, and dropped his voice. Magically, the music didn't seem so loud over here. 'Tell me about these layers.'

'What do you want to know?' she asked, leaning towards him too. Her fingers itched to trace the line of his jaw.

'Everything.'

And so they talked and laughed. His laughter was a sound that warmed her skin and made her stomach flip over. At some point a bottle of champagne appeared on their table, which Matt popped and poured into their glasses. Not once did he look away from Hannah. There was unconcealed hunger written in every line of his face. It felt as if they had slipped into an alternative reality where they were completely alone. A reality where any minute their chairs would fly out and they would meet in a clashing of teeth and tongues. A reality she was very much enjoying.

As if he suddenly realised where they were, Matt looked around—Hannah following suit—and they laughed, finding they were in fact alone. Looking over to the dance floor, she couldn't see Emma at all. Their friends had left. She had no idea when that had happened.

'It would appear that we have been abandoned.' Matt

smirked. 'Well, since we no longer have to concern ourselves with being rude…'

'I'm not sure we were concerning ourselves with it,' Hannah said, deadpan.

He simply shrugged his shoulder. 'Like I was saying, since we're alone, would you like to dance?'

Dancing would distract her from the maddening urge to rip his shirt from his body. 'I'd love to.'

She placed her hand in his and instantly felt the current pass through her at the very touch. His eyes darkened and more than ever she wanted to know what it would be like to press herself up against him. To press her lips to his. To taste him. But he broke the spell, leading her into the throng of people.

His hands settled on her hips and he spun her around, pressing her back into his chest. His warmth filled her. His arms ensconced her. Matt made Hannah feel tiny. He also made her feel safe, which was crazy. She'd only just met him. How could she have such a visceral reaction to someone she barely knew?

Now wasn't the time to care. Right now, she just wanted to feel the beat thrum through her as her hips moved with his, his arms wrapped around her and his lips at her ear. In this moment she felt electrified. She raised her arms above her head, swaying with the rhythm, and he guided them around his neck, slowly running his fingers along her arms and down her sides, sending her pulse into the stratosphere.

Oh, how badly she needed him to touch her, this stranger with his captivating eyes, his strong arms and his hard body. And, just when she couldn't take this thing building between them any longer, he spun her around and cradled her face. Matt's eyes were locked on her lips. Without thinking, she sank her teeth into the soft flesh. He closed his eyes and she could see him take a breath.

'I need to kiss you. Please tell me you want me to.'

Oh, and how! Every cell in Hannah's body was screaming out for his lips, his touch. Her skin burned where his hands sat. Her breaths already shallow.

'Kiss me, Matt.'

The words had barely left her lips before his were on her. She expected a crushing, bruising kiss. Something hard and over-excited. Something to show her how powerful and masculine he knew he was. Something she knew. But it was none of those things.

His lips lightly brushed over hers, parting to take hers between them. He was gentle and tender, taking his time, making her crave him even more while he gave himself to her bit by bit. She felt one of his hands slide down her neck, over her bare shoulder, down her arm to land on her waist, pulling her against the length of him. Every sound, every person in the club, died away. It was just them in this space, in this moment suspended in time.

Hannah wrapped her arms around his neck, trying to get even closer, and then she was pressed against him. Bands of solid muscle wrapped around her back, keeping her safely against him and, as she felt his warmth dip into every part of her, his tongue sought hers out, entwining with hers. Heat exploded in her core. Her body tingled as she felt his fingers splay then fist the fabric on her back, as though he was trying to control the need to rip the damned thing off.

Matt kissed with his whole body and now she was desperate to feel that body on hers.

'Matt...' She moaned into his mouth, feeling his hardness press against her belly. 'Take me home.'

His lips left hers and she wanted to revolt but then she saw how dark his green eyes were and she knew he would take her. That he was feeling this mad intensity too.

His fingers laced with hers and she grinned when he adjusted his suit jacket to hide the evidence of his arousal. 'Lead the way...'

* * *

'Ma'am?' The taxi driver's voice broke through the fog of her memory of the first night they had spent together. 'We're here.'

They were parked on the kerb outside her hotel. Hannah hadn't noticed at all. She cleared her throat, paid the driver and walked into the building.

CHAPTER FOUR

Seven months ago

MATT'S FOREHEAD WAS pressed against Hannah's. He could hardly catch his breath. Shattering…that was what he was doing. Hannah's naked body was laid out before him. Her eyes were glistening with everything he wanted to hear her say but knew he never would. In this hotel room, Matt couldn't think. This was the last time he would be with her. The last time he would taste her skin. Tomorrow he would be gone.

And then it dawned on him that all he felt was her skin. He hadn't even thought of protection. How could he have lost control like that?

'Hannah, I'm so sorry. We didn't use—'

'It's okay, Matt.'

Her hand rested on his cheek—a gentle touch he wanted more of—before her fingers brushed through his hair. He closed his eyes, relishing the feeling.

'We're okay.'

'I'll go to a pharmacy.'

'You don't need to,' she said with a sad smile. 'I can't have a baby.'

'Hannah…' His voice was a broken rasp. 'I'm sorry.' He pulled her into his tight embrace, feeling her sorrow as his own.

* * *

Matt sat at his desk, reading the same line on the report in his hands for the tenth time. Heaving a sigh, he took off his glasses and pinched the bridge of his nose.

This was ridiculous. He couldn't concentrate on anything. From the moment Hannah had walked in it was as if the solid ground beneath him had turned into quicksand.

Matt's focus was usually legendary but now he wasn't even sure how he'd made it through his afternoon meeting.

A baby! He was going to be a father. Well, he didn't know that for certain yet. The paternity test hadn't yet been done but Hannah seemed convinced.

But she was lying. She had to be.

The look on her face that night, though, had been real. Hadn't it? Could she just be that good an actress?

How on earth was he going to deal with this? What would his parents have said about their son now if they'd still been alive? Would they have had a word of advice, or would his father have been disappointed in him?

He was fairly certain he knew the answer. His father had made no secret of what he thought of Matt's life choices, how poorly they reflected on the Taylor name. A hedonistic lifestyle was not what they'd been about. A solid man, according to his father, was one who created a strong family, made a successful name for themselves, didn't act on passions or whims. And that wasn't Matt. According to his father, his were the actions of a boy, and not one to be proud of.

His family had been a strong unit. Matt didn't even know what he was to Hannah any more.

He ran his fingers through his hair. The muscles in his back and shoulders were bunched. His heart hadn't had a regular beat since she'd left.

He was about to try to read the report again when his phone rang. He stared at the name on the screen. For the first time in his life he wanted to reject a call from this person, but the blood was pounding in his ears.

'Alex. Is this the call that should have come months ago?' Matt had never in his life been this angry at his friend. This was his brother, someone who was always honest with him. Someone he could count on with his life. He'd never felt so betrayed.

'I wanted to tell you, Matt, but it wasn't my place.'

'That's an excuse and you know it.' He was fighting to keep his voice level but he could hear the tremble in it. Surely Alex did too?

'You have every right to be angry, mate. I'd be too, but it wasn't about just you or Hannah.'

'Did you even try to get her to tell me? Or did you just happily keep this secret so you didn't have to get involved?'

'Of course I tried to convince her. For months, but it was her decision to make. Not mine.' There was a pause on the line. 'She didn't have it easy, mate.' Alex's tone was placatory.

Matt pushed out his chair and stormed to the window. Silence stretched on the line. He had no idea what he would have done had the roles been reversed but Matt didn't feel like being generous now. Everyone who mattered had known but him. And it hurt. Even if it wasn't his baby, he'd cared for Hannah back then.

'Matt? Are you okay?'

'Am I okay? No, I'm not okay. I could be a father. And it's not just because I had no plans to ever be one—I only get a couple of months to get used to the idea!' he raged.

'I get it, I do, but whether you like it or not this is happening, so what are you going to do?'

Matt rested his palm against the cool glass, taking a deep breath. What was he going to do? He couldn't leave things as they were. He needed to talk to Hannah. As angry as he was with her, he couldn't deny that carrying this secret couldn't have been easy. Carrying this child through doctors' appointments and morning sickness. Had she suffered with morning sickness? Had it been bad? Who had she leaned on? It surprised him that he felt robbed. Surely he was just feeling this way because it was Hannah, and his body craved hers. He didn't want a child, but he had left Melbourne still wanting her.

'I don't know yet, but I'll figure it out. *If* the baby is mine.'

'Matt, you know she isn't like that. Hannah isn't trying to trap you.'

'I don't know anything right now.'

He ended the call and slid the phone into his pocket. Matt knew the first thing he needed to do was to talk to Hannah. Have an honest conversation. There would be no hiding behind secrets now. She had to know where he stood. The next thing would be a paternity test. He'd have no rest until it was proved he was or wasn't the father. If he was, he would need a plan.

Looking out at the sprawling city beneath him, the events of the day replayed in his mind. Everyone wanted something from him—the women who came onto him, the investors, media. Everyone. Now there was Hannah—pregnant even though it shouldn't have been possible.

But according to whom? He only had her word to go on. It seemed as if she was just like everyone else attempting to use him. It wouldn't be the first time but he would make sure it was the last.

The thought that Hannah could be like all the others was like a knife in his chest, but he knew who he was. The circles he moved in with the rich, famous and vastly powerful. His best friend might have brought him into the limelight, but it was own actions that kept him there. The money, the fame—people always wanted to cash in on them.

Stress had him pulled as taut as a bow string and a plan began to form in his mind. He walked back to his desk and pressed the button for his PA.

'Clear my schedule for the rest of the week.'

'Yes, sir.'

The meetings could wait. The company that he had built from the ground up deserved his full attention. His employees deserved a boss who made the right calls. He needed to deal with the crisis in his life so he could return in full force to his work. In the meantime, he could give Hannah his attention. For what they'd shared in Melbourne, he'd give her that much.

Despite the months, Matt couldn't forget their time together. He had never felt such an instant connection to anyone. The moment he'd laid eyes on her in her gold dress he'd known he was in trouble. The glittering fabric had showed off her soft curves that he'd wanted to touch, to explore. Pulling out her chair had been the first excuse to get close to her. He'd had enough one-night stands in his life to know that she was interested too, but then she'd spoken to him; and everything she'd said had always been so unexpected.

Then there was the taste of her lips. The feel of her arms around his neck. He'd missed that. He had missed her. Except now she was pregnant when she'd said she couldn't be. If this baby wasn't his, he would have to question the integrity of every person he let into his life.

He knew what he had to do.

Matt stormed over to his desk, snatched up his keys and left his office, stopping only briefly to speak to his PA, whose eyes trailed up to meet his. He knew the look well. She was too much of a professional ever to act on it but the want in her gaze grated on him.

'I will not be available for the next few days. Don't forward any calls to me.' Before she had the chance to answer, he left. She probably thought he had lost his mind. Maybe he had.

Getting into his sleek sports car, the only thought Matt had was to see Hannah.

No sound came from the large-screen television. Hannah had no idea what was on or what she had watched before it. Her stomach was in knots. Her eyes were puffy. She was exhausted and still upset after the meeting with Matt earlier, but even so, she couldn't stop thinking about him, about their time together. That he'd wanted her before but now he seemed so different.

She worried for her baby. If Matt said he would have nothing to do with them, she could provide everything her child needed currently, but money didn't last for ever.

Life could change on a dime—she knew that better than anyone. Her family's wealth had dried up with her grandparents. The house in Toorak was all that was left of a fortune she had never seen and even that was gone. After her parents' untimely death while she'd still been at university, Hannah had been forced to sell it.

Still, she was confident she could be smart and plan for change as best she could.

Other thoughts had her far more anxious. What would she do when her child grew and asked her about his father? Would she lie to him or tell him the truth and watch it devastate him? He would hate Matt. Well, she would make sure he would never miss him. That Matt never got the chance to see him. She would protect her baby from him with everything she had. She would never speak his name again.

No one needed to know about how she had thought about him and wondered how he was. Or that she would sometimes close her eyes and picture him kissing her belly even when she felt unattractive—especially then.

Those were her secret thoughts, things she hadn't even told Emma. She never again wanted to rely on a man to make her feel beautiful or seen. None of it would matter if he turned his back on their baby.

Hannah placed a hand on her belly, revelling in the little movements she felt. 'I'll make sure you're loved. You will always be able to trust me, I promise.'

As if her baby had heard her, she felt a little kick and chuckled to herself, but a knock on the door shattered her quiet moment.

She padded over to her room door, pulling it open. 'Matt.' She wasn't surprised that he'd been able to come up to her room without her knowing about it. There wasn't much he could do that would surprise her.

CHAPTER FIVE

'MAY I COME IN?'

Hannah was torn. She didn't know if she wanted to let Matt in, but she couldn't bear to leave things as they were. She needed his answer about their baby. Fear was a powerful thing and it coursed through her. She did not know if this would be the last time she would see him. If he would reject her child. It didn't matter to her that their best friends were together. If Matt didn't want this baby, she would make sure he never saw her either.

'I just want to talk.'

His voice was still calm, but he seemed tentative, so Hannah held the door open and stood aside. The hotel room had seemed comfortable to her moments ago but now, with Matt standing inside, it felt cramped, as though he took up all the space.

She moved past him to sit on the arm chair in the corner. It didn't help the ache in her lower back.

God, this tension was going to eat her alive. She watched Matt pluck a pillow off the bed and come over to her. He eased her forward and she gasped as his touch made her whole body tingle. He placed the pillow behind her back and she could tell from the look in his eyes and set off his jaw that he felt something too. Whatever this was between them hadn't fizzled in their months apart. But things were different now. This wasn't a pause in reality, like his vacation had been. This was real life.

He sat on the edge of the bed, as close as he dared get without touching her, and she hated that she wished he would.

After a moment of neither of them knowing what to say, she saw him take a breath.

'You caught me off-guard earlier, Hannah.'

She knew that. Her gut twisted with guilt, and yet she hadn't forgiven him. His accusations still stung.

'I'll be honest with you, I never wanted children…'

There it was. A buzzing erupted in her ears. She'd told everyone that he didn't want a child. There would be no reason why it would change now. What made her special enough to be the exception to his rule? She should never have come.

'Just hear me out.' Matt was staring at her with his assessing gaze. 'What I wanted doesn't matter now. If this baby is mine, I will be in their life.'

'He is yours, Matt,' Hannah insisted impatiently. She couldn't help snapping but she recognised Matt was attempting to be civil. They would get nowhere if they bickered.

'He? Do you know?' There was a strange expression on his face—sadness, maybe wonder, or apprehension.

'No, I just have this feeling. From the start it felt right to think of him as my little boy.'

Matt nodded.

'I suppose it's not a very scientific answer.' Hannah was always logical. It had served her well in her career. Science and medicine were irrefutable, feelings entirely fallible. Just like the feelings in her first real relationship.

How wrong she had been then. She didn't want to be that Hannah again. She hadn't been in a long time. Hearing Matt say he wanted to be in her baby's life made her heart soar and that was terrifying. She needed to stick to the facts and any happiness had to be reserved for her baby.

'Would you be opposed to us finding out for certain?' he asked.

Would she? It would probably make it easier. She still had to decorate the nursery in her flat in Melbourne. Everyone kept asking her if she knew what she would be having. It would be nice to have an answer. Hannah didn't care one way or the other as long as her baby was healthy.

'No, I wouldn't.'

Matt broke into the first real smile she'd seen on him all day and it was every bit as potent as the first time she had seen it. It lit up his face, made his green eyes sparkle. Hannah realised the tension she had been holding for months had melted away.

'I'm glad.'

'But I'm sure this isn't all you came here to say.'

No, it wasn't. He just didn't know how she would respond to the rest of it.

'I wanted to discuss how we would move forward.'

'That's reasonable.'

'After the paternity test, if the baby isn't mine—'

'The baby is yours, Matt!' she said irritably. Anger flared in her brown eyes.

'Just humour me, please.' When she crossed her arms and fell silent, he continued. 'If the baby isn't mine, you will have a lot to answer for. I don't take well to attempts to trap or use me. I've dealt with it enough and it *will* be the last time.'

'And if the baby is yours?' she asked with a cocked brow. The threat should have made her nervous, but all he saw was defiance in her eyes.

'Then everything changes.'

'How so?'

His voice dropped. His gaze became intense. '*If* the baby is mine, Hannah, I will be in their life from the moment of that test to my very last breath.' Matt watched her swallow thickly. He meant every word. A child needed a stable home. A father who understood his duty. Someone who would provide for it.

'Know that there will not be any more of this travelling alone nonsense.' He watched her roll her eyes. 'You can roll your eyes at me as much as you want; it won't change anything. What if something had happened to you and affected my child?'

He wanted his baby to have the privilege he'd had. A father who provided everything his sister and him could have wanted—the best schools, a large house, a stable family. Matt was determined that no child of his would grow up in a broken home—half a home when he could provide a whole one.

Will Hannah end up like your mother? a voice at the back of his mind questioned. He ignored it. Feelings weren't a priority.

'Matt…' Her eyes glistened but he could see she didn't want to give in to those tears and it made him want to know how big of a load she was carrying. The problem was that he was still stuck with the anger from being kept in the dark all this time. He still couldn't trust her.

'If this baby is ours, they will have everything they deserve. Everything they are owed for being mine.'

Hannah closed her eyes and when she opened them the softness in her stare called to him. He reached over and took her hand in his.

'I didn't dare hope that you would feel this way.'

He wanted to ask her how she'd thought he would react but it wasn't important. She needed to know what awaited them.

'There's a lot we will have to do in a short time. The first thing will be the paternity test tomorrow morning.'

'That soon?'

'Yes.' The uncertainty was like a sword suspended over his head. Any moment now it would fall but, as the day had progressed, and now with him sitting here with Hannah, he could no longer tell which wound would be greater—the baby proving to be his or someone else's. The idea that she might have been able to move on so swiftly from him made him want to rage. Just as the thought that she would so callously manipulate him.

'And after?'

'After, we convince the world that we were keeping this pregnancy quiet because it's our first child. We show everyone that we are a family. We'll start with a few small public appearances.' Matt had it all figured out. He could control the narrative, make sure the media reported what he wanted them to. 'And, once we have everyone convinced, we will get married.'

'Married?' Hannah all but yelled.

'Do you have a problem with being married to me?'

'Of course I do! Matt, we had a holiday fling seven months ago!'

'I know, Hannah. I was there.'

'That doesn't mean we should get married! What reason would we have for doing something like that?' she sputtered.

'A baby?' It was a suitable solution, the best way to give his child a stable home. A family that could springboard it to greatness. Maybe he could finally make his father proud. The thought almost made him laugh. Wanting any sort of validation would have been seen as a weakness by his father.

'A man doesn't get emotional, Matthew. It's a weakness. Control makes you strong. Remember that when you're out partying your life away.'

A stoic, controlled family man, that was what his father had wanted him to be. It wasn't too late to try and be that man.

Hannah made a choking sound. 'People have babies every day without being married or engaged, Matt. We're not even—'

'Not even what?'

'In love!'

'I told you, my baby would have a family,' he said evenly. There was no way he would budge on this. No one would change his mind. And love wasn't essential. He knew better than anyone.

She snatched her hand back from his and he frowned at the

loss of her warmth. 'How would this even work? I live on the other side of the world! I doubt you'd leave your company and move to Melbourne.'

'You're right. I wouldn't. That's why you will be moving in with me.'

Hannah was sure she was going mad. He couldn't have just said that, could he?

'Move in? Matt, I'm leaving in a couple of days. Going back to work.' What Matt was suggesting was outrageous.

'You will be staying right here in London,' he countered.

'I can't just leave my job in Melbourne!'

'You'll walk into another, I promise.'

'I'm not working for you, Matt. I've earned my position. This baby won't change that.' She didn't want his promises. She had worked damn hard to get where she was. Nothing had ever been handed to her so, even though Matt had a tech company that most software developers would dream of working at, she wouldn't accept his hand-out.

'Then don't work for me. But you're staying here with me. My child will have their father around for every moment of their lives. I won't be scheduled in.'

Oh, he was impossible!

'I can appreciate that, but I have a life.' One she was reluctant to abandon at the demand of someone else.

'And we can have one here, together.'

Hannah awkwardly stood, too riled up to care about how ungainly she felt. She needed some space from him.

'I'm happy you want to be a part of our lives. Really, I am. But I can't say goodbye to everything I know. My home. My friends. My job.'

But he was willing to be there for their child. Her baby could have things most people could only dream of. They wouldn't know a single moment of 'not today, sweetheart, maybe next week'. And, with her as a single parent, that would be a real possibility for her child.

She hated the thought of having to rely on anyone. Not when she had worked so hard to succeed on her own. Still, it was undeniable that Matt could provide more. Be there to catch their child regardless of what they wanted to do.

And he was exceptional in so many ways; he could be an exceptional father. Did her wanting to go home mean that she was being selfish? Would she be depriving her child and their father of a real future together?

This was all too much!

Her head swam and she slammed a hand against the wall to steady herself. Instantly Matt was beside her, guiding her back to the chair. There was a concerned look on his sculpted face as he leaned over her.

'This is a lot, Matt,' she said.

'I know it is, but we have to do what's best for the baby.'

She glared at him. Of course she knew that! She was the one carrying him. Her temper flared. She tried telling herself he was only doing what he thought to be the right thing, even if he was being an arse about it. And he did have a point— a stable family was important. Her father had read to her at night when he'd tucked her in; her mother had taught her how to drive. They'd taken turns bringing her to extra-curricular activities.

She could do those things for her child. But that would all pale in comparison to what she and Matt could provide to-gether. His name, his wealth, would open doors for her baby to which she could never give him access. He was right—he could provide a great life.

Except the part where they were in love. Love was some-thing that happened to a fortunate few and she was just not one of those people.

Hannah raised her chin defiantly. '*If* we do this, I have conditions.'

'I'm all ears.'

'No marriage. We can have an engagement to see if this could work. We have two months until the baby arrives, all being well. We can try a two-month trial period. But I need to think about it. I'm not agreeing to this now.'

She could see Matt thinking it over, a line forming between his brows as he studied her.

CHAPTER SIX

HANNAH EXPECTED SOME sort of reaction from Matt now that she had agreed to consider his crazy proposal. She got nothing. Instead, his hands were braced on the arm rest, crowding her. Slowly he lowered himself to his knees.

'Have you eaten?'

'What?'

'You heard me.'

Now that she thought about it, the last thing she'd eaten was a small lunch before she had gone to Matt's office. Since she'd got back to the hotel, she hadn't been able to deal with the thought of food. Her stomach was in knots. There was no way she'd be able to eat. It was the last thing on her mind right now. She had just agreed to the possibility of leaving everything she knew behind her.

'Hannah, you might be carrying my child. I asked you a question.'

'You already know the answer. It's fine, Matt, I'll get something in a bit.' She should at least have had an afternoon snack, but it wasn't as though she was in the habit of missing meals. Today was an exception. She could take care of herself.

'You have a choice—either I get us room service or, if you're up for a little walk, we could go somewhere.'

Matt had been so easy going in Melbourne. She didn't know who was this high-handed, demanding person kneeling before her. Eating out did sound good, though, maybe even a little air. Being so close to Matt messed with her brain.

'I'd like to go out.' If she was going to eat anyway, she might as well go some place nice.

Matt nodded and stood, offering his hand to help her up. 'Are you okay?'

'Yes.' His touch made her feel as though she were holding onto burning embers, except there was no pain. Just a licking heat that travelled over her skin. She tried to pull her hand back, but he held on tightly, and she allowed herself to enjoy this moment. To lean into this support he offered while it lasted.

She grabbed her bag and slipped the room key into it as Matt closed the door behind him. He was quiet as they made their way to the lift and as they stepped into it. Hannah wondered if maybe a bit of space between them might have been the better plan.

The lift slowed and she tried to step away from him but he wouldn't let her. The doors slid open and an old couple walked in. The impeccably dressed woman gave her a warm smile as she noted their joined hands and Hannah's belly.

They must have looked like a real couple. Was this what it would be like, pretending for the world so everyone knew they were a real family? What about when the baby was born? Would they keep pretending?

They finally reached the ground floor and Matt kept the doors open, letting the couple exit first before his voice penetrated her thoughts.

'Whatever you're thinking, don't let our situation spook you. Let's just take this one step at a time.'

He looked down at her and all she saw was a man who looked like the Matt who had spent nights in her bed. The Matt who—in just over a week—had been able to glimpse the real her. But this man had so much more distance in his eyes.

* * *

Matt could tell the cogs were spinning in her head. He knew what he was asking of her would be difficult—demanding, even—but it would be best for the child who was possibly his.

He led them out into the crisp evening air. People were milling about and he had to ignore how good it felt to have Hannah with him in his home city. How he had missed this for months. How he had chastised himself for it. He'd never looked back at a fling and wished for more except after he had left Hannah. Now more was upon him and he would never have guessed it would happen like this, without a choice.

Despite her possible manipulations, he was glad to see her, which frustrated the hell out of him. He wouldn't act on this attraction. Not when he couldn't trust her. He might have a responsibility to the child and that was all he would focus on.

They reached a dimly lit Italian restaurant and were warmly ushered inside to their own private booth, where they ordered quickly and were left in peace.

There was so much he wanted to talk about and yet so little he could find to say. It seemed to him that Hannah was struggling for words that needed saying. So, they settled for silence until their food arrived.

He filled her glass with water from a carafe left on the table before filling his own and took satisfaction in the fact that Hannah didn't spare a moment before spearing a *raviolo* with her fork.

When he saw that she had almost cleared her plate, he finally asked the one question that he had wanted to all day.

'Why did you wait so long to tell me?' There was no accusation in his voice, no anger. That had faded somewhat. Maybe she wasn't trying to trap him in a relationship, given how reluctant she was to accept his terms, but there had to be something she wanted.

'I didn't know until the end of my first trimester and then I still couldn't believe this was happening. I didn't want to burden you if there was no reason to…'

He clenched his teeth at that. If something had happened to his baby, he would have wanted to know. Would she have kept it a secret?

'But then I saw the scan and I knew this was real. After that I was scared, I guess, that you would reject us. I mean, we only spent a week together. I didn't want you to think that I'd manufactured this situation to trap you, given who you are, which is what you think anyway. I couldn't trust you would just be there. And there was so much on my plate.'

'Didn't you think I deserved to know sooner?' Had anyone? Alex had said he'd tried to convince her to tell him; he had that knowledge at least.

'I know you did, but Matt, we spent such a short time together. We didn't plan for this. A baby doesn't exactly fit your lifestyle. You don't even want a child. I still don't understand why you want to be a family!'

He wanted to shout that she should have taken the risk. It wounded him deeply that she hadn't trusted him enough to tell him. He reminded himself that those feelings were useless now. It wouldn't turn back the clock so they could do it all over. All that mattered was what they did now.

'Why wouldn't I want us to be a family, Hannah? Don't you think a child deserves that?'

'Of course I do, but what am I supposed to think when *you* don't want a baby?'

'Where I come from, Hannah, that wouldn't matter. What's important is having committed parents, and I plan to provide that if it's mine.'

'With your plan,' she said.

'Yes. I won't let you or this child down. I need you to trust me.'

'I do—'

'Don't just say the words.' He cut her off, not wanting to hear an obvious lie or a placation. 'If you did, you would have told me about the baby the moment you knew. But it's okay. I plan on proving to you that you can trust me with this child.'

'If it's yours,' she threw back at him through clenched teeth.

'Yes.' He wasn't taking her at her word but he also never shirked his responsibilities. Growing up, he'd seen the duty that came with being a parent. The immense sacrifices that had to be made. An image of his mother popped into his head— her soft smile. Her life that had revolved around him and his younger sister. They'd been her everything.

You know why. Is that what you want for Hannah?

It wasn't. He hadn't wanted that all. Exactly why he had never wanted his own family, and yet here he was.

Hannah heard his words but she didn't want to believe them. It was easy to say she could trust him. It didn't mean anything. Hadn't she heard those very words before? All that had happened afterwards was her heart breaking in a million pieces. Trust didn't come easy to her any more and, as much as she wanted to reach out to Matt, to touch him and have him hold her, take care of their child, she couldn't trust him. She couldn't trust that he would go from not wanting children to just accepting theirs. No one accepted what they didn't want. No one.

And this plan of his to be a family... He was never short of female company. Would he give all that up for a family life without love? Of course not. He would get bored; there was no doubt in her mind about that. So would she then have to deal with him seeing other women? Something in her railed at the thought but she had no claim on him.

What about now? Was he seeing anyone? Maybe she could deal with all of it if he was discreet. After all, she couldn't be upset when they weren't in a real relationship. Her priority was her child and her career. That would keep her more than busy enough not to care what Matt was up to.

Liar! a voice shouted in her head. She would always care. Even now he affected her. Hadn't she looked him up on social media every time she'd missed him? When she'd seen him with breath-taking Glamazons she'd felt the sharp pang of jealousy. If she lived with him that feeling would only get worse, because how could anyone be in Matt's orbit and not be sucked in by him, by his easy-going nature?

Well, that had changed since her arrival. She was definitely seeing another side to him. A harder, unyielding part that had been so well concealed in Melbourne.

'Would you like to go back to the hotel?' Matt asked, cutting through the silence.

'Yes, please.'

'We'll fetch your things and head home. I would rather have you somewhere I know the baby will be safe.'

'No.'

'No?'

She could see a mix of frustration and amusement on his face. Of course she wanted to be closer to him, which was exactly why she shouldn't be. He was not going to dictate to her, and she needed a moment to think.

'I appreciate the offer, if you can call it that, but the hotel room suits me just fine, thank you.'

'Stop being stubborn, Hannah. You're going to need to move in at some point.'

'Possibly. But, like you said, you want a paternity test first. So until then I think I'm free to do as I please.'

Hannah could see a vein throb in his forehead. Given how high-handed he'd been, she couldn't bring herself to care overmuch. She wasn't a variable he could control.

'Let's go,' he bit out.

CHAPTER SEVEN

MATT PAID FOR their dinner and escorted her back to her room, where he loitered, looking as if he wanted to say something more. It was probably best to say goodnight now.

'Thank you for walking me back. You didn't need to.'

His hand twitched as if he wanted to reach for her but had thought better of it. 'I don't like that you're here alone.'

'Good thing I'm fine with it, then.' Hannah smirked.

Matt shook his head. She could see he was fighting a smile. 'Hannah…'

'Goodnight, Matt.' She walked him to the door, holding it open as he walked through.

He turned round, placing a palm against the door frame. 'I'll be here early tomorrow to fetch you.'

'I'll meet you there. Text me the address,' Hannah countered.

'Can you not concede just this once?' Matt closed his eyes, as if he was praying for patience. She supposed he was. 'Meet me for coffee first. It'll give us a chance to talk.'

'Fine, I'll see you then. Let me know where.'

He looked at her for long moment before saying, 'I really would prefer it if you came home with me.'

'Well, we can't always get what we want.'

'We'll see about that.'

Matt walked into the coffee shop to find Hannah already seated at a table in the corner. The place was empty save for the staff. One call was all it had taken for them to open earlier for him. It meant they could get a little privacy before customers began to arrive.

Taking the only other chair at the table to sit opposite Hannah, Matt noticed the dark circles under her eyes the moment she looked at him. He didn't have a chance to comment on her obvious lack of sleep because the waiter placed two cups on the table. The scent of his double espresso was enough to wake a sleeping army. He couldn't help but smile.

'I ordered for us while I waited,' Hannah explained. 'I hope you don't mind.'

'Not at all.' It was a small thing, ordering a coffee. So why did the fact that she remembered his go-to order make his heart do something funny? 'Before we go anywhere, I need to know if you're agreeing to my terms.'

Hannah sighed, wrapping her hands around her cup. 'I know you really want this, Matt, but I don't see why it needs to be this way. You're you. Even if I was in Melbourne, you could see your child whenever you want. Help me understand.'

Matt wanted to say it didn't matter, but then out of the window he saw a woman stop her pram and pick up her baby. A little boy stood beside her, holding up a dummy that he'd fished out of the seat cushion. The scene brought back memories of his own childhood. Matt had never wanted this, had told himself he couldn't have it—not when he refused to put someone through what his mother had experienced. Yet now he could possibly have a child—something he did not want—so why did it feel good? It made no sense.

He tore his attention away from the street, fixing his gaze on Hannah. Something about the way she looked at him made him want to talk to her.

'My father was a great man, Hannah. Widely respected. Successful. Stoic.' He remembered him with no fondness. 'There were certain things he expected of us. Perfection by his standards, but no less than what he himself gave. I can't say that I've lived my life in the way a Taylor should, and even though he's dead...'

'You want to make him proud,' Hannah finished for him.

'It's more than that.' He reached across the table to take Hannah's hand, an instant spark crackling between them which he was determined to ignore. 'We're good together, Hannah. Don't you want to see what we could be? Chemistry like ours doesn't come along every day.'

It was the one thing he could use to leverage her decision.

He was right. Their connection was special. It felt as if he wanted to continue what they had started in Melbourne. Maybe that goodbye at the airport didn't have to be an end. Maybe it could be a pause. If he wanted to be in his child's life and explore their connection, maybe it would be worth spending these next couple of months with him.

Heaven knew how badly she wanted him even now. She was about to agree when the café door opened and a tall, sophisticated woman all but screeched Matt's name. A fleeting look of annoyance crossed his face as he closed his eyes and let out a small sigh. A tight smile formed on his lips. This wasn't her Matt. This was Matt with several feet of wall around him.

Despite neither of them inviting the woman over, she sashayed her way to the table, pretending not to notice Hannah at all.

'How are you? I saw you through the window and just had to say hello,' she purred, touching Matt's arm.

Hannah saw the shudder pass through him as he pulled away. 'Well, thanks, and yourself?'

'Oh, just wonderful. It was so good to see you at the St. Michael's dinner. I thought you'd call.'

'I don't recall making any promises,' Matt replied in a polite tone. 'It was nice seeing you, but I'm in the middle of something with Hannah.' Matt turned to look at her. It was obvious he was dismissing the woman who only now deigned to look at Hannah. Sensing that Matt wanted the woman to leave, Hannah reached over and held his hand. His fingers locked around hers tightly.

'Yes, of course. Good to see you,' she said awkwardly, before leaving them in peace.

Hannah wanted to ask what his aversion to her was. Objectively, she was stunning, and she'd looked at him with such blatant lust, but he didn't even check to see that she had gone. *Curious*.

'I'm sorry about that.'

He had nothing to apologise for. He had shown less than zero interest and, when he looked at Hannah, she could see he focussed only on her.

Don't you want to see what we could be?

Despite everything, she really did.

'Don't worry about it.' She tried to pull her hand away but Matt wouldn't let go.

'You were about to say something before we were interrupted. It was an answer, wasn't it? Tell me.'

'I'll give you two months.'

The smile he bathed her in was worth her acquiescence. 'You won't regret it.' He took a sip of his coffee, a thoughtful look crossing over his face. 'What was it like when you found out?'

'At first I was shocked, but then scared.'

'Of what?'

'Going through this alone. Of complications, since I wasn't meant to be able to conceive. The changes my body would go through. But soon fascination overtook the fear.'

Matt nodded, saying nothing more. Hannah supposed there wasn't much he could say.

'Shall we leave?'

'After you.' Matt held out a hand, which she took as she stood. The café spun sharply. Her vision blurred. Everything turned black…

* * *

Matt reacted like lightning. 'Hannah!' he shouted as he caught her. Her lifeless body spiked fear through him, as if he was being impaled. Eternal seconds stretched while his brain caught up and he thought to lower her to the floor on her side. Her eyes fluttered open and she looked around, clearly disoriented.

Without another word, he scooped her up, taking her to his car, which he raced through the streets to the office of the doctor they were to see.

Matt burst through the door with Hannah still in his arms. She was more alert now, and complaining about him carrying her around, but he tuned her out. He had never in his life felt fear like this. She would be seen to immediately.

A doctor rushed out to see what the commotion was about and spotted Matt. Wordlessly, he gestured towards his room, where Matt laid Hannah on the bed.

'Hold your arm out for me.' Hannah couldn't concentrate on anything the doctor was doing. She was so very tired. Matt stood at the foot of the bed, his face unreadable, arms crossed. Was he mad that she had fainted?

Her attention snapped back to the present when a rubber tourniquet was tied around her upper arm and a needle pierced her skin. She looked up at Matt who was still staring at her.

Hannah had no idea how he'd managed to get her to the doctor so quickly, but here she was. Getting a thorough check-up at Matt's insistence and having the blood drawn that would prove to him that the baby she carried was his.

'That's all we need,' the doctor said as he removed the third vial. He had explained why he would take three, but she hadn't had the ability to pay attention then.

He taped a plaster to her arm and placed a long sticker on each vial.

'Remember, I want a rush on those results,' she heard Matt say in a tone that brooked no argument.

'I'll make sure the lab puts priority on it.'

'Thank you.'

Hannah was no longer listening to the exchange between them as she rolled her sleeve down. She thought she heard the doctor saying she would be fine. That she needed rest. Everything else was a sleepy haze.

They left the doctor, stepping into a lift that was already on their floor, when Matt rounded on her.

'You're coming home with me.'

'Matt—' she tried to protest.

'No. I'm not hearing it. What if I wasn't there? You could be carrying *my* child.'

Hannah wrapped her arms around her stomach. 'Fine.'

When they reached the parking garage, the doors slid open and she saw a low, sleek sports car that would have filled her with excitement before. Now it looked difficult to climb out of. It was funny—she had arrived in it but had obviously been too out of it to pay any attention.

'I'm sorry about the car,' Matt said in a gentler tone.

'It's okay.' She didn't need his apology. She was sure the way his day had turned out was nothing like he'd expected. She accepted his help getting into the shiny car. He folded himself into the driver's seat and, when both doors were shut, leaned across her.

His scent slammed into her. Light and fresh, like the open sea under a blue sky, but underneath that there was something more, something comforting. It was the smell that had clung to her sheets after he had left—his scent. Hannah had to bury the need to nuzzle into his neck. She hoped desperately that he didn't notice how deeply she breathed him in.

Then he leaned away. Her seat belt had been clipped into place, making sure the lap sash sat below her belly and the shoulder strap was between her breasts. There was no breath left in her now, just a pounding heart and need powerfully coursing through her veins.

Almost in a fugue, she heard him clear his throat and start up the car which came to life with a loud growl. This space was too confined. The air was thick with the attraction that clearly had not died. His scent seemed to be embedded in the very leather she sat on. And suddenly it became very real that she was with Matt, in his car, going to his home, carrying their child.

London was a blur Hannah didn't then have the capacity to notice. She tried to close her eyes and keep everything she was feeling at bay. It was like trying to hold a tidal wave back with nothing but a fence—impossible.

Damn hormones!

'Hannah, are you okay?'

She swallowed hard. 'Fine, it's just been a tiring morning.' Matt didn't buy the lie; it was clear on his face but he didn't push. Out of the corner of her eye she watched his gaze return to the road, taking the time to admire his profile—that strong jaw. The tousled hair that she wanted to run her fingers through now just as much as when she'd first met him.

He must have sensed her looking at him, because he gave her a smile at half-wattage, but it still made her tingle. How did he always do that?

'We'll stop by the hotel to fetch your things first.'

Matt waited for her with his nose buried in his phone. Hannah figured that he would try to get in as much work as possible after his day had most likely been derailed by her.

She walked into the bathroom and began shoving her cosmetics into a small vanity case when she caught her reflection in the bathroom mirror. There were dark rings under her usually bright brown eyes—evidence of how badly she had been sleeping. It was a struggle to find a comfortable position and, when she did find one, her over-busy mind would run through her situation with Matt and everything she needed to get done.

Her eyes drifted down to her rounded belly and she curled her arms around herself. Despite everything else going on, this little bundle inside her made her happy. It was a happiness un-like anything she had felt before, a fierce love. This baby was a miracle—her miracle. Even so, she no longer felt attractive.

'Hannah?'

'I'll be there in a moment.' She hastily put away the rest of her things and tried to leave the bathroom just as Matt appeared in the doorway. Face to face, barely a breath between their bod-ies, he towered over her. She watched as his hand lifted, coming to rest on her cheek. His head dipped lower almost impercep-tibly but she felt it, as if a piece of herself was reaching out.

'You were taking a while. I got worried,' he said, voice low and soft.

'I was just getting my things,' she replied breathily. His eyes were fixed on hers as if he was looking deep into her soul. She wanted to feel that gaze all over her. Then she remembered what his dates looked like and it felt as though someone had tossed a bucket of ice on her head. She pulled away first and watched him slowly drop his hand.

'I suppose you would like to get going.'

'Whenever you're ready.' He stepped away, allowing her to walk past him.

She shoved the vanity case into her suitcase and shut the lid, doing a quick sweep of the room to make sure she hadn't forgotten anything, then made to heave the bag off the bed, but Matt nudged her aside. He took hold of the handle, placed the case on the floor as if it weighed nothing then wheeled it along behind him, permitting her only to carry her handbag. She had to admit, it felt good, being taken care of even if his concern was only for the baby.

* * *

'We're almost home,' Matt informed Hannah.

She noticed the London Eye looming above them as he turned into the parking garage of his South Bank apartment building and brought the car to a stop in an empty bay.

'Wait,' he instructed when Hannah's fingers curled around the door handle. She watched him walk round the car and open the door before scooping her up in his powerful arms, extracting her from within.

She opened her mouth, but didn't know what to say, so she said nothing. As they finally rode up in the lift, she was completely wrung out. He'd saved her from the indecency of awkwardly having to get out of the car on her own. He'd brought her to his home so she would be safe and, more than ever, the guilt of keeping the news from him ate at her. She knew this agreement was his idea, but that didn't make her feel any better.

After a ride that seemed to take for ever, Hannah and Matt stepped out of the lift and inside his apartment. He led her down a long passage that had two doors and took her into the first one.

'That's my room down there. I want you as close as possible.' It seemed as if he wanted to say more. She couldn't imagine what that could be.

The room was magnificent. Her hotel room had had nothing on this—not the view, the immense bed or the *en suite* bathroom that was a mix of dark marble and glass.

Matt sat her on the bed then wheeled her suitcase into the walk-in closet, disappearing for a moment.

'If you need anything, I'm just down the passage. Make yourself at home.'

It was her home—temporarily at least. And this was her own room. She should have been happy but all she could think of was how this beautiful room was for her alone. They would be engaged and living separate lives. Yet Matt wanted her to see what they could be. How could they do that if they spent their time apart?

She could see the future clearly in that moment. They would be a family, a convenient one. Hers would be a role played.

'Thank you, Matt,' she said from the bed.

He frowned. 'What's wrong?'

'Nothing,' she said quickly.

'It doesn't seem like nothing to me.'

Matt didn't like Hannah holding anything back from him. Not again. Not any more. At the door he turned back towards her, determined to get an answer.

He watched her eyes linger on the bed before meeting his. 'Really, it doesn't matter.'

It mattered a great deal to him. He saw nothing wrong with the room. She would be comfortable in here and he was close by in his own room. He was providing a safe space. If she yelled out for him, he would be here in an instant.

But you wouldn't be here with her.

Could that be what bothered her—their separate rooms? After all, he was the one who said they would be a family *if* the baby was his. But he didn't know that yet. He needed a moment to himself to think about everything.

It didn't help that being around Hannah made his blood sing. Yet she had been the one to pull away. He'd been so close to kissing her in the hotel, he could almost taste her lips. As far as he could see, she wasn't ready to be with him, and he still didn't know what her game was, but this infuriating attraction would not abate.

He stalked towards her and pulled her off the bed. 'Hannah, I'm giving you your space because I think you need it right now. We both do. But if I thought for one second you wanted to be in my bed, if I knew I could trust you, that's exactly where we'd be.' It pained him to admit it.

'You don't have to say that, Matt.'

Was she blind? Did she not understand how much he wanted her? How buckling her in the car, being so close to her body that he knew so well, had nearly undone him? She looked away, making him think maybe she did see, but it made little difference. Grasping her chin, he turned her face, forcing her to look at him.

She tried to push away from him. 'I'm not the same person you knew in Melbourne. I've changed.'

'What are you saying?' he asked, temper fraying.

'I know you've been with other women since me. I don't even know if you're seeing someone now.'

And that was when the tether snapped. 'Do you think I would be unfaithful?' Did she see him the same way his father had—a partying playboy? It stung that she would think so.

'It's just—'

'It's just nothing, Hannah. I am not seeing anyone.' The growl of his voice was ringing in his own ears. 'I'm not in the habit of seeking the company of several lovers. I'm not the one who could be lying.'

'I didn't mean... I just know you've been on dates.'

'Yes, I've been on dates, but I haven't been with anyone since you.' He could see the shock of that revelation on her face. 'I meant what I said. *We* will be a family.'

Her eyes widened as he stepped closer to her. She retreated until her back hit the wall and his face was directly in front of hers. 'When I put that ring on your finger, I will be announcing to the world that we are together.'

He saw her lips form his name; nothing but breath escaped. Those lips that haunted him—those lips, those eyes and that voice. He'd tried to forget her. The dates he'd taken to events had been poor stand-ins. He didn't just want a pretty face, he longed for the conversations he'd had with Hannah, her teasing sass.

And the fact that he thought she was the most beautiful thing he had ever seen since the moment his eyes had landed on her in the club had never once changed. Hannah had done something to him seven months ago. He didn't want fake smiles and inane small talk. He didn't want lust-filled stares—not any more. He was tired of it. If only he could trust her.

Matt crowded her, palms resting flat against the wall beside her head. 'Do you want me to tell you how many times I've dreamed of you? How often I've thought of you? Your lips...'

He leaned down, his breath skimming over her lips. 'Your taste.' He ran his nose along her jaw, listening to how her breathing increased. 'Would you like to know how badly I want to explore your body? Sink my fingers into you?' His mouth was at her ear. 'Because I want to, Hannah.'

She let out a quiet moan and he felt himself harden. 'I want to learn every new curve.' One of his hands came off the wall and trailed over her side, making her shiver. 'I want to hear you call my name when you come for me. Again.' He ran his fingers over her hands which were rigidly splayed against the wall. Her body arched towards him.

Matt pulled away, keeping his face a breath in front of hers, and she finally opened her eyes to look into his. Christ, he wanted her, but now was not the time. Not when she had admitted to being afraid to tell him about the pregnancy. When she pulled away from him. When he was still unsure if she was lying to him.

'But it won't happen.' Matt tore himself away. His own breathing had turned ragged, and he knew he had to leave her alone for the rest of the day just so that he could get back some semblance of control.

'Get some rest.' With purposeful strides he entered his own room and shut the door. Despite how cool his apartment was, his skin was overheated. He was painfully aroused and decided a cold shower would be the best thing for him.

Goosebumps raised on his skin as beads of cold water streamed over him, doing nothing to calm him or the ache between his legs. Slamming his palm against the wet marbled wall, Matt grasped his hardness, remembering the feel of Hannah's skin. The overwhelming pleasure of sinking into her.

His hand stroked his length and he grunted. The sound was drowned out by the jets of water pelting down on and around him. Images of her spread out underneath him in her Melbourne flat played out in his mind. The memory of her moan in his ear had him pumping his hand faster. A taste of those soft curves that he had licked and kissed flashed across his tongue and he moaned at the vivid memory. Eyes screwed shut, his release burst from him with a muted shout.

Panting, he dropped his head, watching the water flow down the drain. The orgasm only barely took the edge off his need. Matt stood there with water raining off him for ages until it was clear that nothing would calm him. Touching himself wouldn't sate his hunger for Hannah.

Nothing would bring him peace until he had that test result in his hand.

CHAPTER EIGHT

HANNAH STRUGGLED TO fall asleep. It had nothing to do with the room or the bed, both of which where more luxurious than anything she had experienced before. Rather it was what had happened before Matt had left.

After he had walked out, Hannah had lowered herself into the arm chair beside the bed, breathing heavily and trembling with need. She'd been beyond aroused. Matt had lit her up like a Christmas tree and, just when she'd thought he might kiss her, give her anything to ease the want rushing through her, he'd left.

How had he been able to tear himself away like that? The answer was plain. He wasn't nearly as affected. All his concern had been for the baby, not her. That was the only reason why she here in his home.

Even after she climbed into bed Hannah couldn't get the sight of him so close out of her mind, nor his voice or the predatory look on his face.

'Predatory' was not a word she would ever have used to describe him before but he'd very much seemed as if he'd been only barely restrained.

She squeezed her thighs together to relieve some of the ache. It did nothing. She tossed and turned, eventually giving in to touching herself. Not that it helped. Now, as the sun went down, she lay on the bed, wondering if she'd made the right choice.

A sharp knock on the door startled her out of her thoughts.

'Hannah, meet me on the terrace.'

'Be right there,' she called back.

Matt had only intended to be out for a short time while Hannah slept, but he was restless. He couldn't be in his penthouse without confronting his attraction to Hannah every moment he saw her. So he'd stayed away until the lab called, giving him an excuse to drive through the city, steeling himself for whatever they would say.

He lowered himself onto the plush outdoor couch, waiting for Hannah to appear. Thankfully she didn't make him wait long. He patted the seat next to him, placing an envelope on her lap when she sat.

It was their reckoning. 'Have you looked at it yet?'

'No.' He picked up the innocuous-looking letter and pulled his glasses out of his pocket, slipping them on his nose before tearing the envelope open and unfurling the page. Quickly reading through the contents, he felt his breath die in his lungs.

Matt was unequivocally the baby's father. He was going to have a child.

He was going to have a child.

A family. His eyes snapped to Hannah's which didn't show a hint of worry. She had known, hadn't she?

'Are you okay, Matt?' she asked him.

He wasn't sure. He'd expected to feel angry, cheated of his choice. This inexplicable feeling blooming in him was completely unexpected and far scarier. Had he wanted this? He couldn't have. He'd never wanted marriage and a family.

But this family was different. This was with Hannah, now a permanent fixture in his life. The mother of his child.

His own mother's face sprang to mind and he tried to shake the memory away. His mother had been far from perfect but she'd loved her children, as Hannah would.

That's not what you want. You don't want Hannah to be unfulfilled like she was.

He pushed the thought away.

'If it weren't for the children...'

The words he'd heard as a child came back to him. The words that had made him want to make life easier for his mother. Words that had made him behave like the perfect son and take care of his sister so that she would always come to him first. His father had expected perfection. He had given them every advantage to achieve it, but not much else—no affection.

What would he be like with his child? He had about two months to decide what type of father he would be.

'Yes.' He dropped the letter to the side and ran his fingers through his hair. 'Everything changes now—you understand that?'

'Nothing has changed. I knew what I agreed to.'

'Good.' Matt walked to the railing and looked up at the fading sky. There was still one thing he needed to know for sure. 'Did you lie to me that night?'

'No, I didn't. It shouldn't have been possible, but it happened.'

Remembering her sorrow, Matt accepted her answer.

'It feels like the universe is laughing at me, that it would happen with you, and I'm sorry that it is. I know who you are, Matt, know what this must have looked like—but I'm also not sorry that I'm getting the one thing that I thought I'd been denied.'

A baby. His baby. His own flesh and blood. Vowing he would know everything about his child, protect them from every invisible threat, he set out to plan his next step with Hannah, because now they were bound together.

CHAPTER NINE

'MATT, I DON'T need an ultrasound. I'm fine and so is the baby,' Hannah argued.

'Yes, that's why you fainted,' Matt said, deadpan. 'I need you to do this. Please.' Matt had stayed up for most of the night with his laptop perched on his lap, researching everything he could. He wanted to be well prepared for his baby's arrival.

'I want to know my baby like you've been allowed to.'

Every day of his life he dealt with facts. Whether those facts were problems or successes, he was able to deal with them because he knew exactly what to expect. It was what had made his tech company so successful and why it continued to grow. Right now, all he knew was that he was going to have a baby. It wasn't acceptable.

'You will, Matt, I promise; but I had my last ultrasound weeks ago. Everything is fine. Beyond fine.' Despite arguing that this scan was unnecessary, Hannah slipped on her shoes to go.

'If everything is fine, it should make no difference to you to have another.'

She rolled her eyes at him. 'I miss laid-back Matt,' she mumbled.

He placed his hand on her back and led her to the lift. 'Laid-back Matt didn't have a child on the way and a stubborn fiancée-to-be.'

* * *

Hannah shook her head but said nothing more. She had already had her moments of madness; Matt was owed his. So she would allow him this.

She felt lighter this morning. Matt having accepted the baby was his and that she hadn't lied to him took a massive weight off her shoulders. It made her feel as if their arrangement was completely doable. After all, they liked each other and got along well enough. More importantly, they both understood that their child deserved their all.

When they walked into the parking garage, Hannah looked at his car and whispered under her breath, 'Right.' It had been low. Had it magically got lower? It seemed like it.

She went to open the door but Matt beat her to it. 'I got it.' Then his arms came around her and she had to try not to sigh at the feeling of being surrounded by him. His scent comforted and aroused her at once. Taking most of her weight, he smoothly helped her into the seat. She clicked the seat belt in place once he closed the door and, when he folded himself into the driver's seat, he made sure the belts were secure.

'Comfy?'

'Yes.'

He was fussing and it made her eyes fill with tears. She tried to look away so he wouldn't see them but he did, as if he had a sixth sense when it came to her.

'Hey, what's wrong?' He reached over, cupping her cheek, making her look at him.

'Nothing. Hormones.' She gave him a teary chuckle and he brushed the tears away with his fingers. Her body sparked at his touch. Somehow, in the seven months they had been apart, Hannah had forgotten how treasured he made her feel. 'Drive or we'll be late,' she instructed.

'We have time. Talk to me.' His thumb brushed back and forth on her cheek.

The words fell out before she could stop them. 'No one does anything like this for me. It makes me feel…special.'

Matt kissed her forehead. 'I will always take care of you. No matter what.'

A fresh wave of tears fell, which he wiped away with a soft smile, and in that moment she was so vividly reminded of the man who had held her on her couch in her apartment.

Matt eased the car out of the garage and into the road. He let his hand drift onto Hannah's lap, keeping hold of the steering wheel with the other, his heart clenching when she threaded her fingers in his.

On the drive to the hospital he felt caught in some sort of time warp because it took far too long yet wasn't quite long enough. When Hannah's fingers left his, it felt wrong. The moment he scooped her out of the car, her hand was back in his. Whether Hannah realised it or not, this would be their first foray out into the world together, where they would be spotted. They needed to look like a couple.

But, even when they stepped into the sonographer's office, he didn't let go. He helped her onto the bed and sat beside her as the doctor started moving the probe over her swollen belly. Hannah's hand squeezed his as images of the baby flashed on the screen in the darkened room. Never had he experienced anything like this. The doctor typed words onto the screen while explaining what they were seeing but it was all static to him.

There was the little human whom he'd helped create. And then they heard the heartbeat and he had never heard a more joyous sound. A tear escaped Hannah's eye and he looked at her in wonder. He couldn't help himself. He bent down and kissed her forehead, not sure what he was feeling. Was there even a name for this emotion?

Matt loved computers. They were easy to understand—uncomplicated. Code was logical. Technology was logical. But all that logic and simplicity seemed like a wasted life when he could feel like this.

'Would you like to know if it's a boy or girl?' the doctor asked as she hit a few more buttons on the keyboard.

Matt and Hannah looked at each other. Smiles mirrored on each other's faces. 'Yes.' Of course he wanted to know. He wanted to know everything. And this would be one thing, one massive thing, that he and Hannah would find out together.

The doctor moved the probe around and suddenly a profile became clear on the screen.

'Congratulations, you're having a boy.' She smiled.

'Told you so.' Hannah laughed. Tears still sprang from her eyes as she looked at him.

'Yes, you did.' He grinned.

A boy.

My son, he thought to himself. His eyes were glued to the screen, and he couldn't remember not wanting children, because suddenly that unnamed emotion had a name—or several. Protectiveness. Excitement. Maybe even love.

For two days he had struggled to come to terms with the possibility of having a child. All it had taken for that thought to settle was hearing a heartbeat.

The image was printed out and handed to him and he could still scarcely believe it.

'I'll give you both a moment.' The doctor shut the door behind her and Hannah adjusted her clothes when Matt helped her to her feet.

He placed his hand on her rounded belly. This was all his, his family. And, in that moment, he knew true happiness.

Matt stared at the ultrasound printout in his hand. There was a lump in his throat he couldn't dislodge, a sting in his eyes. He had just seen his son for the first time. The static outline of a perfectly shaped little human was burned into memory. His baby, who had developed so much without him. All that time he'd lost... He could have been there for the first ultra-sound and met his child then. Maybe he and Hannah would even have had that first trimester together if he'd been there.

Matt ached for all the time he'd missed. All the time Hannah had been scared to call him. He would give anything for that now.

He released a deep breath then stowed the picture away in the centre console, started up the car and drove home. A muscle was flickering in his jaw. Maybe he should never have said he didn't want to be a father because, no matter what his own childhood had been like, those words seemed ridiculous now. When he'd heard their baby's heartbeat, he had stopped breathing altogether.

All those words had done was motivate Hannah to keep his child away. And he couldn't rage at her for what had been his fault. He felt like raging, though, so he clamped his jaw shut. She didn't deserve that, and it certainly wouldn't heal his heart which was breaking for what he'd missed.

'What are you thinking about?'

He heard her question but couldn't respond. Not right now when his baby was suddenly so real. When he couldn't understand why he hadn't wanted this before. When he'd been trying so desperately to control the grief for what he wished he could have experienced.

'Matt, about this plan, I don't want you to feel pressured into doing anything. I can deal with the baby myself.'

Matt still wasn't answering her, and his hands were tightly gripping the wheel. No; she wasn't going anywhere. He wanted every single day with his son.

Out of the corner of his eyes, he saw Hannah twirling the hem of her dress around her fingers, looking out of the window until the car came to a stop. Sadness hung over him like a storm cloud but didn't stop him from helping her climb out and, once they were back in his apartment, Hannah broke the silence.

'Tell me why you're so angry.'

'I'm not,' Matt replied softly. He rounded on her in the large, airy lounge, sliding his hand into his pocket, feeling the scan against his palm. 'But I don't want to hear all your talk about doing this on your own. You don't just get to make an excuse and leave,' he said lowly.

'What are you talking about?' she asked, closing the distance between them.

He dropped the scan photo onto the coffee table. 'You've kept me away all this time, Hannah. From taking this journey with you. With my child,' he ground out. Hearing his son's heartbeat, seeing the proof of his existence and how much of it he had missed out on, hurt.

How could Hannah have kept this from him?

'Matt, that's not what I meant to do!'

Matt forced himself to push away the emotions clouding his head and, in the wake of the quiet that settled in him, there was calm rationality. 'Then what did you mean to do?'

'You know why I couldn't tell you.'

'I heard what you said. And after everything we experienced you didn't trust me enough to tell me. You trusted me with your body but not this.' He pointed at the image lying benignly on the table. 'And it was trust. Trust that went both ways. I never once slept with anyone without protection until you.' Sex had always felt good, but the lust had never been so overwhelming that he'd lost control. Yet, he had with her.

'Why couldn't you have taken the risk to tell me?' His voice was a near-whisper.

'I'm sorry, Matt. If I could do it over, I would. But we're here now. We can only move forward.'

'You're right. We can only move forward, and we'll be doing so as a family.' He was determined to embark upon this new life. 'And we'll start tomorrow. I happen to have the ideal event to take you to to kick things off.'

CHAPTER TEN

WITH A STEAMING cup of herbal tea in her hands, a sleepy Hannah thought she would enjoy the morning on the sunny terrace. Except, when she walked into the lounge, she could barely see the glass door that led outside.

Racks upon racks of clothes had been wheeled in. Matt was leaning against the couch, eyeing the rails.

'What's all this?' She was suddenly a lot less sleepy.

'Come here.' Matt beckoned. She went to him and he spun her round, his hands landing on her shoulders as she faced all the clothes. 'It occurs to me that you need something to wear tonight.'

'These don't just look like evening dresses, Matt, unless this gala of yours is exceptionally casual. In which case, I'm deeply grateful.'

His chuckle next to her ear sent her heart into a frenzy. 'No, smart-arse, I want you to choose a wardrobe off these racks. Whatever you want, for every occasion.'

She turned. 'I have clothes.'

'Not nearly enough. That suitcase will barely get you through the next two months. Or year.'

'Year? What happened to our trial period?'

'Let's just say I'm quietly hopeful.'

Hannah gestured around the room, a challenge in her eyes. 'Quietly?'

Matt sank down into the couch, draping his arm along the

back rest. 'Pick,' he instructed. 'Or I'll buy everything in this room.'

'That's outrageous!'

He simply smirked in response. Hannah rolled her eyes 'I am quite capable of buying my own clothes, you know.'

'I am well aware.'

'I'm not sure how comfortable I am with you spending so much on me. I don't think I can owe you that much.'

'You will owe me nothing,' Matt said firmly. 'Believe me, I can afford this, and I want to give you everything you need.'

That sounded dangerously like a promise for more. Hannah approached the clothing racks. Flipping over a tag on a dress, she nearly passed out at the eye-watering price. And he wanted her to fill a wardrobe with this?

She looked over her shoulder and saw him watching her intently, that smirk still in place. He thought he had her outplayed, but she could call his bluff, and if he really did buy everything, well, that might be a problem. But she could donate the excess. He probably didn't care.

A part of her did enjoy being spoilt like this. Owning one item off these racks would have been impossible for her.

'Are you just going to sit there and watch?' she asked, while flipping through hangers.

'That's the plan.'

'Whatever floats your boat,' she said nonchalantly.

'Would you like to try them on?'

'Can I?'

'Of course.'

Hannah selected several garments that she took to her room, each more beautiful than the last. She stepped out of her clothes and pulled a long, flowing, teal dress off a hanger. This was ridiculous. She didn't really need all these clothes and yet she couldn't stop smiling. It meant something that Matt wanted to spoil her this way, and that was exactly what this was. Merely providing for her would have been very different, but Matt didn't do anything halfway.

She slipped the dress over her body, doing up the two little buttons at her nape, and stepped in front of the mirror. Hannah could scarcely believe she was looking at herself. The dress was cool and comfortable but the woman in the mirror was elegant and striking. Her red hair contrasted vividly against the patterned colour. The floral details brought colour to her normally pale skin.

She'd never owned anything quite this nice before and, despite herself, she grew a little excited at trying on the other items. Her eyes landed on a jumpsuit, something she had missed wearing since she'd fallen pregnant. She could never find one that worked for her. So she shed the dress she wore and stepped into the soft cream fabric that draped over her body as if it were part-liquid, light as air. She tied a knot in the soft belt under her breasts and closed her eyes.

Turning to face the mirror, she let out a small breath and opened them. She took it all in. The deep V-neck showed off her bump and still made her look so effortlessly poised. Her hands travelled over belly as she turned this way and that, examining herself from every angle. Admiring the flutter of the fabric. It was so perfect.

This was what Matt was offering her—a life where he gave in the way he knew how. Feeling this good could be hers all the time if she became Mrs Matthew Taylor. He wasn't offering 'enough', he was offering the best of everything to their baby and her.

Hannah looked to the bed where the rest of the clothes she'd brought with her lay. She was seeing them for what they were now—the start of a future she couldn't possibly have dreamed of.

When she walked back into the lounge there was a pile of clothes neatly placed on one of the chairs. Clearly Matt didn't think she had chosen enough.

'Do you like what you picked?'

'Yes! I love them.'

'Good. And you have something for tonight?'

It was the very first thing she had taken off the rack. She only hoped that Matt would like it on her.

'You don't have to do all this, Matt.'

Matt rose from the couch. 'I know I don't have to. I *get* to.' He helped her take all of her new belongings to her dressing room, where he hung them up. Hannah had followed him in, trying to find the right way to say thank you...but before she could he announced that he had work to do and left.

Matt sat outside on the high-up terrace, elbows on his knees, head bent, phone clasped in his large hands. His impeccably pressed dress shirt was pulled tight over his broad shoulders. Tonight's annual Summer Gala, held by Command Technologies—Matt's company—was an opportunity for investors, management and clients or potential clients to mingle. A glamorous affair which gave everyone an opportunity to look and act their best.

The dinner had been Matt's idea, from the company's first summer, and after the success of that first one it had become an annual tradition. Now it was the ideal showcase for Hannah and him. The world's hawk-like gaze would be fixed on them both. When Hannah looked back at the pictures, he wanted her to see how well they fitted together. See an image that would make her believe this thing between them would work.

He turned the phone over and over between his palms before he scrolled through to find the one person who always made him feel better.

'Bear!' came the happy greeting he loved hearing.

'Hey, Shrimp.' Matt adored his sister. From the moment he'd seen her when his mother had retuned from the hospital, she'd been his favourite person.

'What's up? Need another non-date to a society event?' Sarah teased.

Matt huffed a laugh. 'You know there aren't any tonight.' With a head full of memories all centred around Hannah, he had taken Sarah to the first society event he'd had to attend after returning from Melbourne. After that he'd pushed himself to take other dates. There'd always been someone willing, but he'd hated the way they'd looked at him like a possession to be owned. Just the thought of taking them home had had him shuddering. He couldn't bear it. So, after a while, he'd taken Sarah if she'd been free.

He hadn't told her how he had been feeling. Which was strange because, even though she was five years younger than him, she was his rock. He told her everything, but not this. And she never asked, which only made him love her more.

'I know.' There was a pause on the line. 'You sound off. What's wrong?'

Matt was quiet for a long moment. How much should he tell her? She should at least know that she was going to be an aunt.

'I'm going to be a father,' he eventually said.

'Oh, Bear, I'm sorry.'

Sarah knew better than anyone that he'd never wanted a family. Not with the childhood they'd had. Not when there was the possibility that the mother of his children could end up like his own.

Matt was quiet for a moment. 'I'm not. Does that shock you?'

When Sarah answered, he could hear the smile in her voice. 'Not even a little.'

'No?'

'No. My brother is the best guy I know. You should have seen the way he took care of me. Scared a few dates too.'

'Sounds like a tosser.' Matt smiled despite himself.

'Eh, he has his moments.' She laughed. 'Bear, you were always there for me. You took care of me even though you were a kid too. You have so much love in you; I know you'll be a good father. Always have.'

'Should I rewind this conversation to your sympathy when I told you?'

'Because that was never what you wanted for yourself, and I'd never push you. I think you've had enough of that. But I know this can't be the only thing weighing on you. Talk to me, Bear.'

Matt was never more grateful that she knew him so well. When he opened his mouth, everything came flooding out—from Hannah walking into his office to their getting ready for the gala, their first appearance together.

'I'm glad she talked you down from marriage. Just remember that the baby isn't the only important person in this. You have feelings too. You both do.'

'I'm not giving her false hope. But my child will grow up with both his parents. Like we did.'

'You don't want them growing up like we did. At least we had each other,' Sarah said. 'Just be careful. That's all I'm asking.' There was no judgement in her voice. It was one of his favourite things about his sister—no matter what he did, she would be in his corner, just as she knew he would be in hers.

'I will be.'

'And I know you're mad at Alex right now, but it really wasn't his place to say anything. You know that, right?'

Matt hadn't spoken to his best friend in days. Not since Hannah had arrived. And he certainly didn't want to hear why his friend hadn't been able to tell him. Knowing that he could have felt what he did now for his child months ago was a tough pill to swallow. Especially when one of the people who had known was supposed to have his back.

'Bear, you there?'

'I don't want to talk about Alex.'

'Okay,' Sarah allowed. 'You know, there's a few good things about this whole situation.'

'Oh? What's that?'

'Firstly, you can stop using me to hide from the society vamps…'

He laughed softly, pressing the phone to his ear.

'And, secondly, I get a nephew in a couple of months!' Sarah squealed with excitement. 'That isn't much time to prepare but we'll figure it out.'

'He's not even born yet and you're already planning on spoiling him.'

'Of course! That will be my job as the cool aunt. Oh, and you have to bring Hannah out here.'

'We'll see.'

'No, you will,' Sarah ordered. She dropped her voice to a gentle tone. 'Everything will work out fine, Bear. Good luck tonight.'

'Thanks, Shrimp.' He ended the call and pocketed the phone, feeling slightly lighter, as he often did after talking to his sister. He hoped she was right.

Easing back against the cushions, Matt recounted his plan in his mind. Convincing Hannah that they really could be a family wouldn't be hard. He could barely keep his hands to himself; chemistry like theirs couldn't be faked and it couldn't be hidden. Tonight's dinner would be fine. He would make sure of it…

Seven months ago

Rays of light beaming on his face woke Matt up. Blearily, he peeked one eye open, squinting against the bright morning sunshine. It was nearly blinding. He turned his face away, seeking the shadow that fell on the pillow. Slowly, he blinked, finally able to see clearly, and his lungs ceased working.

Hannah was fast asleep, curled towards him with her head resting on his shoulder, lips slightly parted, red lashes fanning over her cheek. Her red hair was draped over his arm like a waterfall of silk. This close, undisturbed, he could see the light freckles across her skin, an entire constellation over her shoulders and her chest.

Light and shadow fell over her. Never in his life had he seen anything so beautiful.

Her naked breasts pushed against his side and the taste of them flashed across his tongue. They had left the club in a hurry to get back to her place. From the lift to the cab, even up to her apartment, they had been locked in what seemed like one embrace until they'd tumbled through the door in a tangle of limbs and lips.

A moan escaped those lips now and she shifted, her leg resting over his. Her sex brushed against his thigh, instantly making him hard.

Even in her sleep she was a vixen. Beautiful, perfect and sexy as hell.

He threaded his fingers through her hair, watching a frown form between her brows. He wanted to smooth it away, knowing just how soft her skin was. More than anything, he wanted to kiss her, but how could he wake her? That would be entirely heartless.

Matt knew he should wake her, get out of bed and head back to Alex's penthouse. But he just couldn't. He wanted to lie in this bed watching Hannah for hours. Feel how she clung to him. Watch how her lashes fluttered as she dreamed.

He wondered what she was dreaming about. A strand of bright-red hair fluttered onto her face, making her nose twitch. A deep chuckle escaped him as he brought his other hand up to brush her hair back. Had he ever seen anything more adorable?

Matt had no intention of waking her. But he couldn't stop his hand from caressing her cheek, running over the curve of her neck and down her arms until his fingers threaded in hers. He had had her several times the night before, but he was nowhere near satiated. He ached to claim her again and, when they were done, do it one more time.

As if she sensed the need in him, her eyes fluttered open and she looked up at him, with an open expression full of warmth and a hint of vulnerability, before she smiled and it was gone, replaced by that focussed look she'd had just before they kissed.

If anyone had asked Matt what his favourite colour was before, he would have said that he didn't much care. This morning, if he'd had to answer, without having to think the answer would be brown. But even that was too simple a word. There wasn't one he could think of to adequately describe the rainbow of amber, caramel, cognac and honey in her eyes as it reflected the morning sun.

She was so beautiful, it was as if something in him cracked.

'Looks like we forgot to close the blinds.' Hannah yawned.

'Oops.' Matt smirked. They'd both been too far gone to care about anything other than each other. Just as he didn't care right now. He tilted her face up to his and claimed her lips, urgently, powerfully. He felt her small hands on his chest as she raised herself towards him. Her lips parted on a gasp when he squeezed her arse and he swept his tongue into her mouth, tasting her sweetness.

'Do you have to get back?' Hannah asked against his lips.

He let out a laugh somewhere between a huff and a moan. 'I can't think of a single place that could pull me away right now, Hannah. I'm all yours.' He pulled away from her, folding his arms under his head as he rested back on the pillows. A teasing smile curved his full lips. 'Do with me what you will.'

Her smile was devilish, making excitement course through him. Matt watched her hand slip under the covers. Her fingers trailed over the hard ridges of his abdomen, tickling as they went lower and lower, until he felt her grasp his hardness and his body automatically thrust into her grip.

'I like the way you think,' he said, voice rough and raw.

He closed his eyes, the image of her victorious smile burned into his memory. Hannah really was the most perfect thing he had ever seen…

Matt opened his eyes, the memory squeezing his heart. For a moment London had dissolved into nothing and he'd been back in that flat with Hannah, when things had been simpler. His arms missed the way her body felt in them. He still wanted her, but he had to be so careful. He couldn't allow himself just to lose control with her, like he had on holiday. Life outside that bubble was different. It wasn't all about lust now. It was about duty and being the man his child deserved. If he had his way, the man a proper husband should be.

Matt sighed quietly into the warm, still air of the summer's evening. It was nearly time for them to leave. Convincing himself one more time that everything would go to plan tonight, Matt pushed to his feet and stepped inside.

It was quiet. The voices of the hair stylist and make-up artist were completely absent. Matt supposed that meant Hannah was ready. Quietly, he made his way to her bedroom as he slipped on his jacket, buttoning it as he walked. His hand raised to knock on the door frame, but his body ceased as his gaze landed on her in front of the mirror.

Her eyes were cast down as she swished the skirts of her flowing emerald dress. One of her hands travelled up the satin fabric to land on her belly. A delicate smile was in place on her face. Red hair, so soft Matt could still feel it on his skin months later, curled and fell in waves down her back. Straps of striking colour against her light skin fell off her shoulders, and his gaze followed them to the neckline that met in the dip between her breasts.

And then he caught the reflection of her face in the mirror. And, oh, her face! It wasn't so much the make-up that made her breath-taking—because the make-up artist had done a fine job—it was the open expression. She thought she was alone.

None of her barriers was up. All he saw was happiness and love as she looked down at the evidence of their growing child.

The Hannah he had met in Melbourne had smiled often, broadly. She'd laughed hard and without care. He had glimpsed a different side to her back then, a softer side, where her smiles were gentle and had somehow punched through him more powerfully. Where her breathy chuckle had seemed like a secret. That Hannah only came out in unguarded moments. That was the Hannah at whom we was looking now.

She still hadn't noticed him staring at her from the doorway, so he looked his fill. All he could do was shake his head at her beauty. That first morning it had struck him so hard and now he felt the very same way.

Matt wanted to step up behind her and wrap his arms around her waist, peppering kisses along her bare shoulder. He wanted to sweep her off her feet and carry her to his room, where he would lay her down and show her more pleasure than she could imagine.

He wanted to mark her. To lose himself in her. Matt didn't know if it was just his heart that was pounding wildly in his chest or if his entire body had started pulsing with the need to be with her.

Except he couldn't. Not now.

There wasn't nearly enough time to enjoy her if he did act on his impulses, something he rarely ever did. He wasn't a man that relished giving up control, not even to powerful urges that squeezed the breath from him.

More than that, he needed tonight's appearance to go well. What if he did kiss Hannah, if she came willingly into his bed, only to regret it immediately after? That would destroy any chance they had. No risks could be tolerated now. So he took a deep breath and reined in the thundering want coursing through him.

'Hannah.' His voice was low.

She spun round at the sound of her name.

'Are we leaving?' she asked.

'In a moment,' he replied, entering the room.

She nodded and sat in the arm chair, leaning to drag over her gold heeled sandals. Matt walked over and kneeled on the plush carpet, taking the shoes from her. He lifted her foot and slipped one shoe on before buckling it securely.

'Is that okay?' He looked up at her and she nodded, her lips pressed tightly together, but he saw her swallow.

Fighting the urge to kiss her instep, then her ankle, he quickly did up the other shoe and returned her foot to the floor. He helped her up as he stood and took a step back, as if any amount of space could stop the combustible heat between them. Trying his best to ignore it, Matt stuck his hand into his pocket, toying with the small box in there.

'It's important tonight goes well, Hannah. I need you by my side all night.'

'In order to convince everyone we're the perfect family-to-be,' she said evenly.

He said nothing. Tonight was about so much more than that. It would signal the start of their two-month trial for Hannah to make her decision. Matt was certain he could make sure that she stayed, but he still wanted her to see the family they could be.

'Yes,' he replied as he pulled out a square velvet box from his pocket, opened it with a click and removed a ring from within. Grasping her hand, he slid it onto her finger.

'Now everyone will know we're engaged.'

'What? No getting down on one knee? Romance is dead,' she teased.

The corner of Matt's lip quirked up slightly. He should have been glad that Hannah was taking this so easily in her stride, with no big explosion of emotions or demands. Logic had driven her, served her well, and Matt was grateful for that. Which was why he couldn't understand why he was so unhappy.

She had accepted the ring as if it could have been any-thing—a plastic circle—which was fine because he knew all he really needed was a symbol. Any ring would have done.

She's engaged to Matt Taylor.

That was all it should mean.

He hadn't even intended to get it himself. The purchase of it was an errand he could have delegated to his PA or he could have simply ordered the damn thing online. But it hadn't felt right.

This arrangement might be for appearances and duty, but it was still Hannah's finger that it would go on. So, Matt had ended up putting a lot more thought into it than he'd origi-nally intended.

He had gone to one of the oldest and finest jewellers in London. Spying just who had entered the store, the jeweller had shown him their most extravagant rings. None of those had appealed to him. None of them had screamed 'Hannah'.

Until the last one, a rare red diamond that was set in a plat-inum ring. The stone was like flame. From the moment he'd seen it, it had reminded him so much of her. It had taken him back to a moment when they'd been tangled together in be-tween her sheets, sweaty and relaxed, when he'd played with her hair.

'Red is my favourite colour,' she had said.

'Like your hair.'

'Like the rarest diamond. It makes me think of fire and passion and danger.'

So, when he'd held that ring, he'd known there could be no other for her.

'It's beautiful, Matt. I've never seen a ruby this shade.' She twisted the ring, admiring how the light caught it.

Matt didn't correct her. How could he without admitting that he remembered every little thing she had said to him seven months ago without this gesture seeming as if it could mean more than it did? He didn't need the misunderstanding.

* * *

Hannah couldn't help but look at the ring again. The agreement was about an engagement, so she wasn't surprised there was a ring. But she was surprised that it was so beautiful. The trilogy ring was stunning. With two clear stones on either side of a large red one, the emerald cuts kept refracting the light a million times over.

It felt good on her finger. Too good.

She was trying to keep things light between Matt and her but this ring made her want to weep. Being proposed to like this made her feel hollow.

This isn't a real relationship, she reminded herself. *It's not real. It's just a trial run.*

She repeated it to herself until she believed it. But the truth was that, with this ring on her finger, the old wound that she was sure had long ago healed ached anew. Once upon a time, she'd thought she would wear a ring, something pretty and treasured. That dream had been destroyed as if it had been blown up with explosives. A catastrophic system failure with no way to restore the data—ever. That dream had been a corrupted file.

Yet now she was wearing a ring more beautiful than she could have ever imagined and a small, ridiculous part of her wished that dream wasn't dead.

Except Matt had said they would be a family. That he would do his duty to his child. There was nothing romantic about this. She wasn't being chosen to share a life. Still, it was a pretty spectacular ring purely for appearances. She needed to know what Matt wasn't sharing with her.

When she finally spoke, she found Matt studying her intensely.

'Before we go, I want you to tell me what this is really about. I know you said that this whole plan is about the baby, but you and I both know we could co-parent. So it's more than that. Why is it so important that we seem like a family?'

Matt sighed. 'Hannah.'

'The truth, Matt. It won't change anything. I just want to know.' She could see him thinking it over. She waited patiently. Silently. Not willing to speak until he did.

'Being my father's son means something. The type of man I should be. What my parents provided for me made me who I am. I want to provide for my son. I want him to grow up knowing that...'

'That?' Hannah pressed.

'That he can rely on me.' His eyes were burning into hers, but she could see a trace of sadness in them. 'I want to provide him with everything I can. I want everyone to know that he's wanted, that he matters, and I want them to know that before he even enters the world. I want you to know I'm worth taking a risk on.'

'You are worth the risk. After all, I'm here, aren't I?' Hannah was learning how important family was to him. The fact that Matt was willing to settle down because of this situation told Hannah a great deal. He felt deeply, that much was clear. She wondered if there was more to the relationship he'd had with his father. 'Well, Mr Taylor, shall we?'

With a smile, Matt offered her his arm. Linking hers in his, they left the penthouse.

CHAPTER ELEVEN

THEY REACHED THE parking garage and Hannah expected Matt to lead her to his flashy sports car. Instead, they moved towards the car beside it. Matt had sworn to be there for their child. To give his all. Now Hannah understood what Matt's 'all' might look like. He pressed a fob and the largest Audi she had ever seen came to life. He opened the door of the S8 for her, which she saw was so very spacious. Even in her evening dress, she easily slid in.

Hannah sank into the leather seat that held her like a hug. When Matt climbed in, he fiddled with the touch screen and the seat morphed into the comfiest thing she had rested on in seven months. Then he pressed another button and the back rest began to move like little hands easing the aches in her back. The seat was giving her a massage!

'Good?' he asked.

'Great.' She moaned. 'Can I live in here?'

'I'm sure you could.' He laughed.

'When did you get this?' she asked with her eyes closed, focussing only on how good her back felt.

'Yesterday.'

One simple word meant so much more to her than he could ever realise. He'd bought it after he had seen his son. It meant he really did want to be there for their child. Not just that, but that he had seen how uncomfortable she had been in his other car and made an investment for her and their baby.

She hadn't been treated like this before. Not when she'd thought she was in love and had been left utterly devastated, and certainly not with anyone she'd been with since. No one had made her feel anywhere near this special. Not that she'd given anyone a chance. A night, maybe a week or two, was all she'd been willing to risk. Every male companion had known that from the start so why would they have treated her as anything but a temporary interest?

The thing was, to Hannah, once you identified a problem, the only logical solution was to remove said problem and make sure it never happened again. Falling in love was the biggest problem she had found in her life. It had left her open and vulnerable and, once it imploded, it had irrevocably broke parts of her.

Yet with Matt she struggled to remember those lessons she had learnt. He made her want to believe, which made him a danger to her. At the same time, he was the father of her child, so she could never be completely closed off to him. As much as she'd refused his suggestion to marry, Hannah really did want to make their arrangement work.

Clearly Matt was trying too. Trying to prove that he would be a good father, that he would be a dependable provider. So maybe for one night it wouldn't be such a bad thing to pretend they were a loving couple ready to settle down.

For one night, she could believe.

Hannah twirled the ring round and round on her finger, trying not to tear up. She tried to ignore the feeling of Matt's eyes on her, succumbing only to the wonderful sensations of sitting in this magical seat.

She was certain Matt could see her warring emotions. It always seemed as if he was able to look right through her, as if her shields were made only of glass, but he said nothing and for this she was grateful. She felt the car glide forward and only once she was certain she could speak without feeling emotional did she open her eyes.

The lights of London flashed around her, bringing a small smile to her lips. Hannah had never considered living anywhere but Melbourne. She loved everything about the place but now there was the possibility that she would leave it behind.

'Hannah,' Matt said, and she turned in her seat to face him. 'I was serious earlier. I need you by my side all evening.'

'Don't worry, I intend to make life easy for you,' she teased.

'I'm not sure I believe I that.'

She could tell it was meant to be a joke, but the muscle flexing in his jaw had her wanting to ask what was on his mind, except it didn't look as if he would tell her now. Hannah hoped that maybe he would learn to talk to her, but that wasn't going to happen if she pushed all the time. Maybe he just needed to know she was in his corner because, even though she hadn't spoken to him for months, there was still something special between them.

'Don't worry, Matt. Everything will be fine.' Without thinking, she reached over and gave his hand a quick squeeze. The touch was like a lightning bolt through her and she snatched her hand back. Matt's hands tightened on the steering wheel and she knew he'd felt it too.

Silence fell between them. Neither was willing to break it until they reached the paved roads in front of a glittering building. They followed the line of cars until they reached the front, where a valet opened Matt's door. Hannah watched him hand a young man his keys before rounding the car to open her door.

She accepted his proffered hand and, once she joined him, he laced his fingers in hers. One small, innocent touch was enough to set her heart aflutter. The electricity between them made everyone and everything else seem duller, softer. And yet, his fingers in hers felt strong, safe, as though he had her.

Matt led them through the doors into a modern, minimalistic reception area but he didn't stop until they reached open glass doors that welcomed them into a spectacular grand hall. There were round tables as far as the eye could see. The space was magically lit so that it was dim and moody, and the walls were cast in shades of purple and blue. Even the crystal chandeliers were bathed in hues of arctic blue. But each table was bright enough to clearly see everyone seated around it.

Matt pulled out a chair for her at a table all the way at the front. There were several women and men already seated, oozing power and wealth from their high-end clothes to the way they held themselves.

Hannah felt their assessing gazes rake over her from head to toe. Several disapproving expressions greeted her. Once Matt had pushed her chair in, he took his seat beside her and warmly greeted everyone at the table, before introducing everyone to her. Apart from a couple of executives, she realised most of these people were his investors.

'This is Hannah Murphy,' she heard Matt say from beside her, his arm draping over the back of her chair possessively. 'My fiancée.'

'Nice to meet you all.' Hannah smiled in the most pleasant manner she could. She looked over to the side and found Matt staring at her, a gleam in his eye like a lit wick. Those eyes were a web and she was trapped in it, being pulled further and further into its depths, until he blinked. He looked at an older gentleman, who must have said something she hadn't heard, because Matt started talking to him.

She took a breath, praying that she wouldn't do or say the wrong thing and embarrass him in front of these people. Thanks to Emma, Hannah had been to her share of fancy events. But this was an entirely different animal.

That was when she felt Matt's thumb caress her shoulder, a reminder he was next to her, even though his discussion didn't pause for a second. She lifted her chin and plastered a confident smile on her face.

Hannah could feel the stares on her at the table. Inside, she was a wreck, feeling judged, wondering what these people actually thought of her. Outwardly she radiated nothing but calm serenity, a woman happy to be beside the man of her dreams, knowing that she would soon welcome her little miracle. If there was one thing Hannah was always able to do, it was to seem completely confident when she felt none of it. It was how she'd survived after she'd been so brutally destroyed by her 'Prince Charming'. Compared to the heartbreak that had so changed her, this would be a cake walk.

'Matthew, we had no idea you were engaged,' an elegant blonde woman said. Hannah thought she must be in her forties. She had a low, husky voice and spoke in a tone that made her think she probably never had to raise her voice to be heard in any room.

Matt's lips pressed against Hannah's temple and she had to fight the shock passing through her body. She felt the heat of the blush creeping up her neck.

'Recently engaged,' she heard Matt say. 'We've been something special for quite a while.' The meaning of his words was lost on the table but not on her. *They* were special. That week in Melbourne had been the most incredible of her life. Maybe it had been for Matt too.

'So I see,' the woman said, looking at Hannah. 'You never mentioned anything.' Clearly, she was sceptical about their union. After all, Matt must have been on dates.

'I didn't want to expose Hannah to the public scrutiny of my world. I kept up my usual appearances so no one would look at her.'

He paused and Hannah turned to look at him. When he spoke next, she felt as if the words were being said to her. 'But they were just that—appearances. This is our first child and I want to protect them both.' His eyes ripped from hers and she had to fight the urge to pull him back to her. 'I'm sure you can all appreciate that,' he finished, his tone harder, colder.

'We just wish you had said something earlier,' said a well-dressed man with kind eyes, but Matt just shook his head.

'So why now?' the lady pushed.

Hannah's hand found his under the table. 'I convinced him to. Better now than in a couple of months when there's speculation about why he's entering a hospital. It was just the right time.'

'It was,' he agreed, and Hannah wondered if that meant that she was forgiven for having kept this secret. Or maybe it was something else entirely. All she knew for certain was that sitting here with Matt, in this place that seemed so magical, it was getting easier to pretend that they were something real.

Hannah guessed her life would resemble tonight a great deal if they lasted past these next two months. She'd have a team mate with whom to raise a child. They'd make appearances together. They'd share looks when something made sense only to them; it didn't seem like the worst idea to live this way. She could do that. Because right now she was happy.

Before their meal was served, Matt was called on to make a short speech. She watched him speak so warmly, as if he were addressing each person in this massive hall individually, welcoming investors and potential clients alike. He encouraged them to mingle and show off the power house that was Command Technologies.

That first night at the club in Melbourne, she had thought him to be a natural charmer: she was absolutely certain of it now. He held the entire room in his palm and she was overcome with pride. Then he looked over at her and she smiled broadly at him. His words halted for just a second before he drew his speech to a close.

When he took his seat she leaned over, whispering in his ear, 'If our son is anything like you, I think I'm in big trouble.'

He grinned. 'Let's hope.'

She laughed and picked up her utensils as their meals were served. Despite being watched so closely that Hannah could tell exactly when someone moved, she was enjoying their night.

She tried to pay attention to the conversations around

the table but all she could really focus on was the accidental touches every time she or Matt moved. Now his leg was pressed against hers and it felt as if her entire being was focussed on that point. It was ridiculous. Her brain was short-circuiting because a non-erogenous part of her body was touching Matt. She knew what his naked body felt like on hers, so why did she feel doused in flame?

Matt's lips brushed her ear, his hot breath sending shivers down her spine. 'If you keep looking at me like that, we're going to get arrested for indecent exposure, and my investors won't be happy.'

She hadn't even realised she was staring. When she looked into his eyes now, they were dark.

'I—I need the bathroom.'

Hannah excused herself from the table. Thankfully there was no queue. Pretending that she wished only to fix her lipstick, Hannah approached the mirror, going through the motions. What she was really doing was getting her breath back. Trying to control her heart, because his words had set her on fire. In that moment she hadn't cared that there were hundreds of people around. All she'd wanted was his lips on hers but throwing caution to the wind was how they had ended up here with a baby on the way.

She needed to get it together. Yes, he seemed to want her, possibly as much as she wanted him. But she still wasn't sure that he would find her attractive any more once he got her out of this dress.

Taking a few deep breaths, Hannah injected steel into her spine and marched confidently back to the table, only to find everyone mingling on the floor. It would be a nightmare to find Matt in the crowd, but she needn't have worried. Her body sensed him first, then her eyes followed. He was standing with a tall, beautiful brunette. Her hand was trailing down his arm and Hannah had to fight the wave of jealousy that threatened to consume her.

She watched Matt's eyes turn cold. His jaw clenched. Hannah could see the warmth she adored so much leave him, but the woman was oblivious, only looking at him with ill-concealed lust. No one seemed to notice that he was tense.

Anger bubbled to the surface. Matt was undoubtedly the most beautiful man Hannah had ever seen, but he was also funny, smart and caring and most definitely not a piece of meat. There was so much more to him than the magnificent package he came in. Actually feeling the confidence she usually tried to feign, Hannah marched up to the pair of them and placed her left hand on Matt's chest, showing off her very conspicuous engagement ring.

'There you are. I've been looking all over for you.'

He pulled her close, instantly turning back into the man she knew. 'You found me.'

'Want to dance?' Hannah asked, determinedly ignoring the woman that Matt seemed to have forgotten was standing with them.

'With the most beautiful woman here? You bet.' He turned them in the direction of the dance floor and, when his arm came around her waist, the woman faded to a memory.

A light projection of the Command Technologies logo was dotted all over the dance floor, moving around the polished wood or catching people in its beams as they swayed under the lights.

Matt pulled Hannah against him as classical music floated around them. She had danced with him before, but it hadn't been like this. Then it had felt like foreplay—the lighting of a fuse for what wound end in an explosive night. This was different. It was sweet and safe, the stoking of a flame.

He dipped his head down against hers and Hannah couldn't help but close her eyes and lose herself to this moment.

'Thank you for that,' Matt said softly so only she would hear. The sincerity in his voice made Hannah look at his face.

His eyes were closed and his jaw clenched. Whatever had happened with that woman had bothered him.

'You know,' Hannah said quietly, 'That's the second time I've seen you shudder at a woman's touch.' The question hung in the air between them.

The seconds stretched. She was sure he wasn't going to answer but then she heard him mutter under his breath, 'Why do I always want to tell you more than I should?'

He took a breath. 'I hate the way they look at me. Though they don't really—not at me. They're looking at what they can get from me—fame and money. I'm tired of it, this vapid world.'

Hannah could see then the man who wanted more. Who wanted something deeper, something real. It was the man she'd met in a city halfway across the world. Convinced now more than ever that he'd never really been the playboy, Hannah was determined to be there for him.

'As long as you have me, you won't have to deal with that any more. I've got you too, Matt. I just hope you'll learn to trust that. Trust me.'

She watched Matt pull away from her. Their bodies came to a stop, the music dying away. His gaze was intense, as if he was seeing into the depths of her. He had looked at her like that before on a dance floor full of people. And, just like then, she wanted so badly to be kissed by him.

He leaned in, closing the distance between their lips but not all the way, waiting for her to meet him, she realised. To tell him this was what she wanted. So she did. The moment their lips met, a sob rose from her and Matt swallowed the sound. This is what she had wanted, had longed for for seven months—Matt's taste, smell and heat.

In Melbourne Matt had taken his time. His lips had been a sweet seduction in that pulsing club. This kiss was raw, full of craving and power, but restrained and tense. It was wild and begging to be unleashed but full of feeling and need. To some tenderness was gentle, to others tenderness was glimpsing a hidden self. And Hannah saw the self in Matt that wanted her desperately. In this most beautiful of surroundings, with such melodious notes wrapping around them, Matt was urgent. She could feel the rise and fall of his chest. This kiss was a stormy sea and they were drowning in it.

This was a different dance, a different city. But it was the same voltaic chemistry between the same people who had become so different. In this moment, they knew each other.

With white-hot need taking hold of her, Hannah pulled away from his lips, a quiet giggle escaping her when she noticed the smudge of her lipstick on his mouth. Reaching up to wipe it away, she heard a growl rip from his throat as his eyes, darkened like a forest in the fading light, landed on the matching smear she was sure was on her mouth.

'You have—'

But her words were cut off by his lips crashing down on hers, plundering her mouth with another fierce kiss that stole all the breath from her lungs.

'Let's go home,' she said against his lips.

CHAPTER TWELVE

LATER, HANNAH WOULD have no memory of the haste in which they left. Of Matt handing the valet ticket over or the fact that the car had been brought round faster than any other.

Now, though, they found themselves rushing through the streets. Matt's eyes were glued to the road while the car rocketed along without complaint. Anticipation had Hannah in a firm embrace. Her breath hadn't slowed from the moment Matt had kissed her. Her skin tingled and all she could think about was how good it would be to feel Matt's hands on her.

She looked over at him at the same time he turned to her. Their gazes locked for a beat and laughter bubbled out of them both. It felt as if they were teenagers, eager for all these new sensations. Except it wasn't really new to them. It was knowing exactly what it felt like to be with each other that made them so impatient now to have the walls come down between them.

It wasn't long before Matt helped Hannah out of the car and laced their fingers together. With his hand firmly holding hers, he took her up to the penthouse, not once letting go until she was in his bedroom with him.

All Hannah could think about was Matt. Her body was sparking from the feeling of her hand in his. She hadn't been into his room since she'd arrived. Somehow that would have felt like an invasion of privacy. As if maybe she wouldn't be welcome in it. Now she didn't bother looking around. She didn't see it; it didn't matter. Not when Matt was raising her fingers to his lips, when he was drawing one into his mouth, kissing the side of it, licking the space between them. Every sensation went straight to the point between her thighs.

And, when he gently dropped her hand to her side, he closed the distance between them and she closed her eyes just as he brushed his lips against hers, a light touch and then he'd pull away. Again and again, teasing her, lighting her body up, making her want him until she could cry. Then he took her lips in his, sliding his tongue along hers, and she shivered. She parted her lips for him, his tongue caressed hers and her entire body went up in flame. She felt him press her body against his, making her moan into his mouth.

'God, Hannah, I missed you.'

His rough voice scraped against her nerve endings, and when he pulled away she said, 'I want you.'

He spun her round, holding her back against his chest. His body was hard, unyielding against hers. Shuddering when Matt moved her hair aside, Hannah sighed as he pressed open-mouthed kisses to her nape, then shoulder. The purr of her zipper unfastening filled the silent room as Matt eased it down, peppering kisses down her back as he went. The dress slid off her body, landing in a pool at her feet. Her skin pebbled from the sudden cool air.

She heard the rustle of his clothes as he stood up. The sound of his voice at her ear.

'You're so beautiful, Hannah.'

Warm fingers traced her back and undid the clasps of her bra, but Hannah didn't let it fall. His hands were on her shoulders now, trying to turn her round, but a sudden panic was gripping her. The body he'd known was gone. Of course he'd seen that, but it was one thing to be seen with your clothes on, a whole other thing to be naked. He had been so caring but that had been for his child, not her.

Matt walked round her and tilted her chin up to look at her. 'What's wrong?'

'Nothing,' she lied. Insecurities she didn't know how to kill bubbled to the surface.

'Do you want to stop?'

No, she didn't. She craved the release only Matt could give her. Fear that he would be turned off by her was battling that need.

She leaned into his hand when it cupped her cheek, his fingers burying in her hair.

'No,' Hannah breathed.

'Then tell me what's wrong.'

Hannah swallowed hard. 'I'm scared.'

'Of me?' He frowned.

'That you're going to see all of me and...'

'And?'

'And realise you don't want me. I've changed so much.' She looked away, not wanting to see the moment he realised that she was no longer sufficiently attractive.

He cupped her chin, forcing her to look at him. 'You are beautiful.' She closed her eyes when his hand skated over her skin, embracing the roundness of her belly, the fullness of her hips. 'Your body has changed but it's no less beautiful now. You're giving me a child, Hannah. You're a goddess.'

Hannah watched him take a small step back, his gaze running along the length of her body, and he shook his head. 'I'm the luckiest man alive tonight because I get to touch you.'

Her lip wobbled and Matt kissed her then, gently sliding his lips over hers. Giving her a taste of what they would feel like everywhere else. And, as he lifted his lips from hers, his fingers curled around the bra and pulled it away, dropping it to the floor.

'You're perfect, Hannah,' he said with vehemence. 'Always.'

To Matt, there could never be anyone more perfect. He needed to make her understand just how crazy she drove him. That she was just as sexy now as she'd been months ago. He held her hand, moving it to the erection that was straining in his pants.

'This is what you do to me.'

He watched her pupils dilate, swallowing most of the brown in her eyes. Those dainty hands that could be so wicked didn't disappoint. His body jerked as she grasped him over the fabric. In a flash, she was pushing his jacket to the floor, unbuttoning his shirt at speed, ripping it off his shoulders. The appreciative gleam in her eyes gave him a rush like nothing else.

It was different when Hannah looked at him. It never felt fake. Never felt as if he was just wanted for his body, his money or his fame. He felt seen, as if she appreciated the man he was without all his power. Wishing with all his might that he could bottle that feeling and pull it out whenever he needed it, Matt trailed kisses down her body.

Coming to his knees in front of her, he relished the feeling of her belly on his hands. He kissed it. He felt more connected to her than ever before. He looked up at her and found her smiling, tears shining in her eyes.

'Hannah?'

She shook her head but he refused to move. He kept his eyes trained on her and simply waited.

'It's just, there were nights I thought about you. Fantasised about this moment…' Her voice trailed away.

A small admission, but one that had his heart thundering. Had he not fantasised about her too? Had he not imagined what it would be like to take her in this very apartment? She had spent all this time wanting him too. Matt felt the smile spreading on his cheeks. Winking at her, his mouth travelled lower. His hands moved to her hips as his lips closed over her sex, kissing and licking her over the silky fabric that still covered her. He was overcome with her honeyed taste, her smell. Fingers sliding into his hair drove him to pleasure her harder. He savoured her every whimper and moan.

'Matt, I need…'

Feeling immensely proud that she wasn't able to finish the thought, he eased the scrap of fabric down her legs and scooped her into his arms. Setting her down on the edge of his enormous bed, Matt piled pillows behind her.

'Comfortable?'

She nodded and he stepped away, kicking off his socks and shoes, then eased down the fly on his trousers, noticing the pout on her face.

'What is it?'

'I feel like someone else is getting to open my Christmas present.'

Matt threw his head back and laughed. His expression was mirrored on her face. 'Well, who am I to deprive you?' He stepped between her legs. Her eyes focussed as she tugged down his trousers. His breathing became rapid as she slowly peeled the black boxer briefs away. A growl ripped from his throat as she stroked him.

This woman was his undoing.

And he wanted to be inside her right now.

Leaning her against the pillows, he caged her with his arms.

'I need you to talk to me, sweetheart. Okay?' As desperate as he was to lose himself in Hannah, he was still very aware of her condition. He wanted her to feel absolute bliss. Pleasure beyond imagining, not discomfort or worry. Or, worse yet, regret.

Once he was certain she would listen to his request, he tried to stand so that he could go to the bedside table, but Hannah stopped him with a curled leg holding his.

'Matt, I want you like I had you the last time.'

'Hannah…'

'I haven't been with anyone since you,' she promised.

'Neither have I. Are you sure?' He needed to know that she was certain. The last time, neither of them had stopped to think about what they were doing. The consequences of that was what had led to this moment and it wasn't as if she could get *more* pregnant. Still, he had to make sure. For his sake as much as hers.

'Yes. I want to feel you.' And, by God, he wanted that too.

Strong arms pulled her to the edge of the bed and he hooked one of her legs around him. Slowly he sunk into her, and he didn't know if the long-drawn-out moan had come from him, her or both of them. All he knew was every memory of being inside Hannah was crashing around him. This…his was the pleasure he'd ached to feel for all this time.

He pulled his hips back and thrust forward.

'Matt,' Hannah moaned, making every hair on his body rise. His lips pressed against hers, sliding them against hers. Their tongues entwined. The bitten-off noises she made were driving him absolutely wild. With Hannah, he could never have enough of this.

Electrified. That was how Hannah felt. Every nerve ending sparked like a naked wire. Matt's lips were tracing a current to her jaw and down to the sensitive point where her neck met her shoulders. His tongue tasted the skin there and she thought she would combust.

'Matt…' It was a plea; she wasn't sure for what. More, maybe—more of all of this. His answering low groan made pleasure roll through her. But it wasn't just the sound that answered her. His hips did too, slamming into her powerfully. Rough moans and harsh breaths filled the space between them as they climbed together.

Hannah felt like a band stretched too taut. Her heart was racing. Her skin was covered in sweat. She arched towards him and Matt caught her against him, driving them further to the edge until undiluted pleasure snapped through her in a husky sob that toppled Matt into his own release and, slumping over her with a grunt, he caught himself on his forearms.

Blond hair stuck to his forehead. Beads of sweat clung to his skin. This man stopped her heart. Raising her fingers to his cheeks, Hannah kissed him. She poured every ounce of what she had felt over the last seven months into that kiss: the missing him, craving him and fearing he would turn her away. Wanting to hear his voice but too scared to call.

When she finally broke the connection of their lips, she found him staring at her, but couldn't tell what he was thinking. It was as if all that rawness they'd just experienced was now locked away.

She couldn't think of it now. Not when he was still buried within her silken depths. Not after he had kissed her tummy so tenderly. Soft lips brushed against her forehead and then she was being lifted up and placed between soft sheets.

A hard, warm body slid in behind her, pulling her against his chest. The last thing she felt was a kiss on her hair before her eyes fluttered closed. She'd think about all of this tomorrow.

CHAPTER THIRTEEN

COLD SHEETS GREETED Hannah as she turned over. Opening her eyes, she found herself alone in the room. It was not hers but Matt's. That was right, he had held her until she'd fallen asleep. Last night coming back to her in a steady stream, she sat up in bed, running her fingers though her hair. They'd had sex. And it had been incredible.

She tried to quell the disappointment of not waking up with him next to her. She had no idea what time it was. Pretty late, judging by the muted grey light filtering through the gauzy curtain beyond the bed. The sky looked ominous. Part of her felt it was a sign after the incredible night she and Matt had shared.

She shook her head. That was ridiculous. She was in London—it rained here. Nothing more than that.

Hannah swung her legs off the bed, wrapping the sheet tightly around herself, when she heard movement at the door.

'You're up,' came Matt's bright greeting. Sweating and dressed only in shorts and trainers, his closed off expression after she had kissed him last night came to mind. Not knowing what that meant just yet, Hannah didn't respond. 'Good. You better get dressed. I have something to show you.' He placed a cup of peppermint tea on the bedside table.

'Thank you.' She picked up the steaming vessel, bringing it to her lips.

'Be careful, it's hot.'

She made an exaggerated motion of blowing the surface before taking a small sip, hiding her little smile. 'What do you want to show me?'

'That,' Matt said, leaning down to kiss her forehead, 'Is a surprise.'

He disappeared into his bathroom and she heard the shower turn on. Thinking this was as good a time as any to make her escape, Hannah went to her room, showering and dressing as quickly as possible. She was ready at the same time as Matt and, after a hasty breakfast, he drove them to an upmarket suburb.

The houses here were much larger, the cars fancier. On the way here, she'd recognised some of the major landmarks they'd passed from a trip she had taken with Emma during their semester break at uni. It felt like such a long time ago. Everything was different now, most especially her.

Back then, she'd still been quiet Hannah. A person who'd thought softness was treasured. That was before her heart had been broken and she'd no longer been willing to trust a person just because they said nice things.

'Are we there yet?' she said, shaking off the memories.

'Almost.' Matt took a turn down a tree-lined street full of expensive-looking townhouses. He pulled up in front of a four-storey building with a white stone exterior on the bottom floor and exposed brick on the other three. It had quaint little Juliet balconies on several of the windows.

He switched off the car and looked around with an indecipherable look on his face.

'Are we visiting someone?' she asked. Whoever they were, she imagined they were vastly wealthy.

'Not exactly.' He was staring out at the park opposite, where a few people were milling about, but for the most part it was empty. Then Hannah noticed it wasn't the adults who had his attention, but a little boy and girl playing together. They were adorable, and Hannah imagined what it would be like when she was out at a park much like this one with their son.

Matt turned to her, his face serious. 'I've been thinking that the penthouse isn't suitable to raise a family. It's not safe enough. I don't relish the thought of our son crawling around on the terrace.'

'Okay,' she replied uncertainly. 'What are you saying?'

'This house belongs to me. I was undecided as to what to do with it, and until recently was fairly certain I would sell it, but now I think it's the best home to raise a family in. What do you think?'

When Matt had said he wanted to show her something, this had been the furthest thing from her mind. She shouldn't be surprised, of course, not given how much he'd proved that he wanted to provide for their child. Seeing this house, though, brought home the reality of them being a family.

'I don't know what to say…'

'You can redecorate as you wish. Pull the entire thing apart. Whatever you want. I don't care what it costs.'

'Wow.' Hannah was lost for words. Right now she was seeing exactly how much Matt could provide. Much more than she ever could, regardless of how successful her career was. This was beyond her wildest dreams. Hannah's hand rested on her belly as she took in the tall house.

'Why do you have this place if you were just going to sell it?' she asked, still not looking at him.

'It used to belong to my parents. I grew up here. It was left to me in the will.'

Her head whipped round to look at him. There was even less emotion on his face than there was in his voice. It was all just fact: it had been his parents'; now it was his. It was useful.

'Will you have a look at it?' he asked.

'Yes. Of course.' She unclipped the seatbelt and as she climbed out noticed for the first time that there was a rear-facing car seat installed in the back behind her, with a rect-angular mirror attached to the headrest.

Her heart squeezed. How could she go on pretending that they would be nothing more to each other than convenient parents for their child when Matt kept showing her how much he cared? Everything he did made her want to take a chance on him.

And it was scaring her.

Even so, this meant so much, and she took his hand but said nothing as he led her past the low, black metal railings to a black door with a shiny gold knocker.

Inside, the house was full of furniture. It was as if who-ever lived here had simply locked the door on the way out. Everything was perfectly in place. Every surface looked ex-pensive, but it had no personality. Not like Matt's penthouse, that had colours, textures and so many signs of life. It was lived in. This place felt cold, as if it had been staged to look like the perfect home.

'Can I look around?' Hannah felt she needed permission. It felt a lot like snooping through someone's life.

'Be my guest.'

She walked through room after room. She admired every-thing from the pristine indoor swimming pool to the back yard she could see her son playing in. It was beautiful; of that there was no doubt.

This had been Matt's home for a great deal of his life. She tried to see him running through these halls. Had he been a happy child? Picturing him as he was now, she couldn't see him as anything but the boy with a ready smile. But she saw no evidence of him here.

Her parents' home had been a shrine to their years together. In fact, an entire wall had been covered in a mosaic of frames, each holding a picture of a different year at school. There was none of that here. This place had been curated by the best in-terior designers money could buy.

Hannah walked into the master bedroom. She could almost see herself in this room—waking up to a bright day, Matt taking their son across the road to the park. He was right—this place was perfect for their family.

Approaching the mantle, she noticed several silver frames—family pictures. They looked as if they'd been taken by photographer. Lots of people did that. It didn't mean anything really.

Curiosity taking hold now, Hannah opened a chest of drawers, breathing a sigh of relief when she found them mostly empty...except one drawer, the bottom one. It held a large, black rectangular box. Taking it to the bed, she slipped off the lid and found a treasure of photographs.

Matt looked exactly as he did now, just smaller. It seemed as though he'd been the tallest member of the family barely into his teens. Those bright-green eyes sparkled as if he held a secret. But every one of the pictures looked posed. There were no unguarded smiles. The family didn't look genuinely happy. It didn't capture a moment. It was like looking at a stock image of a perfect family.

These weren't like her family pictures, where they'd been so happy the memory flew off the glossy card. She thought of how her parents had taken her to the beach on balmy summer evenings. They'd made sandcastles, even when she'd been too old for them, but it had been fun. She remembered how they'd gone up to Falls Creek every winter in her teens to enjoy the snow and spent every day skiing or snow-mobiling. These pictures were nothing like her own.

She looked at his mother's demure expression. No one would ever see that in her family photos. Her family had made funny faces at the camera; they had asked passers-by to take a picture of them as they ran into the cold coastal water, yelped and nearly jumped out. She treasured those memories. Did Matt have any like that?

She gathered all the pictures, stuffing them back into the box, and went downstairs.

* * *

Matt was seated in the lounge, elbows on knees, head dipped down. He knew this house could be everything he needed but, as it stood now, he didn't enjoy coming back here. This was his parents' home, not his. They were both gone. He could speak to neither of them. Couldn't tell them about his baby or his plan to marry Hannah. He wanted to be the perfect father, but he didn't know what that was. A stolid family man, just like his father? He didn't want that for his child, but he didn't know anything else.

It looked as though, at any moment, his mother would walk into this place to talk about some charity fundraiser or other. That his father would pour a scotch and retire to his office to work some more, without a smile or any acknowledgement that he was happy to see his son. But they wouldn't. And this house reminded him of them. They were gone. All he had was Sarah.

Feeling Hannah's presence, he looked up to see her enter the room with a box in her hand.

'There's a lot of stuff here. Not a lot of you, though,' Hannah said.

'I haven't spent much time here since leaving boarding school. After school, Alex and I shared an apartment while we studied.'

'Is that where you started Command Technologies?'

'Yes. Having Alex's buy-in, it was easy to attract investors and the capital I needed. I'm good at leveraging what I have.' He was doing the same thing now. Maybe Hannah would be able to turn this house into a home for them. 'What's that?'

'Photographs. The drawers and cupboards were empty except for this. I was wondering if you'd like to take it with you?'

Of course they were empty. Sarah had wanted very little from here, having inherited the country manor, which she'd promptly sold, unwilling to move away from her own home. Matt had had people come in to remove what had been left. All of it had either been donated to various charities or auctioned off. He thought his mother would have approved. He didn't recognise the box, though.

He fought the urge to lean into Hannah as she sat beside him, pulling off the lid.

'You were always a heartbreaker, weren't you?' she said lightly, handing the pictures over. His body tensed. 'Are these all your family pictures?'

'They must be.' They hadn't taken pictures often and, when they had, it had been a planned-out affair. After Matt and Sarah had been sent off to boarding school, the opportunities for such things had become fewer.

'It's like it's you but not you,' she said from beside him. 'They're so cold.'

He took the pictures, looked at the first one and threw it back into the box, shutting the lid firmly.

'Do you want to talk about it?' Her voice was tentative.

'Do I want…? No, Hannah, I don't,' he said sharply. 'This doesn't concern you.'

'Matt…'

'Are you done snooping? You were supposed to be taking a look at this house to see if it could suit our family. Not digging around for answers to questions no one asked,' Matt said with pure ice in his voice, tossing the box on the large coffee table and storming out of the room. With no real idea of where he was going, he simply followed his feet until, having stepped into his childhood bedroom, he shut the door. It reflected nothing of him. It hadn't for years.

He sat heavily on the edge of the bed, regretting the way he had spoken to Hannah. Christ, he hadn't meant to snap, but their agreement was never meant to include talking about his family. There was no need for it.

What he was starting with Hannah was meant to be purely for the benefit of his child. He didn't need to rehash his past. Life before all of this really was none of Hannah's concern. She needed to be a good mother, he needed to be a good father and that was all there was to it. He didn't rely on anyone and had never asked for anyone's support. He sure as hell wasn't about to start now.

Emotions were a weakness. A man stood strong—resolute.

CHAPTER FOURTEEN

THE TENDERNESS OF the night before was lost. Hannah could see that. Since she had kissed him, Matt had pulled away. It was the last thing she'd seen before falling asleep. And this morning he had put so much more space between them.

She had always associated Matt with warmth. From the moment they'd met she'd been able to see he was someone who made people feel comfortable. Not this person who, sure, looked like him yet seemed positively arctic in comparison.

Hannah pulled out one of the pictures from the box and studied Matt. He stood up straight, spine like steel. She was so used to his relaxed posture whenever he was around her that she'd never really noticed until now. The serious expression on his face also seemed at odds with who he really was because usually he smiled, winked and pursed his lips when he was thinking. The sparkle in his eye that she had noticed before was the only real indication that there was more inside him waiting to burst free.

How was this person her Matt?

She sighed, leaning back against the cushions of the large couch that had looked a lot more comfortable than it actually was, making her wonder if it was ever really used. Digging the heels of her hands into her eyes, she tried to merge the two images of Matt. All she could think about was the man who had seen her in Melbourne…

Seven months ago

Hannah dropped her handbag on the small kitchen table in the flat she shared with Emma, her laptop bag still slung over her shoulder. There was a knock on the door. Depositing the bag in her room first, she rushed to the door to find Matt holding up a bottle of Shiraz.

'I thought I should partake in all Australia has to offer.' He smiled.

Hannah pulled him in and kissed him fiercely. His hands came around her waist, holding her firmly against him. 'I'd love to, but I promised to go for drinks with some colleagues. You could always come with.'

'I could?'

'Yeah, we'll be there for an hour at most, and then I'm all yours.' She purred, pressing up against him.

'All mine, huh?' Hannah held her breath, watching a teasing smirk curve his lips. 'I think I could live with that.'

Hannah worried for a minute that Matt might misunderstand her invite. Work drinks were never a serious affair— it wasn't like meeting friends or family. No one really cared as long as they could let loose, complain or gossip. Relief flooded her when he agreed. It meant he understood and, despite her momentary nervousness, he seemed completely unfazed, happy to change his plans at the drop of a hat.

Well, he was only going to be around a few more days— something Hannah was trying not to think about, certain she would miss him. But this was a vacation romance and those always ended.

'Great. I'll just grab my coat.'

A short time later, Matt held the door open to a moodily lit bar in one of Melbourne's stylish alleys. Stepping through, Hannah immediately spotted her group and, pushing her shoulders back and holding her chin up, she plastered a broad smile in place as she approached them.

'Hannah! We wondered what was keeping you!'

'Had to stop by home first.' She looked up at Matt, who was studying her with an unreadable expression on his face. Supposing it would be rude to expect them to introduce themselves, she placed her hand on his arm, pushing him forward slightly. 'This is my friend, Matt. He's visiting for the week.'

Everyone from her department stared at him with gaping mouths, but she had to admit she was impressed when Matt showed no reaction at all, except to say, 'Nice to meet you all.'

She had to fight every impulse to respond to his voice when he leaned down and said, 'I'll get our drinks.'

Nodding, she made her way with the group to one of the tall standing tables where they could huddle together and share war stories from their week. Hannah laughed brightly at every complaint, touching the arms of the people she spoke to, all the while keeping the smile that everyone had come to expect from her firmly in place. And, when she looked over at the bar, she caught Matt watching her.

Soon enough, he joined their crowd, handing her a cold bottle of beer. Clinking the bottles together, she and Matt took a long draught of the chilled drink. She watched him place his bottle on the table, keeping one large hand around it while his thumb traced the beads of condensation collecting on the glass. His other hand slid into his pocket.

How was it possible for one man to be so effortlessly sexy, to be so comfortable and at ease all the time? Hannah was so busy watching him that she stopped hearing what was being said around her. She forgot about her bright smile or the confidence she needed to exude at all times. Matt's presence made her body react to him without thought or pretence.

It was only her name being called that returned her to the bar and group of friendly faces that she saw every day. She pulled her confidence and smile back on, like shrugging on a jacket before stepping out of her home, and turned to face the owner of the voice. 'Sorry, I was a million miles away.'

'I see that,' said the blonde from Sales. 'I was asking if you had any plans for the weekend.'

'Of course,' Hannah smiled with a vixen's smirk. 'It's been a long week; I think I deserve a little fun.'

'I don't know how you do it, Hannah. You have the busiest social life of anyone I know.'

Hannah simply laughed the comment away, thinking to herself, I don't know how I do it either.

And there was Matt, studying her once again. Why did it seem like those green eyes could see right into her soul? She wasn't sure she liked that. After all, she had gone to a lot of trouble to hide it from everyone. As for right now, it was becoming difficult to keep up who she was supposed to be when her body was fighting to make her reach out to Matt.

She almost sagged with relief when he put down his beer and announced that they should go. 'We're supposed to meet up for dinner, remember?'

'Oh, right. I almost forgot about that. We don't want to be late.' Hannah bid everyone a good night and the two of them left, saying nothing at all until they reached her apartment.

She'd felt a shift in Matt since they'd entered the bar, but the silence was making her brain work overtime. To buy herself a little time before, as she was certain, he would address whatever was on his mind, she fed Lucky, Emma's black cat, that was asleep on its fluffy cat tree.

She was about to open the wine when Matt grabbed her hand and pulled her to sit with him on the couch. Draping her legs over his lap, he held her in place, and Hannah had to admit that there were very few places where she felt as good as she did in his arms.

'I'm not going to let you avoid me when you know I saw,' Matt said, tenderly brushing her hair away from her face.

'I don't know what you're talking about.' Hannah couldn't look him in the eye. Her heart was pounding; she was sure he could feel it. He was about to peel a plaster off very slowly and she was sure it was going to hurt.

'Don't you?' His fingers held her chin firmly, forcing her to look at him, but still Hannah tried to avert her gaze. She breathed a sigh of relief when he allowed her to look away. Her body was rigid. She felt his arms curl around her, pressing her to his chest, her head safely tucked into his neck.

'I see you, Hannah. I see you when you're with me and I see you when you're out in the world. I know your every honest reaction when you laugh or smile for me. I know when your touch is the real you and I know when you slip into the role of the other person.' His voice was so even that, even though his words were scaring her, for some reason they calmed her too.

'I don't know why you need to be her, Hannah, and I won't ask why, but you need to know that you don't need her. That armour... Tonight, when I saw you shrug that personality on, it bothered me. I don't like seeing you hide yourself, because you're an incredible woman. And I know it's all a mask. Those flirty touches and smiles and laughter...they're all a mask.'

Hannah's throat was thick with unshed tears. 'Scary' wasn't the right word—this was terrifying. The last person who had seen the real her had found her wanting. He hadn't thought she was special. He'd made sure she knew that it was unthinkable that she could be enough. She couldn't be that vulnerable again. And, though she knew Matt was leaving in a few days, what if he too decided that she wasn't worth the effort, now that he'd seen her? Not even for this temporary romance that was unlike anything she had experienced in her life.

Matt pulled her away from his body, cupping her face in his large hands. She tried to turn her face, to hide the tears, but he wouldn't let her. He wasn't looking away.

His eyes were pleading. 'Hannah, I see you, and you're perfect. Please don't hide.'

* * *

Hannah opened her eyes, Matt's words ringing through her mind. He had seen her then and she knew she had seen him too. Because the man who'd wanted her to find her strength hadn't been cold or distant. That man had been perfect, and she knew like she knew her own heart that this version of him was a mask. But why was he hiding?

CHAPTER FIFTEEN

THE SHORT DRIVE back to Matt's penthouse felt unbearably long. Hannah refused to look at him, afraid of what she might see on his face. Unfortunately, she'd learnt a long time ago that she had very little control when it came to Matt. Out the corner of her eye, she looked over, seeing no expression on his face at all. He was focussed only on the road.

The tension was uncomfortable. Especially since last night had felt like such a revelation. It had felt like progress. Clearly, she'd been wrong. So Hannah refused to break the silence now.

Replaying the scene at the house in her mind, Hannah was more than a little curious as to why Matt had reacted the way he had. Something was going on. Maybe she could help him deal with it. She cared for him, more and more with each day. That was why she hated the second-guessing she was doing because it didn't bode well. Not if he was going to be her husband.

Is this what awaits me? she thought. *Will this be my marriage? Will I have a husband who will always remain closed off to me?*

Patience was something Matt had always prided himself on. He didn't lose his temper with people. He tried to make them comfortable. He hardly ever snapped at anyone. It was how he won people over. When people felt safe, they performed at their best. And yet he had snapped at the one woman who meant more to him than anyone else. It would be a massive understatement to say he was annoyed at himself, because now Hannah was quiet. She hadn't uttered a word since she had told him she was ready to leave, that she had seen all she needed to.

Through parking the car and travelling up to the apartment, Hannah remained silent. Matt noticed just how much further away she stood as they ascended. The physical space irritated him.

The moment the doors slid open, Hannah marched out, making a beeline for her room, but Matt was much quicker. He grabbed her hand and tugged her to him, closing the chasm that was opening up between them. The feel of her pressed against him was exactly right. The only thing that could make this moment any more right was if she hit him with the fiery attitude he so enjoyed. Except she was looking at him with confusion and trepidation.

Do something about it!

He knew exactly what—the best distraction they had. He brushed his lips over hers and felt her stiffen in his arms. Lightly, he grazed his lips over the corner of hers and she relaxed a fraction. Then his lips were trailing over her jaw and she leaned into him. He pressed a peck, barely a tickle, against the soft skin at the base of her ear.

'Hannah,' he whispered, and he was rewarded with a reluctant moan. He felt her jaw flex with frustration at her response, making him smile. She could never hide how he made her feel. And he knew he could pull her back to him now, make her forget about what had happened at the house. Her fingers were twisted in the skirt of her dress. She was determined not to give in to him, Matt supposed.

'Touch me,' he whispered, sucking her earlobe into his mouth. He knew she would remember the last time he'd said those words to her—seven months ago in a hotel room in Melbourne.

'Now.' The low, rough command aroused her. He could see

it in her eyes when he pulled away to look at her. The fingers at her sides loosened, slowly raising to slip under his shirt. Muscles tightening at her touch, Matt swallowed down the plea for more. He was in control here. He would make Hannah focus on all the ways they were so good together.

Matt watched the fabric of his shirt lift higher and higher as her hands travelled up his chest. They glided over his skin, leaving behind a trail of blazing heat until she bunched it in her hands and pulled it over his head, leaving his torso gloriously naked.

He loved how confident and demanding Hannah was when it came to her needs. There was nothing sexier than a woman who knew what she wanted. And, despite his slip-up earlier, it was obvious she still wanted him. He would do anything for that look. He couldn't show his emotions to her or talk about what he felt. What he could do was show her with his body that he was sorry. That he wanted her.

Cradling her face in his hands, Matt covered her lips with his, glorying in that instant high he got every time he kissed her. Her fingers curled into his sides, nails scraping his skin making him growl deep in his throat, an animalistic sound. But that was what Hannah did to him—reduced him to primal want and need. Her touch could turn him to ash and, God, did he want that!

Wanting to taste her, Matt slid his tongue along the seam of her lips. Instantly she parted them on a mewl laced with desire. He wanted to plunder her mouth with his tongue but, after what had happened earlier, he knew that would be wrong. Hannah deserved tenderness. His tongue glided over hers, tasting her sweetness, feeling her shiver against his body. Their breaths were coming in short pants as the electricity between them climbed, charging the very air around them. His lips roved against hers, fingers threading through her hair, a sweet seduction. Her body melted against his a little more with every dance of their tongues.

But Matt was impatient to feel her body on his. When he had stopped her from walking away, his only intention had been to quell her anger. To show her they had something she shouldn't walk away from. He should have known that a few kisses and touches would never be enough between them. This chemistry they had was more powerful than any will or plan. It consumed them. So it was no surprise that now all Matt wanted was to be with Hannah...inside her.

Lips connected, Matt's hands travelled down her body, grasping her hips, bunching the fabric of her summer dress. His fingers inched it higher until it was all fisted in his palms. Breaking away only long enough to pull the dress off her, he dropped it to the floor. Standing there in just her underwear, Hannah was a vision, a Botticelli painting brought to life.

But he needed to see, feel, more.

He peeled her bra off her, fusing his lips to hers once more. His fingers traced patterns until they found her nipples. Teasing to the rhythm of his tongue, Hannah sighed his name, and he slipped the fingers of his other hand to her sex, finding her wet and needy.

'Oh, Hannah...' He groaned.

Matt wanted to draw this out. Savour every moment until she was drawn taut and could think of nothing but her lust for him.

Hannah had other ideas.

He had a split-second to wrap his arms around her as she pushed up onto her tiptoes, fisting one hand in his thick hair, making him hiss. The sensation was somewhere between pleasure and pain. The other wrapped around his neck as she kissed him hard in a clash of teeth and tongue, biting his lower lip as she pulled away.

'I'm pregnant, Matt, not fragile.'

That was all she needed to say to tear the animal in him loose.

Matt grabbed her lace panties, ripping straight through the

flimsy material. He spun Hannah round and she pressed her hands against the wall, arching her back. In a breath his jeans were open and his erection free. The irony wasn't lost on Matt that he had wanted to make Hannah come undone but instead she was the one who'd torn his control to shreds.

With no preamble at all, he thrust into her. An animalistic growl echoed through the passage. He barely heard Hannah's breathy chuckle, that soon dissolved into incoherent moans with his hands on her hips, and the sound of skin on skin clapping through the still apartment.

His rhythm was punishing but, when he heard her whimper, 'More, please,' he reached around her, teasing the bundle of nerves until she came apart spectacularly, taking him right along with her.

Neither of them said anything. They couldn't. Not through their harsh breaths.

Matt kissed her shoulder, amazed at how completely he could lose himself in Hannah. Pulling out of her, he realised that, while the fly of his jeans was open, he hadn't even taken them off. Her panties were entirely unsalvageable and hanging uselessly around her hips.

He shook his head at himself. He hadn't lost control like that in a long time—maybe ever. How could he still want her?

He scooped Hannah up in his arms, kissing her forehead.

'What are you doing? I can walk.'

'I know, but my way is better.'

'And why's that?'

He marched them into her room. 'Because we're only getting started.' Matt smirked.

The sky was black, London lit up around him. Up here, the world was quiet, the apartment bathed in darkness. Matt gripped the rail of his terrace. His mind was busy.

The phone in the back pocket of his jeans buzzed incessantly until he answered.

'Shrimp.'

'Hey, Bear, how did it go last night?'

'Good,' he replied, looking up at the sky. 'Today not so much.'

'What happened?'

Matt didn't hesitate a moment before telling his sister about the trip to the townhouse, and she listened without interruption.

'Why did you get so angry?' Sarah asked, her voice soft.

'I don't want to look back. Living through it was enough,' Matt said, pinching the bridge of his nose. 'I hate it when she's silent. There's so much fire in her; I don't want to be the one to extinguish it.'

'What do you want?'

'I want the best for her and my son. I want her to have everything she deserves, but I don't want to talk about our family. It's the past. What does it matter?'

He certainly didn't want to dwell on those pictures that were now locked away in the boot of his car. 'I want her. I think we could have a good life.' One with chemistry and fun. What better person was there to have a family with than a friend? Even though he knew Hannah was so much more than a friend, what she was exactly, he wasn't sure.

'What kind of life is that, Bear? One where you don't rely on anyone? Curiosity isn't a crime, especially if she's going to have your child.'

'Dad relied on no one.' He'd never once showed any emotional weakness. Wasn't that the kind of steadfastness he would need in his own life? And yet he hated the miserable life that would force upon his family.

'You're not Dad,' Sarah said firmly.

No, he wasn't. But Matt had to be controlled. He hadn't seen love, so he'd leaned on showing affection the only way he could—protecting his sister; behaving perfectly for his parents. Sex…it was the one place he could be unleashed, unrestrained, fully himself.

'I'm not. I don't want to be, but he's the only example we have.'

Sarah sighed. 'Just give it more thought. Maybe you don't need an example at all.'

Matt slipped the phone back into his pocket, deciding he could control this. He would deal with the house so Hannah could change it as she wanted without digging around his past.

Hannah awoke in her room, feeling a contented sort of ache. When they had reached the apartment she'd been resolved to give Matt the space he needed to work out whatever it was that had bothered him so much at the house. She hadn't wanted to talk; hadn't wanted to push just then. And when he'd kissed her she'd been determined not to get caught up in their magic. But he had set her alight.

'Touch me.'

That was what he had said. Just like that last night in Melbourne, when he had been completely naked with her, as she had with him. She'd been the real Hannah that night, the truest version of herself, and she was certain the same was true for him.

And, while she'd allowed him to distract her, the moment his lips had touched hers there'd been no force in this world that could have stopped the white-hot heat that ploughed through her, curling in her belly. No, that couldn't be controlled, nor could it be faked. If nothing else, the way they reacted to each other was honest so, while she hadn't used words, she'd pushed Matt in a way she'd known he would respond to.

And respond he had. He hadn't been sunshine yesterday, he'd been the sun. Powerful, uncontrollable and a pure force of life.

Her Matt was in there. She just needed to reach him. Destroy his mask, as he had hers.

This life that they were embarking on for their family required honesty to work. More than that, Hannah cared too deeply for Matt for him to continuously shut her out. Maybe the house was exactly what they needed to bridge the gap.

Hannah flung the covers off, ready to take on the day. She wanted to explore the house some more. It might not reflect the warmth she would like, but that was what they were going to fix and, through it, she would uncover pieces of Matt.

She didn't find him in the kitchen, which was odd, considering how early it still was, so she made herself a cup of herbal tea that she wanted to enjoy out on the terrace. Only to find Matt working in the lounge instead of his office, with the laptop sitting on his thighs.

'Good afternoon.' He smirked.

'Funny.' She rolled her eyes.

He placed the computer on the seat next to him and crossed his legs, ankle over knee. 'I take it you slept well?'

'I did. What's got you in such a good mood?' She sat on the couch opposite him, blowing on her drink.

He didn't answer, changing the subject instead. 'Have you made a decision about the house?'

'I have.' Hannah bit her lip, deciding how much to say to Matt. She didn't want to describe the images she saw in her head of him playing in the pool with their son. Or of family picnics in the park just outside. Those seemed like dreams far too domestic for the man in those stiff photos. 'I love the house. I think it would be perfect for our family.'

Matt said nothing but he was smiling from ear to ear.

'I already have a few ideas, if you're interested in hearing them.'

'Of course I am.'

'Great! I don't really want to knock any part of it down. It's a beautiful property but I would like to redecorate... What?' she asked, seeing the look on his face.

'I want to knock part of it down.'

'Of course you do,' she said, deadpan.

He laughed but explained his vision, which Hannah had to admit she really did like, and it wouldn't be a massive undertaking either. They talked about how they could turn it into something that reflected them. Matt wanted to install every smart device he could think of, which quite frankly excited Hannah too. She could let herself believe that this would be their home. A happy place, Matt's, hers and their son's.

'I've already hired a crew to clear out the place.'

'You did what?'

'I want this done before the baby arrives, Hannah. We don't have time to waste.'

Oh, but this was about so much more than that. 'I wanted to go back to the house, Matt.'

'Now you don't need to. You can deal with everything from here, so you won't have to be on site until after it's completed. You have *carte blanche*.'

Hannah huffed a laugh. Just when she'd thought there would be a way for her to bridge the gap between them, he went and put up another wall. It felt as if they were playing emotional chess. He had a move to cover himself at every turn.

'The architect will be in touch. She will meet you here.'

How could he go from being so open with her when their bodies were connected to so closed off at any other time? It made those old wounds unstitch. Was it possible that she simply wasn't enough for Matt? She wouldn't even be here if it weren't for the baby. Maybe he really didn't want her, not in any real way. Except he was the one who'd proposed marriage. Though, yet again, for his son's sake. But what they'd done last night had felt real.

'Are you doing this just to keep me away? To prevent me from learning anything about you?' She hadn't meant to ask the question out loud but the words were swimming in her head. As soon as they were out of her mouth, she wished she could take them back. Yes, she wanted honesty, but this was too honest. It showed him that she wanted to be closer. Allowed him a weapon with which to penetrate her already beaten armour.

But what was so wrong about wanting to get closer to Matt? They'd had something special from the start.

Matt's face darkened. 'Are you seriously going accuse me of trying to keep you away? *You* were the one who kept me away, if you remember. I'm the one trying to build something with you.'

Hannah's lips pressed into a thin line. 'I thought we were past that, Matt.'

'Maybe you were. Do you know what it's like for me? I'm going to have a son in two months, Hannah! I was raised to know what a family should be, should look like, and yet I didn't get the chance to know my son as he developed because of you! But, even so, I'm still trying to make a home with you.'

'Really? Is that what you're doing? Because to me it seems like you want a mother for your son and a convenient partner on your terms. You shut down every time I want to know more. Aren't families supposed to have no secrets?'

Hannah shot to her feet and moved behind the chair she'd been sitting on, digging her fingers into the soft back rest. 'And you're trying to make a home with me? Matt, you've been dictating to me! You know my life is in Melbourne; you have all this wealth and power but, instead of using it to move closer to us, you've forced me to make the sacrifice. You keep asking more of me and yet you want to give nothing in return.'

Matt's eyes were blazing now. 'Nothing? Are you sure?'

'Yes! I don't even know if you trust me!'

'How can you question that?' Matt fired at her.

'How could I not? I asked you about a picture I found in the house you want us to live in and the first thing you did was to shove me aside! You want me to choose you, choose us, but you don't want me to know you.'

'Of course, I want you to know me. You're the only one I

want, and it's driving me insane, because I don't know if you really want me or are just responding to our chemistry. I don't know if you will choose us. All I can do is make you see why we would be good together.'

'If you want that, then be honest with me. Please. Open up to me a little. Let me show you how much I care about you. Stop backing me into corners. I'm not someone you can control! Why do you want to?'

She saw him flinch as if she had struck him. Watched him push off the couch and stalk towards her, his expression grave.

'I don't want to control you,' he said gently. 'I just want you and our son with me in our home.'

'Matt...' She began to protest but then his lips were on hers, his fingers tangling in her hair. 'Stop trying to distract me,' she ground out on a cracking voice. 'Why do you always do this?'

He was still cradling her face, foreheads touching. His breath was kissing her skin. 'I'm trying to find a way to be the man I should be, and the man I want to be when I'm with you, but they are different men, Hannah.'

'They don't have to be.' She closed her eyes. 'Don't hide from me.' His own words aimed back at him. Hannah knew he would understand what she was asking.

His eyes scrunched tightly together. Their breaths mingled, his lips caressing hers in a feather-light touch.

'I'm sorry.' Matt kissed her lightly. 'It's all I know,' he whispered before claiming her. She let herself get lost in his kiss. And his kiss was demanding. It demanded that all her attention focus on his tongue coaxing hers, his insistent lips. On his hands holding the side of her face. It demanded that she let everything else go, be with him in this moment, so she did.

In the weeks that followed, Hannah and Matt seemed to find a pattern that worked for them. He worked from home as much as he could while Hannah focussed on the house. Her days were taken up with constant meetings, emails and calls with the architect and interior designer. She would trawl through hundreds of websites, finding things she wanted to incorporate into the house that she was determined to make a home which showed their personalities. More especially, one that showed Matt's warmth. Even now, when she thought about it, she hated the idea of him in that cold house.

It was hard for Hannah not to get swept away. Especially when they came together every single night, losing themselves in their mad passion.

Every night she slept in Matt's bed, and every morning she woke with him holding her. He was trying; that was clear. He even bought her a ridiculously large SUV, despite her protests, so she wouldn't feel trapped in his apartment. The size of the car was for his piece of mind.

But he still held back. Something was preventing him from breaking free of those restraints, but Hannah was willing to be patient.

CHAPTER SIXTEEN

ONLY A COUPLE WEEKS remained before Hannah was to give birth. The house was coming together quickly and, from the daily updates, she loved what she saw. It also meant that she would soon have to make a decision as to whether she married Matt or not. A decision that was becoming increasingly difficult. At times she wanted that life, because she wanted Matt. Sometimes she couldn't picture her life without him by her side. Other times, she questioned their connection.

So, when Matt told Hannah about Sarah's party, a part of her silently celebrated. Here was a huge part of his life that she would get to experience. Sarah was massively important to him. Hannah had overheard their calls, the frequency with which they spoke. The tenderness in his voice even when she could tell he was riling Sarah up.

'Should I be worried?' Hannah joked as they drove to Virginia Water early on Saturday morning. The car was packed with an overnight bag and her hospital bag just in case. In fact, they were more than prepared for their baby's arrival, with Matt having turned one of the guest rooms on the opposite wing of the apartment into a nursery.

Hannah had insisted he didn't need to, when she would have the cot in her room, but he had insisted on a back-up plan in case there were any snags with the house. Not that there would be, but Hannah had let it slide.

The only thing they didn't have was a name and they could not come to an agreement on one.

'Of Sarah?' Matt rubbed his smooth jaw, thinking over the answer. The morning sun glinted in his green eyes. Hannah was struck by how beautiful he was. Then he turned to her and smiled and she couldn't breathe. If she was going to spend her life with this man, she really needed to get a handle on her reaction to him.

Not that she wanted to. Even if the lack of oxygen killed a few brain cells.

'Umm…' Hannah had to remind herself that she had asked a question.

Thankfully, Matt wanted to say more. 'She can be a bit protective…' he rolled his eyes '…but you'll like her.'

Anyone who was protective of Matt was all right in her book.

'Are you nervous? It's just a garden party. There'll be a few of her friends there and us,' he said.

'No, of course not.' Hannah batted away his concern.

A large hand squeezed her thigh.

'It will be fine.'

Such a small touch had the power to calm her, ease her worry for just a little while, make her feel safe. The air in the car grew thick. His hand was starting to sear her through the fabric of her jumpsuit, making her skin come alive. As if Matt could feel it too, he removed it and cleared his throat.

'You know, we still haven't agreed.' Hannah tried to bring back the lightness from before. This was probably the best way, especially since the comically loud groan from Matt made her laugh.

'Not this again.'

'Our child needs a name. What about Jack?'

'No.'

'What's wrong with Jack?' she protested.

'It goes in a box,' he mumbled.

'You're being ridiculous. Okay, fine…' She turned in her seat to face him. 'What do you think is a good name?'

'Off the top of my head? Matthew.' He grinned.

'Of course you'd say that. Vetoed.'

'What's wrong with Matthew?'

'Nothing. I just don't think our child will have a big enough head to be named Matthew.'

Matt barked out a laugh. 'Fine,' he conceded, wiping a tear from his eye. 'What about Travis?'

'No!' Hannah tried to hide her horrified expression, but Matt saw it anyway.

'Definitely not Travis. Okay, what about Oliver?'

'Oliver. I like the sound of that.' She looked out of the window, saying the name to herself. It felt as if it fitted.

'We're here,' Matt announced, turning onto a long driveway that led to a magnificent white stone mansion with peaked roofs and flowing stonework.

Hannah's mouth was agape. Once Matt removed their bags from the boot and shut the lid, a stunning blonde with familiar kind, green eyes stepped outside.

'Bear!' She ran up to Matt, who caught her in a crushing hug. 'You're early.'

'Hey, Shrimp.' He extended a hand to Hannah who took it, allowing him to pull her close. 'This is Hannah. Hannah, my sister Sarah. Don't let her bully you.'

Hannah couldn't help but laugh when Sarah smacked his arm. Just like that, her Matt, the man she'd met months ago, was standing before her. She wished Sarah was around all the time, if this was the effect she had on him.

'I would do no such thing,' Sarah said with mock-outrage. 'Before we go in, I should warn you there are a few more people here than I mentioned.'

Hannah expected a scowl, some sign to show his displeasure. After all, this was the man who tried to control everything. Instead, he laughed, a warm sound. His eyes filled with affection.

'Why am I not surprised?'

'Sorry,' Sarah said sheepishly. Hannah was certain she wasn't sorry at all.

'It's fine.' Matt wrapped his arm around Hannah's shoulders. 'Lead the way.'

Hannah was still smiling when Sarah showed them to the guest rooms on the opposite side of the house. 'For privacy,' she announced with a wink.

She liked Sarah a great deal already.

Hannah closed her eyes, turning her face to the sun as she basked in the warmth soaking into her bones. She really did love summer. It was made all the more special by their beautiful surroundings. The back of Sarah's home opened onto a massive green lawn with large trees and picture-perfect flowerbeds. Sarah, Hannah had learnt, was a jewellery designer, and the white orangery in the corner of the property had been converted into her studio.

Taking a sip of her chilled mocktail—Sarah had made sure plenty of the drinks were pregnancy-friendly—she heard squeals of laughter. Sarah had invited a horde of people—her closest friends, she'd assured Hannah.

Matt rose from the table, kissing Hannah on the cheek as if it was the most natural thing in the world, when a family arrived, the two kids bursting through the door and making a beeline for him. The little boy leaped on and clung to his back while his younger sister insisted on swinging from his arms.

The sight made her smile. She could see with crystal clarity what an amazing father he would be. He was so relaxed here. Every strain on him had simply vanished.

'They love him,' Sarah said, watching the children, just as Hannah did. They sat at a long table set on the grass with all manner of summery foods upon it.

'I can't imagine anyone who wouldn't.' She pulled her gaze away from the man who was making her feel all sorts of things, even though he wasn't even looking at her. 'You have a beautiful home.'

'Thank you,' Sarah replied, looking at the behemoth of a house. 'It's so beautiful and tranquil out here. I feel a lot more inspired to design here than in the city.'

'I can understand that. Was this a family home?' Hannah imagined it must have been. Estates like these were normally passed through the generations, weren't they? This place felt different from the townhouse. There were bright pops of colour everywhere, while still oozing glamour. It felt welcoming.

'Heavens, no.' Sarah laughed. 'I bought this place a few years ago, before Mum got sick. After she passed, I inherited their estate. It's quite far from here, or London for that matter, and I hated it. Sold it as soon as I could.'

Hannah didn't know how to respond to that. There seemed to be so much that Sarah wasn't saying. Why had she hated it? And why did her mother's death seem so matter of fact?

'You can ask, you know,' Sarah said. 'I can see the questions on your face.'

Hannah laughed. Seeing through people seemed to be a gift both siblings possessed. 'Just trying to wrap my head around it. Why would you hate a family home? Even Matt was being weird at the townhouse.'

'I'm not surprised.' Hannah watched Sarah's expression soften when she looked over at her brother, who was now flat on his back, being wrestled into submission by the two kids whose energy showed no signs of running out. 'Matt doesn't have too many happy memories there. I know I certainly don't. Or rather, all the ones I do have are with him. He used to take me across to the park to play.'

Hannah remembered seeing the children and how far away Matt had seemed that day.

'He was always my best friend and protector. It made me think I was invincible. I mean, look at him.' Sarah laughed.

Hannah had to admit she could definitely see why Sarah called him Bear. 'You two have always been close?'

'Since day one,' Sarah replied. 'I think he wanted to make sure I wasn't lonely. Our dad never spent any time with us. He demanded certain things that he felt were necessary of us. Wanted Matt to change who he was, because someone as warm and openly affectionate as my brother was a disappointment. Insisted my mother stop working to look after us and get involved in a society approved charity. It was always about the image. She didn't even work when we were sent to boarding school. I think she threw herself into her projects even more then.'

Hannah was starting to see a picture emerge of a young, lonely Matt, not receiving the attention he deserved, so he became whatever his sister needed. Sarah looked as though she were far away, seeing a reel that no one else could.

'He used to come see me at my school whenever he had a pass to go out. Sometimes he'd come with Alex but most of the time by himself. We'd just go get milkshakes and talk. Make sure I was okay. Our parents never came unless they had to. Not even at the end of term.'

'I'm so sorry,' Hannah said, grasping Sarah's hand. She wasn't sure what made her do it, but she ached for them. 'It's not fair that you had to go through that.'

'You're right, it's not. Even less so for Matt.' Sarah took a sip of her drink and placed it back down on the table, running an elegant finger around the rim of the glass. 'The thing is, we had nothing to complain about. Not when Matt's best friend was Alex, you know?'

Hannah nodded. She'd heard all about that story. 'Our parents were in our lives. They provided for us. Made sure we wanted for nothing. On the surface, it all looked absolutely perfect.'

'But it wasn't.'

'No, it wasn't. I never once saw my father so much as hug or kiss my mother. It was like they were business partners, and the business was the family. He was emotionless and she was restless. We could tell. You don't just take a career woman away from that world and expect her to be fulfilled. Don't get me wrong, Hannah, we had an amazing mother who loved us tremendously. But I think she harboured some resentment towards us for the life she lost.'

Hannah couldn't picture it. Even if she had to give up Melbourne and her life there so her son could have all he needed, she would never feel that way. And she had been everything to her own parents. She could feel it in her bones, even now. They had loved her unconditionally until the day they'd died. 'Why do you think that?'

'There was this one time, the weather was particularly bad, so Matt and I had to play inside. He must have been about ten, I think, and Mum was on a call with a friend of hers. Anyway, Matt was nearby, and he heard the conversation but he didn't realise at the time that I was hiding closer. I remember being so proud of my hiding spot. Mum said that sometimes she felt that, if it weren't for us, she could have had everything she'd strived for.'

'Oh, Sarah.' Hannah gasped.

'I didn't fully understand what she was saying but I remember the look on Matt's face. He made sure he was exactly what they wanted all the time after that. Told me to come to him if I needed anything. When I got older, I understood that he'd wanted to ease the burden on her.'

Hannah felt as though she had swallowed hot coals. She felt sad and angry for that little boy who'd taken the world on his shoulders. He'd become a man who did the same. As if struck by a lightning bolt, Hannah understood why he refused to open up to her. Every vulnerability was his own because he wasn't meant to show any emotion.

Except that wasn't who he was. She thought back to Melbourne, the ultrasound, his smile and affection when he held her... Matt's heart wasn't meant to be caged.

'Matt.' She mouthed the word to herself, not realising she had turned her entire body towards him. He looked right at her, bathing her with his beaming smile. She so desperately wanted to wrap her arms around him and tell him it was okay. *They* weren't his parents. They couldn't be because she had fallen for him.

Uh-oh.

She had fallen for him.

When had that happened? Hannah rifled through her memories, but she couldn't find that single moment. All she knew was that it was an absolute truth.

'You love him, don't you?' A soft voice came from beside her.

Hannah's throat was closing up. Love meant trust. Did she trust Matt?

'I...' She didn't know what to say. There was no denying it. But she didn't have to admit it either.

'It's okay. I can see you do,' Sarah said kindly.

Hannah looked at the young woman with a soft smile on her face.

'I'm happy he's found someone who makes *him* happy. And you do, Hannah. Even if he acts like a complete arse, know that you do.'

Hannah watched Sarah pick up her glass and go over to her friends by the pool, leaving her with a maelstrom of emotions and thoughts from their conversation.

She loved Matt.

CHAPTER SEVENTEEN

THE SUN WAS going down over the estate. Everything was quiet now. Sarah was bidding her guests farewell and Matt, well, he just needed to be alone. Which was why he was currently leaning his elbows on the balcony rail on the terrace that ran along the full length of the house.

Memories of his childhood swirled in his mind. Perhaps it was because of the children he'd so enjoyed entertaining. Maybe it was this house, that reminded him of their family estate.

Whatever it was, it had him on edge. He was certain it was because his own son's arrival was imminent. Being a father was still a terrifying prospect. His father had provided for them and given them everything except what they'd needed emotionally.

Today when he'd played with the kids, it had felt so good. He'd loved every minute, and when they'd tired they both run to their father, who had scooped them up and held them until they'd fallen asleep.

Matt didn't have a single memory like that, not of himself or Sarah. There hadn't been any loving words or hugs. A solitary pat on the back was what he'd got when he'd graduated with first class honours, a singular moment of pride.

Most of the time his father hadn't really interacted with them at all. He'd been far too busy with his job, stocks or society. Taylors didn't just have, they earned. There was no nobility in their blood, just hard work. But, surely even if his father had worked hard, he could have spared a few minutes each day for his children or at the very least, for Sarah? Matt had never felt loved by his father. In fact, his disappointment in Matt was all Matt had been sure of. So why did he feel so guilty for hating his childhood? For not wanting to subject his son to that?

Matt had seen those couples today, parents married for years, and he'd been able to see their love. Had seen it when they'd looked at their kids, as if they were the physical embodiment of it. How was he going to provide a loving home for his son? Each memory of his childhood was a splinter under his fingernail, making him worry he would cause his son the same unhappiness.

Neither he nor Sarah had ever wanted to visit their parents, who'd done what they'd needed to in order to be successful. To show off the perfect marriage, perfect family and perfect children. So. Damn. Fake. Maybe that was why he hated it so much when those women who wanted nothing but his power and fortune threw themselves at him. It was all fake, not a real emotion in sight. They wanted something to make them look good, something they could benefit from.

Matt squeezed his eyes shut. Was it wrong to go ahead with his plan, knowing that he and Hannah weren't in love, even if everything about her drove him crazy? Then again, how could he not? He didn't want to repeat his parents' mistakes but their duty to their child superseded everything, surely? After all, he'd turned out just fine without love.

He dropped his head, running his fingers through his hair, fisting the strands until it hurt.

'Matt?'

The soft call came from behind him. Hannah… Hannah was real. Their chemistry was real. She wasn't even wearing her mask today. She was herself—his Hannah.

He loosened his grip and turned around, schooling his face

into a neutral expression, despite fraying at the edges. Coming apart.

Her eyes softened and he watched her slowly step towards him, but he turned away. He felt her when she stood by his side.

'Are you okay?' Hannah asked.

He hazarded a quick glance at her, could see concern shining in her eyes and had to look away. No, he wasn't okay, but he wasn't about to display that vulnerability. He couldn't do it. He could feel a muscle ticking in his jaw. Control couldn't abandon him now. Not when it was his closest ally.

'Fine.'

Hannah touched his cheek and he leaned into it, his brittle control disappearing like a wisp of smoke.

'You don't have to say that if you aren't.'

'What are you talking about?' Matt was certain his concerns weren't written on his face, and his first instinct was to put up his guard.

'Everyone is leaving. Your sister is inside and you're out here all by yourself. You can talk to me,' Hannah said gently.

'I don't need to talk.'

He felt the loss immediately when she removed her hand, turning back towards the railing. 'You do,' she said softly. 'Your emotions aren't a weakness; they don't have to be hidden from the people you trust.'

'What would you know of it?' He growled.

'What I know is that someone who shines as brightly as you do, feels as deeply as you, shouldn't ever have to hide that away.' She turned to him then, fire in her eyes. 'Regardless of who told you that you need to.'

'Hannah…' Matt warned. He had seen her talking to his sister, relieved that they seemed to like each other from the moment they'd met. Now he wondered exactly what Sarah had said.

'Why do you want to hide what you're feeling?'

'Because the past has no bearing on what we're doing.'

'That's not true. Your parents—'

'I had a mother who loved us and a father who provided for us.'

'And was that all you wanted?' Hannah asked patiently.

Matt looked into her eyes, the words flowing out before he had a chance to stop them. 'My father always told me a man doesn't get emotional. He said that one day when I had a family I would have to change.' He had been trying but she made him ache for more than he should want.

Hannah took hold of his face, closing the distance between them and, automatically, Matt held her against him. 'You don't need to try to be that way. Don't you see how people respond to you? Sarah, Alex, me: you've pulled us all in by being you. What you feel and share makes you who you are, and you *are* perfect. You don't need to change to be.'

'You don't understand,' he said, pulling away. 'If it weren't for me, my mother wouldn't have lost her career and been unhappy. If I could have been different my father…'

'What? Wouldn't have been disappointed? Tried to change you?'

Matt said nothing.

'It's you who doesn't understand.' Hannah's hands fisted in his shirt. 'You didn't ask to be born. They decided to have children. None of this is on you. Don't you see? You were just a child. Innocent. And, because you have such a big heart, you tried to take on the world for everyone else too. You weren't responsible for Sarah or your mother's happiness or your father's distance.'

Matt tried to look away. His throat had dried up.

'Children love their parents so much all they ever want is some of that back. You didn't get it from your father, Matt, it's okay to be angry about that.'

She was right. The guilt he felt for being angry about his childhood clearly was because he still loved his parents. Why would he have held onto that townhouse for so long if he hadn't?

'Would you ever try to change our son to suit your wants?'

'No, never.' Matt was certain he would accept him unconditionally. He already loved him; yet Matt would never know if his father had loved him.

The fervour in Hannah's eyes called to him. He crashed his lips down on hers. Yanking her to his body, he spun them round, pressing her against the solid railing. Snaking one arm around her waist, his other hand at the back of her head, Matt pinned Hannah to him. There was no escaping this kiss. Not that she was trying to. She opened up beneath him, accepting his rough, controlling kisses. His tongue dominated hers, lips sliding together, bruising, punishing.

This…this was what he needed. For now, he could think of nothing but the taste, feel and scent of Hannah.

His breathing was coming in ragged pants. His jeans tightened as he grew hard, pushing his erection against Hannah, who moaned at the contact. Then her hands were under his shirt, asking, pleading for more of him and, God, he wanted to take her right here. This woman ignited his blood. And heaven help him if this wasn't what he lived for.

He pulled away, making her whine in protest. Normally he'd have a chuckle, smirk or witty comeback for the reaction. Not now; now he just wanted to be buried all the way in her. To bask in this realness.

'Come with me.' His voice was barely a growl and she nodded, threading her fingers in his. Matt tugged her along to the open French doors along the terrace on their wing of the house. Every step was torture until they made it to their room. The door was shut, locked and Matt had his clothes off all within seconds.

'Take off your clothes,' he ordered, and Hannah obeyed. 'Take it all off.' She did as she was told. The cream jumpsuit pooled at her feet. She stood in front of him, glorious in her nudity. He dropped to his knees, looked into her eyes then leaned forward and kissed her deeply. Hannah smacked a hand over her mouth to stop the drawn-out moan escaping.

'No, I want to hear you.' His tongue delved into her sex once more and he noticed that she was now biting on her finger. It wouldn't do. He stood and lifted her, wrapping her legs around him as he took her to bed. Settling against the pillows, with Hannah straddling him, he held her face and kissed her. Let her taste herself on his tongue.

'You're not hiding anything from me tonight.' This was what he needed. Understanding lit her eyes. He was baring himself to her in the only way he knew how. Then he was the one moaning out her name as she lowered herself onto his hardness. Matt was lost to sensation. The world fell away and all that was left was them.

CHAPTER EIGHTEEN

HANNAH KNEW MATT had been scraped raw on the inside. That kiss had proved it. The sex that had followed, even more so. The moment his lips had taken hers she'd vowed to be exactly what he needed. She hadn't measured her responses to him. She never could anyway. Hannah had responded to his every touch. The more she had, the more he'd seemed to want it, that unfiltered honesty. So she'd given and given, and he'd taken and taken.

The problem was he was still holding back. Not with his body; that had been unapologetic in its honesty. But his heart, his feelings—they were sealed tight.

When they had awoken, Matt had been entirely pleasant and it had annoyed her endlessly. After everything she'd found out about is childhood, the way she had found him on the terrace, Hannah was certain he was hurting. Except he was trying to hide it.

It probably would have bothered her less if she couldn't see the lines of tension around his eyes. Light bruises coloured the skin beneath them, betraying how little sleep—if any—he had got.

If Matt wasn't going to come to her, then she would go to him. She would be brave for both of them. Show him that vulnerability didn't have to be a weakness.

Hannah was adamant she could do this. It was a risk, but she was strong.

* * *

'Join me for a drink on the terrace?' Matt asked the evening they returned to his apartment.

Smiling softly, Hannah nodded. She watched Matt pour a glass of wine for himself and ginger ale, which she accepted. Taking a deep breath, she convinced herself she could do this, and followed him out.

Matt had seated himself on the chaise end of the couch, inviting Hannah to sit between his legs. She leaned against his chest. His warmth seeped into her back.

Hannah was deep in thought, figuring out how she would tell him the hardest story in her life, when he presented her with a burgundy box.

'What's this?' She placed her drink on the table beside them before picking up the box that obviously held a piece of jewellery.

'A reminder.' Matt's deep voice reverberated through her.

A click sounded loudly in the still night. 'Matt...' Hannah breathed. Sitting on the black velvet cushion within the box was a stunning pendant. A white-gold, diamond-encrusted teardrop that surrounded a rose-gold flame inlaid with pink diamonds. It was beautiful, elegant. She was staring at the exquisite piece when Matt's hands plucked it out of the box.

'When you wear this, I want you to remember who you are, Hannah. You're a flame. Never hide it.' He fastened it around her neck, gently pulling her hair out from underneath the chain, sending goose bumps racing along her skin. Fingers tracing the shape, Hannah didn't know what to say.

'I love it,' she managed, touched beyond measure.

'I'm glad.' His breath caressed her ear.

Matt made her feel safe and protected, strong enough to be herself. She was more determined than ever to get him to open up.

'I really enjoyed meeting Sarah.' Hannah clasped the pendant firmly in her hand.

'Thank you for not hiding who you are. I know you would have thought about it.'

Hannah huffed out a laugh, unsure about how to respond. Of course, she'd thought about it. It was how she dealt with the world. Naturally, Matt saw that. He saw everything about her because she didn't need that mask around him.

'You're perfect as you are,' Matt said, kissing her head.

'No, I never was,' she said in small voice. Yes, she had decided to share this story with Matt. It didn't make it any easier to say.

He looked at her then. Hannah knew he would see apprehension in her eyes. 'What do you mean?'

'Back in Melbourne you said I wear a mask and you were right. You saw right through it. Nobody else ever had.'

'I was looking.'

'You were.' Hannah took another sip, steeling herself to say the rest. 'I had to wear it. I needed it.'

'Why?' Matt took her drink from her, placing his and hers on the nearby table. She let him. She also let him pull her across his lap, tucking her head against his neck. Sitting like this brought back memories.

'When I was young we didn't have much, but I had the best family, and then I met Emma, which I wouldn't have if it weren't for the scholarship that made attending the same school possible. That was hard, being the ordinary kid when everyone else was so vastly wealthy. I didn't belong in their world.'

Hannah didn't want to linger on the bullying. It didn't mean much to her any more. 'I pretended like it never bothered me, which was easy when I was so reserved. I could go home and be myself around my parents and Emma.'

Hannah hazarded a quick glance at Matt, who was sitting very still, refusing to interrupt.

'Then, towards the end of uni, I met someone. He was funny and popular. For some reason he was interested in me. I didn't understand why at the time. I was quiet—I loved being on my computer more than socialising—but he still asked me out. It was flattering, you know? My parents had died in an accident not long before and I was vulnerable.'

Hannah played with a button on her dress. She didn't realise she was doing it until Matt's thumb stroked her fingers. 'We went out for a long time. I was certain I would marry him; I mean, I loved him with my whole heart, and he said he loved me. After we graduated, he pushed me to accept a job at a much more prestigious company than his, but he said he was happy for me. In fact, I thought he was going to pop the question soon after.'

'What happened?' Matt's voice had grown low. It resonated through his chest into hers.

'He broke me,' she all but whispered. 'He often worked late or had to travel out of town. I trusted him implicitly so I never thought to question it. Turns out he wasn't travelling at all. One time, I had forgotten something at his place and, since I had a key, I went in. I don't think he ever expected me to use it. I knew he didn't like anyone going in when he wasn't there. Except he was…with another woman. She was pregnant, Matt.' Her voice cracked despite how hard she tried to remain strong.

Matt's arms tightened around her. 'Hannah.'

'You know what he said when I confronted him?'

'What?'

'"Did you really think you would be enough for me?" I gave him all my trust and he shattered it.' Hannah felt the growl that came from Matt.

'I don't understand.'

'he wasn't gifted at all really, but he was exceptionally entitled and lazy. He only asked me out after news of the attention I was getting from companies got out. He saw an opportunity. It was clear my career trajectory would surpass his, and here was an easy way to get what he wanted without having to work for it. That job he pushed me to take was purely because he liked the money on offer. I didn't want to accept it when there was an offer from my dream employer on the table. All I asked for was his affection and I thought I had it. I was wrong.'

She could hear how Matt's breathing changed. Feel the anger radiating off him. Having this reaction made her throat feel less dry. It was as though this story was losing power over her because she was telling Matt.

'He made me feel special at first but, over time, bit by bit he broke me down and I didn't really notice until after. He made me feel like I was nothing without him. Told me I wasn't the type of person he normally dated so I would be grateful to him. Told me no man would ever want a "useless" woman who couldn't bear children so I was lucky to have him. And I believed it all. Caved to his every demand because I wanted to make him happy. I was an idiot, wasn't I?'

Hannah laughed humourlessly, realising just how little she'd asked of Travis and how much he'd taken from her. How little she'd asked of anyone after him because she refused to trust. She wasn't naïve any more.

'No, you weren't,' Matt said forcefully.

'It was Emma who showed me exactly how badly I'd been treated when I was finally ready to see clearly. After Travis, I gave up on the whole idea of a relationship. It was so much easier to just have flings. No commitment meant no one would get hurt.'

'*You* wouldn't get hurt,' Matt stated, kissing her temple. Hannah felt the tremble, from his lips to his arms to his voice. She had never seen fury in Matt and was slightly afraid to look now. So she didn't, she just kept talking.

'Yes,' Hannah whispered. 'I changed who I was. Became more outgoing, bubbly. I always had a ready smile and a thick skin. People liked that, and it felt safe, because they couldn't see me and that was the most important thing. It was exactly as you said—it was my armour.'

'But it's exhausting.'

'It is,' she agreed. It had been, always having to remember to keep that persona perfectly in place, never to show when she'd felt something real. When she'd been tired. It was draining.

Then she'd met a man who shone like the sun with gorgeous green eyes and everything had changed. 'You saw me,' she said softly, mostly to herself, but she knew he had heard her when he forced her to look at him.

His eyes were dark, nostrils flaring, a tick going in his jaw, and even though he still held her Matt's hands kept curling in and out of a fist. His anger was savage. If Travis had magically apparated out of thin air, there was no denying that Matt would have ripped him apart.

'I'm sorry you went through that. You deserved so much better.'

'Yes, I did.'

Hannah looked at Matt then. Really looked at him. At how he was furious at the treatment of her, as if he was ready to fight the world to protect her. She recognised that his every atom of attention was all focussed on her. That love, that she was so afraid of feeling for him, burgeoned into something so consuming it was scorching her from the inside out, wiping out the existence of everything else.

She hooked her hand at his nape, pulling him to her, sucking his lips between hers and hearing his gasp which made sparks fly in her belly. Pressing herself against Matt or pulling him closer—she wasn't sure which she was doing—Hannah licked his lips, seeking permission, which he granted with tightening arms. Her tongue brushed against his, sweetly at first, but the jolt of current that passed through them made her ravenous for more and Matt obliged, offering more of himself to her. She was melting. Growing more aroused with every strangled, choked sound he made. They had to stop, or she would want him right now, outside, in full view of the world.

She pulled away first, but Matt pressed a kiss to her forehead, letting her rest there against his lips.

'I have never told anyone that whole story, but I told you,

Matt. I trust you. I just hope you know you can trust me.' It was an opening for Matt to talk to her. She'd proved she could expose herself to him and he could do the same.

'I do trust you.' There was hesitancy in his voice. Hannah studied his face, seeing the openness that had been there a moment ago disappearing. He wasn't going to say a damned thing. She'd bared the deepest wound inflicted upon her soul and still he couldn't take that next step.

Hannah felt a fool. Why did she think this was a good idea? Just because she was in love with him didn't mean that he loved her.

Fool. Fool. Fool.

She swung her legs off him, awkwardly getting to her feet.

'Hannah, wait…' Matt called after her, but she was already at the glass door.

'Goodnight, Matt.'

Hannah rushed to her bedroom and closed the door. That was where she stayed.

CHAPTER NINETEEN

AFTER HAVING HAD Hannah in his bed every night, the sheets felt cold without her in them. She had shut Matt out and now he was lying in his darkened room, staring at a pitch-black ceiling.

Though he was utterly still, inside he was trembling. His skin felt too tight, too hot. His breathing hadn't evened out at all and, despite being in his cool, comfortable bedroom, he kept rubbing his knuckles as if he could punch something.

Fury still roiled through him.

The idea that anyone could treat Hannah so vilely made him ache for violence. Which was surprising, because violent was not how he would ever have described himself. Not even during all the years he'd played rugby and sometimes tempers had run high. He had been the guy who'd defused a situation. Not now. Now he wanted some sort of retribution for what Hannah had gone through. Matt wanted to find the guy and make him pay in some way. He could—it would be easy.

After she'd left him on the terrace, he had contemplated going down to the gym to pummel the massive punching bag. Except he couldn't leave the apartment. It would have felt too much like walking away from Hannah when her wounds had been reopened.

His perfect Hannah had turned herself into something else because of some arse who'd exploited her goodness and walked all over her. It had been then when Matt had understood her terms. She couldn't allow herself to be pushed around by another man. And he had forced her hand, hadn't he? Was he no better than…?

Travis. Matt felt ill when he thought of the name. He hadn't suggested it with any seriousness in the car. He'd just carelessly tossed out a name. Then he had seen her face and instantly regretted it. How could he have known? It didn't excuse him. If he had been taking the naming as seriously as he should have been when she'd brought it up, he wouldn't even have said the blasted name.

Hannah never needed to be reminded of that again.

It was no surprise that she couldn't trust. Tonight, though, she'd proved that she trusted him. Putting herself out there like that was the bravest thing he had seen. He knew what she was trying to do. Hannah was only trying to be there for him, and he'd pushed her away when she'd been vulnerable. He never remembered being such an arsehole before.

He needed to apologise—first thing in the morning, because it was late and she needed rest. Also, he couldn't talk to her feeling like this. He needed to get himself under control. If he was being entirely honest, part of his anger was directed at himself for hurting her tonight. But she was asking for something he just couldn't give her. All he wanted to do was to force away all the feelings from yesterday. Hannah already got more of him than anyone else. His mind drifted back to his last night in Melbourne and that night had proved as much. They had been so consumed by each other. They still were. All Hannah had to do was walk into a room to rob him of breath. She distracted him from work constantly, with his thoughts of how he had explored her body. Of what she would be doing. And he could see the attraction in her eyes when she looked at him.

God, that look.

Yes, they were still consumed by each other, but things were different now.

Still, the memory of that night played behind his closed eyelids…

* * *

A room away, Hannah lay in bed, thinking of the same night…

Seven months ago

Hannah had spent most of the day with Emma. Matt had wanted to spend time with Alex, and she understood. He had come all this way to see his friend until she had stolen him away. Hannah couldn't bring herself to feel bad about it. Not when he was the only thing she could think about today. In twenty-four hours he'd be gone and she was trying not to fall to pieces. She missed him already. Stupid, really, because he hadn't climbed aboard the plane yet. How could you miss someone who was still around?

It felt as if the first breath she'd taken that day was when the four of them met for dinner. She and Matt sat side by side, holding hands under the table all night. He barely looked at her and, when he did, despite the smile on his face his eyes seemed dull. She felt the same.

Trying so hard to be as ebullient as she was known to be, Hannah forced smiles and laughter, but inside she was crumbling. Matt's hand gripped hers tighter, as if he would pull her into himself if he could. She wanted the world to disappear. Wanted to pause time so they could take something for themselves. Maybe live in that stationary moment for ever.

'I'll be home in a bit,' Emma said when dinner was done, and she left with Alex. Hannah turned to Matt, not ready to say goodbye. She couldn't.

'Come with me?' Matt asked her. His voice was low, cutting out, as if he couldn't get it to work properly.

In bed now, Matt ran his fingers through his hair, folding his arms behind his head, his gaze firmly on the past…

Hannah's hand was held tightly in his as they walked to a nearby hotel. He needed to be alone with her, have her all to himself. He didn't want the distraction of friends or cats. It needed it to be just Hannah and him. Neither did he have the patience to make it back to her flat or Alex's.

It barely took any time at all for him to get the key card to the last available room, a suite on the top floor. Maybe the universe was giving them a small gift.

In the lift, Matt didn't kiss Hannah. He wasn't sure he would be able to stop if he did. Instead, he pulled her against his body, resting his head on hers, inhaling her scent so he could commit it to memory. When they finally entered the suite, neither of them took the time to look around. It didn't matter. They simply sat on the couch in silence for just a moment. This was breaking Matt apart.

'Hannah,' he said. It was one word, but it so honestly conveyed exactly what he felt: sadness at having to leave her; regret that they couldn't be more; happiness that he found her at all.

He wasn't sure who moved first, all he knew was that their lips met somewhere in the middle. He yanked Hannah over so she was straddling his lap. Aching to feel her closer, he held her against him, lips desperately moving over hers, swallowing every bitten-off sound that was driving him insane. He needed to feel her right now but there were too many clothes in the way.

'Touch me,' he whispered breathily against her lips, pleading, and she did. She made short work of the buttons and pushed his shirt and coat wide, exposing his body. Then her hands were on his face, scraping lightly against his jaw, and Matt's eyes fluttered closed. Her fingers skated over his neck, and then every contour of his chest and stomach, and there was nothing. Nothing existed in this world except Hannah and her touch that was heating his skin and making his heart race.

Every thought was blown from his mind.

It was as if she was forcing her fingers to remember every bit of him and Matt understood that. His every sense was focussed on her. On the sounds of appreciation for his body. On the scent of her hair, her skin, her arousal tinting the air. On the look on her face and the flame of her hair. His hands slid up her thighs…he'd never forget the silk of her skin. And then he kissed her and was consumed by her taste…sweet.

Matt was coming apart for her. He shrugged off his shirt and coat while Hannah moved off him, taking his trousers and underwear with, making his hardness spring free. She settled between his bare feet, taking his length in her hand, licking him from base to tip. He couldn't take it any more. He missed her lips on his and pulled her up, kissing her hard, but she pulled away, shucking off her clothes while never once taking her eyes off him.

He held his breath as she climbed on him once more, holding herself just above his hardness.

'Don't hide anything from me tonight,' he begged her.

'I won't.'

His body tensed like it never had before when Hannah lowered herself slowly onto him but she didn't move.

'Please, Hannah…'

In her bed now, Hannah turned onto her side. A tear trickled down the side of her nose, falling onto the pillow…

Hearing Matt so desperate, knowing he sounded that way because of her, made Hannah feel euphoric as nothing else ever had. Matt was all there was in her heart right now.

'Take me, Matt.'

She needed him so badly. Needed him to unleash himself upon her. To have him bare himself to her; maybe that would keep her glued together. She needed to feel whole with him.

Hannah wrapped her legs around his waist as he picked her up and walked them to the bedroom, where he laid her down gently on the covers.

She had never seen his eyes so dark. That handsome face

that always seemed to have a smile didn't have one now. All she could see was heat in his eyes and sorrow on his face. It was impossible not to be moved by this man. In a week she had gone from dancing with him in a club to wishing he would never leave, but she knew that he had to. His life was in London and hers was here in Melbourne.

Reaching up, she cupped his cheek and he leaned into the touch, kissing her palm. And then her wrist. And then her shoulder. When he sucked down her neck, she gasped, and when his lips closed around her nipple she arched into his mouth.

'So perfect,' he said against her skin. Hannah's whole body was shaking with need. A light breeze might have made her explode.

'Matt, I...'

'Shh,' he soothed with more kisses before pressing his forehead to hers and entering her with a hard thrust. 'You will always be perfect.'

Tears sprang to her eyes from his words and the feel of him rocking into her with the full power of his hips. Unintelligible moans were pouring from her as he took them both to the edge and then over, falling, shattering together. Hannah clenching around Matt whose strangled groan as he filled her made electricity dance over her body.

It had never been like this with anyone, and she was sure it never would be again.

Both Matt and Hannah lay in the dark of night, trying to reach for that perfect moment that had changed everything.

CHAPTER TWENTY

THERE WAS A pounding behind Matt's eyes that refused to abate. He leaned his forehead against the upper cupboards as rich, dark coffee spilt from the portafilter into his cup. He'd had to make it stronger than usual this morning. He hadn't got a wink of sleep. All he could think about was their last night in Melbourne and what Hannah had recently told him. The trust she'd placed in him. Matt lifted his glasses, pinching the bridge of his nose.

He needed to talk to Hannah, clear the air. She was so important to him and not just because of their son. He pulled his cup out from under the spout just as the machine clicked off. Shuffling footsteps sounded behind him and he sensed Hannah enter before she uttered a tired, 'Good morning...'

Turning round, he saw she looked exactly as he did—puffy eyes with dark bruises underneath. Her shoulders were slightly slumped forward. Apparently neither of them had got any sleep the night before.

Matt placed a cup of peppermint tea next to her. He had to apologise before he said anything else. 'Hannah.' She turned to face him, looking so tired he felt his heart clench at the sight. 'I'm sorry about last night. I didn't mean to hurt you, but I am glad you told me.'

'It's fine, Matt. I shouldn't have—'

'No.' He cut her off. 'You should have. I'm always in your corner. I just don't know how to do this. Be what you're looking for.'

* * *

Hannah fought the urge to shake her head. She accepted his apology. How could she not? But he wasn't being honest with himself.

All night she'd lain in that bed, thinking about their week together in Melbourne. The things he'd said to her. How he had touched her. That last night, nothing had come between them. He had asked her not to hide, and she hadn't, because all week he had shown her who he was.

Matt couldn't stand here and tell her that he didn't know how to be what she wanted—which was just himself—when she had seen the real Matt in Melbourne. That was who he was, not this person who hid his emotions.

Feeling bold, she took a step forward—just one—and placed her hand on his bare chest over his heart. Gazing into his eyes, she said, 'Yes, you do, because all I want is you, but you've locked yourself away.'

Hannah saw the shift in his eyes, from apprehension to scorching heat, hands at his sides curling and uncurling into fists.

He took a small step towards her, and then another, closing the distance between them entirely. Hannah licked her bottom lip and his eyes darted to the movement before meeting hers once more. A warm finger curled under her chin, tilting up her head. She watched him lean closer until he was kissing her. Slowly. Gently. Thoroughly.

A jolt of electricity passed through her body, settling into a constant flutter in her belly. Matt was taking his time. The part of her that was still capable of thought was reminded of their first kiss—how deliberate that had been. But this one was different too. He'd been learning her, seducing her, with that kiss in the club. This was more. It felt as though he was worshipping her with his mouth, saying things with it he couldn't say aloud.

She raised her other hand to his chest, wanting to grab hold, but there was no shirt, just planes of muscle. They were hard and comforting and so very Matt. His skin was growing hotter beneath her touch and all she wanted to do was hold onto to him so tightly.

He must have sensed it because he picked her up and sat her on the kitchen counter, moving to stand between her legs. His mouth never once left hers. Here, she was practically as tall as he was. She wrapped her arms around his neck, feeling his large hands on her sides. His thumbs caressed her belly and she could have cried.

His lips skated over jaw, down to her neck, and she threw her head back with a sigh.

'I can feel your pulse racing.' There was wonder in his voice. 'My Hannah.'

He licked her there. Hannah's whole body was on fire now and, when Matt's mouth closed over the cotton fabric covering her sensitive nipples, she mewled. His tongue laved her, wetting the night dress she wore, until she felt she would come apart just from that. But he pulled away, only to press his forehead against hers.

'The things you make me feel,' he said under his breath. Hannah wasn't sure she was meant to hear it.

'You make me feel too, Matt.'

'I'm sorry,' he whispered.

'I know.'

'I need you, Hannah.'

'Then have me.' She was craving his touch so badly that if they stopped now she would likely expire. It was more than that. Last night she had realised how much she wanted Matt. How much she wanted him to love her back. And these touches made it feel so much as though he did that Hannah wanted to stay in this space. She had seen glimpses of the man she knew him to be over these last two months, had seen what they could be, and it made her want to stay.

Her breath left her in a giggle when he scooped her off the

counter in a bridal carry, taking her into his room. Their cups of tea and coffee were long forgotten.

He set her on her feet only long enough to get rid of her night gown then laid her gently in the middle of his enormous bed. He removed his trousers and underwear then slid in beside her.

Hannah reached up and removed his glasses. 'These things are unfair.'

'Why?' he asked with a frown.

'Because you're so damn beautiful, you don't need to make me want you more.' She huffed.

'You think I'm beautiful?' Matt smirked.

'Shut up! You know you are.' Hannah laughed, utterly connected to Matt right now…

The sound of her laughter would always be his favourite thing. Just hearing it did something to Matt's heart.

How did I get so lucky? he thought to himself, seeing Hannah look at him the way she was doing.

Her touch in the kitchen had seared him right to his soul. She could see him, and it felt so damn good to be seen, but he still couldn't let go. Love was a foreign concept to him. He didn't know how to do it but this woman made him feel everything so intensely.

Like he did right now with her brown eyes that could hold a whole universe, fixed on him. Matt brushed her hair back, losing himself in her flame.

'I know *you* are,' he said, voice like gravel. He could do nothing but kiss her then. Every force on earth acted to pull him to her lips. He felt so out of control. He wanted to devour her, but at the same time to take his time. To make her feel treasured yet ravish her. So it was no surprise that he was trembling when he swept his tongue into her mouth and she moaned. Lips sliding against each other's, heart hammering against his ribs, Matt skated his hand to her breasts, teasing her nipple with his thumb, so careful not to make it uncomfortable. Pleasure…this was all about pleasure. And trying to show her what she meant to him.

Satisfaction curled around his spine when she panted, her voice coming in broken little pieces. It wasn't enough. Running his hand over her round belly, he moved lower still, hovering over her sex. Hannah was writhing below him. Trying desperately to reach his hand that he deliberately kept away from her.

'Please, Matt,' Hannah begged.

This woman, so capable and confident, would never have begged anyone else—just him. The thought was both sobering and made him high. 'I'm going to make you feel so good, sweetheart,' he whispered in her ear at the same time his finger slipped into her folds. Her keening whine shot through his body as she pressed her face into his neck.

Matt held her firmly, telling her she was safe, that she could let go while his fingers slowly slid in and out of her, drenched in her wetness. His thumb teased her. And, even though he was the one making her come apart, his breath was just as rapid as hers.

'I…' was all she got out before she fell apart in his arms and the sight was the most beautiful thing he'd ever had the privilege to witness.

Taking his fingers from her, he pulled her against him so her back was against his chest. They fitted so perfectly together. Right then, he knew joy.

Matt peppered kisses along Hannah's neck and shoulders. Each touch fired off a thousand different sparks until she was craving his touch again. It wasn't just the touch that was currently shredding her heart in the best way. Hannah had been feeling uncomfortable, less sexy with each passing day, but Matt blew right through her insecurities. He was so gentle and considerate. Being on her side like this, with his hard warm body pressed up against her, was the most comfortable she'd been in days. That didn't take away from the fact that she could feel his erection and wanted it inside her.

Thank God she didn't have to ask, because she felt him at her entrance, then slowly push into her with a strangled groan.

'Hannah. How are you so perfect? It's like you were meant for me.'

How she hoped she was. Rocking his hips, Matt slid in deeply and out. A curse flew out on his rushed breath. Her own was sticking in her throat. She was being carried away on a cloud of sensation where she was above everything, yet tethered to this bed, where Matt was taking her apart and putting her back together with every thrust.

Then Matt laced their fingers together, making her touch herself with his guidance. It was so utterly intimate. She was racing towards release and, from the sound of Matt's gruff pants, so was he.

'With me, sweetheart—' he choked.

Always! her brain screamed at her, but she couldn't get the words out, not when she was climbing, climbing, climbing, then shattering around Matt, bearing down on him as his muffled shout sounded against her neck.

Her body went limp in his arms. Sex with Matt was always amazing, but this time it was so different. It wasn't just sex. He had taken care of her. He had apologised and worshipped her.

This wasn't sex at all. This time, they'd made love, and it made Hannah's heart sing.

CHAPTER TWENTY-ONE

LYING TOGETHER, bodies pressed tight, the thumping of their hearts could be felt, rocketing through each other as if they were one, their hearts fused eternally.

Hannah had never felt so at one with Matt than she did right now. And given how tightly he was holding her—one arm possessively around her belly—she imagined that he was feeling the very same way.

She wanted to lie here with him and forget the world. Bask in this moment for as long as she could. She'd been so hurt the night before but now that seemed like aeons ago.

Needing to look at Matt, Hannah turned around in his arms. Fingertips scratching through the stubble that had grown overnight, she watched him slowly open his eyes. There was something in the way he looked at her that made warmth spread out from her chest. As fun as it had been, they had shared something powerful.

She wanted him to know how she felt. The words coalesced on her tongue.

'Matt...' His name came out softer than she had meant but somehow it seemed like the loudest sound in the world. That one word was all it took; she could see him withdraw. Whatever emotion had been in his eyes just a second ago evaporated until his face was a neutral mask, and she wanted to scream.

He still held back. After what they'd done in this bed, with his arms still around her, he couldn't open up.

Hannah wasn't sure what he could see on her face. She never could hide anything from him. Whatever he saw was making his jaw tick. All that peace from a moment before was incinerated, replaced with anger and frustration.

'You know what? Never mind.' She climbed off the bed, pulling the sheet with her.

'Hannah, stop.'

'I need a shower,' she said stiffly, not bothering to meet his eyes. Wrapping the soft sheet tightly around herself, she looked around for her night dress, only to find it pooled on the floor. It was fine, she didn't need it.

She rushed out of Matt's bedroom without a backward glance. There was no way she was going to show him how much it hurt her when he shut down. She was going to ignore the burning behind her eyes. As soon as she was in her own room, she closed the door and stepped into the *en suite* bathroom, closing that door too for good measure. She didn't bother locking it. Why would Matt follow her? He had nothing to say to her.

The sheet was dropped unceremoniously to the floor then she stepped under the jets of hot water, letting the torrent fall over her, shutting out the world.

Steam clouded the bathroom, fogging up the mirror, until she felt totally alone. The warmth was barely enough to chase the chill that had crept under her skin. She stood there under the water, trying to collect her thoughts, arrange them into something that made any sense and push away the emotion that was making it hard to think. She needed the logic now that she had so relied on for her whole life. It was her greatest strength.

She pushed her hair back, turning her face up to the water. How could Matt be so tender and giving, be the man she wanted so much who kept saying he wanted to be a family, and still shut her out?

Wanting wasn't loving, was it? *She* was the one who'd fallen in love, not Matt. He hadn't promised her that. But he confused her. If they'd never succumbed to their chemistry, things would be clearer. That had been impossible, though. From the moment she'd seen him, she'd wanted to be back in his arms. Except he just wanted to do the right thing for his child.

Hannah cursed herself. Maybe she was so blinded by her feelings that she didn't see this for what it was. But, even if that was true, the way he touched her made her feel treasured. The way the Matt from his holiday had done. Those touches had made her consider a life with him. How long would that life be? He wanted to be a family for their child but children grew up. So would this be their life for eighteen years? Twenty?

Hannah curled her arms around her belly. She agreed to two months and that time was almost up. Her due date was just around the corner. She had coloured three weeks before and a week after her due date in red on the calendar. The red zone. She was well into that now which meant their trial period was ending and a decision had to be made.

Matt was doing everything right for their child. There was no denying that. From accompanying her to every doctor's appointment, renovating the house, buying the car and babyproofing the apartment and the other house. It was amazing. There was already an assembled cot, drawers full of clothes sized from new-born to six months. She couldn't forget the feeling of seeing the car seat for the first time. Two months out and it had already been in place just in case.

He was a provider all right. Seeing Matt in 'caring dad' mode was one of the most incredible things to witness. It made her love him more, which was why she was hurting now. He was a loving family man. There was no doubt about that. The weekend at Sarah's home had more than adequately proven that. Having heard what their childhood had been like, it was completely understandable why Matt had been reluctant to have his own children, but he was thriving in this role.

At least, she'd thought he was. Herein lay the problem. Yes, he was making the right gestures for the family, but would she ever know what he was truly feeling? When he was over-whelmed, nervous or hurting? She wanted to be there for him so desperately. Unfortunately, that wasn't something she could force. He had to want it, want her that way.

At the moment, he only wanted their chemistry. It felt as though they were some weird combination of friends with benefits, who were also having a baby and starting a family that needed to be stable and perfect. Definitely not normal and far from enough.

At least for her.

Hannah shut off the taps. Wallowing in this steamy bath-room was accomplishing nothing. She didn't hide. Didn't shy away from a challenge. There was no way in hell she would start now.

She stepped out of the shower cubicle, wrapping a towel around herself and towelling her hair dry with another. She was determined now. She needed answers from Matt. Infor-mation was the only logical way to make a decision. Finding a way forward was dependent on honesty. Whatever that way would be, Hannah was certain she would be able to do it.

CHAPTER TWENTY-TWO

HANNAH DRESSED QUICKLY, giving little thought to what she wore or how she looked. None of that was important now. Her hands were trembling as she ran a brush through her damp hair.

Was she afraid of the answers Matt would give her? Of course she was. But she was done living in limbo. Done fooling herself that she could believe they were a family.

'You can do this,' she said fiercely to her reflection in the bathroom mirror.

Taking a deep breath, she slipped on her sandals, straightened her aching back and went in search of Matt.

She found him in the lounge, instead of his office as she would have expected. It was the first place he went when he wanted to enforce the distance between them. Hannah watched him for a moment. His damp golden hair stuck up at odd angles as if he had rubbed a towel through it and subsequently forgotten its existence. A deep groove sat between his brows, glasses on his nose.

Her heart gave a lurch but it was time. She couldn't put this off any longer no matter how much she wished he would look up from the laptop on his legs, set it aside and say he was wrong to shut her out.

Wishes were ridiculous. They provided neither knowledge nor comfort. All they did was make her pine for the impossible.

'Matt?' she called as she entered the room.

He looked up at her and somehow his frown grew deeper. 'We need to talk.'

He closed the laptop, placing it on the table, and patted the cushion next to him but Hannah shook her head. Proximity to Matt was dangerous. She needed a clear head and the moment she smelled that cool scent on him her thoughts became foggy. She would remain standing.

'Hannah…' he started, but she held up her hand and he stopped. She didn't want another apology or an excuse.

'Before we say anything, I want you to promise you will be honest with me now.'

His face softened. 'I always am.'

That wasn't technically true, but she wasn't getting into that just yet. She was about to take his words as agreement, then she thought better of it. 'Promise me.'

'I promise.'

She nodded, looking out of the window at the morning sunlight. It was still morning. With everything that had happened, it was hard to believe so little time had passed since she'd been in Matt's bed, with him making love to her.

No! Focus! she scolded herself.

'When you proposed marriage, I thought you were crazy. I thought a trial period would work better. A relationship alpha-test, if you will. Our two months are almost up.' Hannah kept her voice even, held all emotion back. She didn't want Matt to comfort her or feel as if he needed to shield her from his thoughts, as she knew he would if she showed the slightest hint of being upset. He always picked up on what she needed. Well, now she was going to use his own tricks against him. Everything she felt was being shut away.

'I know,' he said carefully, eyes searching her face. But Hannah knew he would see nothing there. 'I think we could be a great family.'

Wasn't that the truth? They could be.

'The house is almost done. We could move in by the weekend.'

The vision Hannah had seen when they'd visited the house in Belgravia flashed before her eyes. Matt and her son playing, strolling through the park. Family picnics. But after? Matt in his office. Hannah in her own bedroom after a day of work. Being with Matt only with their son in tow or when they had sex.

It wasn't enough.

'That's soon,' she said.

'It is.'

'But that won't help me make this decision,' Hannah stated plainly.

Matt's face fell before he schooled it into something emotionless. 'What are you saying? Are you considering us not being a family? I told you—I won't lose my son.'

'We will always be a family whether we're together or not. We have a child together. Maybe it won't be a traditional one, but it will still be one.' Hannah looked down at the glossy hardwood floors before meeting Matt's gaze. 'I'm not going to keep our baby from you. Not ever. You can see him whenever you want.'

'You do want to leave.' His voice was hard.

'I didn't say that.' She didn't *want* to leave. How could she? No one ever wanted to leave the person they loved. That would be crazy. Except Matt didn't know she loved him. She hadn't told him so.

'Then what are you saying?' His eyes were burning right through her now.

'I'm saying I haven't made a decision, but I would like to, and only you can help me do that.'

'What about our son?' he fired at her.

'No, not even him.' She took one step towards him. 'Do you trust me?'

'You know I do,' Matt snapped.

'No, I really don't. You told me you're always honest with me, but you don't ever tell me everything. You have such impenetrable walls around you, Matt, that no one gets to see all of you.'

'Hannah, listen—' he said impatiently.

'No, you listen. You wanted us to be a family for our child, to prove you could be the man you should be. It's not enough to build a life.'

'It could be,' Matt said softly, fire still blazing in his eyes. His posture had gone rigid, as if it was taking everything he had to stay seated.

'I need you to answer me honestly.'

'I already said I would.' There was impatience in his tone.

Given how Matt had grown up, what his father had been like, Hannah had to ask this question. 'Will you love our child?'

'Of course I will!' Earnestness poured out of him that warmed Hannah's heart. A heart that was now hammering in her chest.

'Will you ever love me?' she asked, working to control her breathing. Keeping calm, as though this wouldn't make or break them.

'I don't know,' he replied, voice rough, regret flashing on his face.

Hannah's heart crumbled. Part of her knew the answer but hearing it just wasn't easy. 'I can't be in a marriage without love.' She swallowed hard and moved to sit on the sturdy table in front of Matt, taking one of his hands in hers. 'I don't want to be loved less than our baby, Matt. I've already not been enough for someone; I won't put myself through that for the rest of my life.'

Matt brought her hand to his lips, whispering brokenly, 'Hannah, please.'

'You'll be a great father. I know you will.' She placed the palm of her other hand on his cheek. 'You mean so much to me, but I don't need you. I can be enough for myself and our child. And he will be the luckiest little boy in the world, because both his parents will love him very much, but I can't do this. So my decision is made. I'm sorry.' Hannah pulled away from Matt and strode from the room.

CHAPTER TWENTY-THREE

MATT RUSHED AFTER HANNAH, following her into her room. She pulled her small suitcase out from the dressing room and began haphazardly packing it with her clothes. Hers, Matt noted—not any of the garments he had purchased for her. She was walking out and not even letting him do what he'd promised to—provide. His stomach was turning over. He couldn't let her go.

'Hannah, please. Reconsider.'

Her eyes met his and they looked so tired. This was wrong. It was all wrong. He tried to reach for her but she stepped away, shaking her head.

'What about our son? I don't want to miss anything.' Matt was trying so hard to rein in the panic in his gut. Hide the fact that he was breaking apart, watching Hannah dump the contents of her closet into the bag, but that control seemed like such an alien thing right now. No matter how hard he reached for it, it wouldn't come to him.

'You won't, Matt. You can see him whenever you want. I would never keep you away. But "us" can't happen. It can't be one-sided. This is for the best.' She slammed the hard-shell case shut and placed it on the floor. Matt looked around wildly for any bit of divine inspiration to keep her here. To stop her from walking out of his life.

Hannah looked at the ring on her finger and pried it off, placing it gently in his hand that she had taken in hers. She made to remove the necklace given to her the night before, but Matt wouldn't let her.

'No. You're keeping that.'

Hannah grabbed the handle of the suitcase and turned to leave.

Matt's throat was thick, burning. 'At least let me drive you wherever you want to go.' He ran his fingers through his hair in desperation. 'Go to Sarah, then. I promise not to call but you'll be safe. She'll take care of you.'

Hannah's eyes softened then, filled with tears, and his heart desiccated.

'Bye, Matt.'

She turned around and walked into the lift and, as much as he wanted to follow her, he knew she would turn him back.

The doors slid closed and then there was silence pressing in on him from every side, deafening, suffocating. He was so utterly broken. He stared at the closed lift doors, polished and sealed shut, taunting him. He wanted to rip it apart. He wanted to rip apart this whole goddamned apartment. His family was gone.

In a daze, he went back into Hannah's room. Her scent hung in the air. In his hand, twinkling as if the world wasn't ending, sat her ring. He curled his fist around it until it felt as though the diamonds would tear into his skin. At least that pain would feel better than this.

He couldn't breathe. Couldn't stay here a moment longer.

Grabbing his wallet and keys from his office, Matt left the apartment as if he were being chased by the hounds of hell. He needed out. Pressing the button on his key fob once when he got down to the parking garage, he realised that, without thinking, he'd taken the keys for the S8. Hannah was everywhere. But it wouldn't matter which car he took, she would be on his mind, an unrelenting spectre.

He started up the car and Matt drove to the only person he wanted to see now.

* * *

Tyres crunched on gravel as he brought the car to a stop and as soon as he shut the door he saw Sarah walk outside, her hair messily tied on the crown of her head, in jeans and a tank-top. Her feet were in flip-flops. She must have been working in her studio.

'Bear? I saw you on the security camera.'

'Shrimp,' was all he could say before engulfing her in a hug.

'Come on, let's go have some cake, and if you want to talk we can do that.' There were no questions. No comments about how busy she was or about work. Matt loved his sister so much and, in that moment, didn't know what he had ever done to deserve her. He was just grateful.

A short time later they sat at the round table in Sarah's spacious kitchen, a mug of steaming black coffee in front of Matt and Sarah was cutting into a cake that looked far too good to eat and placing it on two plates.

Only then did he realise how hungry he was. So much had happened this morning, the day felt ten years long.

Sarah handed him a plate and fork but, despite how good the cake looked, Matt couldn't bring himself to eat. He didn't want a confection; he wanted his family. He stabbed at the cake with his fork until his sister reached across the table and squeezed his hand.

'She left,' he heard himself saying. Sarah didn't reply; Matt took that as an invitation to go on, so he told her everything, from the moment they'd met in Melbourne to Hannah walking out now. Of course, he had told her about it before, but this time Matt filled in every little omitted detail. When he was done, Sarah moved their plates aside and held both his hands.

'She's right. You have locked yourself away. You did when you were ten years old. It seems to me like you opened up to her in Melbourne but now you've shut her out. Let me ask you this—all those women you dated before, you had no problem with them then, why does it all bother you so much now?'

'I'm just tired of it. None of them know me. It's all so superficial,' Matt answered, avoiding his sister's eyes.

'Don't you see? You were honest with her in Melbourne because that's what you wanted. You were entirely yourself with her because there was no other way you could be.'

Sarah was right. He knew she was.

'You know what your problem is? You're so busy trying to be perfect. The perfect brother, perfect son, perfect friend, perfect boss. Our parents are gone, Bear. You don't have to be that any more. You're trying to live up to the impossible demands of an imperfect father.'

'Sarah...' He pulled his hands out of hers, rubbing his face.

'Matt, don't you get it?' Sarah never called him 'Matt', not unless she was well and truly frustrated with him, and he smiled a little. 'Our father was more demanding than he had any right to be. What he asked of you was wrong. Being emotionless doesn't make you a man, it makes you a bad parent.'

'We turned out okay.'

'Did we? I only felt truly loved when I was around you. Did you ever feel that way?'

Matt didn't answer.

'And now you're trying to fight that, be someone you're not, and all it's done is make you lose Hannah. You need someone who will challenge you, Bear, and she needs someone to show her it's okay to trust someone with her heart. Would you ever treat your child like our father treated us?'

'Never!'

'Then be open with her because that's exactly what you're doing now.' Sarah shook her head, her voice dipping to hushed tones as she said, 'I hate our parents so much for what they asked of you. I hate that Dad wanted you to be an emotionless robot like him. You've never been that. You love so openly, it makes us want to do anything for you.'

'Us?'

'Me, Alex, Hannah.'

Matt shook his head. He had avoided thinking of his friend. While the sting of the betrayal had dulled, it was still there. He had always thought they were honest with each other, would have each other's backs. That was what brothers did—they would do anything for each other, including protecting the people that were important to them. Matt cursed.

He finally understood. Alex hadn't told him Hannah's secret. She'd asked for trust and Alex hadn't betrayed it. Not even for his best friend. Alex had protected Hannah—even though she wasn't his to protect—for Matt.

'You can't say you don't understand love when you practically raised me, tried to make sure Mum was happy. You do know what love is. Always have, despite our parents. You understood what she and Dad had wasn't good. Why else would you be afraid of doing that to someone else?'

'But I did the same, didn't I?' Matt covered his eyes with a large hand, shame curling in his belly. 'I did exactly what he did to Mum.'

'You can fix this. It's not too late. She loves you.'

Matt threw his head back, wetness in his eyes. He knew she did. He tried to ignore it, but he knew it, and he'd still let her slip away.

'Bear…' Sarah sounded choked by her own tears, but he couldn't look to confirm. 'You love her too. You wouldn't be in this much pain if you didn't.'

She was completely right. That night he had gone to the bar with Hannah, seeing her hide her real self had bothered him so much, but it had also felt incredible to know she was genuinely herself when she was with him. As if he was special. Thinking back, that was the night he'd known he loved her. Which meant that, even though he'd been telling himself that his baby had been conceived out of lust, in an uncontrolled moment, he'd actually been conceived out of love. He'd been so desperate to show Hannah his heart that night. Because he was in love with her!

God, he was an idiot!

'I have to get her back,' he said, suddenly jumping to his feet.

'Then what are you waiting for?' Sarah gave him a watery smile. Matt hugged her, kissing her on the cheek.

'I love you, Shrimp.'

'I love you too, Bear. Go!'

Matt had to find Hannah.

CHAPTER TWENTY-FOUR

THE MOMENT SHE was out of Matt's building, Hannah sent Emma a message, telling her she had left Matt's and intended to check back into the hotel she had previously stayed at, but she didn't get the chance to. Hannah felt an almighty pain, like a cramp except ten times worse.

'No. No, no, no. This can't be happening today...' She clamped an arm around her stomach, the muscles hardening. Breathing through her mouth, Hannah tried to keep calm until it passed.

Hannah was well acquainted with Braxton Hicks contractions. This felt different, more intense. She set the stopwatch on her wrist. There was no need to panic, she tried telling herself.

A deep ache set in her lower back, a band of pressure forming in her abdomen. Theoretically, she was well-prepared. Emotionally, she started feeling out of control on the side of the road.

Hannah pulled out her phone and called an ambulance.

Now lying in a private room, Hannah was trying her best to keep herself together. Not to cry over losing the man who meant everything to her. She loved him so much she could barely breathe, but she wanted to be strong. Not just for herself but for her baby too. A baby that she loved fiercely. She clutched the covers, not knowing if she should call Matt. Could she? She wasn't sure. They weren't together. He would need to be there when the baby was born but not to hold her hand. She would just have to get through this on her own.

Through the tears, she was grateful to him for something at least. Holding the pendant in her fist, Hannah was determined to show her baby how to be brave in this cold world. He would be proud to call her his mother.

She lay in the bed gripped by fear, hoping that this panicked feeling might distract her from the way she was crumbling on the inside. Then she hit another contraction and figured that, nope, she was fully capable of crumbling and being torn apart at the same time.

Matt had only just folded himself back into his car after his quick pit stop when he received a call from the hospital saying Hannah was in labour.

Never in his life had he ever driven so fast through the streets of London. He couldn't bring himself to care about the blaring horns and yelled curses he left in his wake. Hannah needed him. Whether she wanted him there would be another issue entirely but, if everything went his way, maybe she would allow him back into her life.

The car screeched to a stop and, once inside, he ran the maze that was the hospital wards until he found Hannah in a private room. A blood pressure cuff was on her arm and a sheen of sweat on her forehead.

He'd made it.

'Matt?'

'I'm here.' He took a seat beside her bed, taking her hand. 'I was so worried I wouldn't make it in time.'

'I didn't know if I should call you.'

'Oh, sweetheart, there's never a time when you can't.' He kissed her forehead, seeing tears well up in her eyes. It took all of a moment for her posture to become rigid. Her chin to set.

'You don't have to be here for all of this. They will call you in when he's born.'

Panic flared when he saw how badly he had messed up. 'Please don't throw me out. I want to be here with you.'

'After this morning...' She swallowed thickly.

'You were right. I was holding back, Hannah. I'm an idiot because it took you walking away to realise I don't want to. I swear, I'm usually smarter.' Hannah was unmoved and Matt sighed. 'You were right about everything, you know. I thought I could be the man my father wanted, but I don't want to be him. I never did. I want to be better. I wanted to be a provider like he was, but I don't want our son to have the miserable childhood I did. I've been worried that I would do the same. And I feel so disloyal for thinking it. Today Sarah told me she hated our parents and I thought, if our child ever thought that of me, it would kill me.'

'They won't ever hate you.'

'No, because I will be there for them. I will love them and create memories with them and you.'

'Me?' She looked at him dubiously. 'You can't want that purely on your terms. It doesn't work that way.'

'I know that, Hannah. You've given me everything I've ever wanted but never dared dream of. I couldn't let myself, not when I was determined never to put anyone in my mother's situation.'

Matt felt a tear run down his cheek. What was wrong with him? He'd never cried this much in his life! 'And I was conflicted. Wanting this with you but still wanting to live up to my father's expectations. He told me I would never be good enough if I didn't change.'

Hannah brushed away the wetness with a whispered, 'Matt.'

'I went about all of this wrong. When you said marrying you was about more than the baby it was true. I want *you*. I've wanted only you from the start. That's why I couldn't bear the touch of anyone else.'

'Why?' Then Hannah gripped his hands so tightly, he was

surprised none of his fingers broke. He rubbed her back as she breathed through the pain, settling back once it passed.

'We can talk about this later.'

'No. Now.'

'So stubborn.' His lips quirked up. 'I didn't want them. That life wasn't enough for me any more, not after I had a taste of what was real with you. I could see no one else since I saw you walk into that club. I've been in love with you since a small bar in a Melbourne alley, Hannah. I just didn't know how to show it and then I made excuses to keep you in my life, but the truth is I can't picture my life without you. You're my missing piece, and I behaved abominably. I should have given you the chance to say goodbye to your life in Melbourne. To leave on your own terms.'

'Why didn't you?' Hannah searched his face.

'I was so desperate to have you in my life. I still am. I can't let either of you go. You're my everything. You both are. I love you so much, Hannah. Please, please forgive me.'

'I can't live my life wondering if you're ever going to trust me with all of you. I won't let myself be in the position where I could be left picking up the pieces of my life if you change your mind. I'm worth more than just settling for half a relationship.'

Matt took her face in his hands. 'You're right. You're worth all of me, and more, and I'm promising that to you now. Every moment of every day you will have all of me. No more walls. No more masks. To prove it to you, I'm not okay. Letting go of what I was taught to be is hard, and I'm probably going to need time to work it all out. I feel like I'm standing on a ledge, terrified that I could be as bad a father as mine. Of disappointing you or our son.' Matt closed his eyes and took a shuddering breath.

'Then take my hand. Let me pull you back.'

'I feel so selfish for wanting you to.'

'It's not selfish to want to lean on someone. To show your heart to them. That's what a relationship is.'

'I love you so much, Hannah.'

'I love you too, Matt. I was scared to tell you.' Tears streamed down her face.

'Because I was an arse.'

Hannah laughed, a deep belly laugh that shook her shoulders. 'Sarah said you would be.'

'She knows me pretty well.' He grinned. 'We have so much to talk about, and I promise to tell you anything you want to know. I want to share everything with you. Tell me you want that too. There will only ever be you and, if you say no, I will wait all my life if I have to.'

'I do. So much!'

And then Matt couldn't help himself: he kissed her as if it was their last kiss and their first. As if she was the source of all life in his universe. As if she was all that kept the pieces of him together, because she was. As soon as his lips left hers, her hands were squeezing his again, her teeth clenched together tightly.

'That wasn't even five minutes.'

The words barely left his lips before a nurse was returning with a veritable army in tow. This was it. He was about to get the family he wanted.

Hannah was exhausted. Never in her life had she ever felt quite this tired before. Fatigue ran down into the marrow of her bones. She could barely keep her eyes open. She was sweaty, and her hair was a mess, but she couldn't care less. Not when she was looking over at Matt, who held their baby boy in his arms with wonder on his face and tears in his eyes.

Oliver William Taylor.

The baby looked almost comically small against Matt. And yet, she had never seen a more perfect sight. She felt so buoyant, she was honestly not sure if she was tethered by gravity any more. Matt was smiling down at their little boy. Her Matt. He loved her. This amazing man was hers. And he'd been so vulnerable with her, trusting. The image of his tears was carved into her memory for ever.

As if he could sense her staring at him, Matt turned to look at her and smiled that smile, the one that shone like the sun. It blinded her and made her heart leap.

'You did amazing,' he said, happiness so clear in his voice. 'I can't get over how perfect he is.'

'Careful or he'll wrap you around his little finger,' Hannah teased.

'Too late for that.' Matt laughed. 'It's to be expected, since his mother already has that power over me.'

'Oh, really?'

'Yes, and I sense it might only get worse.'

'And why's that?' Hannah was smiling so much, her cheeks were beginning to hurt, but man it felt good!

She watched Matt reach into his pocket and pull out her ring.

'I did this wrong before, but I want to make it right. I love you. I love you so much, sometimes I think it might break me. I promise to support you in the career you want to have or don't want to have. Whatever you want and whatever you choose, I will be beside you, right in your corner. I need you in my life and promise to be everything you need too. Hannah Murphy, will you marry me and spend the rest of our days in that house that you redecorated so beautifully?'

Hannah's breath was stuck in her chest and, for what felt like the millionth time that day, tears slid down her cheeks.

'Yes,' she croaked out. 'Yes,' she said, stronger this time. 'A million times yes!'

Matt beamed at her as he slid the ring onto her finger—somewhat awkwardly, because he refused to put Oliver in the bassinet—and kissed her fingers.

This day had gone from incredible, to anxious, to devastating, to scary only to end more spectacularly than Hannah could have ever imagined. She wiggled her fingers, admiring the emerald-cut stone in the middle of her ring.

Matt was watching her closely and she could see him pondering something.

'What is it?' she asked.

He smiled shyly, as though whatever he was about to reveal was a closely guarded secret. Which only made Hannah more curious. 'In light of our complete honesty, I should tell you, the red stone is not a ruby.'

Hannah laughed. 'Is it some sort of semi-precious stone?' She gasped dramatically. 'Is it coloured glass?' She was enjoying teasing him immensely, especially as his ears had gone slightly pink.

Matt rolled his eyes, but his lips curled in a smile. 'It's a diamond.'

Hannah's teasing smile fell off her face. 'Matt!' His name came out all strangled. It was a guarded secret because he'd remembered. Even though she thought their engagement had just been a formality, Matt had bought her this ring. He really had loved her all along.

Matt took her hand while she tried not to cry again today. Really, she was going to dehydrate from happiness. 'Three diamonds for the three of us. We're indestructible together.'

They really were. When she thought of all they had been through together and apart, she couldn't help but feel they were meant to be. Everything had just been a lead-up to this. Maybe she needed to know real pain to understand true joy.

'Before I forget, I got you something else,' Matt said, reaching into his pocket.

'You mean other than everything?'

He smiled another of those shy smiles that she was starting to think was more devastating than the others, and handed Hannah a box.

She lifted the lid and burst out laughing. Tissue paper was

roughly pushed away so she could remove a vintage cartridge video game.

'I love it!' She was still chuckling. 'But you know we have nothing to play this on, right?'

'Ah, but that's where you're wrong.' Matt smiled. 'I believe you were meant to show me your appreciation of vintage games. A woman has layers, after all,' he teased.

Hannah plastered a dark smile on her face, covering up just how much this meant to her. 'I'm going to whip your butt, Mr Taylor.'

'I look forward to it.'

EPILOGUE

Five years later

HANNAH SAT AT the patio table, listening to the sound of splashing coming from the indoor pool. Outside the sun baked the lush garden. They had spent five wonderful summers in this house. No longer did it look staged. It was an actual home. There were pictures of friends and family on the walls. Every room reflected Matt's and Hannah's personalities. And, no matter how much they tidied up, there always seemed to be a toy to be found. Hannah loved it.

She looked down at her baby girl, Daphne, who was happily drinking from her bottle. After several years, and with no luck in getting another miracle, Hannah and Matt had adopted their second child.

'What time is Sarah coming over?' Emma asked from beside Hannah. Her own baby boy—born just weeks before Daphne—was asleep in her arms.

'Any time now.'

Hannah had grown attached to Matt's sister, the women becoming close friends. And, when Emma and Alex had moved back to London, the three ladies had become almost inseparable.

'They really are having fun, aren't they?'

Hannah followed Emma's gaze to the pool where Matt and Alex were playing with their little boys, looking far too much like catalogue models.

'I'll always be grateful to Matt—he brought my best friend back to me,' Emma said, her voice sounding far away. She had been there when Hannah's heart had been broken, changing her, and then had seen her friend heal with Matt.

'And Alex helped mine find herself.' Hannah smiled at her best friend.

'Well, aren't we lucky?' Emma said with a chuckle.

They really were. Their lives were nothing short of perfect. Not in the stiff photo-snapshot way that Matt's had been, but rather that they got to be themselves. Loved unconditionally for who they were.

Hannah had found a job without much trouble at all four months after Oliver's birth—without Matt having to step in—and her career was soaring, with her now managing a team of developers. Command Technologies had continued its sky-ward trajectory with Matt at the helm. He no longer hid his feelings away. Matt was wholly and completely himself and he was happy.

They were happy. Content in this incredible life.

Hannah and Emma watched their husbands help both boys out of the water, dry them off and slip a towel-poncho over their heads. Alex, with his son perched on his shoulders, and Matt, giving a piggy-back to Oliver—who had a shock of blond hair and green eyes to match his dad's—walked over to their table. Droplets of water fell from Matt's blond hair, running down his sculpted body. Even after all this time, the sight made Hannah's mouth turn dry. Green eyes winked at her, and he gave her his most wicked smirk. Truly there had never been a sexier man to grace this planet.

A ring sounded through the house.

'That must be Sarah,' Hannah said.

'I'll get it. I need to put the baby down anyway,' Emma offered. Alex, carrying their son, turned to follow his wife when Oliver wriggled off his father's back.

'I wanna come too!' he announced excitedly.

'Come on then, Squirt.' Alex held out his hand, which Oliver held tightly, and off they went, leaving Hannah and Matt alone with their baby daughter who was now fast asleep. Hannah tucked her into the nearby bassinet and was then pulled against Matt's hard, wet body. His lips trailed down her neck, making Hannah shiver and sigh.

'Is it bad that I want to kick everyone out and take you to bed right now?' he whispered in her ear.

'Yes.' Hannah spun around in his arms. 'But I'd like that too, husband!' She grinned.

'Hmm…' said Matt. 'Looks like we'll have to make do with a bit of this, wife.' He slid his fingers into Hannah's hair, tilting her face up to his, and covered her lips with his. He tasted of mint and chlorine and Hannah couldn't help but moan into his mouth.[a]

'I love that sound,' he said, voice low.

'I love you.' And how! This man, her little family, was more than she could ever have wished for. She'd been so wrong before. Wishes weren't ridiculous. They were dreams that you needed to work a little harder to make a reality.

Matt smiled against her lips, kissing her again.

* * * * *

COMING
SOON!

We really hope you enjoyed reading this
book. If you're looking for more romance
be sure to head to the shops when
new books are available on

Thursday 22nd
June

To see which titles are coming soon, please visit

millsandboon.co.uk/nextmonth

MILLS & BOON®

Coming next month

PENNILESS CINDERELLA FOR THE GREEK
Chantelle Shaw

'I had the impression on the beach a week ago that you want us to be work colleagues and nothing more.'

His dark blue eyes were unfathomable, but she noticed a nerve flicker in his cheek. He sipped his wine before he said softly, 'Is that what you want, Savannah?'

She was about to assure him that of course it was. Anything other than a strictly work based relationship with Dimitris would be dangerous. But she was transfixed by his masculine beauty, and when he smiled she felt more alive than she'd done in ten years. 'I don't know,' she admitted huskily.

The band had been playing smooth jazz tunes during dinner, but now the guests had finished eating and the tempo of the music increased as people stepped onto the dance floor.

Dimitris pushed back his chair and stood up. He offered his hand to Savannah. 'Would you like to dance?'

Continue reading
PENNILESS CINDERELLA FOR THE GREEK
Chantelle Shaw

Available next month
www.millsandboon.co.uk

LET'S TALK
Romance

For exclusive extracts, competitions and special offers, find us online:

f MillsandBoon

𝕏 @MillsandBoon

📷 @MillsandBoonUK

♪ @MillsandBoonUK

Get in touch on 01413 063 232

MILLS & BOON

THE HEART OF ROMANCE

A ROMANCE FOR EVERY READER

MODERN

Prepare to be swept off your feet by sophisticated, sexy and seductive heroes, in some of the world's most glamourous and romantic locations, where power and passion collide.

HISTORICAL

Escape with historical heroes from time gone by. Whether your passion is for wicked Regency Rakes, muscled Vikings or rugged Highlanders, awaken the romance of the past.

MEDICAL

Set your pulse racing with dedicated, delectable doctors in the high-pressure world of medicine, where emotions run high and passion, comfort and love are the best medicine.

True Love

Celebrate true love with tender stories of heartfelt romance, from the rush of falling in love to the joy a new baby can bring, and a focus on the emotional heart of a relationship.

Desire

Indulge in secrets and scandal, intense drama and sizzling hot action with heroes who have it all: wealth, status, good looks…everything but the right woman.

HEROES

The excitement of a gripping thriller, with intense romance at its heart. Resourceful, true-to-life women and strong, fearless men face danger and desire - a killer combination!

To see which titles are coming soon, please visit

millsandboon.co.uk/nextmonth

MILLS & BOON

Desire

Indulge in secrets and scandal, intense drama and plenty of sizzling hot action with powerful and passionate heroes who have it all: wealth, status, good looks…everything but the right woman.

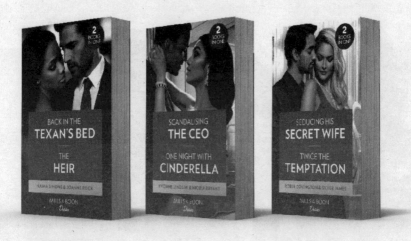